DARE TO FALL

CHURCHILL BRADLEY ACADEMY BOOK THREE

L. ANN
CLAIRE MARTA

DARE TO FALL

Cover design by Honey & Sin

Interior Formatting by Crow Fiction Designs

Back Page Blurb - Tami Thomason

First Edition: February 2023

ISBN: 9798375512730

This is a dark high school bully romance. The warnings from book one continue for book two.

Did we leave you breathless, broken, and stunned? Secrets still wait to be answered. The monster of Churchill Bradley Academy roams the halls, but he is not alone. Others watch from the shadows. An angel in the dark with shattered wings is lost to despair on a path to destruction.

Do you see a glimmer of light in the dark?

Red or green, dear reader?

Playlist

OBLIVION - PALAYE ROYALE

TRAITOR - DAUGHTRY

I'M OK - CALL ME KARIZMA

OUTRUN MYSELF - JACK KAYS

UNDER THE GRAVEYARD - OZZY OSBOURNE

FIRE OUT - CALL ME KARIZMA

Dedication

One book turned into two, then three, and oops, now we have four.

This series took on a life of its own. A world we fell into and brought to life.

To all the readers who have messaged us saying how much they love the story.

Grab those tissues. It's not over yet.

1

Eli

Kellan is swearing, loud and colorfully, while Miles and I pin him in place on the bed so the nurse can stitch the gash above his eye.

"I've given you worse when we spar," I tell him when he tries to pull away again.

"Like fuck," he snaps. "You've never hit my face."

"Then I'll add it to our spar sessions in future."

"Don't you fucking—ouch, fuck. That fucking hurts."

"Almost done." The nurse's voice is cheerful, like she stitches people up every fucking day. Maybe she does. I don't know. "Just one more. Hold still, honey." And then she's straightening and pulling off the surgical gloves. "There we go. All done."

She takes a step back. "Your ribs are badly bruised, so they're going to ache for a while, but they're not broken."

"And your nose wasn't broken either." Miles perches on the side of the bed. "Just a lot of blood." He has a white-knuckled grip on Kellan's hand.

"You're going to have to come clean, you know." I turn my glare on him.

Miles ducks his head.

"I'm serious. They'll try and fuck him over again if you don't."

"I know."

My gaze drifts over the room, pausing on the wall clock. "What time is it?"

"Three am," Miles tells me.

I frown. Something about the time bothers me. Three am …

Fuck.

I pull my cell out of my pocket. There are seventeen text notifications from Arabella. Why would she be texting my main number?

I tap into them.

Ari: Fuck you.

Ari: Fuck this situation.

Ari: You got what you wanted.

Ari: You humiliated me.

Ari: Hurt me.

Ari: Took my virginity.

Ari: Twisted everything with your hate.

Ari: All I did was exist, and you hated me.

Ari: You judged me without even getting to know me.

Ari: All I wanted was to belong.

Ari: It shouldn't have felt good to fuck you.

Ari: You became a bad habit I didn't want to give up.

Ari: Then you took it all away.

Ari: I hate you for that.

Ari: Well, you win.

Ari: I'm done.

Ari: You got what you wanted.

My jaw clenches. Does she know I'm Sin and thinks I've left her alone on purpose? I need to call her. I *should* have called her earlier, but I was so focused on Kellan and getting him to help.

I find the other cell and swipe the screen. There are … *Holy fuck* … forty-three texts.

My hand is shaking when I open them.

Kitten: Where are you?

Kitten: Please, Sin. I need you.

Kitten: Why are you ignoring me?

Kitten: It's been thirty minutes, and you're not here.

Kitten: I'm not leaving the cemetery until you come.

Kitten: They're texting me orders. They want me to go to the ball tomorrow night.

Kitten: I'm nothing but their puppet.

Kitten: They want me to confront Eli. They want to see him react.

Kitten: I hate this school.

Kitten: You're the only thing I'm clinging to.

Kitten: Please don't take that away from me.

Kitten: Please come.

Kitten: I'm still waiting. It's been an hour.

Kitten: I'll do anything you want.

Kitten: I'll get down on my knees and suck your cock like a good girl.

Kitten: I'll suck your friend's cock too.

Kitten: I'd do anything for you.

Kitten: Please don't abandon me.

Kitten: It's two hours now, and I'm still here.

Kitten: I don't know who I am anymore.

Kitten: It hurts so much.

Kitten: I can't stop crying.

Kitten: I love you.

Kitten: Please don't do this to me.

Kitten: Sin, I love you.

Kitten: I feel so lost and alone.

Kitten: They've made me do things I'm not proud of.

Kitten: They have the videos.

Kitten: Please talk to me.

Kitten: Eli hates me so much.

Kitten: Maybe I deserve his hatred.

Kitten: Am I such a bad person?

Kitten: Is that why this is all happening to me?

Kitten: I can't do this anymore.

Kitten: I can't keep fighting.

Kitten: I'm so tired.

Kitten: I'm sorry.

Kitten: I'm weak.

Kitten: I'm not the strong girl you wanted me to be.

Kitten: I'm sorry if I did something wrong.

Kitten: I'm sorry if I'm a disappointment.

Kitten: I messed everything up. I'm not a bully.

I didn't want to hurt anyone.

Kitten: I always make everything worse.

Kitten: Did they hurt you too, like they did, Miles? Is that why you haven't come?

Kitten: Please tell me you're ok.

Kitten: I'm sorry. I'm so, so sorry.

Kitten: I'm going to keep Zoey company.

Kitten: I like it out here, surrounded by trees.

Kitten: I'm so numb.

Kitten: I want to see the colors playing on the stone floor.

Kitten: It has to stop. I need to make this stop.

Kitten: Maybe it will just hurt for a moment, and then I won't feel anything anymore.

The last text was sent over two hours ago. The cell falls from my fingers.

"I have to go." I whisper the words, and don't wait for an answer, turning to run from the building.

There's a shout behind me, but I ignore it as I sprint across the grass and into the trees. She's not at the bench when I get there, which I shouldn't be surprised about. I stop and look around.

Think.

She can't get in the crypt because I have the only key. That leaves …

The chapel.

I take off again.

My lungs are burning when I skid to a stop outside the chapel doors.

"Ari?" My shout echoes through the trees and I push the door open and step inside.

The interior is silent, *cold*, and at first, I think it's empty, but then I hear something. A soft breath, maybe?

"Ari?" I repeat her name, quieter this time and walk quickly to the altar, to where she was the last time I saw her in here.

My heart stops.

She's on her knees, head bowed, her back to me.

"Ari?"

She ignores me. I move closer and crouch down beside her. "Hey. I'm sorry I'm late. Kellan was hurt and I … I needed to make sure he was okay. It took longer than I thought it would."

Nothing.

"Ari …" I clear my throat. "Kitten, please look at me."

That gets a response. Her head jerks up, and I get a quick impression of white features before she tumbles backward, one hand outstretched.

"No! Get away from me. Leave me alone."

"It's okay." I catch her hand in mine to stop her crazy scramble across the floor.

"Let go of me." She tries to fight, but she's cold and tired, and I'm stronger.

I pull her toward me, then wrap an arm around her waist. "Stop fighting me, Kitten."

"No. You can't say that. You *can't*." She twists her hand free and thumps it against my chest. "I can't do this anymore. Please. Just let me go."

"It's okay." I press my face into her hair and hold on tight while she twists and fights against my grip. "Ari, stop."

"I can't fight anymore," she whispers, and sags in my arms. "Just do whatever you came here to do."

"I know." I loosen my grip and cover the hand curled against my chest with mine. "No fighting, I promise. But I need you to come with me."

She doesn't reply.

I rise to my feet, tugging her up with me. She doesn't resist. When I link my fingers with hers, she doesn't stop me. Doesn't fight when I walk toward the doors, taking her along with me. Doesn't even question me when I lead her through the cemetery to the entrance of the tunnel, which will take us into the dorms without being seen.

I cast careful looks at her as I guide her inside. Her face is blank, eyes dull, lips almost slack, and I'm worried that something has broken inside her. Something I won't be able to fix.

We walk through the tunnel in silence, and she waits while I check to make sure no one is in the hallway before I lead her out and down to my room.

Her silence is unnerving. I don't like it. I'd rather she fought with me, but I don't say anything until I've got her in my room and locked the door.

She's standing where I left her, in the center of the room, hands loose at her sides, when I turn to face her.

"Ari?"

She doesn't respond to me.

"I need you to get out of those clothes. I don't know what you were doing, but they're filthy." The knees of her pants are covered in dirt, her sneakers the same. "Will you sit down for me?"

She drops onto the mattress, but still doesn't say anything. I kneel in front of her and ease her feet out of the sneakers, and peel off her socks. "Pants next, Kitten."

There's no reaction to the nickname, and I don't know if it's because she isn't hearing me or …

Or what?

Wrapping my fingers around hers, I tug her back to her feet, then slowly push the pants down her legs. The entire time, I'm waiting for her to react, but she just stands there and lets me strip her out of them.

"Back on the bed." I pull back the sheets. "Lie down, Kitten."

She follows every command I give without comment.

I hate it.

I hate the fucking silence. The lack of argument. The absence of fire in her eyes.

Kicking out of my sneakers, I crawl onto the bed beside her and pull her into my arms. She's stiff, unresponsive, and so fucking cold.

That worries me. I reach down for the sheets and tuck them around us both.

"Close your eyes, Kitten. Try to sleep, okay? You're safe now. I've got you."

2

Arabella

A soft voice whispers in my ear, and a hand strokes my hair. I'm so cold, and the body next to mine is a furnace burning through the ice, cocooning me in its heat. My thoughts are sluggish. All I can think about is how I'd waited for Sin for hours out in the freezing wind, while hope died a slow and painful death as time trickled by.

"Close your eyes, Kitten. Try to sleep, okay? You're safe now. I've got you." The voice is familiar.

I don't respond.

"You're like a fucking ice cube," the voice continues. "I'm going to try and get you warmed up, but I want you to close your eyes and rest."

A hand moves over my side, the heat burning a path along my skin. It hurts. He continues to whisper to me, and eventually, my eyes grow heavy, and I give myself up to exhaustion.

***

Consciousness returns slowly—memories awaken a sliver at a time.

Sin didn't come.

The realization swallowed me whole and set me wandering through the woods like a lost ghost. I walked and walked until I found the chapel. Something inside me felt broken, the fragments of hope wearing down to a fine powder. I knelt on the stone floor with no will to go back to school. I wanted the cold to take me. To lie down and let it take me away from all the pain.

"She's been asleep for eight fucking hours," a voice rumb

from behind me. "She shouldn't be out of it this long."

"You said she was out of it when you found her," a second voice replies.

"She was like a zombie."

"You know she might not be the same Arabella after all this."

"I know."

There's a moment of silence.

"At least we don't have to worry about anyone looking for her." The second voice is closer. "The way she's been acting, they won't expect her to come out of her room."

"Until the ball tonight. She said something about the ball in her texts."

"We should check her phone, but first, I need to go down and make an appearance. I'll bring some lunch back up. Miles will join us when he can get away."

"Be careful."

"Oh, don't worry. I'll be ready for them this time."

"Text me when you get there and when you're on the way back."

"Yes, mother."

"I mean it, Kell."

"Okay, okay. I'll see if I can get her some soup and a bowl of plain rice. We just have to make sure she eats it."

"I can feel how much weight she's lost."

"She must have been starving herself for weeks with all the stress of what she's been dealing with."

"It stops now."

"I'll be back soon."

A door opens and closes.

Awareness creeps in. I'm lying on a mattress on my side. I can barely move under the weight of the blankets heaped on top of me, but it's the body curled up around me that holds all my attention. A hand is stroking my hip gently, and I can feel a face pressed into my hair.

I frown. *Where am I?*

All I remember is the chapel and the cold. I open my eyes slowly and focus on a wall.

A dorm room?

It's not mine because I don't recognize the hoodie hanging on the back of the chair.

"Hey, Kitten. Are you awake?"

Sin?

Turning my head, my gaze collides with a pair of intense green eyes.

Eli.

I stare at him, my brain trying to process what I'm seeing.

Eli is in bed with me. I'm in his dorm room. Why does he sound like Sin?

Realization comes in a creeping wave of horror.

"No. No." I shake my head in denial.

He holds me against him when I struggle. "Don't be frightened. It's okay. I'm not going to hurt you."

"You can't be him. You *can't* be him."

"It's going to be okay." He doesn't deny my words.

"Why? Why would you do this to me?" I whisper, eyes wide but dry. I have no more tears to shed. Jumbled memories of everything I'd done for him, *with him*, surge up, and my head spins with anguish.

Eli's jaw is tight. "Ari, *stop*."

"I trusted you." My voice rises hysterically. "I *trusted* you, and I *loved* you."

Subduing my struggles with his body, he pins me down and presses a hand over my mouth. "Please, Kitten. You need to be quiet. No one knows you're in here."

I twist my head away to the left. "Don't call me that. You're not Sin. You're *not* him."

"I am." His words are rough.

"*You're* doing this to me. *You're* the one behind everything. *You're* the one who's blackmailing me. You're the one who broke me. It's you. *All you*. You're behind everything. I can't do this anymore. I *can't* ..."

I don't want to look at him.

He made me fall in love with him. *Why did I let it happen?* Eli Travers became my bad habit. Sin became my addiction. The same person, and I didn't know.

I was blind to it.

How stupid can I be?

I let him have my body. I let him crawl inside my heart. Only to have him burn me from the inside out until I have nothing left to give. The truth threatens to crush me.

I stop fighting, going limp beneath him, the weight of my thoughts sliding away into emptiness.

"Ari?"

I close my eyes, and don't respond.

"Ari? Talk to me, please." Eli's voice is barely above a whisper, and he cradles me against his chest. A hand strokes my face and my hair. Lips press gently to my forehead.

He continues to talk, but my mind shuts down, and darkness washes over me.

3

Eli

I'm not sure if she's asleep or just ignoring me. Her body temperature is back to normal, there's no reason for her to still be sleeping.

"Ari?" I keep my voice low.

She doesn't acknowledge me.

"Kitten?"

Her entire body stiffens. That answers that question, then. She's ignoring me.

"I know you're angry with me. But I swear, I'm not behind the texts or the threats."

"You've lied about everything else, why should I believe you about that?" Her voice is toneless, but I can't stop a surge of hope.

She *answered* me. It's a step up from the silence.

"Why would I tell you to key my car?"

"To make sure I don't think it's you."

"Have you any idea how much it cost to repair the damage?"

Her shoulder moves in a shrug.

"Will you at least look at me?" I lean up on one hand and brush her hair off her cheek.

She turns her head and buries it into the pillow.

"Ari, please?"

She twists to face me. "Answer one question."

"Anything."

"*Why?*"

I frown. "Why what?"

"*Why* did you do it? Why pretend to be a stranger? Why do the things you did to me? *Why* did—"

The door swings open and Kellan walks in, juggling two bags and three drinks.

"Hey, you're awake." He smiles at Arabella.

Arabella looks at him, then at me, and the little color that had returned to her face drains away.

"Oh my god," she whispers. "If you're Sin, then *he* …" She scrambles from the bed, sways, and drops heavily back onto the mattress.

"Ari, calm down." I sit up and swing my legs off the bed.

"Calm down," she repeats. "You want me to *calm down*? The video … that's you and …" her eyes cut to Kellan again, who carefully sets down the food and drinks, then crosses the room.

"Bella." He crouches in front of her and takes her hands. "Eli wanted to tell you it was him, but he couldn't see a way to do it without making you feel—"

"Used? Lied to? Manipulated? Tricked?" Her voice is hard.

"Yes, all of those." He glances at me. "It might have started as a cruel joke, but it didn't stay that way. You know that, don't you?"

"When did it stop? Was it when you recorded me sucking your cock? Or how about when you were both … *doing things* to me? Maybe you started feeling bad the night I begged you to fuck me, and you refused?" Her blue eyes, when she twists to glare at me, are no longer empty. They're blazing with fury. "*When*, Eli? When did it stop being a joke to you?"

"When I kissed you on Halloween."

1

Arabella

Months ago.

The anger I'm feeling sears through my numbness. "I don't believe you."

I stare into Kellan's face. There are cuts and bruises covering it. I'm sure they hadn't been there yesterday.

He strokes his thumbs over my hands. "Sin started giving you what you wanted after Halloween. Don't you remember? He ate you out on the tomb and touched you in the way you wanted. Did things that were in your diary—"

Pulling free out of his grip, I scoot away from him across the bed. "The diary he *stole*. You twisted all my fantasies up. You did it to humiliate me."

"Yes … No." Eli shakes his head.

"You hate me. You've *always* hated me."

"I can't go back and change the past. I wish I could, but I *can't*. You felt something for Sin. You felt safe with him. *With me*—"

My head is a mess, and I can't think straight. I snatch up a pillow and hug it to my chest. "Sin isn't real. You made him up. He is a lie."

"Ari, no matter which way you look at it, Sin is me." Eli's voice is soft and steady. "You had feelings for *me*."

I loved him. Something I'd told Sin in my texts when I thought he'd abandoned me.

I stare at him, raw piercing bleakness clutching my heart. "I didn't know it was you."

"You felt good with Sin, didn't you? He gave you the confidence to be strong. He told you to fight. He made you feel alive."

"Yes, but—"

"It wasn't a trick, Ari. I swear it wasn't. Not after Halloween. I liked being with you. Touching you."

"Sin left me." I hug the pillow tighter, pressing my cheek to the top of it. I'm so confused. From day one, Eli has set out to destroy me.

Why would he change his mind? Why would he help me?

"I *couldn't* fuck you." Eli's voice is low and raw. "Not like that. I wanted you to know it was me. *Eli*, not Sin. That it was *me* inside you, giving you pleasure. That it was me you were begging. I wanted to hear you cry out *my* name when I made you come."

"You were so shitty to me during school." My whisper is soft, fragile, threatening to break.

"You were accusing me of things. The photograph telling everyone you were my stepsister." He rakes a hand through his hair. "And then things changed again at Thanksgiving."

"You took my virginity."

He narrows his eyes. "You were not *drunk*."

"I'd been downstairs, and I wanted something to numb my feelings. Miles told me vodka didn't taste of anything, so I had it with a can of Coke."

"Fucking Miles," he growls.

"It's not his fault." Kellan moves from his crouch to sit on the edge of the bed. "Then the video was leaked, and you ran away."

"I-I couldn't face anyone," I stammer. "They were already

teasing me about you."

"We didn't leak that video either," Kellan tells me. "We haven't shared *anything*. The cloud was supposed to be secure, but someone hacked into it and stole everything."

Eli looks at me for one long minute. "We called a truce over Christmas. You smoked your first joint, and we got to know each other better. We had sex and, no matter what you claim, it wasn't just fucking, Ari."

My bottom lip trembles. "It *wasn't* real."

"You lashed out at me at the Christmas Eve party. You were happy with me until that night."

He'd been the boy who held my hand. The one who made me feel good. He had made me smile. I recall my fear of coming back to school. How angry I was with him for reading out my diary in class.

"But then another photograph was released." Kellan breaks the silence. "And you came back to school. When did they start blackmailing you, Bella? Was it straight away?"

My chest grows tight at his words. "I—"

Eli reaches out and gently strokes my bare thigh. "We figured out what was happening a few days ago. I'm so fucking sorry we didn't see it sooner. You wouldn't have been all alone. You can tell us. It's okay to talk."

My attention bounces between them, but I remain silent.

Can I really trust them? Am I just going to dig myself deeper into the hole I'm in already?

"I got beaten up." Kellan touches his face. "That's why Eli didn't meet you at the right time. It was hard to keep him from tearing down to your room when we figured out what was happening, but you told us you were being watched. We didn't want to tip anyone off that we knew what was happening."

I don't reply.

Kellan smiles. "Let's eat, and then maybe you'll be in the mood to talk." He rises and moves to the table.

"I'm not hungry."

"You need food, Kitten." Eli insists. "No more skipping meals. You need to let us take care of you."

He's so close, I can feel the heat from his body reminding me that he's been holding me the last few hours. He's watching me intently. Part of me wants to melt back into his warmth and seek out the comfort I need. Instead, I hold myself stiffly, still clutching the pillow like a shield.

Eli is Sin?

I'm so mixed up inside—hurt, furious, betrayed.

Is this all another mind fuck? Are they really not behind the texts and orders?

The last messages I received flit through my head. I'm supposed to go to the Valentine's Ball tonight. They want to see the Monster of Churchill Bradley Academy. I don't know what they'll make me do. The thought of attending leaves me feeling sick inside.

5

Eli

"I need to use the bathroom." She stands and drops the pillow she's been hugging onto the mattress.

Kellan waves a hand toward the door. "Through there. If you need towels, they're on a shelf. There's a spare toothbrush in a wrapper if you want to use that. Although I'd suggest waiting until after you eat to brush your teeth."

She crosses the room and slips through the door, closing it behind her. Kellan's easy smile drops away and he faces me.

"She still doesn't believe us." He keeps his voice low.

"She doesn't believe *me*," I correct. "And why should she? I lied to her for months as Sin."

"She'll come around." Kellan empties the bags of food and separates it out. "Soup of the day for Bella, and plain rice. Noodles and chicken curry for you. Satay Chicken for me."

"Did anyone say anything?"

His smile returns. "Of course not. They're waiting for me to retaliate. Now the sun has risen on their fuck up, they're rethinking their recent life choices." His voice is light.

I reach for my food and silverware. "You saw all their faces, right?"

"Every single one."

"What do you want to do?"

"I want to wait. Let their anticipation build. We have other things to deal with right now."

I nod around a mouthful of food.

The click of the door precedes Arabella coming back into the room. She stops in the doorway, chewing on her bottom lip and tugging at the hem of her shirt in a fruitless attempt to cover her thighs as she looks at us both. Setting my food to one side, I stand and cross to the dresser. Without a word, I pull out a pair of sweats and hold them out to her.

Her gaze drops to my hand, then up to my face.

"They're too big, but it'll do until we can get you some of your own clothes from your room.

"Am I a prisoner here, then?"

"Of course not." I shrug and drop the sweats onto a nearby chair. "Look, take them, don't take them. It's up to you."

"Eli." Kellan's voice is a soft warning.

"I'm trying, Kell. But she has to meet me halfway."

She laughs, the sound hard and sharp. "Don't you know you can't change the nature of the beast, Kellan?"

I shake my head. "I'm not doing this with you, Ari."

"Doing what?"

"Fighting with you. I understand why you're angry with me, why you don't believe me, but I'm not going to let you goad me into proving you're right, Kitten."

"Stop it." Her voice is brittle, razor-sharp.

"Stop what?"

"You don't get to call me that. You're not *him*."

I sigh, lifting my eyes to the ceiling and begging to any deity that's listening to give me patience.

"You know there's a way he can prove it to you," Kellan says around a mouthful of food. He waves a hand at me. "Lift up your shirt."

"Kell—"

"We're going to go around in circles, otherwise. Just do it."

It's with extreme reluctance that I pull the front of my shirt up, baring my chest. I know what he wants me to show her. And it's not anything she hasn't already seen … mostly … but she didn't realize it the last time she saw it.

Kellan points his chopsticks at me. "See it, Bella?"

She's scowling, looking everywhere but at me.

Kellan rolls his eyes. "Bella, Bella, Bella." He places his food down and stands. Stepping up beside her, he touches her face gently and turns her head toward me.

"See the tattoo?"

"I was there when he got it."

"Are we done?" I feel like a slab of meat as they both stare at me.

"Of course, we're not done." Kellan flicks his fingers toward the words across my ribs. "Look closer, Bella. What do you see?"

"Exactly the same as you."

"Don't be awkward, pretty girl. Read it out."

She sighs. "It says, *Nasty Little Monster*."

"What else does it say?"

"Kell." I growl his name.

"Show some patience, Elliot Travers the Third."

"What?" Arabella's eyes widen.

"Fuck's sake." I glare at my friend, who smirks.

"You didn't know that? Eli is short for Elliot. It's the family name."

"Shut the fuck up."

He laughs and turns his attention back to Arabella. "You didn't answer my question. What else does it say, Bella?" His voice is soft. "Shall I give you a clue? Look at the colors. Shall we do it together?" He crosses the room and stops beside me. "Which letters did he turn red?"

He taps the word *Nasty*. "Look, the S is red there." His finger slides to *Little*. "The I is red. And …" He flicks the word *Monster* with a fingernail. "Oh look, the N is red there. Say it with me, pretty girl. What does it spell out?"

6

Arabella

I stare at the red letters.

S.I.N.

Eli is watching my expression, and from the way his eyes flicker, I'm sure he recognizes the moment of my acceptance.

It's true. Eli is my lover in the dark. Why else would he have the name written over his body and hidden inside other words? The last thread of doubt drains away, leaving me shaken.

Did he do it to taunt me? Is that why he got it done while I was watching?

I'd been so wrapped up in my problems and anger that the different colors on the tattoo hadn't clicked in my head. Not that I'd seen a lot of it, as Eli had his t-shirt on when we had sex. I'd wanted Sin to fuck me, and he had … as Eli.

I rub my arms up and down, trying to warm the chill inside me. For months he's been lying to me. He'd pretended to be someone else. I confided in him. He became my obsession.

I close my eyes for a moment, emotions struggling to break through the numbness.

"I know this is a lot to process." Kellan's voice is quiet. "You're struggling with it. It's going to take time. We understand that."

My eyes snap open, and I pin him with a glare. "You fucked with my head for months."

"You enjoyed what we were doing." Eli takes a step toward me.

"Don't try and deny it."

He's right; I did, but if his comment is supposed to make me feel better, it fails miserably.

My attention moves to the ink on the other side. *Feed Me. Fuck Me. Fight Me.* is tattooed in bold black letters.

"Why?" I gesture at it.

Eli shrugs, dropping the hem of his t-shirt. "You told me to do it."

"And if I told you to jump off a bridge, would you do that, too?"

"I don't know. Maybe? Do you want me dead, Ari? Do you hate me that much?"

"No." I avert my face from his searching gaze, and move to the chair. Taking the sweat pants, I pull them on to cover my legs. Not that it matters. Both of them have seen me naked more than once.

Their hot seeking mouths on my breasts and between my legs. The silence of the tomb broken by the sounds of my moans and panting.

A traitorous, sharp, low curl of lust flutters through my stomach at the memory. I suck in a shaky breath. It's enough to shock me. It's been weeks since I've felt anything other than depression. I can barely remember how the dares they gave me made me feel.

"Come on, Bella. Your food is getting cold." Kellan returns to the table and pulls out a chair for me.

I sit down without a word. Eli takes the seat beside me while Kellan takes the one opposite. I stare down at the white Styrofoam bowl and spoon in front of me. When I don't move, Eli reaches over and peels off the lid. The fragrant aroma of vegetable soup teases my nose.

"Eat." He pushes the spoon toward me. "If we're going to help you, we need you strong."

"I'm not strong."

Kellan snorts. "You're kidding, right? You've been struggling with what's been happening on your own for weeks, and here you are … still standing."

I shake my head, blinking back tears. "I broke."

"Not completely."

I tear my attention from Kellan and fix my gaze on the table. "I wanted to die when Eli found me. I'd given up."

Silence descends at my whispered, raw confession.

A chair scrapes against the floor, and a moment later, Eli is crouched beside me. Taking my hands, he squeezes them tightly.

"No. No giving up." His words are fierce. "No ending anything. You get angry. Do you hear me, Ari? At the person who did this to you. At us. At *me*."

I glance away from him. "I'm not brave enough."

"The fuck you're not. You are still the girl who came out to the cemetery in the middle of the night to answer the call of a stranger. The girl who was courageous enough to demand what she wanted. To have her fantasies fulfilled in the dark." He lifts my hand and brushes the tear trickling down my cheek away with the pad of his thumb. "You are not broken. Not at the core."

I close my eyes and lean into his touch, savoring the contact. "Just scarred on the inside."

Eli's palm flattens against my cheek, stroking it lightly before he pulls away. "Eat. Then fight. Don't let these fuckers win."

"You have us with you now," Kellan points out as Eli retakes his seat. "The game has changed."

With a shaky breath, I take my spoon and scoop up some soup. For once, food doesn't taste like sawdust in my mouth. Between Kellan's encouragement and Eli's quiet praise, I finish almost all of it.

"You get the orders on your phone, right?" Kellan is watching me play with the rice.

I nod. "From an unknown number, but they managed to delete some when I tried to show Principal Warren."

"Can I see it?"

Abandoning my food, I leave my seat and find my discarded clothes. I don't even remember Eli stripping me out of my sweatpants and hoodie. I search through them until I find my main cell and carry it back to the table. "Here."

Eli frowns when I hand it to his friend. "You don't have a password?"

"No."

"Jesus, Ari, you need to keep things secure."

"I wouldn't need to if people stopped taking my stuff," I snap back.

Kellan is already absorbed in whatever is on the cell's screen. "Okay, kids, let's stop the bickering."

I go back to swirling the rice around my plate.

"Stop playing with your food and eat it," Eli snaps.

I glare at him, but pop a spoonful into my mouth, and chew.

His lips curl in a smile. "Good girl."

The needy ache that rocks through my body surprises me, and I have to press my thighs together to alleviate the throbbing. I don't know what power those fucking words uttered in that husky voice have over me, but I'm not sure I like them. Eli Travers is someone I shouldn't want, but my body doesn't seem to have figured that out yet.

Kellan hums. "They want you to go to the Valentine's Ball tonight and unleash the monster." His eyes flick to Eli. "I wonder how they are planning to do that."

My chest tightens. "I don't want to go. I can't—"

He cuts me off, handing the phone to Eli while he talks. "We need to figure out who is doing this. That means acting like we have no idea that you're being blackmailed."

Head bent, Eli sits in silence, scrolling through the messages. I watch, my insides twisting into knots as his expression hardens into stone, eyes narrowing, and his gaze turns deadly.

They might finally be aware of what's been happening, but from the look on my stepbrother's face, the person blackmailing me might just get what they want. The Monster of Churchill Bradley Academy has woken up, and he's ready to make someone pay.

7

Eli

It isn't that I didn't believe her when she said someone was behind the shit she was doing to me, but seeing it in front of me … reading the texts and her attempts to fight against the demands has fury running through my veins like molten lava.

I toss her cell onto the table and pin my gaze onto Kellan. "Lock down her phone. No more easy access."

He snorts at my choice of words, but I'm in no mood to find it funny.

"I'm not doing it." Arabella's soft voice has me turning on my chair.

"*Yes*, you are."

"No. I'm done." The lack of fight in her voice tips my anger over the edge.

I shove to my feet. "So that's it? You've been dealing with this shit for weeks, letting me believe you're doing it because you hate me—"

"I *do* hate you."

I ignore her outburst. She's full of shit, and we both know it.

"And now you have people around you, ready to support you, fucking *fight* for you … *Now* you're giving up?"

"Eli." Kellan warns.

I ignore him as well.

"Kitten, you're not a coward."

"*Don't call me that!*" she screams, lurching to her feet, fingers clenched into fists.

"Why not?" I step up to her. "What's wrong, *Kitten*?" I drop my voice to the whisper I used as Sin. "Don't like the reminder that you spread your legs for me?" I summon up a smirk. "More than once."

The crack as her hand hits my cheek echoes around the room. It's followed by an irritable sigh from Kellan.

"When you two are done with the foreplay, can we finish eating and then plan our next move?"

"I fucking hate you." She spits the words at me.

I press two fingers to her chin and tip her head up, and smile when I see the spark in her eyes.

"There she is." I brush my thumb over her bottom lip. "You feel that, Ari? That fire in your blood? Hold on to it." I dip my head and touch her lips with mine, a barely-there touch, gone before she can react to it. "Wrap yourself in it."

I drop back onto my chair and pull the container of food toward me. After a second, she takes her seat.

"As we were discussing," Kellan says into the silence. "You should definitely go to the ball tonight. Wear whatever they want you to wear. Do what they want you to do. We'll be there to—"

"Wait a minute." My head jerks up. "*I* never agreed to go to the stupid thing."

"But she can't flirt with you if you're not there, Eli." He speaks to me as though I'm a child. "So you'll dust off your sexy formal wear and turn up, like a good little target." He picks up her cell and taps around on the screen. "I'm pretty sure they've cloned your phone. That must be how they knew Miles was talking to you. We have to assume they don't know about your Sin cell." He laughs at the name. "Use that to stay in contact with Eli. Do *not* text anyone from this one." He waves it at her. "Understand?"

She nods, still pushing the rice around the plate. Dropping my own fork, I reach out and wrap my fingers around the spoon she's holding and take it from her. Her eyes dart up to meet mine. I scoop up the rice, then lift it to her mouth.

"Open up."

She glares at me.

"I'm not above force-feeding you, Hellcat." I tilt my head and smile. "I know a *lot* of ways to get you to open your mouth for me."

I'm goading her, and from Kellan's eye roll, he's picked up on it as well. Her eyes are hot, fiery with anger, as she parts her lips and lets me slide the spoon into her mouth. My dick is hard as fucking stone when she licks her lips.

"Good girl." I fill the spoon again, and feed her another mouthful.

The air in the room turns heavy with anticipation as she takes each spoonful from me. Our breathing is in sync, my eyes locked on her lips as her tongue snakes out again to catch a grain of rice. And then the moment is shattered by her cell vibrating.

She immediately stiffens. Kellan snatches it up before either of us can move.

"Your clothes have been delivered to your room. You're to take a photograph when you're dressed and reply to the number with it."

Her face pales, and she presses her fingers to her lips. "I can't."

"You can." Kellan's voice is firm. "If you want this to be over, you *have* to do this. You need to give us time to figure out who it is. We can't do that if you stop responding."

"Ari." I wait until she looks at me. "Whatever they want you to throw at me, I can take it. I know it's not you."

8

Arabella

"But what if they want me to do something bad?" I croak. "I almost killed you with that coffee."

"That *wasn't* your fault." Eli's voice is firm.

The guilt inside won't let it go, twisting me up inside. "I handed it to you. I watched you drink it."

"They made you do it."

"I wanted to say no. I didn't want to do it."

"Breathe, Bella." Kellan reaches across to touch my arm.

The dorm room door opens then, and my heart jumps in panic. Before anyone can move, Miles slips in, closing it behind him. He leans back against it, his attention on the three of us.

"I managed to sneak away."

"Miles." I lunge at him.

"What the—" He catches me with a grunt. "Hey, it's okay."

I hug him tightly. "They hurt you because of me. I'm so sorry. I shouldn't have dragged you into this mess."

"If you hadn't, then Kellan would never have figured out what was going on."

Cupping his face between my palms, I examine the bandage on his forehead. "Let me see."

He rolls his eyes. "It's fine."

"Don't act all macho with me. Tell me the truth."

He grasps my wrists and lowers my hands. "It hurts like hell, but

I'll survive."

Miles curls his arm around my shoulders, guides me back to the table and to my seat, then he moves around to drop onto Kellan's lap.

Kellan smiles. "Hello, loverboy." He kisses Miles' cheek.

My jaw drops open. "Kellan is the guy you said you liked back in October!"

Kellan laughs. "Busted."

Miles has the good grace to look guilty. "We kind of hooked up, and things went from there."

"But you said you didn't meet him at school."

"I *didn't* meet him at school. The first time I met him was at an introduction to Churchill Bradley thing before we started here."

I twist to look at Eli. "Then that means you've always known about Miles?"

"That he's gay? Yes," Eli confirms dryly.

"But we had you fooled. You didn't know we weren't really dating."

"Not me." Kellan rests his chin on Miles' shoulder. "I knew he was hiding something."

"I can't believe you didn't say something to me." I can't hide the hurt from my tone.

"It's not like you didn't have secrets of your own, sneaking off to the cemetery to meet Eli—" Miles retorts.

My eyes widen. "You *told* him?"

"He thought the guys in the video might be the ones blackmailing you," Eli explains.

I rise from my seat. "I should go back to my room."

He frowns. "You don't need to leave. Stay and finish your food."

"I want to go back." I need to process everything they've told me.

"I can check to make sure there's no one watching," Miles offers. "When you're ready."

I look around the room until I find my sneakers and stuff my feet into them. My hoodie is next, and I pull it over my head. I bundle up my dirty sweatpants and make sure I have both phones with me. Hugging them to my chest, I turn to face the three boys.

Kellan and Eli are standing by the door, Miles beside them.

"Don't forget. Only contact us on your other phone," Kellan reminds me. "But don't use it in public, so you can't take it with you tonight. We don't want them to know you have another one."

I nod. "Okay."

"It's going to be okay. Just do exactly what they tell you."

Eli's gaze is intense. "We will all be watching."

Why does that sound more like a threat than a comfort?

Miles opens the door and peeks outside. "It's all clear."

As I move past him, Eli catches my arm. "Text when you're back in your room, and *lock* the door after you."

Our eyes meet and hold for a heartbeat.

The second he lets me go, I step out after Miles and hurry along the hallway. I don't look back, although I swear I can feel Eli's gaze burning into my shoulder blades.

The hallway is empty, but Miles checks the stairwell before leading me up to my floor. He makes me wait when we hear voices, sticking his head around the door to check.

"It's Lacy. She's unlocking her door," he whispers.

The minute of waiting feels like hours, and I'm shaking with nerves over the thought of getting caught.

"Go." Miles' hand on my back surges me forward out into the hallway. "See you later."

I rush along the hallway and almost drop my key when I fish it out of my pocket. Unlocking the door, I slip inside and lock it behind me. There's a long black dress bag draped over my bed and a pile of makeup beside it. A shoe box is on the floor. I dump my armful of clothes on top of the chair beside the desk and find the phone Sin gave me. I text Eli.

`Me: I'm back in my room.`

`Sin: Alright. We'll see you tonight.`

Once I've read his reply, I turn to the bed and pick up the dress bag. I unzip it and reveal a white dress inside. The makeup I've been left with is in neutral, natural shades. The shoe box contains strappy white heels.

Why white?

I'd been expecting something slutty and outrageous. They've gone out of their way to humiliate and use me, so why is the outfit so subtle?

My other phone pings. I pull it out of my pocket and swipe the screen with my finger, bracing myself for whatever is waiting for me.

`Unknown number: You have everything you need. We want you to wear your hair up exactly like this. Copy the makeup. We expect it to be perfect. Do not disappoint us.`

A photo appears under the message. I stare down at the image of a blonde girl in a white dress.

9

Eli

"I don't like it." I spin to face Kellan, who's lying on his bed, ankles crossed and playing on his cell.

"I know. You've said so five times now."

"You can't tell me you haven't noticed the similarities."

He sighs, sets his phone on the mattress, and looks at me. "Yes, I've noticed them. "

"Then why the fuck are you just sitting there?"

"Because there's nothing else I can do right now." He stands. "Look, I know it's hard for you to just watch and not do anything, but you need to keep it together. If whoever it is gets wind of the fact you know what they're doing, it's going to put Arabella in danger."

What he wasn't saying hung between us like a heavy weight. Our eyes meet and jerk away.

"It's different this time, Eli. We know this part of the pattern. We can predict some of what's coming."

"Can we?"

"Have you sorted your clothes out?"

I glare at him.

"Eli. They want her to flirt with you. If you're not there, she can't do that, and that means they'll tell her to do something else." His voice is patient, like he hasn't already said this a thousand times already. "We can control this as long as we know what they want." He crosses to the closet and throws open the door. "Hmm. I forgot most of your clothes were destroyed. You'll have to use mine." He pulls out a pair of black dress pants and a just-as-black shirt. "Here. These will do. Go shower, then try them on, while I work out what we can use as masks."

"*Masks*?"

"Masquerade Ball, Eli." His voice is muffled as he ducks and rummages through the closet.

I take the clothes he holds out to me, grab underwear from the dresser, and retreat into the bathroom.

I don't want to go to the party tonight. I have a really bad feeling about it. We've been here before. Getting ready for a party, a dare in play, and no idea how the evening is going to end.

Stripping out of my clothes, I take a quick shower, towel dry, then pull on the clothes Kellan has given me. We're similar in height, but he's slightly thicker around the waist than I am, leaving the pants a little loose. That's not really a problem, I have a belt I can use.

When I return to the bedroom, it's to find Kellan dressed. His clothes are similar to mine, only he's wearing a white shirt. He passes me a black wooden box.

"What's this?"

"Face paint. I thought you could design your own mask." His lips tilt up. "I'm going for the Zorro look." He waves a strip of black silk at me.

I look down at the box, then walk back into the bathroom. I have a black and white skull covering my face less than fifteen minutes later.

Kellan laughs when I show him.

"Perfect." He walks to the door. "Let's go and see what trouble we can cause."

Kellan veers straight to the tables where the drinks are when we enter the ballroom, takes a silver flask out of his pocket, and pours a little of its content into two glasses, then fills them up with Coke.

"Vodka?"

He smiles. "Might make the night go easier." He hands one to me.

"It's too loud in here."

He angles a look at me. "We've been in here less than a minute. Bella's not here yet, so don't even think about trying to escape. Find a seat, park your ass, and stay there. Make it somewhere that she'll see you when she walks in."

I take a sip of my drink and turn to look around the room. People are already on the dance floor, arms looped around each other, making out. I spot a couple of empty chairs near to where the doors have been thrown open wide, and in a direct line of sight of the door on the opposite side. I nudge Kellan and point. He nods, and we both walk over to sit down.

There's a prickling down the back of my neck, and I twist around, sure someone is watching me, but I can't see anyone looking in my direction, so I'm not looking at the entrance when Kellan swears.

"What?"

But he doesn't need to answer because, as I turn to look at him, my attention is caught by the girl framed in the doorway.

Blonde hair piled on top of her head, and loose, wispy tendrils framing a face with barely any makeup. Her shoulders are bare, aside from the thin straps holding the white silk in place. The bodice dips deep, displaying creamy skin and cleavage, and the material hugs her hips before flowing out around her legs.

My heart stops beating, the breath stills in my throat, and my fingers crush the plastic cup, spilling my drink all over my hands.

"What the fuck?" I surge to my feet, only to be stopped by Kellan.

"Sit the fuck down."

"Why would she do that?"

"*She* didn't. And *you* can't tell her. So, *sit the fuck down* and let the evening play out."

10

Arabella

Why is everyone wearing masks?

The rush of agitation that's been cloaking me since I started getting ready for the ball slides into a panic. My gaze darts frantically across the students inside the ballroom before settling on a macabre face. A skull. The eyes staring at me from the sinister disguise are burning a hole right through me, so intently that I want to turn and run away.

I tear my gaze away and focus on a table filled with spare masks. With the little white purse clutched between my fingers, I hurry over and snatch up the first white mask I see.

Where are Eli and Kellan?

I have to set down the purse so I can put on the mask and tie it behind my head. People are looking my way, and it makes me nervous. I pluck up my purse again, looping the chain around my wrist so I can lace my fingers together in front of me, in an attempt to contain my trembling.

I know what I'm supposed to do. The orders came when I was crossing the campus. Fear and sickness almost caused me to turn back and run to my room at the thought of what is to come.

I scan the masked faces, searching for the person I need. Music is playing, and couples are already on the dance floor swaying to the song. There's a group of students walking toward me, and my heart sinks when I realize who they are. The three girls are clothed in elegant dresses, and the boys with them are in formal wear. All of them wear masks.

"What are you doing here, freak?" Lacy snaps, her eyes flash with anger behind her red mask.

Maggie glares at me.

I raise my chin. "I-I changed my mind about coming."

Tina steps forward and grabs my arm, her sharp nails digging painfully into my skin. "Get out." She starts to drag me toward the door.

"Mr. Drake is coming," Linda warns.

Everyone looks in his direction, and after a moment's hesitation, Tina lets me go and walks away.

"You're going to regret showing up." Lacy's lips twist into an angry snarl.

Brad's frown turns into a leer when she turns away.

"See you *later*, Gray." Garrett smirks before following him, with Bret, Jace, Kevin, and Evan at his heels.

I don't have time to react to his words because Mr. Drake stops beside me. I paste a smile on my lips and stay frozen in place while his gaze crawls over my dress. Eventually, his attention settles on my face.

"Problem, Miss Gray?"

I shake my head, stomach churning with disgust at the way he's watching me. "No, sir. They just wanted to make sure I found a mask."

He nods, smiling. "You weren't the only one not to realize it was a masquerade ball."

"I thought it was a students-only party."

"Someone needs to be on hand to make sure things run

smoothly, and security isn't always up to the task. Enjoy your evening, Miss Gray." He walks away from me, heading for another group of students.

I count back from ten in my head, take a breath and go back to searching.

Where is Eli?

My gaze roams over the room, returning to the boy with the skull face, who's now seated and still staring at me like he's ready to do violence. My focus darts to his friend, and something about the smile teasing at the masked boy's lips brings recognition. It's Kellan.

My eyes return to the boy beside him, taking in the black pants and shirt he's wearing. I'm not used to seeing him dressed up. Usually, he's in sweats and a hoodie or black ripped jeans.

Tonight, Eli is dressed as death.

A shiver of apprehension runs through me. Our eyes lock and hold, and like a sleepwalker, my feet start moving, taking me across the busy ballroom toward him. When I get closer, I realize he's not wearing a mask at all, but face paint.

He looks like a monster tonight—fierce, deadly, *dangerous*. His jaw is tense, and his eyes are blazing. He looks ready to savage someone.

Please don't let that someone be me.

Kellan is whispering something in his ear, but Eli continues to watch me, eyes unblinking. The intensity of his stare makes my steps falter.

He's pretending. That's all. He's acting angry, so whoever is doing this to us doesn't realize he knows.

I repeat the words to myself over and over, but it doesn't stop a thread of wary doubt from worming its way into my thoughts.

"Good evening, Bella." Kellan smiles when I reach them.

I ignore his words and shove my purse into his chest, still staring into Eli's eyes. Grasping the material of my skirt on either side, I pull it up to my knees, and lift my leg so I can straddle his thighs. When I'm settled on his lap, I wrap my arms around his neck. He's like stone under my touch, muscles stiff with tension.

I smile as I've been instructed and start to gyrate, moving against him awkwardly in time with the beat of the music.

Kellan swears beside us, but I keep my focus on El, knowing we're being watched. Voices talk behind us, shocked gasps, and insults.

Are they recording this?

Tears fill my eyes at the thought of more videos of me plastered over the school's social media, but I blink them away.

Eli's hands fly up to grip my waist. "What the fuck are you doing?"

I bridge the gap between us, and tease his mouth with mine, but don't kiss him. Instead, I whisper against his lips. "Lap dance, but I don't know what I'm doing."

Can he hear the panic in my voice?

I'm scared of getting this wrong and then paying the price for my failure.

Eli's tongue flicks out, licking across my lips, and then he smiles. It turns the skull on his face even more monstrous.

"Fuck me with your clothes on, Kitten." His voice is a raspy whisper, and my body comes alive.

Sin.

Eyes screwed shut, I focus on that thought. That's who I'm

dancing for. *Not* Eli, but my lover in the dark—*Sin*. My movements slow, I undulate over the hard ridge pressing up behind the zipper of his pants. The fact that he's turned on by what I'm doing only feeds my body's need to please him. Rubbing my breasts against his chest, I grow wet with excitement.

"That's it, Kitten," Sin whispers. "Just like you're riding my dick."

I tangle my fingers in the hair at the back of his head, and moan, tipping my head back. The fingers gripping my hips flex, and he takes control of my actions, guiding me.

11

Eli

I can feel the heat of her pussy against my dick. Her nipples, diamond-hard, are clearly outlined through the front of her dress. I'm torn between the desire to push her panties to one side and fuck her where we sit, and the pain slicing through my heart at the memories playing in my head.

I've been here before, a girl in white on my lap, desperately trying to make me hard.

"Fuck me, Eli. Right here. Right now."

"You don't want me, Zoey. Not this way."

I shake my head, displacing the ghost voices, and focus on Arabella's face. The girl on my lap right now doesn't need to *try* to make me hard. All she has to do is touch me.

Her blue eyes are dark, locked on me, as she moves. Her hips roll, dipping and grinding as though she's riding my dick. The fingers in my hair tighten, and she pulls my head back so she can lower hers and lick up my throat. Her teeth sink into the lobe of my ear, and then her tongue licks the sting away. My hand slides from her hip, up her spine, and my fingers make contact with bare skin. She shivers beneath my touch, and I flatten my palm, forcing her closer to me.

I pull my head free from her grip and press my lips to the valley between her breasts. The scent of her perfume fills my nose, and I kiss my way over the curve of her breast, pushing my tongue beneath the material to flick against her nipple. Her breath hitches, and her back arches.

My fingers dig into the curve of her ass, pushing her down harder onto my dick. The hands around my neck slide over my shoulders and down my chest. She pushes herself back, writhing on my lap.

"Are you getting yourself off on my dick, Kitten?" I whisper, and goosebumps rise over her skin at my words. "Do you want to come? Right here?" The reason she's on my lap is forgotten. I don't care *why* she's here, only that she is.

Small white teeth sink into her bottom lip and I move my hand, bringing it around to smooth up her leg beneath her dress. There are no panties to impede my progress and my fingers stroke over her pussy.

Her eyes fly up to meet mine when I push one finger inside her.

"Fuck me like you hate me, Kitten." My thumb finds her clit and I circle it, flick it. My mouth finds her throat and I bite down. "Purr for me."

Her lips part, and I push a second finger inside her, feeling her muscles clamp around me.

"That's it," I whisper. "Come for me."

Her movements are jerky, uncoordinated as she fucks my fingers *right there* in the ballroom. When her body tenses, I wrap my free hand around her neck and pull her mouth down to mine. Her cries are swallowed by my lips as she comes.

"Good girl." I ease my fingers free and lean back on my seat.

"Not sure it's quite the reaction they have in mind, but fucking hell, I need a cold shower," Kellan drawls from beside me, and the cold, hard reality of why we're here hits me like a baseball bat.

Arabella slides off my lap, cheeks bright red. She reaches for the table behind her to steady her balance as she stands. Her eyes meet mine, then dart away, and she turns to Kellan. Her hand is trembling when she holds it out.

"I want you to dance with me."

And with those words, I'm back at a different party with a different girl saying the same words to Kellan.

His head tilts, a small smile teasing his lips.

"You know if we dance, it'll upset everyone. The two most beautiful people in the room can't dance together, Zoobles."

"The three most beautiful people," she corrects him. "I want an Eli and Kellan dance sandwich."

I shake my head.

"Please, Eli?" Her voice is soft, cajoling. "Everyone is wearing masks. We can be different people just for tonight."

Against my better judgment, I let her draw me onto the dancefloor with Kellan. She slips between us, reaches for our hands to wrap mine around her waist and his around her neck. I'm behind her, her ass pressing against my dick as she dances. She moves my hand up to her breast, pulls Kellan's head down so she can kiss him.

He's happier to play along than I am. I don't like this. It's not right. It's not her. Something is off. Zoey doesn't like boys. She likes girls. So why is she trying to convince us to fuck her?

I pull my hand free and step away. "I can't do this."

Laughter snaps me back to the present, and my gaze focuses on Kellan and Arabella. They're on the dance floor, not far away from me. He's talking to her, lips quirking up as he smiles, and she laughs up at him.

Unlike when she was fucking my fingers, she looks a lot happier, more relaxed. Her arms are looped around his neck, his hands are resting on her hips. They look good together.

He must sense my gaze, because his head turns and he winks at me, and lets his hand slip down to cup her ass and squeeze. I shake my head and stand so I can cross the room to where the drinks are. Grabbing a Coke, I pop the can and pour it into a plastic cup and walk back to my seat. Kellan's flask is tucked into the side of the chair, so I grab it and top up the Coke with vodka and take a healthy swallow.

If this is how the evening is going to go, I'm seriously considering going back to my room to raid the stash of alcohol we have there because I'm not sure my nerves can take it.

12

Arabella

"You're doing so well," Kellan's whisper of encouragement is right in my ear as we sway together on the dance floor.

My cheeks are hot with embarrassment. I'm still dazed by the fact that Eli just made me orgasm in front of the entire school.

I keep my eyes trained on the front of Kellan's shirt. "I can't believe he just made me come with everyone watching."

"They might act like they're shocked, but most of them are secretly wishing they were in your place."

I exhale in a quiet rush. "They wouldn't enjoy it if they were."

"Eyes up here, Bella."

Lifting my chin, I meet his warm, watchful gaze.

His lips quirk up as he smiles. "There. Isn't that better? Relax. We're just two people enjoying a dance."

I let my shoulders loosen up and laugh. The sound is flat, lacking in humor. "I wish I could enjoy it."

"I'll make sure to dazzle you with my fabulous moves." He glances away from my face and winks. A beat later, his hands are on my ass, squeezing and kneading.

"What are you doing?" I squeak, clutching at his collar.

His head dips to nuzzle my cheek, and then he licks my ear. "I'm guessing this is supposed to be more than a dance."

"I'm supposed to flirt with you."

"And?"

I hesitate, only answering when his fondling hands pinch my ass. "Seduce you into taking me back to your room to have sex."

"Then we better give them a show." He presses a kiss to my lips. It's soft, chaste, and teasing.

"Open for me, Bella," he whispers against my lips.

Kellan's tongue invades my mouth to entwine with my own. It's different from the way Eli kisses me. There's no dominance or anger. I taste passion and heat, but it's not the same. It doesn't want to consume me, like when I'm with my stepbrother.

Kellan raises his head and grins. He spins me around and grinds his groin into my ass, his hands holding my hips. His hard-on presses against me, and an unexpected ache fills my body.

I catch sight of Eli watching us as Kellan spins me again, his gaze hooded.

"Play with me, Bella. Make him show how jealous he is. That's what they want." Kellan murmurs in my ear, his lips kissing up along the side of my neck. My attention on Eli, I glide my hands up my body to cup my breasts. I keep my focus on him while I dirty dance with his best friend. We're practically dry humping each other to the beat of the song. Kellan's hands bunch the material at my hips, dragging it upward.

My groin tightens with need, my breath hitching, and my heart thumps wildly in my chest. Having Eli watching us is a turn-on I can't deny.

"No panties, Bella? How deliciously shocking." Kellan chuckles. "Are you wet? All it would take is another few tugs, and everyone would see your pretty pink pussy."

I grab his wrists, but he doesn't pull my skirt higher than my thighs.

"Kellan." He stops at my warning tone.

"Maybe they want me to fuck you right here on the dance floor." One hand still clutching the fabric, he uses the other to bend me over at the waist and grinds behind me. "I could, you know. With Eli's blessing."

Pushing back against him, my lips part, my eyes half closing.

A mix of unease and arousal twists my stomach. It pulses between my legs, where an echo of Eli's fingers thrusting inside me scorches me like flames from the inside. It's so strong and painful that I half expect my dress to disintegrate.

Eli's lips thin, his unforgiving eyes watching us as we move. And then he turns on his heels and shoves his way through the crowd toward the exit.

Awareness pours back in. Faces are watching us, phones up and recording. I struggle to free myself from Kellan's arms, mortification burning my cheeks, but he catches my wrists and hauls me back. He pushes hard into the vee of my thighs, the hard ridge of his cock pressing against the thin fabric of my dress.

His gaze drops to my mouth, skimming over my lips. "Put your arms around my neck. We're not finished here. We'll dance for a little longer, and then I'm taking you back to the room."

13

Eli

"Close the door."

I've been sitting in the dark for almost an hour, Zoey's last party playing on a constant loop in my head. The comparisons between then and now. Between her behavior and Arabella's. I can't get how that night ended out of my head. I don't want this one to end the same way.

The bite in my voice is not lost on Kellan. He drops his arm from Arabella's shoulder and turns to twist the lock on the door. She doesn't move, staring at me out of those big blue eyes.

"Did you enjoy dancing with Kellan?

"It's what I was told to do."

"That's not answering me. Did you enjoy it? Is your pussy wet? Did he touch you? *Kiss* you? Did you ride his fingers on the dance floor? Did you *come* for him?"

"What?" Her voice is a shocked whisper.

"It's an easy question. Are you wet? You liked him touching you before. Did you like me watching while he ran his hands over your body? While his mouth sucked on your skin? *Did it make you wet?*"

Her cheeks are bright red. That's answer enough.

"Do you want to play some more?" My words are silky.

"P-play?" Her throat moves as she swallows.

"Red or green?"

"What?" she whispers again.

"You heard me." I stand, and stride across to her. "Take off the mask." My demand is directed at Kellan, who moves up behind Arabella and unties the ribbon. "Answer the question. Red or green? Do you want to play some more … with both of us? Do you want us to fuck you together, Kitten? Red or fucking green?"

Her tongue snakes out over her lips. "Gr-green?"

"Are you asking me or telling me?"

"Green." She repeats the word more firmly.

I hold up my hand and let the strip of black silk roll open. Her recognition is immediate, lips parting as she gasps.

"Remove the dress." I can't touch her while she's wearing it.

"Why?"

"Take it off or I'll fucking rip it off," I snarl.

She flinches.

"It's okay," Kellan's voice is quiet and confident. "It's not you he's angry with." His hands rest on her shoulders. "Do you want me to help you?" He's already sliding one strap down her arm.

"You're in control here, Bella. You say red, and everything stops. You know how it works." He dips his head to kiss her shoulder. "I liked dancing with you tonight. Eli—" She stiffens at the sound of my name, and Kellan clearly notices because he changes his words. "*Sin* enjoyed watching us. I bet his dick is hard and ready to make you feel good."

He steps back and tugs on the lace holding the back of her dress together, but he's moving too slow for me. I hand him the blindfold, take hold of the front of the dress where it splits to display her cleavage and pull sharply. The rip as it tears in two blends with her shocked cry. The dress falls in two parts down her arms to pool at her feet, leaving her naked under my gaze.

Kellan places the blindfold over her face and ties it snugly into place, while I unbuckle my belt and slide it off. Her lips part at the sound of my zipper.

"On your knees, Kitten. Open your mouth."

Kellan presses his hands down onto her shoulders and guides her onto her knees.

"Tongue out."

I fist my dick and pull it out of my pants. Kellan's eyes dip to look, and a smile tilts up one side of his mouth.

Stepping forward, I rest my dick on her tongue. "Open wider. Loosen your jaw. Tip your head back." While I talk, I reach for her hair, tangling my fingers into it and pull her head back, so I can thrust my dick deep into her mouth.

She gags, tenses, and tries to pull back. I tighten my grip.

"Breathe through your nose. Relax your throat."

I glance at Kellan, who's watching my dick sliding in and out of her mouth.

"Spread your legs, pretty girl." He kneels beside her and runs his fingers over her thigh, gently easing them apart so he can stroke her pussy. "You're so wet. I bet you could take both of us at once." He bends his head to lick over one hard nipple.

She gasps around my dick when he pushes two fingers inside her. "Suck Sin's dick, pretty girl, while you fuck my fingers. You look so good. I can't wait to have my dick in your mouth … and your pussy. Would you like that?"

"Keep your mouth around my dick and get up on all fours," I tell her.

She moans softly, rising on her knees and placing her hands down. Kellan's fingers stay buried deep in her pussy, and he moves until he's behind her and lowers his head, tongue coming out to lick over one ass cheek and down until his face is buried against her. I pull my dick from her mouth.

"Tell me what he's doing." I sit on the floor in front of her, my legs either side of her arms.

"He's licking me."

"Where?"

"My … my ass … my pussy … oh god," she groans.

"How many fingers are inside you?"

"I don't know. Two?"

Kellan lifts his head, lips wet with her arousal. "Three. And you're taking them so well, pretty girl. I bet you can take more." He licks his lips. "You taste fucking amazing. It's no wonder Sin is so hungry for you all the time."

I push her head back down onto my dick, and the new angle lifts her ass high in the air. Kellan runs his fingers over her spine, then lifts his fingers to his mouth and licks them. "That pretty ass of yours is just begging to be filled. I have just the thing for it." He holds my eyes as he pushes one finger into her ass. "Fuck, she's tight. She's sucking me in like she's hungry for it."

Arabella gives a soft whine and I stroke her hair. "You're doing so good. Just relax. You can take it. Such a good girl. Suck my dick, Kitten. Make it nice and wet for me."

Her head bobs, tongue lapping along my length, cheeks hollowing out as she sucks. My gaze jumps from her mouth to where Kellan is pumping his finger in and out of her ass. When I feel that familiar tingle in my veins, the tightening in my balls, I pull her head off me.

"Time for you to show Kellan how good your mouth is, Kitten. I want your pussy." I hook my hands beneath her arms and draw her to her feet with me, grip her chin between my fingers and kiss her, *hard*. My tongue slides between her lips, tangles with hers, while Kellan's hands roam over her body, cupping her breasts, stroking down over her stomach, rubbing a circle around her clit.

"You're so incredibly wet, pretty girl," he whispers, stripping out of his shirt and pants. "I can't wait to feel your pussy around my cock. But I think your favorite sin wants to get his dick soaked in you first."

We both guide her to the bed and down until she's lying on her back, with her head on the edge. Kellan wraps a hand around his dick and gives it a slow pump, then runs the head over her lips.

"Open up, pretty girl. Swallow me down."

Her lips part, and she takes Kellan's dick into her mouth. The angle of her head puts her between his legs, his balls brushing against her face as he fucks her mouth. I watch them for a second, before climbing onto the bed and settling between her legs.

Spreading her pussy open with thumb and finger, I give her a long lick. One which has her hips rising up off the bed. A strangled moan escapes her throat. I laugh quietly, and then there's only the sound of her moans, of Kellan swearing while she sucks on his dick, of my groans of pleasure as she writhes on my tongue.

When her body tenses, arches up, and her fingers curl into the sheets beside her, I pull my face away. Her mouth is still full of Kellan's dick, and she's sobbing and crying around it as her body rides through its orgasm. His hands are on her breasts, twisting and pinching her nipples, keeping her on the peak while I reach for a condom.

I'm still fully clothed, so I shove my pants further down my thighs, roll on the condom and crawl up her body. Kellan's hand moves so I can suck a nipple into my mouth, and I reach between our bodies to line my dick up.

"Take off her blindfold," I tell Kellan.

He pulls his dick out of her mouth and reaches for the blindfold. It falls from her face just as I thrust inside her. My hand grips her jaw.

"Open your eyes."

Her blue eyes flutter open.

"Look at me."

I thrust deep, *deeper*, until I can't go any further.

"*Look* at me." I growl the words from between gritted teeth. "Say my name."

"Sin." The word is a moan.

"Naughty girl." Kellan chides and pinches her nipple. "Try again." He lowers his head to take the stiff little peak into his mouth.

Her eyes are clouded with desire, lips wet and plump. I drive into her again. "Say my name."

"*Sin*." Defiance and desire drip from her voice.

"Again." My next thrust drives us up the bed.

"Sin!"

"Who's fucking you? Say my fucking name."

19

Arabella

"Who's fucking you? Say my fucking name." Eli's voice is rough, thick with lust.

I can't. He frightened me with his aggression when we first walked into the room, and I don't want to acknowledge that he is the one making me feel good.

"Sin, Sin, Sin," I chant the name over and over, refusing to let go of the fantasy. He's the one I trust. The one I love. My secret lover in the dark who gave me the confidence I needed to survive in this hell, before Eli snatched it all away.

He continues to move over me, *inside me,* at a merciless pace, fingers clutching my jaw. The painted mask he'd been wearing is smeared across his face in a mess of white and black. I'm limp, his plaything to fuck and play with, and I revel in it.

My pussy pulses around his cock as I come, and the release is so intense that I arch up, and my eyes slam shut. Crying out, I give myself up to the euphoria.

"Open your eyes and keep them on me."

My eyes pop open at the rough command, and I drown in a pair of green eyes that keep my gaze captive.

"I'm not going to fucking stop until you say my name, Kitten." Eli doesn't slow his thrusts.

It's like he's possessed. *Obsessed* with making me say his name. I meet him thrust for thrust, my body trembling as another orgasm starts to mount.

Kellan's mouth is sucking on my breast, teeth grazing over my nipple. My head is light, caught up in overwhelming sensations that he's forcing on me. I can do nothing but feel.

Their hands are everywhere. Lips caress my neck, jaw, and breasts. I'm lost in the pleasure of it. They give attention to every inch of my body—licking, kissing, touching, and feasting on me hungrily. My pleas and moans fill the room.

"Let go, Kitten. Fall for us." His voice makes me throb around his cock, and I climax again, eyes rolling back in my head. I never want the bliss to end.

His movements change, becoming uncoordinated, and a second later, he shudders inside me.

"I'm not done with you yet," he pants in my ear, his body heavy on top of me.

15

Eli

I roll off the bed and remove the condom. Tying it off, I toss it into the trash can near the door, then turn back to the bed. Kellan is between Arabella's thighs, her legs over his shoulders as he feasts on her pussy. I crouch beside her head and fist her hair, dragging her face around to me.

"Say my name."

"Sin." The nickname is a sigh of pleasure.

I kiss her. Hard. Demanding. My teeth nipping at her lips.

"We can do this all night, Kitten. We're going to make you come so much you'll forget everything except the desperate need to say my name."

A smile curves her lips, and I wonder if she has any idea how fucking sexy she looks. Her body is flushed. Teeth marks cover her breasts, her throat, her thighs. Her eyes are heavy, post-orgasm dazed, but there's still a defiant tilt to her chin as she holds my eyes.

Kellan lifts his head and looks at us both. "You should clean his cock, pretty girl. It's all sticky with his cum. Be a good girl and lick it clean."

Her hand reaches out, finds my dick and curls around it. I twitch, not quite ready for round two, still sensitive from coming.

"Suck his dick while I fuck your pussy." He rolls on a condom and kneels up, lifting her ass to rest it on his thighs, and slowly pushes his dick inside her.

She moans.

I wrap a hand around her throat, forcing her head back. "Tell me how it feels."

"Good." The word leaves her on a sigh.

"Better than me?" If she says yes, I might just kill Kellan.

She shakes her head. "Different."

I stand up and press my dick to her lips. "Do as he said. Clean my dick."

Her tongue slides over me, licking me like I'm her favorite flavored lollipop. And I slowly stiffen again in her mouth until I'm thrusting deep into her throat. Her hand lifts to clutch at my thigh as she writhes on the bed.

Kellan's fingers are on her clit as he drives in and out. I lean forward, bracing myself on one arm, while I fuck her mouth in fast and hard thrusts. Her whimpers vibrate along the length of my dick, and then she's coming again, crying and sobbing. Kellan doesn't let up, slamming into her, driving my dick further down her throat with every thrust he makes.

Her nails rake down my thigh, and I grit my teeth against the sting, lowering my head to bite her hip in retaliation and feel her body shudder.

"Fuck. Fuck. Fuck." Kellan collapses on top of us both, shoves up and rolls away.

I'm back in position almost immediately, deep inside her, before I register the fact I'm fucking her bare. When I try to pull out, she hooks her legs around my hips.

"No!" She drags me deeper.

"No condom. I need to—"

"No. Fuck me." She tangles a hand into my hair and pulls my head down to hers. "Fill me up. *Fuck me*, Eli."

And my name on her lips is all I need to send me hurtling over the edge for a second time. I bury my face into her throat, snarling and snapping with the force of my orgasm.

Her rapid breaths, the beat of my heart, Kellan moving around …

Sound slowly comes back to me as I float down to the ground. Arabella's fingers are in my hair. I think she might have left a nail or three embedded in my ass, but I can't bring myself to care … or to move.

I could stay wrapped up in her body forever, cocooned in the dark where the world can't intrude.

"You might want to move before you crush her." Kellan's amused words come from my left.

I roll my head sideways, pressing a kiss to her throat. "Can't."

"Why not?"

"I live here now."

He laughs, and I can hear him moving around. Light fills the room briefly when he opens the bathroom door, then closes it again behind him, only to return a few minutes later.

"Come on. Move your ass and stop being a heathen. That pretty little kitty is going to be sore from the workout she just got. Aftercare is essential." He hands me a warm, wet washcloth. "Your mess, so you can clean it up."

I sigh, press a string of kisses along Arabella's shoulder, then roll off her. She doesn't move, other than to give me a sleepy smile. One I take and store, because I'm pretty sure she won't be smiling at me like that tomorrow when the events of tonight sink in.

I slide down the bed, kissing her hip, her thighs, her stomach as I use the washcloth to clean her up. She's almost asleep by the time I'm done, so between myself and Kellan, we get her settled into the bed, then I strip out of my clothes and stretch out beside her. She curls into my side, face buried against my shoulder. Kellan is behind her, his fingers running up and down her side in gentle strokes.

"A much better ending than the last party, don't you think?" he says softly.

Our eyes meet above Arabella's head.

"It's not over yet," I reply.

***

I wake up, heart racing, the rapid beat loud in my ears.

Did something wake me?

I lay still, straining to hear above the sound of my heart, and slowly Arabella's breathing, and the recognizable soft snores of Kellan become clear.

It must have been a dream. I shift onto my side and look at the girl in my bed. She's sleeping, lips slightly parted, one hand tucked beneath her cheek. Her back is to me, and she's facing Kellan, whose hand is resting on her hip.

She's uncovered from the waist up, and I let my gaze travel over her. Her breasts are clear in the moonlight shining in the room, and I reach out to run one finger over them. She murmurs something and wriggles her ass. A move that wakes my dick up. I pinch her nipple, and she sighs, pressing her breast more firmly into my palm. I squeeze gently, then let my palm slide down to her stomach to press her back into my erection.

My lips find her throat and I kiss my way up to her ear, along her jaw, then turn her head toward me so I can capture her lips. She moans into my mouth, one arm reaching back to hook around my neck. The move arches her back, thrusts out her breasts, and before I really think about what I'm doing, I've got a condom on, and I'm buried to the hilt inside her body, while Kellan sleeps on, oblivious, beside us.

"Say my name," I whisper against her lips, and she smiles.

"Sin. My Nasty Little Monster. *Eli.*" My name leaves her lips on a sigh of pleasure.

We come together, her body pulsing around mine and I bury my face into her throat to muffle my groans while my hand is over her mouth to do the same.

We must have fallen asleep still fucking, because when I next open my eyes, it's to a surprised shout.

"*Kellan*? What the fuck happened here last night?"

16

Arabella

"K*ellan*?"

"It's no big deal."

"No big deal? You're in bed with Arabella and Eli!"

The argument snatches me from sleep. Awareness filters in. There's a heavy weight on top of me, and something hard swelling inside me. My eyes snap open to find Eli above me.

Sleepy green eyes meet mine. "Good morning, Hellcat."

"What the—" My lips part, and my gasp morphs into a moan when he starts rocking slowly in and out of me. Linking our fingers, he draws my hands above my head and pins them there.

"I can't believe this. You fucked them."

My gaze shifts over Eli's shoulder, where Miles is standing by the door, arms crossed, watching us. His face is pinched, angry.

"I fucked Bella, *not* Eli. He doesn't like dicks all up in his space," Kellan replies, and my head turns to find him stretched out beside us on the mattress, the sheet draped over his waist.

What the hell is happening? Why am I in bed with them?

Drowsy memories reel through my head. Images of hungry mouths, and rough hands. The sting of teeth. The building pressure as they'd fucked me into the mattress.

Kellan and Eli. Giving me pleasure. *Together.*

Oh god, what did I do?

Something I've desired in my dark little fantasies, a tiny voice reminds me in my head. *Isn't that what they've been giving you since Halloween?*

"I love feeling you clench around my dick. You're so fucking wet right now. Are you thinking about last night?" Eli's lips find my neck, biting and licking at my skin, still thrusting into me lazily. "You're such a good girl for me. You took Kellan's dick so well. I loved seeing how hard you came for us both."

The praise has my toes curling, and I groan. My legs move of their own accord, wrapping around his waist and driving him deeper inside me. There's a voice at the back of my mind shouting at me to push him away, but I'm hooked on the sweet ache that's growing inside me. It drowns out everything else, until I'm lost in Eli's heat.

"Oh, and that's supposed to make it better?" Miles' shout interrupts the pleasure building in my body, and I tense.

"Ignore them." Eli's fingers squeeze mine and he captures my lips, tongue sliding between them to stroke against mine.

"Miles," Kellan calls after him. "Fuck."

"Come for me," Eli demands, and my body obeys his command without argument, clenching greedily around his length. Pleasure erupts as my orgasm rolls through me.

Eli thrusts into me a few more times before shuddering through his release.

"You look beautiful. All sleepy and sated. Thoroughly fucked."

Am I becoming a sex addict, or is it just Eli that makes me this way?

I stretch, blinking up at him.

A sudden thought turns me cold and makes me stiffen beneath him. "Did you use a condom?"

I try to push him off me, but he doesn't move. "Kellan did, and the first time we fucked last night. But the second time? No. You wouldn't let me pull out." He bites my throat. "You begged me so prettily to fill you up, and then you looked so good covered in my cum."

My cheeks burn with embarrassment as I remember my mindless pleas. "You should have insisted! It's a good thing I'm on the pill. Elena sorted it out before I came back after Christmas."

I'd also been given the chat about being sexually active and not getting myself knocked up. The whole conversation had been awkward and ironic, as that was exactly how she'd ended up with me.

I wiggle beneath him again. "Can you *please* get off me?"

Eli ignores me, kissing a path over my shoulder. "I'm kind of enjoying where I am."

"I need to pee."

His sigh is a soft, warm exhale of breath against my throat. "Fine."

He pulls out of me. I wince at the unexpected soreness. Rolling the condom off his cock, he ties the end and rises from the bed to drop it into the trash can. When he turns away from me, I see the silver mesh of scars crisscrossing his back.

I rush across to the bathroom and close the door behind me. I'm aching all over, and when I glance in the mirror above the sink, I see little dark-red marks from the suction of their mouths. Hickeys cover my neck and all over my breasts, and when I examine lower, I discover more on the inside of my thighs. They marked me all over while they explored every inch of my body.

I recall the look on Eli's expression when we entered the room after we came back from the party. His forcefulness and aggression.

The way he slipped so seamlessly into being Sin. How he ripped the white dress from my body.

A knock sounds on the closed door. "Bella, we need to use the bathroom, too."

"Coming." I do what I need to do, and wash my hands.

Kellan is naked and standing just outside when I open the door.

His gaze runs over my nudity and pauses on my face. "Are you suffering from post-threesome blues?"

"Being fucked by two men was one of your fantasies." Eli is watching me from the bed, now dressed in a t-shirt and boxer briefs.

Spying a hoodie hanging off the back of a chair, I snatch it up and pull it on. It's baggy enough to cover everything.

"You only know that because you read it." I can't keep the accusation out of my voice.

"There's nothing wrong with the desires you have, Hellcat. It doesn't make you your mother."

"Doesn't it?" My voice is sharp. "I recall you telling me I was just like her."

"You're angry that we fucked, and now you want to fight." A lazy smile curves his lips. "I'll feed you, fuck you, *and* fight you, Hellcat. You have my promise on that."

I shoot him a glare and gesture between the three of us. "*This* was a mistake. It's not happening again."

"You're addicted to my dick. Of course, it will."

"You arrogant asshole."

Kellan chuckles. "And we're back to the verbal foreplay between the two of you."

A familiar chime stops any response I have. I freeze at the sound, and my stomach flips. Kellan, who still hasn't bothered to cover himself up, finds my purse on the floor and hands it to me. I locate my phone and check my messages.

`Unknown number: We know you're still in their dorm room. Take a photograph of Eli's back.`

"They want a photo." My voice is low.

Are they close by? Were they listening outside the door?

Kellan peers over my shoulder. "Let me guess. They want proof that my dick is as big as the rumors say?"

"Eli's back."

The boy in question goes rigid. "No."

"But they—"

"I said *no*." The words leave him in a snarl.

I flinch at the venom in his voice. He stands and stalks toward the bathroom, slamming the door. Silence and confusion are left in his wake.

17

Eli

I grip the edges of the countertop, head bowed, as I suck in breath after breath. It shouldn't bother me, not after this many years. Students at school have seen my scars before. *Everyone* has seen them.

Arabella hasn't. Not for long enough to really *see* them, anyway.

Yes, she did. When you were both at the hotel. She asked you about them.

I whirl and bury my fist against the wall.

"What was that?" Arabella's voice is raised and worried beyond the door.

"It's just Eli. Don't worry about it." Kellan's is the opposite, calm and level.

I walk across to the door, meaning to open it, but my hand won't move, won't turn the doorknob. I stand there, frozen, listening to the conversation in the other room.

"After what they wanted me to do yesterday, taking a photograph seems a little …"

"Anticlimactic?"

"Yeah."

"You'd think that, wouldn't you?"

I turn and rest my back against the door, then slide down to the floor, drawing my legs up and looping my arms around them. I should go out there, explain myself, but I can't. I just fucking *can't*.

"Why do you think he's called the monster, Bella?"

My eyes close. I wish I could block out the sound of Kellan's voice, but my earbuds are in the other room.

"Because he's an asshole who does what he wants?"

Kellan laughs. "*Now* he does. But back then …" He pauses, and in my mind, I can see him shaking his head. "That's not where the nickname came from. Most people have forgotten now. Eli made sure he molded the nickname to fit something else, something darker. He took something that started as an insult and turned it into a warning."

"An insult?"

I lower my head and rest it against my knees.

Here it comes.

"What do you know about Eli's past?"

"Nothing really. I heard his mom died when he was fourteen."

"That's right. He was with her. There was a car accident while they were driving here. No one is sure quite what caused it, but the car flipped and rolled down an embankment. It hit a tree. They found out afterward that Eli's seatbelt was faulty. When the car flipped, it came undone and he was thrown about. He went through the window. Those scars on his back are from that and then flying across the ground at however many miles an hour it was."

My back is burning. I know the pain isn't real. That it's not really there. It's the memory of those first few weeks after the accident replaying in my head.

"What about his mom?"

"They think she died on impact."

I swallow against the lump blocking my throat. I want him to speed up, but he won't. Kellan is always thorough in his explanations.

"Anyway, he was out of school for a while, but when he came back, he was still banged up. One side of his face was swollen. Couple of teeth knocked out. Scars all over his back. They looked worse back then. Red and sore. He looked a mess. A couple of the boys coined the term—"

"The Monster of Churchill Bradley," Arabella interrupts him softly.

"You got it. Over time, he embraced it—*became* it. I guess some people remember its origin and want to remind everyone else."

I shove to my feet and turn. I don't want to hear her pity, so I throw open the door. Kellan meets my gaze, Arabella doesn't. But it doesn't matter. I don't want to *see* the pity in her eyes, either.

Striding across the room, I pull the shirt over my head and brace my palms against the wall. "Take it."

"Eli—"

"Just fucking do it." I know what Kellan's about to say. He'll argue, tell us to wait and see what the punishment might be.

But I can't risk it. Because I've fucking *been* here before and I know what's coming.

"Take the fucking photograph."

18

Arabella

I stare at Eli's ruined back. His muscles are tense beneath the skin.

Eli was in the car when his mom died. He'd been hurt in the accident. The students made fun of him when he must have been suffering, mourning inside with so much pain. They'd called him a monster. His life must have been hell, and he embraced it, twisted it to fashion himself an armor to survive. He became the Monster of Churchill Bradley Academy.

Impulsively I reach out to trail my fingertips down the marks just left of his spine. He tenses further beneath my touch but doesn't move.

"What the fuck are you doing?"

Ignoring his low, tortured words, I bridge the gap between us and press my lips to the imperfect flesh. I kiss a path along one jagged set of lines, then I move on to another. Eli moves so fast that I gasp when he spins, grabs my arms, and slams me back against the wall, his hand closing around my throat.

He presses his body into mine, and cages me in. "I never gave you permission to touch me."

I meet his angry gaze warily. "I'm sorry."

"Take the fucking photograph before I change my mind."

"We don't have to do this. I'll say it wasn't possible."

Eli's fingers tighten around my neck, cutting off my air. "You don't know what they might do to you if you fail."

I shake my head, my heart beating rapidly in my chest, fear

spiking. "I'll take that chance. I did what they wanted last night. That has to count for something."

"You're not leaving this room until you take the fucking photograph." The muscle in his jaw ticks, an unspoken threat hanging between us.

"What are you going to do, Eli?" I hold his penetrating glare. "Keep me a prisoner?"

"Yes," he replies without an inch of hesitation. "You are doing this, or I will gag you, tie you up and take you somewhere no one will fucking find you."

A disbelieving laugh escapes me, but it dies quickly when he doesn't smile. "Holy shit. You're serious!"

Kellan sighs behind him. "As much as I'm sure you'd both get a kick out of it, we are *not* keeping her captive, Eli. If we're doing this, it needs to be done now. Your blackmailers will be waiting for a response."

I want to argue more. Tell him that he doesn't have to do this, but the look in his eyes makes it clear he's not going to listen.

I drop my attention from his face. "I-I think if you're lying face down on the bed, it would be better."

"It would look more natural. Like you're sleeping," Kellan agrees.

Eli slides his hand up from my throat and cups my jaw. He rubs his thumb over my lips. "Make it quick."

Releasing me, he stalks to his bed and throws himself down on the blanket. Kellan gives me a firm nod when I glance his way. I move to the end of the bed, aim the camera on my phone at Eli, and snap a photo. The image is of his back and shoulders but not his face or lower half. I attach it to a text and send it off.

"Done." I sink down onto the edge of the bed.

"Did they send you anything else last night?" Kellan pulls out some boxer briefs and some sweatpants from the dresser on his side of the room.

I scroll through the messages on my cell. "Just the lap dance with Eli and flirting with you before sex—"

The phone is snatched out of my hand.

"Hey!" I twist and find Eli holding it. His face is pale, eyes wide and haunted. "What's the matter?"

Kellan crosses the room, rounding the bed to take a look at what his friend is staring at. "Shit."

"What?"

"It's nothing." His smile is tight.

"Don't give me that crap. I can tell from your faces *it's something*."

"The girl in the photograph they sent you. That's Zoey," Eli's voice is quiet.

A sick sense of dread washes over me. "Zoey Rivers?"

He nods.

I frown. "When was it taken?"

Kellan and Eli share a look but remain silent.

I take the phone back from Eli and look at the photo on the screen. Zoey is in a white dress. The same one I'd worn last night. I copied every detail, just as instructed. My hair and makeup. I'd been a living doll for my blackmailers to position and use. It's no wonder Eli had seemed so angry.

Zoey. The dead girl. Eli and Kellan's friend.

They had ensured I was dressed the same way.

Why? What was the motivation behind it?

"When was this taken?" I repeat, my agitation blooming.

"Halloween." Eli's voice is void of emotion. "The night she died."

19

Eli

Logically, I'd known they had to have sent Arabella a photograph of Zoey. And I *knew* everything about her outfit and look was the same as how Zoey looked the last time we saw her. But mentally, I *still* wasn't prepared to see her face staring up at me.

"This is good." Kellan's words draw a frown from me.

"How the fuck is this good?"

He plucks Arabella's cell from her fingers and looks down at the screen. "Because it narrows down the pool of suspects."

I take the shirt he hands me and pull it over my head. "Explain."

"Well, whoever we're dealing with is the same person who connected with Zoey. And, just like last time, everything seems to be linked to *you*."

"That doesn't narrow *anything* down."

"No, but when you add their demand for photographs of your back, that means it's someone who remembers where your nickname came from."

"Still leaves a shit ton of people."

He nails me with an exasperated look. "Will you stop interrupting me? Please and thank you." He hands Arabella her cell. "As I was saying, it means it's someone from our year."

"How do you figure that?"

"Because it was someone in our years who coined the term in the first place. The years below us had no idea who you were, only that you were that shy kid who'd been in an accident and lost his mom. The years above us are no longer here. By process of elimination, that leaves someone in our year."

"What about one of the faculty?"

He shakes his head. "Doesn't make sense. Plus, that video of the two of you fucking in the Hamptons? Pretty sure none of the faculty were there. But that also brings the pool of suspects into a smaller, more manageable amount. We need a list of everyone in senior year and cross-reference it to who was at the club that night."

"Not really." I push off the bed and rummage through my dresser for a pair of sweatpants and pull them on. When I turn back, it's to find Arabella's eyes on me. I hike an eyebrow. "Enjoying the view?"

"What do you mean *not really?*" Kellan says before Arabella can answer me.

I scratch my jaw. "Someone could have posted that video somewhere, and then whoever is behind all this bullshit picked it up."

"All that means is that it could be more than one person, and at least one of them matches my theory."

"But that doesn't narrow it down enough for us to pinpoint where to look. There are over one hundred people in senior year."

"But you don't know all of them, Eli."

"No, but like you said, they *all* know who I am."

The cell in Arabella's hand chimes, and all three of us stare at it. When she doesn't move to read the text, I take it from her and swipe across the screen.

`Unknown number: Well done. Did you fuck Kellan?`

`We know he likes to mark the people he sleeps with. Show us one of his bite marks. One from somewhere "special."`

"They want a photograph of either your pussy or your tits."

"Don't they have enough of me already?" The tremor in her voice is clear.

"It's for control. They must be running out of things to use from the cloud. I don't think we uploaded that much."

"I've got an idea." Kellan stands. "Bella, take your top off."

"Why?" She's bright red.

"Sweetie, I've had my tongue, fingers, and dick inside you. It's a little late to be embarrassed about being naked in front of me. Strip and get on the bed. I'm going to wrap my lips around your nipple and take a selfie."

"I don't want—"

"It won't go any further than that, I promise. Not even if you scream green from the rooftop."

"He's right. Do it his way."

Her discomfort with the idea is written all over her face, but she pulls off the hoodie and climbs onto the bed.

"Pull the sheet up around your waist." Kellan stretches out beside her. "Roll toward me." His hand rests on her hip and tugs her closer. "That's it." He reaches for the cell. "Okay, give that to me. Bella, close your eyes, relive having Eli's dick inside you. His mouth sucking on you." Her nipples harden. "That's it. Good girl. Ready? Okay, here we go."

He licks a wet circle around her nipple, lifts the cell, and snaps a photograph, then immediately rolls away. Arabella drags the sheet up to cover herself.

"There. That wasn't too painful, was it? And check that out! We look fucking hot together." He tosses her the cell. "Send the photograph."

"Why are you so … so *unconcerned* by all this?" she snaps.

I sit down beside her, take the cell, and send the photograph. "He's concerned. This is his way of dealing with it." I meet Kellan's gaze. "We're in unknown territory now."

The humor leaches from his face. "I know."

"Unknown territory? What does that mean?" Arabella twists to face me.

I don't move my eyes from Kellan. His tongue runs over his bottom lip, and then he nods.

"Whoever is sending you these texts did the same to Zoey. They wanted her to fuck Eli. Eli said no."

"I thought Zoey liked girls?"

"She does … *did*. She was having fun with the dares—"

"And then she wasn't." I took over. "But we missed the signs. She thought they were funny at first. And they were. Silly little things. But somewhere along the way, they turned darker. At the Halloween party, she came in … dressed exactly the way you were and did the same things you did. Gave me a lap dance, begged me to fuck her. I refused."

"So, then she dragged both of us onto the dance floor. She was … *handsy*." Kellan picked up the thread again. "Eli called a stop to it before I did. After he left, she said she wanted to have sex with me … just to see what it was like with a guy instead of a girl. Something was off about it. I mean, don't get me wrong, I've known girls and guys who want to give the other side a try, out of curiosity, but it just didn't *fit* for Zoey. When I said no, she started crying, then ran off."

He looks at me again, and I know the pain in his face is reflected in mine. "That was the last time we saw her."

I close my eyes. "Until I found her in the cemetery."

20

Arabella

Zoey played a game of dares. The dares turned into a nightmare. She turned up dead.

This has all happened before. Did her darer kill her, or was her death really an accident?

I press a hand to my stomach under the sheet and try to contain the panic trying to consume me.

"Are you saying that if you hadn't found out about me being blackmailed and gone along with the dares last night, I could be dead right now?"

Eli doesn't answer.

Kellan shrugs. "Maybe? It's possible. We seem to be repeating the game."

Where would they have found me? Out in the cemetery where Zoey had fallen or somewhere forgotten out in the woods. A mirror image of the girl who had already been lost.

A tremor rolls through me. "It could still happen, though, couldn't it? If I stop playing their fucked-up, twisted game, they could do to me what they did to her."

The reality of my situation slams into me hard, and I draw my knees up and hug them to my chest. I can't stop shaking, the coldness enveloping me going bone deep. *What if's* start to circle in my head, the possibilities of what the future could hold chilling me to the core.

Eli wraps his arm around my shoulders and tugs me into his

chest. "Nothing's going to happen to you." He accurately guesses the direction of my thoughts.

"You don't *know* that. How can you be sure? All it would take is one slip-up. If they realize you know what they're doing, anything could happen." The words spill out of me in a terrifying rush. "They already tried to hurt Miles. That was my fault, and they said they'd kill him if—"

Eli's fingers press against my chin and tip my head up. His mouth smothers my words, silencing my fears. He plunges his tongue between my lips, and kisses me thoroughly, until my body melts against him. I feel the contact through every inch of my body. Thinking is paralyzing, and all I want to do is get washed away in the pleasure he can give me. Hide in his arms where nothing can reach me.

"Nothing is going to happen to you." Eli nips at my lips with his teeth. "We'll protect you, Hellcat. I promise."

I have to wonder if he's making the promise to me or himself.

They never saved Zoey.

But they hadn't realized what was happening until it was too late.

Kellan pulls a t-shirt on. "I'll go down and grab us some breakfast. I could do with a coffee."

"If you intend to talk to Miles, be careful." Eli keeps his arms around me, stroking my spine, and I burrow into his warmth.

"Be careful of what? Letting people know he's gay or that we've been fooling around? He's hiding in the closet, and it's not like we're dating. I'm a free spirit until then."

"What are you doing with him?" I lift my head to search Kellan out.

"He sucks my dick, and we've fucked once."

"Miles wouldn't be this upset about finding you in bed with me, if he didn't like you a lot."

"I think he was more upset about finding me in bed with Eli." Kellan rakes a hand through his hair, moving for the door. "He needs to make up his mind, because I'm not going to be his dirty little secret for much longer."

He walks out, and silence descends. Eli tugs me backward until I'm lying on the bed and then stretches out beside me, arms wrapped around my waist. I rest my head against his shoulder, letting his presence keep me from spiraling from all the chaos in my head.

I can't stay in their room forever. The texts are already coming. I'm trapped in this deadly game, and I have no idea what will come next. It might be the weekend, but that doesn't mean I'm safe.

My thoughts shift to the diary hidden in my room. Zoey's diary. Do I tell them about it? I should, but the need to read it for myself keeps me quiet.

I have to know what happens. If she wrote about the dares. When things changed. If she had an inkling of who was behind it. She failed the night of the Halloween Ball, and I can't make that same mistake.

"You can't watch me every second of the day," I break the silence.

Eli's arms tighten around me. "You'd be surprised by how much I watch you, Hellcat."

I lift my chin so I can meet his eyes. "I'm serious, Eli."

He moves down the bed until we're face to face. "Zoey didn't know what was going to happen. You *do* know what could potentially happen, which means you can be prepared for it. Use the other phone to keep in contact with us. Tell us *everything*. No secrets, Ari. That is the only way this is going to work. Do you trust me?"

"No," I reply honestly.

A flash of irritation crosses his face.

"You lied to me for *months*. You *bullied* me. Did you really think a night of wild sex would make me trust you so easily again?"

"Ari, I need you to—"

I place a finger over his lips. "Trust is earned, Elliot Travers the Third. If it's true about the link with Zoey, I'm only in this mess because of you. Would I still have a target on my back if you'd left me alone?"

He doesn't reply.

"Would things be different if you hadn't bullied me from the start?"

21

Eli

Her words are like a perfectly aimed gunshot to the heart, and the pain as they hit rocks through my entire body. She's right, but at the same time she's so very wrong. The irony of the truth is insane.

"Would things have been different if I hadn't bullied you?" I repeat her question, then shake my head. "No."

"Of course, it would! *You* brought their attention onto me."

"I'm not denying that it's my fault, Ari." I keep my voice low.

"But you just said—"

"I know what I said." I reach out to brush a lock of hair from her face. "I understand that you're not ready to trust me. But I need you to remember that you trusted *Sin*."

"Until I found out you're both the same person."

"Exactly."

She scowls. "That makes no sense."

"Sin and Eli. They're just two sides of the same coin."

"But—"

"It doesn't matter. If trust is not possible right now, then I need you to *listen* and believe what I say next."

"You're talking in riddles!" She starts to roll away.

I catch her wrist and tug her back around to face me, then anchor my arm around her waist and pull her closer to my body. She relaxes against me for half a second, before tensing and shifting back, so there's a little distance between us.

"There was no target on your back while I was bullying you."

"Of course, there was. I was nobody when I got here. Then I became the monster's target, and then his stepsister."

I'm shaking my head before she finishes talking.

"Are you denying what you did?"

"Ari, let me talk." I rein in my instinctive need to snap after hearing the word monster leave her lips. "When you were the *monster's* target," my lips twist, "you were safe." I lower my gaze to her mouth. "It was when the monster kissed you that you became a pawn in the game."

"What?"

"Think about it. No one bothered you while you were the focus of … less than friendly … attention. It wasn't until *after* I kissed you at Halloween that things started happening. When *I* stopped targeting you, that's what caught the attention of whoever is behind this."

She stares at me in silence for a full minute. "Is that what happened with Zoey?"

"No. Zoey always liked girls. Everyone knew that."

"That night … Halloween, in the cemetery. You said she was popular until she fell in with the wrong crowd."

My laugh is soft, humorless. "That's right."

"Are they the ones behind this?"

"No, Ari."

"How can you be sure?"

"Because *we* were the wrong crowd. Me and Eli." Kellan replies before I can.

I twist my head to find him by the door. "How long have you

been standing there?"

"Long enough." He places bags onto the table. "Grilled cheese, coffee, and juice." He busies himself unbagging everything. "Out of bed. I'm not letting you heathens get crumbs on the mattress."

I reach for the hoodie and hand it to Arabella, then make my way over to the table and pull out a chair. When she joins us, I wrap an arm around her waist and pull her down onto my lap. She struggles. I tighten my grip.

"If you keep wriggling like that, I won't be held responsible for my actions."

She immediately stills. I nuzzle her neck. "Good girl."

"You're an asshole."

"I thought we'd already established that." I squeeze her hip. "Eat your breakfast before it gets cold."

"Having sex with me doesn't give you the right to manhandle me."

"*Good* sex," I counter.

"*Very* good sex," Kellan adds. "You know, most people would be full of post-coital bliss. You're just a raging ball of aggression, which I'm sure Eli finds extremely hot, but I'm more into after-sex cuddles."

I snort. "That's bullshit."

"Hush." He reaches across the table and places one finger against my lips. "You don't have sex with me, so you wouldn't know."

I push his hand away. "No, but I hear you talk about it. You're the 'sneak out while they're still asleep and then pretend you don't recognize them' type."

He rolls his eyes and takes a bite out of his grilled cheese.

"Did you see Miles?"

His smile fades away at Arabella's question. "No. He wasn't down there. I've dropped him a text. He'll either figure it out, or he won't. We have other things to worry about right now."

As if on cue, her cell chimes. When she rises to scramble off my lap to get it, I hold her in place. "Let Kellan get it."

He scoops it up and reads the text. "They want to know why you're not at breakfast."

"What does it say?" I hold out my hand and Kellan passes it to me.

`Unknown number: Why aren't you at breakfast? You have thirty minutes to get down here. Wear something that shows off your 'war wounds' from last night. We want Eli to see what Kellan was sucking on.`

Arabella turns white. "I can't go down there."

"You have to. Do you have anything low cut?"

"I don't—I don't know. I'll need to go back to my room." Her hand covers her mouth. "I feel sick."

I press a kiss to the side of her neck. "You'll be fine. Wear that pink blouse you flashed Mr. Drake in and no bra. That'll show enough without being totally indecent."

"But they must know you're not down there."

"Unless they didn't see Kellan. Who was in the cafeteria when you got there?" I throw the question at my friend.

He thinks about it. "I don't recall seeing anyone familiar. So, no one from our year."

"That means they might be expecting us." I stand, lifting Arabella off me. "Go and get dressed. We'll go down there now and be waiting for you." I cup her cheeks and tilt her head back so I can press a hard kiss to her lips. “Be brave for me, Kitten.”

22

Arabella

Eli lends me a pair of sweatpants to go with his hoodie, so I don't have to walk through the hallways half naked when I leave to go back to my room. He sees me out of the door, with a quick kiss that turns into a make-out session with me pinned against the wall and his tongue down my throat. I'm breathless and flushed when I finally break away and dash out of the door.

I don't run into anyone on my way upstairs, but when I reach my floor, I discover the door to my room is wide open. My stomach dips in dismay at the sight of it, and I almost turn and run back to Eli and Kellan. Instead, I suck in a steadying breath and force myself inside.

The light blue blankets on the beds are a mess, with odd stains all over the fabric. Both sets of pillows have been shredded, and the stuffing strewn all over the floor. The contents of my dresser have all been pulled out, and my panties are in a messy pile.

But it's the word *whore* spray painted across the wall that holds my attention.

Who did this? My blackmailers? What would have happened if I'd been in my room when they'd arrived?

I shudder.

Moving deeper into the room, I check the bathroom, and pull back the shower curtain. My heart is in my throat, and I sag in relief when there's no one hiding behind it. Once I'm sure I'm alone, I close the door and lock it.

I use the cell Eli gave me to take photos of what I've found and send them to him.

`Me: Someone trashed my bed.`

`Sin: Don't touch anything. Call housekeeping to clean it up.`

`Me: Why?`

`Sin: Because whoever has been in your room jerked off over them. Multiple someone's I'd say.`

My gaze jumps to the stains on the sheets. Bile rises in my throat, and I swallow it down.

The number for housekeeping is on top of a notepad on my desk. I call and explain what's happened, and they promise to send someone up to write a report and clean my room while I'm down at breakfast.

I'm desperate to soak in a long hot bath and unwind my aching muscles, but I opt for a shower instead. I can't relax in here, knowing someone has access to my room. What if they come back while I'm in the tub? My shower is quick, just enough time to wash, and I'm dressed and ready with ten minutes to spare on my thirty-minute deadline.

I match the pink blouse Eli suggested with a pair of black jeans and sneakers. A black jacket my mother bought me is enough to keep me warm as I move between the buildings.

I shoot off a quick message to Eli.

`Me: I'm heading down now.`

`Sin: We'll be waiting. Did you call housekeeping?`

`Me: Yes. They said they'll have everything cleaned up while I am at breakfast.`

`Sin: Good girl.`

There are students already in the cafeteria when I get there, but with it being Saturday morning, the majority will sleep in after staying up late after Valentine's Ball.

Eli and Kellan are at their usual table. Lacy is playing court with her cheerleaders at theirs, surrounded by the jocks. Miles is with them. He doesn't look in my direction or acknowledge my presence in any way. From the look on his face, he's still mad at Kellan, and I'm sure he'll blame me for what happened.

I hate that I've hurt him by sleeping with the guy he likes, but I had no idea they were involved and what happened was out of my control. Between the demands my blackmailer was making and how hungry Eli made me for sex, I ended up doing something I never dreamed I'd do.

I order a coffee and then take it to a table on the far side of the room, away from everyone. The whispers have already started. People peer down at their phones and laugh before shooting glances my way. The videos they took last night must be plastered all over the school's social media. I have no interest in checking.

A prickling sensation creeps up my spine. The feeling of being watched, *judged*, as I slip off my jacket, is strong. The dark hickeys Eli and Kellan marked me with are visible on the pale skin of my throat. More bites are visible in the gap of my shirt. I sip my coffee, eyes lowered, aware that most of the attention in the room is on me.

Be brave for me, Kitten.

Eli's words give me the courage to sit there while everyone stares. As much as I hate feeling like a monkey in a cage at the zoo, I don't want to think about what will happen if I don't obey.

A shadow falls over my table. I lift my gaze and find Garrett, Bret, Kevin, Jace, and Evan surrounding me.

Garrett drops down onto the chair beside me. "I was a little disappointed you weren't in your room last night. We couldn't find you anywhere. I was looking forward to peeling off that pretty dress you wore."

It was them.

Clutching the coffee cup tighter between my hands, I focus on the heat of the liquid inside but don't reply.

They came for me. He'd threatened they would.

"We had a party without you." Evan snickers. "Left you a present."

"Looks like Arabella had some fun with someone else." Bret points out. "Makes me wonder where else he left his mark."

I flinch when Jace's not-so-gentle fingers brush one of the bruises on my neck.

"Did you spread your legs for Kellan last night?" His voice is rough, and I don't miss the hint of envy. "You were practically fucking him on the dance floor."

Garrett's hand lands on my thigh under the table and inches upward. "Bella, Bella, Bella. If you're that desperate for dick, we're more than willing to give you what you want."

I grab his wrist before he can get any higher. "Leave me alone."

He smiles. "But you like our attention, don't you?"

I have to stop myself from darting a look in Kellan and Eli's direction to beg for help. Every reaction I give will be seen. No one is going to help me. No one ever does.

"Slut." The high-pitched shriek comes from the right. I have a split second to raise my free hand to protect myself as Tina throws the contents of the cup she's holding all over me. I cry out as pain sears over my forearm.

23

Eli

Kellan stops me before I wade into the group of boys crowding around Arabella. When Tina comes screaming from out of nowhere, he grips my wrist and pins it to the table.

"Don't fucking move. I've got this."

He rises to his feet, brushes his hands over his thighs, then strolls over to where Tina is screaming obscenities in Arabella's face.

"Ladies … ladies." He slips through a gap between Evan and Bret, putting himself between Arabella and Tina. "I'm sorry, my love." He holds out a hand to Tina. "If I'd known you have feelings for me, I'd have absolutely let you get on your knees and suck my dick. Darling, you should have said something." His fingers clamp around her wrist. "Let's go and resolve that *right now*." His eyes flick toward me.

I stand and move toward the doors.

"Get the fuck off me, Kellan." Tina tries to twist free.

"No, no. That's not how it works, my sweet."

He pulls her toward the door. I slip through it before she spots me. The last thing I want to do is leave Arabella alone to deal with the jackals inside, but I understand the look Kellan threw at me.

It's time for the Monster of Churchill Bradley to come out to play.

If we're right and this is all about reactions, then I'm going to give Tina one she's not going to forget.

Kellan steps through the doors, Tina in tow. My hand flashes out and I have her pinned to the wall by her throat before she realizes Kellan has released her. Crowding close, I press my mouth against her ear.

"How many times do I have to explain to you fucking idiots that you *do not* get to play with my toys. You remember that video of you with the girl? Do you want me to release the other one where you're fucking her pussy with your tongue?"

"Eli!" She squeaks my name.

I flex my fingers. "What you're going to do is go back in there and apologize. If her arm is burned by what you've just done, I'll be doing the same to you."

"What do you care?" She gasps when my grip on her throat tightens.

"That's not your fucking business. Who told you to do it?"

"Do it?"

"Throw the drink on her. I want a fucking name."

"No one!" Her hand comes up to claw at my wrist. "Eli, please. I can't breathe!" Her face is turning purple, eyes wide.

I loosen my grip just enough for her to suck in a breath. "A fucking name, Tina. Now."

"No one! No one. She was fucking mocking us … coming to the party looking like Zoey." Her voice breaks, and tears spill down her cheeks. "And then she's all over you and Kellan, just like Zoey was."

My hand drops, and I step away. Tina sags, one hand lifting to rub her throat, the other dashing away the tears.

Kellan gives a low whistle from beside me. "*You* were the girl she kept sneaking off to meet."

She glares at him. "Until *you* two got your claws into her. She never wanted to spend time with me once she had the two of you."

"Or she realized what a fucking bitch you are." I shove my hands into my pockets. "Get your ass back in there." I jerk my chin to the doors leading back to the cafeteria.

She pouts. "Or what?"

I take a step toward her and she darts sideways. "Oh my god. Fine!"

I'm on her heels as she walks back into the cafeteria and heads to where Arabella is still surrounded by the jocks. I get a quick glimpse of pale features, as well as a hand sliding up her thigh, and … Well, I lose my shit.

My fist connects with Garrett's jaw and the impact sends him over the top of the chair to crash into the wall.

29

Arabella

The burn on my forearm throbs, and I grit my teeth against the pain.

Eli stands over the fallen jock, his hands curled into fists. "I said *no one* gets to play with my fucking toy until I'm done with her. I'm getting fucking tired of repeating myself. "

"Kellan did," Garrett whines.

"What can I say?" Eli's lips curl. "My little Hellcat is hot for big dicks, and I don't mind sharing with Kellan." His gaze sweeps over the boy on the floor. "I'm pretty sure she'd laugh if she saw what you're packing between your legs."

I balk at the venomous hate in his tone, grab my jacket and stand to leave, only to discover Tina blocking my path, Kellan just behind her.

"I'm sorry about your arm." Her voice is sullen, but her eyes are filled with malice.

I don't reply, and step past her, just wanting to escape. Bret, Jace, Kevin, and Evan cut me off just before I reach the door.

"She's trying to run away," Kevin calls. "Travers, come and punish her."

The students around us already have their cameras out and pointed at us in anticipation of the shit show that's unfolding. They all look eager to see what Eli will do to me.

His murderous eyes swing in our direction, and he doesn't see Garrett launch himself off the floor at him. As he's thrown forward into a nearby table by the jock, Kellan puts himself between Eli and everyone else. Kevin grabs me when I try to dash past him. I don't even think and bring my knee up. It connects with his balls, and he doubles over with a pained howl. The second he lets go of me to cup himself, I bolt.

I head straight to medical, where the nurse tries to question me about my burn, and I lie, telling her it was just an accident. She runs cold water over it, then applies something to soothe the pain over the area before covering it with a sterile bandage.

One of my phones pings when I'm easing my jacket over my arms. When I check, relief floods me when I see it's not my main one.

`Sin: Where are you?`

`Me: Medical seeing to my first-degree burn.`

Clutching my bag in one hand and my cell in the other, I walk out of the room.

`Sin: Meet you outside the dorm building. I need you not to freak out.`

I frown down at his words.

`Me: What's happening?`

`Sin: Just trust me.`

`Me: What are you going to do?`

Eli doesn't respond, which sets my anxiety on edge. I cross the campus until I see the dorms. A crowd has gathered outside the main doors, and Eli and Kellan are leaning against one of the walls. The second Eli sees me, he straightens and stalks toward me. The air of determination around him makes the hair on the back of my neck stand up. My pace slows as he comes closer.

What is he going to do? Why did he tell me not to freak out?

His eyes stay fixed on mine, giving away nothing. The crowd follows in his wake, and I force myself to keep my breathing steady when he reaches for me. His hand wraps around my jaw and tips my head up.

"When did I tell you it was okay to fuck Kellan?"

"Don't—" I try to shake my head, but his grip stops me from moving.

"She's shaking." Someone in the gathered throng laughs. "Maybe she's scared he's going to eat her."

Eli smooths the pad of his thumb back and forth across my cheek, eyes cold and unyielding. "Get on the floor and kiss my feet."

Fear uncurls at his demand. "Please don't do this."

I search his face for an ounce of softness, but his expression is aloof, lips set in a thin line, eyes narrow. This is the monster. The bully I've come to know. There's no trace of Sin or the lover I'd been in bed with this morning.

Is this just all for show?

The way he's acting seems so real, and it sends a chill down my spine.

"Do it." His voice is soft. "Get on your fucking knees and kiss my feet."

I blink fast, trying to stem the fall of tears. "No, please."

The fingers on my jaw flex. "Last chance, or I'll make you do something worse."

My mind runs wild with the possibilities of what that could mean. I lower myself to the grass at his feet, and stare down at the ground. Despair is a heavy weight in my stomach.

Fingers tangle in my hair, yanking my head up.

"Lips on my foot *now*."

My chest constricts at the ice in his gaze, its shards piercing my chest. I shake harder, unable to contain the very real fear that's running through my body. The moment he lets me go, I bend down and kiss his shoe, tears spilling down my cheeks.

25

Eli

The moment her mouth touches my sneaker, I press it against her lips and then use my foot to shove her backward. She lands on her ass, hands behind her.

"Did you really think you could cause trouble between me and Kellan?" I keep my voice steady, cool, and embrace the monster they all think I am.

She doesn't respond, staring up at me out of terrified blue eyes.

"Answer me." The words come out like a whip crack, and she flinches.

"N-no."

"No?" I crouch down in front of her and tilt my head. "So you didn't think fucking Kellan would make me angry with him for touching you?"

She shakes her head. I smirk.

"If you're that desperate to be fucked, all you have to do is ask me, Princess. I'll let you ride my dick … but first, you need to *beg* for it." I press two fingers beneath her chin and lift her head. "Would your pretty little mouth like my dick to fill it?" I reach for the button on my jeans and pop it. "Up on your knees."

The crowd around us shifts restlessly, the mood changing from anticipation to discomfort. I lower my zipper. When she doesn't move, I slide my other hand from her jaw to her hair and pull her up onto her knees.

"Open your mouth."

Whispers start, and then Lacy steps forward. “Eli, I don’t think—”

“Yeah, let her go. You’ve made your point.” Another voice speaks over her.

I sweep my gaze over the students crowding around. Every single one of them flushes and looks away. I pat Arabella’s cheek.

“Looks like they saved you … *this time*.” Turning my back on her, I walk into the dorm building, Kellan close beside me.

Neither of us speak until we’re in our room, and then I blow out a breath.

“Here.” He hands me a bottle of water. “I don’t have any vodka, or I’d give you that.”

“It’s too early to drink, anyway.”

“Is it?” His voice is grim.

“If anyone was watching, hopefully, they’ll think she’s nothing to me now.”

“And if they don’t?”

I glance over at him.

“I’m not sure she’ll be able to handle it, Eli.”

“What’s the alternative?”

He has no answer for that. I pick up my cell.

`ME: Ari, are you back in your room?`

She doesn’t reply.

`ME: Kitten, tell me where you are.`

Nothing.

“She figured it out, right?” My fingers are drumming against my thigh.

“Doesn’t mean it didn’t hurt. There’s no way she can’t be upset.

She might need a couple of hours."

"I'm going to her room."

Kellan steps in front of the door. "Eli, you *can't*. You've just put on a show to prove that she's nothing more than a chew toy to you. Running to her room to comfort her will undo all that."

"And what if fucking Garrett and the others are up there?"

He snorts. "Pretty sure the only thing Garrett is concerned with right now is how many teeth you knocked out." He turns and opens the door. "I'll take a walk up there and see what's happening."

I pace the entire time he's gone. When he finally slips back through the door, I pounce on him.

"Well?"

"She's back in her room. She says … quote … 'I fucking hate you, Eli. Leave me alone.' … unquote."

"I told you." I grab my cell and instead of texting her, I call her.

"Leave me alone."

"Kitten, I had to sell it."

"You were going to make me suck your dick in public."

"I wasn't. I knew someone would put a stop to it." Well, ninety percent of me had been sure someone would, anyway.

"It was humiliating."

"I know. That was the point." When she doesn't speak, I sigh. "Listen, do you know the closet at the end of your hallway, near the stairwell?"

"What about it?"

"Go there. Make sure no one sees you and go inside. I'll meet you there."

"Why?"

"Just do it." I end the call.

"You're going to show her the tunnels?" Kellan drops down onto his bed and stretches out.

"We need to talk. I need to—"

"Regroup, I know. Just be careful. It's still early." He fiddles with his cell. "I'm going to see if I can get Miles to talk to me. Drop me a warning text when you're on your way back … just in case." One side of his mouth tips up into a smile.

"That sure of your persuasion skills?"

"That sure of my *seduction* skills."

I'm still chuckling when I leave the stairwell and pull open the closet door. Ari is standing inside, her back to the wall, arms wrapped around her waist. Her eyes meet mine when I step inside.

"What—"

I lift a finger to my lips. "Sound travels," I whisper. I walk past her and press the wall until I find the hidden catch, releasing the door. "Come on." I hold out a hand and step into the tunnel.

26

Arabella

I gasp as the wall slides apart. There's enough light in the closet to see a doorway that wasn't there before. Before I can question its existence, Eli presses a finger to his lips again.

My mouth snaps shut, and I take the hand he offers me. He guides me into the gap, and the door closes silently behind us, plunging into pitch-black nothingness. My hand tightens on Eli's, and the tension inside eases a fraction when a thin band of light pierces the dark. He keeps the flashlight pointed forward as we move. I place my feet carefully, worried I might trip. He doesn't force me to go any faster, keeping pace with me until, finally, he stops. My ears strain, trying to catch any sounds, but the only thing I can hear is my harsh breaths, and then Eli directs me forward again.

"Stay right there." He lets go of my hand.

I shiver, the cold seeping through my clothes, and watch the beam from the flashlight moving away from me. A moment later, there's a tiny orange spark as he lights a candle. Three more follow, and they give off a soft illumination, enough for me to recognize that we're standing inside the tomb.

"There's a tunnel to the tomb?" I can't keep the shock from my voice.

"One of many."

"How long have you known about them?"

"Kellan and I found them in our second year here."

My gaze wanders around the stone walls. "No wonder you were always here before me, and I never saw you when I came out to the woods."

"There's another one which comes out at the edge of the cemetery. I used that one more than this." Blowing out the flame on the match he's holding, Eli turns. "Come here."

Still angry with him for what he'd done to me earlier, I hesitate before moving closer to him. "What do you want?"

"We'll be warmer under here." He gestures at a gray blanket that's been folded up and left on the floor. He stoops, picks it up and shakes it out, revealing another underneath. He spreads that one out, sits on top of it and lays the second across his legs.

"Are you going to stand there and freeze, or are you going to get your stubborn ass down here?" His voice is dry.

I scowl and roll my eyes, but I can't think of a single reason why it would be better to stay where I am, so I join him on the makeshift bed. He draws the blanket over me, then curves a hand around my waist and pulls me close to his side.

"I still hate you," I mutter, pressing my face into his chest. "It's been, what? Twenty-four hours since I found out you're Sin."

Twenty-four hours since he found me broken.

Everything is hitting me in waves, and I feel like I'm being pulled back to how I was feeling when he found me in the chapel.

Eli's lips brush my forehead. "Out there when everyone is watching, we have to act like we hate each other."

"We do hate each other."

"You know it's more than that, Kitten."

"Sex."

His lips smile against my skin. "*Good* sex."

I punch him lightly in the ribs. He grunts.

"Part of me was sure what you did was for show, but another part is scared you are just playing with my head again."

His hand moves to cup the back of my head, his fingers tangling in my hair to force my face up to his. "I had to make them believe you mean nothing to me, Ari. If they think there's nothing but hate between us, they might leave you alone."

I search those green eyes that have both terrified and aroused me with the fire in their depths in the past. "But what if they don't?"

"Then we have to work out our next move."

"You mean you're going to keep being an asshole to me?"

He sighs. "It's the only way it's going to work."

I roll away from him and attempt to throw the blanket off. He grabs my hand and hauls me back until I'm half lying on top of him.

"No. Stay."

I try to move, but his arms wrap around me, keeping me in place. "Why?"

"Because when we're alone, we're Eli and Ari. Out there, I'm a monster, and you're the school whore."

I stiffen at his choice of words. "I'm not a whore."

"And I wasn't a monster until they forced me into the role. Listen to me, Kitten. When we're alone, we can be who we want to be. Out there ..." He glances toward the locked door. "We are who we need to be to keep you safe. We show our hate."

"But you can be so cruel, and the jocks … they…" I shudder, my voice hitching.

He brushes a lock of hair out of my face. "You let me worry about them. We have four weeks until spring break, and then we can get some time away from the eyes watching us."

The next twenty-eight days stretch out endlessly in front of me, and my throat locks up. I struggle to breathe for a second. "That's a long time."

He grips my chin, forcing me to meet his gaze. "Here's the deal. I'll bully you in public, and you can fuck me like you hate me in private. Bite me. Claw me. Mark me. Take what you need to take the pain away and give yourself pleasure."

His lips meet mine, but I pull back from the kiss. "You just want to fuck me again."

His lips curve up. "Don't deny you want me."

"You're such an asshole." But the words lack bite. I wiggle out of his arms and move to lay beside him beneath the blanket.

He doesn't try to stop me. Instead, he reaches for something to his right. I eye the metal tin he picks up. Opening the lid, he plucks out a hand-rolled cigarette and a chunky metal lighter, then closes it and puts it to one side.

He lifts the joint to his lips, and flicks open the lighter. Touching the flame to the end, he inhales deeply, then offers it to me.

"Here."

I take it from him. "A joint?"

He shrugs. "It'll help you to relax. You need it after the last couple of days. It will take off the edge of what you're feeling." He smiles. "I'll make sure you don't float away."

27

Eli

I finish my circuit of the football field, 'Oblivion' by Palaye Royale playing in my ears, and stop next to the bleachers where the cheerleaders are all crowding around the players. Propping one shoulder against the stand, I twist the cap off my water bottle and take a mouthful.

Arabella's contact has been silent since Saturday. My guess is that they're happy with the shit they've made her do and my responses to it all. A small part of me hopes that's the end of it, but I know it won't be. Whoever it is will be watching, waiting, looking for another opportunity.

Earlier this morning, Kellan managed to finally track the access history of the cloud storage we were using and found a masked IP address, which he's been trying to trace. So far, it's bounced him all over the world. He tried to explain it to me, but I zoned out when he started talking about pings, proxies, and host addresses. When he saw me staring at the wall, he sighed and said it meant he had more work to do.

My cell's ringtone cuts off my music, and I tap an earbud to connect the call.

"What?"

"Hi, son. Do you have a few minutes to talk?"

The sound of my dad's voice snaps my spine straight. We haven't spoken since I returned to school. We seemed to be in a good place when I left, but with all the shit going on, that could easily change.

"Hi. Sure. I've just finished a run." Nothing of my concern sounds in my voice.

"How's school?"

"Same old."

"Principal Warren called. He says you're going to all the counseling sessions, but that things don't seem to have gotten any better between you and Arabella."

"It's fine." *Fuck*. The last thing I need is my dad sniffing around. "She's working through some shi—stuff, that's all."

"Elena is wondering whether we should move her to another school."

"What's the point? There are only a few months left until we graduate. Have you mentioned it to her?"

"No."

"Don't. She already feels like she's not welcome here. Having you or Elena tell her you're looking to take her out will only emphasize that."

In truth, Arabella getting out of this place would be the best way to stop the bullshit going on, but then we'll never find out who's behind it. I'm pretty sure she'd leap at the opportunity to get out of Churchill Bradley, because she doesn't think she's strong enough to deal with what's happening.

I know better. She *is* strong enough. She just needs to realize it.

"Hmm. I never thought about it that way." Dad's voice snaps my attention back to him. "I'll speak to Elena."

"Good." I hesitate before speaking again. "How are you? No more health issues?"

He laughs quietly. "No. Elena talked me into reducing my work hours. I'm eating well, and exercising."

I nod, even though he can't see me.

"Alright. Well, you're probably busy with class, so I'll let you go."

"Dad?" I say his name before he hangs up.

"Yes?"

"I'm glad you've managed to find some happiness with Elena."

"I love you, son." He hangs up before I can reply.

"Hey, Travers!"

I look up to find Jace, Evan, and Bret in front of me. They're nudging each other and laughing. I hike an eyebrow.

"One of the girls said they saw Arabella fucking around near your locker earlier. Guess the little bitch didn't learn her lesson on Saturday," Evan says.

Has she received another instruction?

I haven't checked my other cell for messages, and I can't while they're standing here watching me. I summon up a smile while my mind races.

"Guess any attention is good attention when your life is a mess," I drawl. I push away from the stand, shoving my hands into the pockets of my sweats. "Guess I better go and see what she's fucked up now."

I keep my pace slow, knowing their eyes are on me, and make my way back to the building where the senior lockers are kept. My footsteps slow as I approach my locker. There's something stuck to the front of it.

A printout of a photograph.

Of me.

I study it but make no move to take it down. It's the one she took a few days ago. The one of my back, scars on display. My eyes move from that to the handwritten text across the top of the paper.

The Monster of Churchill Bradley. As ugly on the outside as he is on the inside.

Without removing my gaze from the image, I pull out my cell and call Kellan.

"What class are we in next?"

"Math."

"Is Arabella there?"

"Yep. She's looking a bit shaken up."

I grunt. "Has Drake arrived yet?"

"No."

"I'm on my way."

"Eli, you sound weird. Is every—" I cut the call, pluck the photograph off my locker, and set off for class.

28

Arabella

My attention keeps darting to the door and back to my desk as students enter the classroom. Kellan is at his desk, but there's no sign of Eli. I texted him to tell him about the instructions, but he didn't respond.

The photo had been waiting for me in my locker. The instructions were easy enough—pin the photograph to the front of Eli's locker—but it still left me feeling sick to my stomach.

Kellan is playing with his phone when I look in his direction. His lips press together, and then he frowns.

Is he talking to Eli? Has he seen the photo yet?

To distract myself, I pull my math books and pens out of my bag.

It's going to be okay. We just have to pretend to hate each other. It's not real. Just like Eli had said in the tomb, we're just playing our roles in public. He's going to retaliate because he has to.

After smoking the joint, I'd fallen asleep in Eli's arms. We stayed in the tomb for hours before heading back to the school.

On Sunday, he texted me, but I haven't seen him since. I spent most of the day curled up in my bed reading Zoey's diary. She wrote about getting more dares, but things had been changing. She talked about ignoring them, then items she owned started going missing. Silly things at first. A schoolbook, then a ring her mother had given her. A necklace Eli and Kellan bought for her seventeenth birthday.

The noise in the classroom around me dies down, and my stomach twists. Eli is here. I know that before I even look up to confirm it. When I *do* lift my head, he's standing in the doorway. His expression is tight with anger, and his eyes are narrowed into two green slits. The fury I can see in them holds me frozen in my seat. All I can do is stare, paralyzed by fear of how he's going to react.

No matter how many times he told me it's an act, all I can see is the monster.

My heart hammers against my ribs. I feel like prey. *His prey*. Because deep down, I know that's what I've always been since I arrived at Churchill Bradley.

He stalks through the room, the negative emotion surrounding him a palpable force in the air. I know I'm not the only one reacting to it when some of the other students shrink away from him as he passes.

He stops in front of my desk. "Did you get a kick out of it? Let me guess. You took it on Saturday morning, after you were done fucking Kellan? Was that your little plan all along? Do you think it'll hurt me?"

My stomach drops. "I—"

Before I can finish, he continues past me. My shoulders sag with relief. Maybe he's not going to do anything, after all. The thought has barely formed when a hand wraps itself in my hair. My head is jerked back so viciously that I cry out in pain. The second my lips part, Eli stuffs something into my mouth.

"Eat the photograph, Princess. Then later, since you're clearly hungry for my attention, you can eat my dick too."

I try to push the paper out with my tongue. He presses his palm over my mouth to stop me from spitting it out. Bringing my hand up, I grab his wrist to shove it away, but it won't budge.

He releases his grip on my hair and pinches my nose closed. "Chew."

I struggle to breathe, black spots dancing before my eyes. My lungs burn with the need for oxygen, but he doesn't release me.

"Dude, she's going to suffocate," someone calls out.

"Travers, stop!"

Eli ignores them. "What's the matter, Princess? I thought you wanted a piece of me inside you. Eat the fucking photograph."

I chew the paper and swallow it, gagging when it gets stuck in my throat. Eli forces my mouth open and pushes one finger inside, checking to make sure it's all gone. I'm tempted to bite him, but the gleam in his eyes warns me against it. When he's probed every part of my mouth, he pulls his finger free and lets go of me. Coughing and spluttering, I hunch over my desk.

Eli rounds the desk until he's facing me, and his hand moves to my face. I flinch.

He pats my cheek gently and smiles. "See? That wasn't so hard, was it?"

I'm sure my anguish is right there in my eyes when I stare up at him. "I hate you."

"I live for your hate, Princess." He walks over to his desk and drops down beside Kellan.

Lacy, Tina, Maggie, and Linda snicker. The jocks are grinning at each other, reveling in my suffering, and it feeds the growing rage inside me. We're nothing but their entertainment. My gaze connects with Miles, and he gives me a sad smile. I don't return it.

Mr. Drake arrives before anything else is said. I drop my attention down to the books on my desk and that's where I keep my focus for the entire class. The second the bell sounds, I gather my things and run for the door.

"What's your rush?" Bret calls. "Frightened Travers will make you suck his dick in front of us?"

"Oh my god, don't encourage him." Lacy snaps. "We all know he'll do it."

Jace rises from his chair. "I'd fucking pay to see that."

"You that desperate to see Travers' dick or Arabella giving head?" Brad laughs.

"I just want to see those pink lips wrapped around my cock."

"Fucking asshole," Garrett mutters, shooting a glare in Eli's direction, but it's loud enough for me to hear.

Every inch of me is aware of Kellan and Eli still sitting at their desks, listening to the interaction in silence as I dash for the door. I've just reached my locker when my phone pings. I ignore it, put away my books and then lock up. I can still hear the jocks laughing and joking further down the hallway.

The second the back of my neck prickles, I know Eli is watching me, but I don't look in his direction. I storm along the hallway and into the girls' restroom. Once I'm safely sealed in one of the stalls, I check my messages.

`Sin: You did good, Kitten.`

`Me: Fuck you.`

`Sin: You'll get to do that later when we're alone.`

`Me: What you did wasn't funny.`

`Sin: I gave them what they wanted.`

`Me: You're an asshole.`

`Sin: You already know that.`

Stuffing the phone back in my pocket, I clench my fists and brace my arms against the wall. I want to punch him for what he just did to me. Make him hurt. I take a few deep breaths to steady my nerves. The cell pings with another message, but I ignore it.

I have a session with Counselor Clarke soon. I'm not in the mood to listen to him coaxing me to spill all my secrets and darkest thoughts. None of the time I've been spending with him has helped.

I can't get the image of Eli's face as he walked into the classroom out of my head. The way his eyes had burned with malice and fury.

He's acting … right?

29

Eli

She refuses to answer any of my texts for the rest of the day, won't look in my direction and avoids me as much as she can.

"I think you upset her," Kellan says as she walks stiff-backed to a corner table with her dinner tray, gaze fixed straight ahead.

"Isn't that the point?"

His eyes shift from her to me. "You don't think it was over the top? You knew they were going to use that photograph at some point."

"It was do that or something more violent. I went with the approach that would hurt her the least."

He rubs his jaw. "I'm not sure you were successful in that."

Squashing down the frustration I feel, I reach for my drink. "What are you saying? I need to tone it down? Ignore it? Wait until she goes missing and then find her dead in the cemetery before I react again?"

"Eli—"

"Don't fucking *Eli* me." I shove to my feet.

"Where are you going?"

"To do what I do best."

He sighs but doesn't stop me as I stalk across the room to where Arabella is sitting, alone, hunched over her food. I wrap a hand around her arm and drag her to her feet. Her drink spills, sloshing over the front of her top. I don't stop, don't speak, just drag her across the room to the sounds of catcalls and cheers from the watching students.

She struggles the entire way, twisting and turning in my grip. I ignore her, pulling her along beside me until I find the first available restroom. Pushing her through the door, I step inside, take a quick look around to make sure it's empty, and twist to slam the lock, to stop anyone else from entering.

When I turn back, Arabella is glaring at me, fingers clenched into fists either side of her hips. I look her over.

"Want to hit me?" I lift my chin and tap it. "Right there. Take your best shot."

Her swing is wild, and her fist glances off my jaw. I sigh, and grip her arm, bend it and then angle her wrist.

"Lock your wrist, tense your hand. Take your thumb out. If you leave it tucked under your fingers, you'll break it." I peel her fingers away and move her thumb. "That's better. Now try again. Keep your wrist locked. And fucking aim, don't just swing and hope."

Her second punch is a little better, but still barely a love tap.

"Again." I take a step toward her, she retreats. "Don't fucking run away. *Hit* me."

Her third attempt connects with my mouth and knocks my head sideways. I taste the coppery flavor of blood in my mouth, and smile. "Much better."

"You're a fucking asshole." She swings for me again.

"I know." I take another step closer. "Hit me again."

"There's no way you were acting."

"I *was* acting, Ari." This time when she throws a punch, I catch her wrist and twist it up behind her back, pulling her into my body. "Meet me tonight."

"No. I don't want anything to do with you."

I dip my head to brush my lips over hers, leaving a smear of blood behind. "I'll make you forget why you're angry." Adjusting my grip, I spin her so we're both facing the mirror. My thumb wipes the blood on her lips, turning them red. "My blood looks good on you."

I stroke along her jaw, down her throat, and slide a hand into her top, my eyes holding hers in the reflection of the mirror. Settling it over her breast, I squeeze, feeling her nipple harden against my palm.

"Look at the way you come alive in my arms," I whisper against her ear.

My other hand finds the hem of her shirt. I pull it over her stomach, her ribs, and up until I uncover her breasts cupped in a lacy bra. My mouth tracks a line of kisses down her throat.

"You're so fucking pretty." I seal my lips around the pulse beating in her throat and suck, my tongue licking over her skin.

A sigh leaves her, eyes fluttering closed, and her head drops to rest against my shoulder.

"Touch me, Ari. Feel how hard you make me."

She reaches backward, presses her fingers against my dick, and I groan against her throat. "I need your hands on me. I want your pussy sliding up and down my dick. Are you wet right now, Kitten?"

"Sin." The nickname leaves her lips on a soft moan.

Turning her in my arms, I grasp her waist and lift her onto the countertop, then step between her thighs. I cup her jaw and tilt her head back so I can kiss her, my tongue slipping between her lips to tangle with hers. Her hands wind around my neck, her legs hook around my hips, and she pulls me closer so she can grind her pussy against my dick where it's straining against the front of my jeans.

"When things get too much," I whisper against her mouth. "Think about this. This is the reality, Ari. This is me, not the monster."

"Open up!" Someone rattles the door and shouts, jerking us apart.

Arabella's eyes fly up to meet mine. I lick my lips and suck in a deep breath.

"Get ready." I stroke a finger over her lips. "I'm sorry for what I'm about to do. I swear to you, I don't like this any more than you do."

"What are you—"

I pull on the mantle of the *monster,* lift her off the countertop, and stride across the floor of the restroom. Unlocking the door, I throw it open and shove her out into the hallway beyond.

"Next time you want to fuck with me, I won't be as gentle." I stalk away down the hallway, leaving her to face the cluster of students alone.

30

Arabella

Sin: Go to the closet at the end of the hall on your floor an hour after curfew.

Scowling at my phone, I drop it onto my bed and storm for the bathroom. If he expects an answer, he's not going to get one.

He can't boss me around.

Eli has been nothing but a jerk to me all day. If this is what it's going to be like for the next three and a half weeks, I wish I could stay locked in my room. He says he doesn't enjoy what he's doing to me, but I'm not sure I believe it.

He's cruel and brutal. Hard and cold.

"Does he think his magic dick is going to make me forget the way he's been treating me?" I mutter to my reflection. "Is that his plan?"

I want your pussy sliding up and down my dick. Are you wet right now, Kitten?

My nipples harden as I recall his words. Yes, I *had* been wet, needy, and throbbing. If we hadn't been interrupted, I'd have let him fuck me right there in the restroom. I hate him for the power he has over me. That he can make me feel good and then shatter me a second later with a snap of his fingers.

I sit on the edge of the bathtub, and twist on the faucets, then dump a generous amount of my favorite scented bubble bath into the running water.

"He's so fucking annoying." I strip off my clothes and climb into the tub, the heat enveloping me in its comforting embrace. "I'm not going tonight. No way. I'll just go to bed early."

Once the bath is full, I turn off the water and sink right down until only my head is breaking the surface. The heat works its way through my body, loosening the tension holding my muscles taut. Sighing softly, I close my eyes and listen to the silence. Images of Eli fill my head. His hands on my body. His lips on my skin. How it feels when he's buried inside me.

Touch me, Ari. Feel how hard you make me. When things get too much, think about this. This is the reality, Ari, not the monster.

My anger fades, but my hurt remains.

I shouldn't still want Eli after what he's done. It's an addiction. I'm hooked on what he can give me—of losing myself in the sweetness of Sin. It takes me away from all the pain. All those dares in the tomb. I'd eagerly gone back for more every time he summoned me.

I wash my hair and body, lingering in the water until it grows cool. But eventually, I have to get out. I towel off and go back into the bedroom, where I brush out my hair, then use the hairdryer until every strand is dry.

I ignore my phone for as long as I can, but my willpower crumbles once I'm dressed. I have ten minutes until the time we're supposed to meet.

I should stay in my room. Forget about meeting him. It's not going to change anything. He's still going to be a bastard to me tomorrow, no matter what happens between us tonight.

I pace up and down in front of my door.

Look at the way you come alive in my arms.

The weight of everything that's happening threatens to crush me. I hate this. I hate Eli Travers so much that it aches in my chest.

He confuses me.

Taunts me.

Kisses me.

Drives me insane.

After today I don't know if I want to fuck him or punch him.

When I next look at the time, there are five minutes to go.

"Screw it." I stuff my phone in my pocket, open the door and step into the hallway.

I go straight for the closet and walk inside, then lean back against the wall. I close my eyes and almost miss the soft tread of footsteps coming in my direction. Eyelids parting, my spine turns to steel when Eli opens the door.

"You said you'd make me forget why I'm angry. Prove it."

Eli

My smile at her words makes her eyes grow wide. Coming to a stop in front of her, I press a finger against her lips.

"Sound travels in here. You're going to need to be *very* quiet." And with that warning, I drop to my knees and pull down her yoga pants along with the scrap of lace covering her pussy beneath them.

"Eli!"

I catch her hands when they land on my shoulders and flatten them against the wall.

"Keep them there or cover your mouth. Whichever works best," I say and bury my face between her legs.

A startled squeak comes out of her, and I chuckle against her pussy. My tongue works its way between her lips to find her clit, and I flick over it a couple of times.

She gasps, and her legs widen slightly, as much as she can in the pants that I've only lowered to her knees. Her hips tilt, chasing my tongue as I swirl it everywhere except where she wants it the most.

I push a finger inside her and lean back to look up at her face. Her lips are slightly parted, eyes closed, and there's a slight flush to her cheeks. A second finger joins the first, and I stroke a circle around her clit with my thumb. Her legs tremble, so I add a third finger to the two pumping leisurely in and out of her pussy.

Reaching for one of her hands, I place her fingers on her pussy. "Spread yourself open for me. Offer me your sweet little clit. Ask me to lick it."

Her fingers scissor, opening herself up to my gaze. Her clit peeks out from its hood, wet, pink, and needy. I touch it with the tip of my tongue.

"Beg for me, Kitten."

"Please."

"You're so greedy, sucking my fingers inside your body. So fucking hungry for my tongue. Your pussy is dripping with your need. Admit it. You've been wet all day. Every time you saw me, heard me speak, you wanted to come."

My tongue laps a path around her clit, and she whimpers.

"Tell me you hate me."

"I hate you." She moans the words.

"Do you want to fuck everyone you hate?"

"No."

"When I had a hand wrapped into your hair and the other over your mouth today, how wet were you?"

"I wasn't."

My fingers stop moving.

She reaches for my wrist. "Please … don't stop."

"Then don't fucking lie to me."

"I wasn't wet."

"Liar." I blow a breath over her clit and she jerks. "I bet if I'd spread your legs and put a hand into your panties, they'd have come away soaked." I lick her clit again. "You like it when I'm mean."

"No, I—"

"Naughty Kitten. I should spank you for that." I tap her clit lightly with two fingers. "Play with yourself."

Her fingers dance over her clit. I watch for a minute and then lean forward to join in with my tongue. When her legs start to shake, I pump my fingers in and out faster, sucking and flicking her clit until she cries out, grinding her pussy against my face.

"That's it," I whisper. "Fuck me."

I grab her hips and hold her in place when she tries to move away.

"Fight me."

I pull my fingers free of her body and replace them with my tongue, fucking her with it the way I plan to do with my dick later. Her entire body is shaking, her fingers digging into my shoulders. Her pussy is soaked, and I lap up every last taste of her, then press a kiss to her clit.

"Feed me."

Her gasps are loud in the closet, little panting breaths and whimpers. She doesn't stop me when I rise to my feet and pull up her pants. Gripping her jaw with my fingers, I kiss her, pushing my tongue between her lips so she can taste herself. She clings to me, sucks on my tongue, moans into my mouth.

When I pull away and take her hand to draw her into the tunnel, she doesn't resist.

32

Arabella

Eli must have visited the tomb and set everything up before I arrived in the closet because the candles are already lit. The instant I step out of the tunnel, he turns and grasps my chin between two fingers. His mouth meets mine, tongue plunging savagely between my lips.

"Fuck me." I snarl between kisses.

He thinks what he's doing to me in the day is making me wet. That I enjoy the torment.

My anger surges, and I fight him the only way I know how—by causing him pain. I sink my teeth into his lower lip and bite down until he hisses. When I let him go, he slams me back into the stone wall of the tomb. Clawing at his shoulders, my mouth finds his again. The kiss is as savage and violent as the emotions he invokes in me. He feeds my need, not backing down from the fierceness. His hands are all over me, groping, molding, squeezing.

"You want my dick, don't you, Kitten?" He hooks his hands beneath my thighs and brings my legs up to wrap around his hips. "I bet you've been thinking about it all day."

Instead of answering him, I attack his neck with my teeth. He swears and sucks in a breath.

I want to hurt him. Shred him to pieces until he's as raw as I'm feeling. This is our battlefield, and I won't back down from this fight.

He moves, carrying me across the space, and then lowers me onto the waiting blankets. I fight him as he untangles my legs and arms from his body. Squirm and twist as he strips me of my sneakers, yoga pants, and panties. Once I'm naked, he kneels between my spread thighs.

"I hate you." I snarl, my gaze locked on him as he pushes down his sweatpants. His cock is hard and ready, growing even harder when he rolls on a condom.

His gaze connects with mine. "Say it again."

"I hate you," I repeat.

He leans over me, one hand beside my head and he teases the tip of his cock over my wetness. He torments me, and the worst part is how much he makes me want him. My body comes alive under his touch. It's his to play, but even with the fiery passion between us, there's a tiny voice screaming inside me that this isn't right.

"I can't hear you." Eli taunts.

"I hate you."

He thrusts into me in one smooth glide that has me arching up off the blanket with a moan.

"I want you to remember this tomorrow when you're sitting in class. I'm going to leave you aching. I'm going to fuck you so hard, you'll feel the imprint of my dick inside you for days." He pulls back his hips, then slams into me so hard he rams me into the floor. Pleasure and pain shoot through me, and I clutch at his back.

"Give me all your hate," Eli growls.

I sink my teeth into the material of his hoodie while he fucks me slow and deep. Every time he draws back and thrusts forward, I feel every single inch of him. And every second of it makes me hate him more.

"Such a good fucking girl."

His growl causes my pussy to contract around his cock and my entire body floods with heat, almost dragging an orgasm out of me.

His pace increases. "Your orgasms are mine, Kitten. Every. Single. One." He punctuates each word with a thrust of his dick. "Whether I give them to you with my dick, my fingers, or my tongue, they belong to me."

He reaches down between us and rubs my clit with his thumb. Releasing my bite on his shoulder, I groan in pleasure.

My hands skim down his back to his ass to pull him deeper inside me. The pain, the roughness of our coupling, is animalistic in its nature.

"I hate you so much."

33

Eli

My bed shakes at the force of Kellan's kick.

"Fuck off." I don't move from where I'm lying, one arm thrown over my face.

"Get up."

"No."

It's been three days since I fucked Arabella in the tomb. Three days since she came all over my dick, then rolled away and walked out. Three days since I stoked her anger and let it burn me alive.

"Get the fuck out of bed."

"It's Saturday."

"And we're going into town."

"Like fuck." I roll onto my side, presenting him with my back, and close my eyes.

"Eli, you can't stay hidden in here forever." His voice is thick with exasperation. "You've skipped classes for two days."

Because I don't want to face Arabella and deal with whatever new bullshit her anonymous puppet master is going to force her to do. Which, in turn, will force me to retaliate.

"You could just say fuck it and ignore the demands." Kellan knows me well enough to guess the direction of my thoughts.

"Because the last time we did that, it ended so well."

"Then let her do what she needs to do and fucking ignore it."

"Have you seen what happens when someone ignores another

person's attempt to bully or humiliate them?"

"Oddly enough, yes."

"Then you know why I can't do that."

He sighs. "The fact you haven't been seen in two days is making people talk. You need to show your face."

My mattress bounces, then a hand touches my back. I twist and grab his wrist. "You know better."

One eyebrow arches above amused eyes. "Touchy much?"

"Fuck off, Kellan."

"So, that's a no on the trip to town?"

I don't answer him, and a few minutes later the door clicks as he walks out.

I shift onto my stomach, bury my face into the pillow, and let sleep pull me back under.

***

"Jesus Christ, have you been there all fucking day?"

My eyes snap open at Kellan's voice. I push upright, yawning. "What time is it?"

"Four … *in the afternoon*. Did you sleep all day?" He dumps a bag onto his bed.

"I guess I did."

He folds his arms and shakes his head. "Okay, enough of this." Spinning, he pulls open my dresser and throws a t-shirt and jeans at me. "Get dressed."

"Why?"

"Just fucking get dressed!" he roars.

I stare at him, then slowly swing my legs off the side of the bed.

"Fine. If it's that important to you."

I pull on the clothes he's tossed at me. "Now what"

"Now we go and eat." He throws open the door and stalks out into the hallway beyond.

I grab my cell, shove my feet into sneakers and follow him. "What's wrong with you?"

"Nothing. You're the one who's avoiding the world."

"I'm not avoiding the world." I push open the door and step outside, squinting as the sunlight hits my eyes.

"No, just one corner of it." He jerks his chin, and I follow the direction he's indicating to see Arabella sitting on a bench, head bowed over a book. Her blonde hair is falling forward, hiding her face. "I cloned her cell. She hasn't had any texts since Wednesday, but now you're back in view, I bet that changes fast."

"Does she know?"

"Yeah. She agreed it would be easier than her needing to text us every time they contact her. The problem is I can't track them unless they text her. And they won't text her if you're out of the picture."

"So, I'm the bait?"

"Something like that."

"For fuck's sake." I scrub a hand down my face.

"What happened to being able to handle it?"

"I *can* handle it." I shove my hands into my pockets and turn toward the cafeteria.

"Are you sure?"

I stop. "Do you need me to prove it to you?"

"You don't need to prove anything to *me*."

My eyes stray to Arabella, who hasn't noticed our presence less than a few feet away from where she's sitting.

"Are you asking me to make a scene?" My voice is soft. "She hasn't done anything for me to need to target her."

Kellan shakes his head. "Eli, the shit you did to her on Wednesday … and I'm not talking about making her eat the photograph. When you came back to our room that night, you weren't right. You haven't *been* right since then. Whatever happened afterward … You need to clear the air with her before it starts up again."

I'm shaking my head before he's finished. "We need to sell this, Kell. If I make her comfortable with me, she's never going to believe I'm serious about the things I do in retaliation to her puppet master's commands."

"So, you're going to let her think you're enjoying it? Getting off on it?"

My gaze shifts from her to my friend. "She said something to you." It isn't a question.

"We talked yesterday. She thinks you like what you do."

My laugh is low and bitter. "Of course, she does."

39

Arabella

I want to tell Eli and Kellan what's happening, but I can't. Whoever is behind the texts have already threatened to hurt them. I've even had to push Tina away after she had an allergic reaction to something she ate. She looked so scared when her face swelled up. I dread to think what would have happened if they hadn't gotten her to medical in time. Only a small group of us know of her allergy to shellfish. There's no way it was accidentally put in her sandwich. If I can narrow down who was there when it happened, maybe I can figure out who is stalking me.

I don't know what to do. Why is this happening to me?

Zoey's words resonate inside me. The deeper I delve into her diary, the more I see the similarities. I understand her fear. I know her thoughts. They mirror mine. I'm living her terror, trapped in the same nightmare.

My phone pings and the slither of peace I've had for the last few days dissolve in an instant. I close Zoey's diary and slide it into my bag before I take out my phone. A text is waiting for me when I swipe the screen.

`Unknown number: Go to your room.`

I rise from the bench and walk in the direction of the dorms. Eli and Kellan are heading toward the cafeteria in front of me. There's no need to message them because Kellan will know I've been given a task now that he's cloned my phone. I haven't heard from Eli since we fucked in the tomb. He's been skipping classes, and although part of me is relieved, I'm also angry.

Did he catch a conscience? Does he feel guilty for what he's doing?

I've talked to Kellan about what happened, and he assured me Eli is putting on an act. But even though he was wearing an easy-going smile, he couldn't hide the doubt lurking in his eyes.

After he found me broken in the chapel, Eli told me to fight, to be strong. Was all that a lie? Does he just enjoy being a bully, relishing in his retaliation and causing my tears?

I go straight to my room, and when I reach it, I enter cautiously, bracing myself for something unpleasant. Nothing looks out of place, and it takes me a second to spot the key on my pillow. I pick it up and examine it—I'm sure it's a room key.

My cell chimes again.

`Unknown number: The key is for Eli's room.`

Unease creeps up my spine.

`Me: What am I supposed to do with it?`

`Unknown number: Find his sketchbooks. Pick the most disturbing drawing and tear it out.`

That doesn't sound so bad.

`Me: What if he comes back to his room?`

`Unknown number: He's in the cafeteria right now. We'll message you if he moves.`

It has to be someone in there with Eli and Kellan right now. I hope Kellan is reading these messages and searching for who it could be.

`Me: Ok.`

I stuff my phone back into the pocket of my hoodie and clutch the key tightly in my palm. Hurrying out of my room, I take the stairs down to the senior boys' floor. I have to wait in the stairwell for the hallway to empty of the few students entering rooms. The second they're gone, I dash along to Eli's room. It takes a couple of seconds to get the door open because I'm shaking so much. I make it inside just as a door opens somewhere to my left.

Heart beating rapidly, I press my back against the wood and listen to the sounds on the other side. Minutes slip by, and no one comes to demand why I'm in Eli's room. I relax a fraction and take a look around. Kellan's side is neat, while Eli's is a chaotic mess.

I cross to his desk and trail my fingertips over the hoodie hanging on the back of his chair. I've seen him wearing it so many times. It must be his favorite.

My attention lands on the pile of sketchbooks. Picking up the top one, I flick through the pages. There are ones of Kellan in different poses, and some of a girl I now know is Zoey. The next book is filled with images of the tomb and chapel, the vibe moody and dark. In the third, I find doodles, half-finished pictures as though his mind had moved on elsewhere and he's lost concentration. When I pick up the final book, my breath hitches.

Jace, Brad, Garrett, and the other jocks are on the floor, limbs broken, and bloody faces twisted in anguish. The next page shows Lacy, Tina, Maggie, and Linda tied to wood stakes, flames licking upward to consume them as they scream. The violence in the drawings leaves me disturbed and uncomfortable. Dark drawings fill the pages, each one more violent than the next.

My heart stops when I see my face staring back at me from one of them. Blonde hair spilling down my naked shoulders, I'm on a cross covered in blood. The malice behind it is clear.

Does he loathe me that much? Want to see me in that much pain?

My phone pings.

I drop the sketchbook in panic and pull out my cell.

`Unknown number: Destroy his drawings. We want a photograph of proof when you are done. Remember to keep one.`

The thought of destroying Eli's artwork leaves me with mixed emotions. He's spent hours pouring himself into them, but at the same time, the darkness I see in the last set leaves me agitated and troubled.

They want one of the violent drawings, and the book is full of them. Ripping out the one of me, I fold it in half and tuck it in my hoodie pocket, then grit my teeth.

Eli is an asshole.

I rip the first drawing in half.

Eli is an asshole, and I hope seeing his precious art destroyed hurts him the way he's hurt me.

I go to town on the rest of the sketches, tearing them into fragments.

The only book I leave untouched is the one of Kellan and Zoey. I carry that one to his dresser and tuck it underneath his t-shirts.

Once I'm done, I take a photo of the mess I've made, and send it off to my blackmailer.

35

Eli

"It's someone in here." Kellan's voice is low as he hands me the cell to read the texts.

I sweep my gaze over them, tensing when I read the command to destroy my art.

Will she look through it all?

I try to remember whether I've left all my sketchbooks out. I don't *think* I have. I usually have four or five on the go at any given time, one for each mood, and another full of sketches of Kellan and—

I stand abruptly.

"Where are you going? Sit the fuck down."

"My sketches of Zoey are on the dresser."

Kellan's eyes close briefly and he sucks in a breath before he opens them again and looks at me.

"We can't stop her, Eli." His voice is soft. "She has to do this."

I sit back down, and the air between us is tense while we wait for her to say she's done. Ten minutes pass, fifteen … and then the cell chimes. My eyes jerk down to it, then up to Kellan.

"You look."

He picks up the cell and swipes across the screen, then silently turns it to show me. A photograph of my sketchbooks strewn across the floor; the pages inside torn to pieces.

My jaw clenches. She accused me of enjoying my role in all of this, but how the fuck can she expect me *not* to react emotionally, even while I know she's not at fault? This is my life, my *soul*, they're shredding.

An alarm dings on my cell, and I pull it out of my pocket. "I have an appointment with the counselor."

"Keep it together."

"Yeah." Easy for him to say. He's not the one who has to keep up this fucking act.

I drain my coffee and make my way to the counselor's office. He's waiting for me when I get there.

"Come in. It's been a couple of weeks since we caught up. How are you feeling?"

Angry. Exhausted. Drained.

"Fine." I drop into the chair opposite him and stretch out my legs.

"I heard there was another clash between you and Arabella last week."

I shrug.

"Eli, this won't work unless you talk to me."

"There's nothing to say, other than it's difficult to stay away from someone who won't leave you alone."

"Retaliating just escalates the situation."

I tip my head back and look at the ceiling. "You think I don't know that?"

"Emotional reactions are never helpful. You need to take a step back when she does something. Stop being reactive and start being proactive."

I frown and slowly lower my head until I'm looking at him.

"You already know that she's angry with you. She is lashing out because of what she thinks you've done. Being reactionary is only going to make things worse."

"You mean I should be prepared in advance, and just lock down every emotional response I want to react with?"

"I … no, that's—"

"You know." I straighten in my seat. "That makes sense. I should plan in advance how I'm going to respond to the shit she pulls. That way I'm not clouded by emotion when she finally makes a move." I nod. "Yeah, I like that. Thanks, doc."

I jump to my feet, already thinking about the ways I can prepare in advance. If I have a plan of action, I can retaliate quickly instead of having to wait. Maybe even preempt their plans. If I get Kellan to go through the original texts, maybe we can pick up on what their endgame is.

"Eli, I—"

"You've given me a lot to think about. I'm going to cut this one short and go do some work on my art project. Thanks." I'm out of the door before he can say another word.

My cell chimes with an incoming message just as I reach the room housing my sculpture. I check it while I unlock the door.

Kellan: You should come back to the cafeteria right now.

Me: Why?

Kellan: She's pinned the sketch you did of her nailed to a cross on the noticeboard. Just sashayed right in and stuck it up there.

A photograph is attached to the text—my drawing in all its glory.

Me: Is she still there?

Kellan: Yep, sitting at a table nearby with a drink.

Me: So they're expecting me to respond now.

Kellan: I'd say so. They sent a text telling her to pin it up in here, then take a seat and wait for you.

I relock the door and turn away, the counselor's words running through my head.

Me: Fuck them. I'm going for a run.

If they want a response, they'll get one. But this time it'll be on my terms and when I'm fucking ready.

36

Arabella

The fog swirls around my feet, and I can barely see the gravestones in the sea of blackness. Zoey is standing by the crypt, dressed in a beautiful white dress. Her tears glisten on her pale cheeks, and she beckons with one hand for me to join her.

I jerk awake, my heart pounding and my mind empty of everything other than fear from the nightmare. The room is pitch-black. A heavy weight is on my back, pinning me down. Exploding into panic, I open my mouth to scream, only to have something shoved in my mouth. No matter how much I shake my head, I can't dislodge the gag. Rough hands grab my arms, forcing them behind my back.

Wriggling and kicking my legs on the mattress, I can't get free. Something encircles my wrists—*rope*? It's tied tight, biting into my skin. My screams are muffled as I try to buck my attacker off.

And then the weight on my back disappears.

My ankles are grabbed and secured, more rope binding them together. My legs are forced up behind me. I fight to lower them, but I can't, and it takes me a second to realize the rope around my ankles is bound to the one around my wrists.

Chest rising and falling with fear, I try and concentrate, listening for anything that might give a hint to who my attacker is. And then it dawns on me … something is over my eyes.

A blindfold?

Eli.

Is it Eli?

Is this his retaliation for the drawing I pinned on the cafeteria board on Saturday?

I sat there for three hours waiting for him to react, but he didn't show up. Now, on Monday evening, he's finally retaliating?

I stop fighting and wait for him to speak. He *always* speaks.

But the minutes tick by, and the silence stretches.

Is he getting off at seeing me so helpless?

Fingertips brush my bare thigh.

I tense.

All I'm wearing is a baggy t-shirt and a pair of panties.

The bed dips beside me. I twist my head in the same direction and listen *hard*, but Eli doesn't speak.

Is he trying to scare me? Is this one of his games?

A finger glides down my cheek and stops just above the strip of material gagging my mouth. The warm touch vanishes and is replaced by something cold, flat, and hard.

What is that? A knife?

Terror paralyzes me in place.

Why isn't Eli talking? Why isn't he taunting me? Making me angry?

If he's enjoying seeing me so vulnerable, he'd tell me.

What if it's not Eli?

The thought is like a shout inside my head. I whimper, the sound muffled by the gag. Panic quickens my pulse, sending my breathing into short, sharp pants.

My captor moves off the bed, and a hand strokes its way along my spine down to the curve of my ass. The hem of my t-shirt is yanked up past my hips, and the edge of my panties is lifted. Cold metal touches my inner thigh a second before the sound of cloth being cut reaches my ears. The cotton is ripped away, and cool air washes over the sensitive flesh between my legs.

No, no, no!

My eyes are screwed shut behind the blindfold, but tears leak out, spilling down my cheeks. I renew my struggles, twisting my wrists from side to side, but that only makes the ropes cut into my skin harder.

The knowledge that there is no escape ... I'm at their mercy … is like an ice-cold bucket of water.

A sob tears from my mouth, muffled by the gag.

All I can do is wait. Wait for what they are going to do to me.

I'm shaking, crying, so lost in terror that I lose track of time. I don't know how long it takes for me to notice that there's no other sound in the room. No movement.

No one has touched me again.

Have they gone? Please, God, let them be gone.

Sniffling, I rub my cheek against the pillow, trying to dislodge the gag and blindfold but neither budge. My muffled shouts and screams for help do nothing but make my throat raw.

Time crawls by.

My legs and arms ache, slowly morphing into numbness, and I must have fallen into a fitful doze because the next thing I know, the sound of my door opening breaks the silence.

There's a gasp. "Oh my god! Sarah, call security."

I try to move my head, but my neck is stiff, and I let out a muffled whimper.

"It's okay." The voice is closer. Female and soothing. "It's all going to be okay, sweetheart. I'm going to untie you."

The blindfold is removed, and I blink against the blinding light.

Is it morning already? Have I been bound and gagged most of the night?

It takes me a second to focus, and when I do, I see a woman dressed in the school's house cleaning staff uniform. Her face is pale, and there is pity in her eyes.

The second I see her face, I start to cry.

37

Eli

I check my cell, but there's still no reply from Arabella. She still hasn't spoken to me since the night in the tomb. My retaliation plan is prepared. I'd planned to carry it out yesterday, but she didn't turn up to class. When Kellan commented on her lack of presence, one of the teachers said she was sick and staying in her room. We know there's been no word from her puppet master since Saturday. I guess they're waiting to see how I respond.

When I walk into math, she's at her desk. Her appearance throws me for a second. She's back to the hoodie and yoga pants of her first few months at school, instead of the goth-girl look she's been sporting since Christmas. Her hood is up, pulled forward over her head and I can just about see a curl of blonde hair peeking out.

I glance at Kellan, who closes the door and positions himself just outside. My lookout, just in case Mr. Drake is early.

All eyes are on me as I cross the room. There's a sense of anticipation in the air when people realize I'm on a direct course for Arabella. Before she realizes I'm there, I curl my fingers into the neck of her hoodie, haul her to her feet and shove her forward until she's half sprawled across her desk.

She struggles, and I press down, forcing her face into the cool wood.

"Ripping up my sketchbooks, Princess? *Really*? How fucking childish are you?" With one hand holding her firmly in place, I smooth the other over her ass. "I was going to let this one go, but if you insist on behaving like a child who's fucking acting out because their daddy didn't pay them any attention, then I'll fucking punish you like one." My palm comes down in a sharp slap across her ass.

She yelps and tries to scramble away.

"Oh no, Princess. You'll take your fucking punishment, and then you'll apologize." My palm connects with her ass again.

"Let me go!" Her demand is muffled by her hoodie.

I lean closer. "Stay fucking still. Don't make me take this up a level."

She ignores my plea and continues to struggle, swearing and cursing my name.

I release a long sigh, hook my fingers into the waistband of her yoga pants and drag them down over her ass. I'm careful not to take her panties with them, but she freezes all the same.

I stroke my palm over one rounded cheek. "Count to ten, and we'll call it even." I bring my hand down.

She cries out but doesn't count.

"Arabella …" I tut, shaking my head. "If you don't count, this won't ever end. Let's try again. *Count*, Princess." The sharp crack of my palm hitting her ass echoes around the room.

"Stop! No, please. Stop!"

I make a show of rolling my eyes.

"Do you want Mr. Drake to come in and find you like this? You know he'll add it to his spank bank. Last chance before I carry on until I feel like stopping." I need her to fucking count for me. I spank her again.

"One!" The number is torn from her throat.

I pat her ass. "Good girl. Again."

"T-two."

I can hear the tears in her voice, but I stiffen my spine, forcing myself to continue. "And again."

She's sobbing by the time we reach seven. The class around us is silent. I'm not even sure any of them are recording what I'm doing.

"E-eight. Please, Eli. Please stop."

But I can't. I have to see it through.

I stroke my hand over her ass. It's on fire. I'm sure my palm prints would be visible if I pulled down her panties to check. I lift my palm to strike her again.

"Eli, stop. You're going too far."

I stop, hand hovering in the air and nail Garrett with a glare. "And who the fuck do you think *you* are?"

"It's not funny anymore. Just let her go."

I hold his gaze and bring my hand down, *hard*, across her ass.

She cries out.

"What number was that? Someone distracted me. Do I need to begin again?" My lip curls when Garrett flushes.

"No! It was nine. *Nine*, Eli. Please, no more." Arabella's voice is frantic.

"How many did I say I was going to do? How many are left, Princess? Your knight in shining armor has made me forget."

"Y-you said t-ten. There's one … o-one left."

I grit my teeth. One more, then it's over. My palm rises.

The door bangs off the wall.

"Eli." Kellan's voice slices through the silence. "Put her down. We need to talk."

My eyes drop to the cell he's clutching in one hand. I pat Arabella's ass. She flinches.

"Looks like we'll have to finish this some other time."

I tug her upright and straighten her clothes, then lift a thumb to wipe away the tears on her cheeks.

"Don't fuck with my stuff."

I turn my back on her and walk out.

38

Arabella

My ass is on fire, and I can feel the imprint of Eli's palm searing into my skin. I scrub a hand over my eyes, my shoulders quivering as I sob. I can't believe he spanked me in front of the entire class. When he pinned me to the desk, I had a flashback to the night of the attack. He'd been so cold, *so remote*. The thought of him touching me again in any way leaves me nauseous.

After what happened Monday, I've been jumpy. The school wants to keep the attack on me quiet, and I feel like they are just sweeping it under the carpet.

It's just Arabella Gray again. She's trouble.

Maybe they think I deserve what is happening?

The gasps and murmurs that erupt around me tear me from my misery.

"Holy fuck."

Glancing at Jace, I catch sight of the cell in his hand. There's a photo on the screen. A blonde-haired girl hogtied, blindfolded, and gagged. Another image appears at a different angle to display the ruined cotton of my panties on the blanket, giving the photographer a clear view of my pussy.

They took photos of me?

My head spins, and I sway on my feet. The harder I blink, the more black dots dance before my eyes.

A strong hand grabs my arm and steadies me. "I got you."

My eyes jerk up and meet Garrett's. "No, please."

"It's okay, Arabella. I'm not going to hurt you." His voice is soft and subdued. "Did Eli do that to you?"

He's talking about the photo.

I don't reply to his question. At this point, anything is possible. Maybe he did? I just don't know anymore. My head is a mess, and my ass hurts. I'm mentally and physically exhausted.

"I need to go." Tears streaming down my face, I grab my bag and make for the door. I'm relieved to see no sign of Eli or Kellan out in the hallway. I duck my head and limp for the exit, praying Mr. Drake won't catch me.

"Hey, wait up."

I flinch at the shout and keep moving forward.

"Hey." Garrett touches my arm.

"What do you want?"

His eyes are troubled as he scans my face. "You're white as a sheet, and you look like you're about to faint. You shouldn't be alone."

My laugh sounds brittle to my ears. "You're one of the last people on the planet I want with me right now."

"Where are you going?"

"I-I don't know." My strength falters.

If I go to the tomb or the chapel, Eli will find me.

The thought of seeing him after what just happened makes me want to run in the opposite direction.

Garrett touches my arm lightly. "Come on. This way."

"Why should I trust you?"

My phone vibrates in my bag, but I ignore it.

"Because I'm done with watching Travers tear strips off you. It's not funny. He's a fucking monster, and it needs to stop." He gestures toward the other end of the campus. "I know somewhere we can go that he won't think to look for you."

The prospect of going back to my room leaves me feeling miserable.

What if he's my blackmailer?

I hesitate for a heartbeat, before I nod, a reckless need to have control over *something* driving me. "Okay."

Garrett leads me to the gymnasium and then around it. We end up at a side door which he opens. It leads into a storage area where boxes and spare equipment are housed.

"That door back there leads into the main building. It's unlocked if you want to try it, if that makes you feel safe to be in here with me. There are some mats to sit on right next to it." He points further in. "It's pretty comfortable."

I hug my bag to my chest and follow his directions. "I don't think I can sit down."

Garrett grimaces. "Shit, I should have thought of that. Maybe I can find a cushion. It might be gentler on your ass."

There are empty beer bottles tucked away and other signs that the place is being used by students. When I reach the door, I push it open a crack and peek out into the gymnasium. There's a class in session, a group of students playing basketball.

I leave the door ajar and turn back to him. "Why are you being nice to me?"

"I don't like what Eli is doing to you."

"Isn't it the same as what you want to do?"

"No." He rakes a hand through his hair. "I'd have never gone that far, and your room wasn't my idea. That was Jace's."

I freeze. "J-Jace's?"

"I think he was pissed you went off with Kellan at the Valentine's Ball."

He's not talking about Monday night.

He glances around. "You hungry? I can grab something from the vending machine. I could do with a drink."

I offer him a wobbly smile. "Not really."

"I'll bring you back something anyway. Just make yourself comfortable, okay?"

As he turns away, I call his name. "Garrett?"

He glances at me. "Yeah?"

"Please don't tell anyone where I am."

He nods, his expression serious. "You got it."

I wait until he's gone to check my phone. Eli has left me a bunch of messages.

`Sin: Ari, where are you?`

`Sin: Tell me where you are.`

`Sin: Why the fuck didn't you tell us what happened?`

`Sin: Who was it?`

`Sin: You know it wasn't me, right?`

`Sin: Ari, tell me where the fuck you are.`

I close the text conversation, not wanting to see anymore.

Fuck Eli.

I don't want to lay eyes on him again. The sooner spring break arrives, the quicker I can go back to the Hamptons. If it comes down to it, I'll find a hotel somewhere, so I can stay away from him the whole time we're off.

I take out my other cell and copy Miles' number into the one that Eli gave me and send Miles a message.

`Me: It's Arabella. I'm with Garrett. I'm okay, he's brought me somewhere quiet behind the gymnasium. Don't tell Eli or Kellan. But if anything happens to me, you know who I am with. He's not being an asshole.`

A ping comes from my other cell as I shove it back in my pocket.

I half expect it to be Miles asking why I'm using a different number, and everything inside me turns to ice with dread when I read what's written.

`Unknown number: Next time you don't get Travers' attention, we won't just leave you tied up with a few bruises. Play the game properly, Arabella, or we'll do worse.`

39

Eli

I rub a hand down my face. "For the last time, it *wasn't* me."

I must have been in the principal's office for at least an hour, answering question after question about the photographs posted on social media.

"When did you last speak to Arabella?"

"Speak to her? Wednesday."

"Other students report that you've clashed a lot, even though your return here was under the agreement that you would stay away from her."

"It's hard to stay away from someone who shares every class with me and is going out of their fucking way to destroy everything I own."

"Ah, yes." Principal Warren looks down at the piece of paper he's holding. "I've been informed of the petty back and forth between you."

"Petty back and forth." My voice is flat.

"It ends now, or I'll have you both removed from the school."

"I *didn't* fucking do it."

"You said that about the videos at Christmas as well."

"Because I didn't fucking do them either."

There's a pain behind my eyes. I pinch the bridge of my nose.

"I swear to you this wasn't me."

"Spring break is in two and a half weeks. You have until then to sort this issue out. I do *not* want to see you in my office again." He nods toward the door. "Out."

Kellan pushes away from the wall when I exit and falls into step beside me.

"Did you find her?"

He shakes his head. "She's not answering calls or texts. She's not in her room, the tomb, or the chapel."

The pain in my head is getting worse. I rub my forehead. "Where the fuck could she be?"

"It's not important. What did Warren say?"

"That if all the bullshit doesn't stop, he's kicking us both out." I stop. "What the fuck am I supposed to do? If I retaliate, she thinks I hate her. If I don't retaliate, they're going to do much worse than …" I shake my head. I can't even finish the sentence.

The pain behind my eyes is spreading. I press the heel of my head to the bridge of my nose.

"You don't look well." An arm wraps around my shoulders. "Let's go back to our room and talk this out."

"And what if they come for her again, Kell? Because I'm hiding away where she can't fucking cause shit."

He pats my shoulder. "We'll worry about that later."

***

It's three am. Kellan is asleep across the room, but I've been tossing and turning all night. My head is still throbbing. I've taken a couple of painkillers which eased the headache for a little while, but now it's back.

My cell … *Sin's* cell … is in my hand. I've lost count of the number of texts I've sent. All ignored. I swing my legs off the bed and stand. Pulling on a pair of sweats and a t-shirt, I slip out of the door, and creep up to the next floor.

The lights are dimmed in the hallways and everywhere is silent. When I reach Arabella's room, I stop and rest my palm against the door, pull out my cell with my free hand and text her.

`Me: I'm outside. Open the door.`

I wait.

Nothing. No response via text, and no sound coming from the room. Chewing on my lip ring, I study the handle, then pull out a bunch of keys. It takes four attempts before I find one that fits the lock, and I click it open and step inside.

"Ari?" I keep my voice low as I move across the room to her bed.

She's huddled beneath the sheets, barely visible. I sit on the edge of the mattress.

"Ari?"

She doesn't move. I sigh.

"I'm sorry. Why didn't you tell me?" I scrub a hand down my face. "It doesn't fucking matter. I crossed a line today. I'm so fucking sorry. I thought I could control it, but I can't."

I glance over at her. Her eyes are closed, breathing steady. I stand and brush a finger over her cheek.

"I'm sorry."

Standing, careful not to disturb her, I walk out, locking the door behind me and head back down to my room.

90

Arabella

"What's going on with you and Eli?"

I glance up from the book I have spread out on the table in front of me. Miles settles in the seat beside me.

"Nothing."

Eli is poison. Not an antidote. I'm not going to swallow down his bullshit like a jagged little pill. If I do, it might just kill me quicker than my blackmailers.

"No, seriously. You haven't made eye contact with him since Wednesday. It's like he doesn't exist for you anymore." His voice drops to a whisper, joining the low buzz of conversation at the other tables around us in the library. "Kellan says—"

"Fuck what Kellan says. I don't want to hear it." The memory of the spanking leaves a bitter taste in my mouth. "It's Saturday. Shouldn't you be off seeing him or something?"

He ignores my question. "What about your blackmailers?"

I shrug. "They haven't sent me any more messages. Maybe they're finally done."

Lies.

They're just waiting for the right time to make me do something awful to Eli. The threat they gave hovers over my head every single night when I go to bed. I've resorted to sleeping pills, just to be able to rest because if I don't, my mind won't let me. No dreams are better than nightmares about monsters under my bed.

Miles frowns. “What did Principal Warren say to you yesterday?”

“That he’ll kick me out of school if my feud with Eli continues.”

“Maybe you should tell him the truth.”

My attention returns to the book in front of me. “I’ve tried that before, and it didn’t end well. At this point, I’d rather get kicked out.”

Not that my mother or Elliot would be happy, but I’m at the stage I really don’t care. My life is in danger, and my privacy is violated. Every second of every day, I’m waiting for something bad to happen.

“If you’re here to be their spy, you can leave.”

He fidgets with one of the pencils on the table, flipping it between his fingers. “What are you doing with Garrett? He’s been hovering over you since Thursday morning.”

“He’s kind of sweet.”

“He was bullying you only a few weeks ago.”

Lifting my chin, I meet his gaze. “He’s being the friend I needed.”

He flinches at my hard tone.

Garrett surprised me by staying with me all day Wednesday and playing hooky from classes. He fed me and talked about random things like books and movies, just to keep my mind off what happened. For someone who tormented me for so many weeks, he’s actually gone out of his way to make me feel safe. When Thursday morning rolled around, he was at my door, waiting to walk me to breakfast.

I snatch my pencil from his fingers and place it back in my case. “If you don’t mind, I’m trying to study.”

I might have been able to avoid Eli for the last few days, but it’s the weekend, which means I don’t know where he might be. I have no intention of walking into him. If I have to spend all my time in the safety of the library, I will.

He huffs. "I am your friend too, Bella."

A shadow falls over us.

"Is he bothering you?" Garrett is glaring at Miles.

Miles straightens at his question. "I was just asking her a question about our English assignment. All done now."

Garrett grunts and holds up a plastic bag. "I got us some lunch."

"Thanks." I close my book and put it away. "Bye, Miles."

Garrett falls into step beside me when I stand and walk toward the entrance.

He holds the door open for me.

"Where do you want to eat? We could find a bench."

I stop in front of him. "Only if you tell me why you haven't left my side since Wednesday."

He glances away. "I told you I'm going to make sure Travers doesn't touch you like that again."

"Why?"

"Arabella—"

"I'm not moving until you tell me, because you haven't been my knight in shining armor, Garrett. You've been a villain since I arrived here. And don't tell me it's because we like the same kind of sit-coms."

A nerve pulses in his jaw. Grabbing my wrist, he tugs me outside and doesn't stop until we're away from listening ears.

"My dad used to hit my mom when I was younger. I was too small to defend her from him. Seeing Eli hit you … I couldn't just stand by and watch. Not this time."

I pull my wrist free from his grip and squeeze his fingers. "How old were you?"

"Eight. He walked out when I was twelve."

The raw pain on his face tugs at my heartstrings. I wrap my arms around him and hug him, offering comfort. He freezes in my embrace, then hugs me back just as fiercely.

"I may not be a knight in shining armor, but I'll be your shield against the monster," he whispers into my hair.

If only that were possible.

There's more than one monster at Churchill Bradley Academy. One who wears the title proudly, and another who lurks in the shadows.

What happens if someone protects me from Eli's retaliation? Do I really want to put a target on Garrett's back?

No. Even though I'm desperate to be saved, I can't let him do that. The risk is too high. I need to push him away. Keep him at arm's length as I've done with Miles.

The hairs on the back of my neck rise, the feeling of being watched washing over me. Still lost in Garrett's warm, safe embrace, I turn my head and see Eli and Kellan watching us from a bench. My stepbrother's expression is carved from stone, void of emotion, but his eyes—his eyes burn me alive with his rage.

91

Eli

Fucking Garrett. What the fuck is she doing hanging around with him?

Is this another order? I dismiss that thought immediately. We'd know if that was the case. Nothing has come through on her cell. *Then why the fuck is she with him?*

"It could be nothing."

I slice a look at Kellan, who shrugs.

"Maybe he caught a conscience. I'll ask Miles if he knows anything. He was talking to her a few minutes ago."

It took Kellan a week to wear Miles down after our threesome with Arabella, but eventually, the swim captain gave in and agreed to give Kellan another chance, as long as he promised they would be exclusive. Kellan tried to argue that Arabella was a girl, so it didn't count, but Miles was having none of it.

If I wasn't so fucking stressed over everything going on, it would have been funny to see my friend scrambling. He likes Miles, *a lot* more than he's admitting.

"Look, there's Miles. Go and spend time with him. I'm going for a walk." I turn toward the trees and set off.

"Eli," Kellan calls after me.

I ignore him and pick up my pace. I need some time alone, away from people, from the constant stares and whispers about the *'monster.'*

My steps take me to the cemetery, and I stop in front of Zoey's plaque. I trace over the letters of her name with one finger, then sink down to sit in front of it.

"Everything is fucked up, ZoZo." I loop my arms around my knees and tip my head back against the gravestone behind me. "It doesn't seem to matter what I do, things just get worse. Ari hates me, and it's not the kind of hate where she still wants to fuck me. She *hates* me with every fiber of her soul. It's there in her eyes every time she looks at me.

"And now she's spending time with fucking Garrett. You remember him, right? The asshole who got caught putting recording devices in girls' showers. Yeah, yeah. I know there was never any proof it was him, but all signs pointed in his direction."

I fall silent for a few minutes, pretending she's there and replying to me. I know what she'd say. Zoey saw the best in everyone.

"I know … you're right. All signs point at me being responsible for the videos being leaked about Ari. But it's not the same."

But it *is* the same, and deep down, I fucking know it.

I sigh and lean forward to rest my head on my knees.

"I don't know what to do, Zo."

My eyes land on something. A splash of color in the dirt to my right. I stretch out an arm, pluck it out of the ground and lift it. Brushing the dirt off the charms, I uncover a butterfly, a heart, and a four-leaf clover.

Arabella's charm bracelet. *Is it a sign?*

"Are you telling me to talk to her, ZoZo?"

But, of course, there's no answer to that. I pocket the bracelet and push to my feet. Leaning forward I press a kiss to the plaque.

"I miss you, ZoZo. Thanks for the chat."

As I turn to walk toward the gates, there's a snap of twigs behind me. I spin around and scan the cemetery, but can't see anyone. The fine hairs at the back of my neck lift.

"What the fuck do you want?" I say the words out loud, but only silence answers me.

Maybe it was an animal. Maybe I'm imagining it. I don't think I am, though. I'm sure there's someone there, watching me, but wherever they're hiding, it's completely out of my view.

"Fine. Lurk like a fucking creeper." I continue on my path toward the gates and back to the school grounds.

There's a group of students crowded around the front of the dorm building when I reach it. They melt apart as I approach, leaving a path for me to walk through. Tension zips through my spine, but I keep my shoulders loose and my walk casual as I move through them toward the door.

There's a sheet of paper pinned to the wood, and I slow as I near it. A photograph is at the top of the sheet.

I pull it off and study it. It's a close-up of me, of my face, a look of fury contorting my features. My gaze drifts to the words beneath.

How did Zoey Rivers really die?

Maybe you should ask the monster.

42

Arabella

Unknown number: There's a key in your locker.

My stomach twists with trepidation at the message. Six days have passed since they sent the threat of what would happen if I don't get Eli to react. One hundred and forty-four hours of hanging in limbo. I've caught him staring at me. Every time he passes my desk in class, he knocks my books off my desk. He's lashing out at me even when I haven't been told to do anything to him. The shittier he is to me, the more it drives away any warmth I had toward him. I can't stand being anywhere near him. Garrett has been growly and protective, even though I've told him just to stay away. I'm not sure what to do to get the message across for him to leave me alone.

I weave my way through the flow of students, aiming for my locker. It's Tuesday afternoon, and I have a free period. Whatever my blackmailer has planned, they've timed it perfectly.

When I open the door to my locker, there's a key on top of my books. I slip it into my pocket just as my phone pings.

Unknown number: Go to the art department.

I frown at the message. Why are they short? Usually, the instructions are more detailed. Why the change?

I do as I'm told and head for art.

My phone chimes again.

Unknown number: Take a can of spray paint from one of the storage closets.

It takes me a couple of minutes to find the right one. Once I do, I rummage through the equipment until I find a can of red spray paint. I hide it in my shoulder bag.

Unknown number: Go through the gym and find room C5. You have the key to unlock the door. Eli's sculpture for his art project is inside. Ruin it.

My breathing turns shaky. I'm not sure what to do. Ruining more of Eli's art is not something I want to do.

Me: But he's been working on it for months.

Unknown number: Don't fucking care. Destroy it. Send a photograph as proof or pay the price.

Terror lodges in my throat.

Eli will kill me if I do this.

Months ago, when it had just been me and Sin, I'd enjoyed the danger, the risk. It feels like forever ago. This twisted game is out of control. But if I'm to survive, I need to play.

I leave the art department and head for the gym, and room C5. When I enter, the first thing I catch sight of is the dust sheet covering the sculpture in the center of the room. I circle around until I'm in front of the statue, and pull off the sheet.

All I can do is stare.

The monster's face is grotesque, its body just as disturbing, but what it's holding has my heart pounding in my chest. A woman is in the beast's arms. One clawed hand around her waist, the other gently cradles her head. She's naked, hair spilling down her shoulders, and the tail of the creature is wrapped around one of her legs. Chin tipped up; she's staring at the monster with a look of absolute adoration.

Me.

I'm gazing at the monster in worship.

My features are captured and immortalized in marble.

Eli made this?

Did he carve it with his own two hands?

Has he made me his art piece to display at the end of school?

Why?

The questions echo inside my head with no answers to be found.

My lips tremble.

It's beautiful, haunting, and macabre. I've never seen anything like it before.

I can't defile it.

Tears flow down my cheeks. I cannot destroy it. I just can't. As much as I hate my stepbrother, destroying this work of art would be like ripping out a piece of his soul. The attention to detail, the hours he's poured into it, would be for nothing.

I'm *not* a bully. I'm *not* heartless. I'm not the monster they're trying to mold me into.

Why did he use me as his muse? Is this another cruel joke?

I've been in the arms of the Monster of Churchill Bradley Academy more than once. Every time has been different and volatile. There's nothing sweet about the relationship between us. I'm not sure there ever will be.

I scrub away my tears and glance around the room until my attention lands on a small slab of black stone in the corner.

I take the spray can from my bag and shake it before popping off the lid. Crossing the room, I stop in front of the small slab. It's the same color as the marble, so hopefully, they won't know I haven't touched the sculpture. My hand is shaking as I spray a dick on the surface and write the word *monster*.

Please let this work. Please let this work.

When I'm done, I snap a close-up so that only the graffitied part of the stone is visible, and press send.

I don't give myself time to think. I flee from the room … from the scene of the crime.

They are going to know I didn't do it. Why did I just risk everything for a statue?

The question repeats over and over in my head, but I can't answer it.

93

Eli

I'm waiting for her when she comes out of the building. For once, I don't have to pretend I don't know what she's done, because Lacy is quick to inform me she'd seen Arabella letting herself into the room where my art project is.

There's a malicious smile on her face when she delivers the information, and I'm confident it's because she wants to see Arabella put down and *not* because she's concerned about my project.

When Arabella appears out of the door and dashes along the path toward the dorms, I step out in front of her, arms folded, and cock an eyebrow. She skids to a stop. My gaze slides over her, and I know I'm successfully channeling the *monster* when she pales and tries to back away.

"Show me your hands."

"Eli, I—"

"Show. Me. Your. *Fucking*. Hands." I don't have to pretend to be angry. I *am*. If my sculpture is ruined … I don't even want to complete that thought.

When she doesn't move, I reach out and wrap my fingers around her arm so I can pull her hand from her pocket. She has her fingers clenched into a fist, so I tighten my grip and peel each finger away from her palm. There are flecks of red paint on her fingertips. My eyes lift to meet hers.

"What did you do?" My voice is soft.

She shakes her head. My fingers flex on her wrist, tightening until she gasps, and I know she'll be left with bruises, but it doesn't stop me from dragging her along with me as I walk back to the building.

She's trying to peel my fingers off her wrist, when I unlock the door housing my sculpture and pull her in. There are people trailing behind us, so I slam the door shut on them and pull down the blind. I don't want any witnesses to what might happen next. My eyes move immediately to the sculpture in the center of the room. The dust sheet hangs over it, and I release her so I can pull it off.

"Eli—"

"Shut the fuck up." I stalk around the marble, searching for damage, but can't find a single mark. "What did you do, Ari?" My gaze swings to her, and her eyes dart to the left.

I turn my head to follow the direction of her gaze and see the dick she's painted on the piece of stone I'd cut off from the base. My eyes snap back to her.

Whirling, I push all my tools off the workbench. The clatter as they hit the floor is loud and she jumps.

"Run," I tell her quietly. "And don't fucking look back." I pick up a chisel and throw it at the wall. "*Go*!"

She aims for the door, throws it open and runs out.

"You *fucking bitch*!" I roar, throw the dust sheet over the statue, lock the door and then take off after her.

Right on cue, Miles and Kellan appear and grab my arms to haul me backward, stopping me from catching up to Arabella, who disappears through the door of the dorm building.

"Get the fuck off me." I shake Miles off and shove him away.

I catch his eye roll, but he steps back, lifting his arms. "Leave the girl alone, asshole."

"Or what?"

"Leave the pretty boy alone, Eli." Kellan steps between us, the hint of a smile tilting one corner of his mouth.

We've worked this out in advance, although if she *had* destroyed my work, it could have gone in a very different direction.

"I'm going to fucking kill her." I say it loud enough for the people closest to overhear. "She's destroyed it. I've been working on that piece for fucking months, and she's *ruined* it." I hurl a chunk of marble to the ground. "What the fuck am I supposed to do now?"

"We'll work something out. I'm sure Mr. McIntyre will give you an extension." Kellan pats my shoulder, and we turn toward the dorm building. Miles has melted away during the distraction, his plan is to meet us inside without being seen walking with us.

"Why don't you stop picking on girls." I swing around at the words and find Garrett standing behind me.

I lift an eyebrow. "Did you say something?"

He tips his head back, glaring at me. "I said, leave Arabella alone."

I let my lips curl up into a smile. My anger over the statue might all be for show, but I need an outlet for the frustration the entire situation is causing me. If Garrett wants a fight, I'll fucking give him one.

"Are you going to stop me?" I take a step toward him. "Why are you sniffing around her, anyway? Think she's going to put out for you? That little pussy is not for you." I advance toward him, and he steps back. I nod. "Yeah, that's what I thought. Go back to hiding behind your friends."

I turn my back on him and stalk toward the dorm and up to our room. Miles is already inside when we get there. I close the door and sag against it, blowing out a breath.

"She didn't touch it."

"What? But she sent them a photograph." Kellan shows me the image on the cell.

I shake my head. "That's a random bit of stone I cut off. She took a close-up photograph of that. She didn't touch the actual piece."

"So why did she look so fucking terrified?" Miles demands.

I run my palm over my face. "That's her default setting right now. I think she's forgotten the reason behind my behavior and believes I'm doing it on purpose."

99

Arabella

"Got you mac and cheese."

A plate appears in front of me. "Thanks."

When I look up, Garrett smiles. "You're welcome." He drops into the seat beside me.

It's Friday. Three days since my last instructions. I've received no backlash or threats from my blackmailers, so they must have bought my lie about destroying Eli's statue.

Eli has been picking on me more and more. He throws my food over me whenever we're in the cafeteria at the same time. Insulting me, taunting me, he's the asshole I know him to be. But no one has stopped him. Everyone just turns away. Everyone but Garrett.

He still hasn't taken the hint, and keeps trying to protect me, getting in between us. No matter how hard I push, he won't stop. He needs to leave me alone. To just give up.

I poke at my food. My appetite is barely there, but Garrett seems set on making sure I eat.

"Ah, shit." His muttered words shift my attention to the two boys walking toward our table. I tense.

"What the fuck, Garrett?" Jace snaps, coming to a stop in front of us. "Every time I look, you're with her. You're like her pet puppy."

"She must be good at sucking dick, or maybe she's finally spread her legs for someone other than Travers and his minion." Evan snickers.

"Is that it?" Jace's gaze slices my way. "Are you fucking him?

Using our friend to protect you from the monster?"

Garrett's jaw clenches, and he rises from his chair. "Dude, stop it. You've got to see that Travers is going too far. Bella doesn't deserve what he's doing to her."

"Deserve it?" Jace laughs. "She keeps provoking him. You have to be insane to do something like that."

I push back my chair and stand. "Thanks for lunch, Garrett."

Ignoring the other two jocks, I walk across the cafeteria for the door. I can't explain why I'm doing what I'm doing. It's too exhausting trying to defend myself when everyone sees what my blackmailer wants them to see. They've painted me as a girl desperate for the attention of a bully. Someone who will go to any extreme to get what she wants.

Does anyone remember the Arabella Gray who first arrived, or has she been erased in the charade I'm being forced to play?

"Hey, freak!"

I peek over my shoulder at Lacy's call. She's sitting at her table surrounded by her friends, a smirk on her lips.

A hand shoves my shoulder. Off balance, my hip smashes into the side of a table, and I cry out. When I swivel my head to see who pushed me, my heart plummets.

"Watch where you're fucking going," Eli snarls.

I shrink away from him, backing away to put the table I'd crashed into between us. There's no flicker of emotion on his expression as he stalks to his table. Kellan follows him, shooting me a troubled look as he passes.

The second they move, I scurry out of the cafeteria. Pain radiates up from my hip, but I ignore it. As soon as I'm locked inside my dorm room, I strip off and check. Touching the dark red bruise forming on my skin, I grimace. Another one to go with all the others I've suffered over the last few weeks. How many more will I get before the year ends?

I throw myself down on my bed, and don't bother trying to fight the negative thoughts that fill my head. My phone rings. I hesitate, then reach for it.

"Hello?"

"Hello, sweetheart." My mother's voice is happy.

"Hi, Elena."

"Can you start calling me Mom?"

I frown. "I thought you didn't like me calling you that?"

"It's something Elliot pointed out," she replies. "I've become so used to you calling me by my first name that I never really thought about how wrong it is. I should have done this sooner. So, please, Bella, call me Mom."

Now she wants to play at being a mom after all the years she's missed? I'm too tired to argue about it. "Okay."

"How's school?"

"Good."

She takes a breath. "Do you want to tell me what's going on with you and Eli—"

"Nothing is going on," I reply robotically, repeating what I've told the principal, the counselor, and my teachers.

"We've had reports of you fighting."

"That's what stepsiblings are supposed to do, right? Like any other family."

Elena is silent for a beat. "I'm here if you want to talk. If something is going on, you can tell me."

"It's nothing. Just stupid stuff."

And I can't tell you because if I do, someone will end up getting hurt, and it will be all my fault.

"I know something happened between the two of you at Christmas. Then things changed. I'm not blind, you know."

Does she know Eli and I had sex?

Closing my eyes, I clench my fingers around the phone in my hand. "I don't want to talk about it."

I do. I do. This is tearing me apart. Help me. Please help me.

She sighs softly. "If you change your mind, I'm here."

"Thanks, Ele—Mom."

"Elliot wants to go away for spring break. Just the two of us. I wanted to call you first before letting him book something."

"Why?"

"Because it means you and Eli will be home alone."

"Oh." The thought of being alone with him scares me. Anything could happen with no one there to stop it.

"We don't have to go—"

"No, you should. I might just find somewhere else to stay. Head to the beach or something. Somewhere peaceful. I quite like the idea of being alone for a while."

Somewhere I can think. Catch my breath without eyes watching me all the time. It's everything I yearn for.

Elena hums. "Charge it to your credit card. Maybe go shopping?"

"I will."

"I can order a car to come to pick you up from school on the last day, if you like?"

Her offer makes me smile. It feels strange on my lips. When did I last smile? "Yes, please."

"Okay, darling. I'll arrange it for you and text you the details."

"I hope you both have fun," I whisper. "I better go. I have a session with Counselor Clarke soon."

"Talk to you soon, sweetheart."

"Bye, Mom." Ending the call, I roll onto my side and stare at the calendar pinned to the wall. My gaze follows the red crosses over the dates and the ones yet to be ticked off—my countdown until freedom.

95

Eli

"When did you last speak to Arabella?"

"What?" I drag my eyes away from the sketch I'm doing and search out where Kellan sits across the table from me.

"Arabella. When did you last talk to her?"

I shrug. I stopped texting her a while ago. I don't remember when, but she hasn't been speaking to me since I spanked her. Something changed that day. It had to. To make it believable, I had to cut off any feelings I have for her. It's the only way I can make whoever is watching believe the role I'm playing.

The days are blurring together into a constant repetition of see her, hurt her, walk away from her, while the words '*it's to keep her alive'* roll on a loop through my head.

"Eli!" Kellan's clipped voice drags my attention back to him. "Have you been with her at all when you're not in her face?"

"She wants nothing to do with me, so … no." I focus back on the sketchpad.

"*Eli!*" He snatches the pad out of my hands and stuffs it in his bag. "For fuck's sake."

"*What?*"

"Look at me."

I frown. "Why?"

"You've been acting weird for days. What's going on?"

That makes me laugh. "What's going on? Seriously?"

"Not *that*. I mean with you."

"Does there need to be anything else?"

He's silent for a second, and I can feel his gaze on me. "The agreement was that you'd retaliate to things she does." His voice is soft.

"And?"

"And she hasn't done anything for days."

"Your point?" I know what his point is. I just want to hear him say it.

"You dumped yogurt in her hair yesterday. The day before, you poured coffee into her bag. Today you sent her flying into a table. She has bruises on her arms from where you've grabbed her and shoved her out of your way."

I look at him, but don't say anything.

"Fuck's sake, Eli. She *hasn't* done anything to you."

My lip curls up on one side.

"This is what you were like when she first joined. You *liked* hurting her. Is that what's happening now? Have you gotten a taste for it again?"

The words were almost a mirror for something Arabella said a couple of weeks ago. I squash down the spark of guilt it brings up and reach for my drink.

"I'm doing what I need to do. That's all."

"And where will it end? We need to find a better way."

I stand, bracing my hands on the edge of the table, and lean close to Kellan. "There is no other fucking *way*. Driving her out of the school is the *only* thing I can do at this point. It's either that or she ends up next to Zoey." I should have let my dad take her out when he mentioned it.

"And the way you're behaving, you're the one who will put her there."

"Fuck you, Kellan." I shove away from the table and stalk out of the cafeteria.

I'm halfway to the cemetery when my cell chimes. I swipe on the notification to ignore it, only for it to chime again seconds later. I ignore that one, and I'm bombarded with more.

"Fuck's sake."

Unlocking the screen, I tap one of the notifications without reading it. It takes me to a video. A quick glance tells me it's been sent as a mass group text, outside of the social media app, which was shut down after the last video of Arabella was released. I hit play without looking at the thumbnail.

Oh, my darling boy. Look how smart you are. I can't wait for you to go to school. It's where me and your dad met.

I freeze. Another voice, robotic sounding, talks over the feminine one.

Before the Monster of Churchill Bradley, there was a boy called Elliot Travers the Third. Short, shy, and scared of everything.

I lift the cell and stare down at the video.

A woman, dark-haired and slim, is standing next to a boy in dark jeans and a navy t-shirt. His hair is messy, flopping into his eyes as he ducks his head away from the camera pointed at him. She's smiling directly at the screen, and a man's voice can be heard chuckling.

"Come on, Eli. We need to keep this as a memory. Maybe you'll

meet your soulmate there like I did."

I swallow.

But he couldn't hide the truth of who he was for long.

The video changes. In this one, the boy is a little older. He's dressed in a dark suit, with one arm in a cast strapped across his chest. I know without looking that the left side of his face is swollen, both his eyes are bruised, and his nose is broken. He moves carefully, and tosses a single red rose down into the hole in the ground.

This, students of Churchill Bradley, is where the monster was born. Brought to life by the death of his mother.

The video changes to a set of photographs—of my face after the accident, my broken bones, my back.

Look your fill, students of Churchill Bradley. Behold the Monster.

The cell phone drops from my hand.

***

"*Oh my god!"*

"Let her go!"

"Fuck. He's going to kill her."

"Eli!"

"Eli. Stop!"

I blink, and the voices reach me as though through a wall, muffled and faint.

Where the fuck am I?

I shake my head.

Blue eyes, wide and fearful.

Red lips parted on a silent cry.

A hand wrapped around a throat.

Everything comes into focus in a rush of noise and images.

I have Arabella pinned against the wall, my hand around her neck. My face is close to hers and I'm swearing, snarling, and snapping at her. Her fingernails are biting into my wrist as she tries to break free.

Hands are on my arms.

People are shouting.

And then one voice reaches me.

"Leave Arabella alone!"

My fingers flex and drop from her throat. She sags, sucking in gasping breaths. But she's no longer my focus. I turn slowly, eyes searching out the person who'd called out.

There he is. Ginger hair, and freckles across his nose. A nose my fist connects with almost as soon as I see it.

One punch becomes two, becomes three. Blood sprays from his face and my knuckles. He raises his hands, trying to protect himself, while others try to drag me off him, but I'm beyond reason, beyond fury.

And then a voice I recognize reaches me.

"Eli, enough. You have to stop." A hand touches my shoulder.

My next punch falters and I drop my hand to the ground, bracing myself while I catch my breath. I don't stop Kellan from hauling me to my feet. Words are being spoken, but they're unintelligible, washing over my head. All I can hear is one voice, over and over.

Look your fill, students of Churchill Bradley. Behold the Monster.

96

Arabella

People are screaming and shouting. I'm down on my knees, sucking in air, as I try to focus on what's happening, but my brain is sluggish, dazed. My heart is pounding in my ears. I can still feel the imprint of Eli's hands around my throat. The feral look in his eyes when he pinned me to the wall is branded in my brain.

When I lift my head, it takes a second for me to understand what I'm seeing.

Eli is kneeling over someone on the floor, his fists flying, blood spraying.

Garrett.

The other boy's face is a mess of red, and he's struggling weakly beneath his attacker. Some of the jocks try to pull Eli off of him, but he's snapping and snarling like a rabid animal.

Eli is going to kill him.

I try to cry out, to beg him to stop, but my voice is a small croak, swallowed by the other shouts and noise.

What is happening?

I don't understand.

He'd attacked me out of nowhere without any provocation.

Horror chills my blood, tears spilling free, as the jocks struggle and fail to drag Eli off their friend.

Oh god, he's going to kill Garrett.

He tried to kill me.

Kellan emerges from the gathered crowd, pushing his way past the other students with Miles a step behind him. He strides over to my stepbrother, but instead of grabbing him, he touches his shoulder. "Eli, enough. You have to stop."

"Bella, are you okay?" Miles crouches in front of me, blocking my view.

Crawling into his open arms, I sob into his chest. "Garrett! He's going to kill Garrett." My voice is raspy, and it hurts to swallow.

His arms close around me, and I'm wrapped in a tight hug. "Kellan stopped him. What the hell happened?"

I shake my head. "Don't know. I don't know! Keep him away from me." Confusion and fear tear me up from the inside out.

Eli tried to kill me.

His eyes had been empty of everything except fury. They burned with rage.

I sob harder into Miles' chest.

Eli really is the monster everyone claims him to be.

97

I don't know what hurts more—my head or my knuckles. My hands are swollen. I can barely lift a pencil, which worries me for a while until the nurse says I haven't broken any fingers and the swelling will go down in a day or two.

Painkillers aren't helping the headache, though, so I'm lying on the bed, covers over my head with the curtains closed and the light off.

The scrape of a chair warns me that someone else is in the room. I don't move from my position to find out who it is.

"I know you're awake."

I stay quiet. If I don't say anything, he might go away.

"Eli. I'm not leaving until you talk to me. What happened yesterday?"

I don't want to think about yesterday. I don't remember a lot of it, but the flashes of images I *do* have make me nauseous.

"Okay, if you don't want to talk, then listen. One of the students said a video was sent around to the entire school."

"Not the faculty." I can't help but correct him. My voice is rough, *hoarse*, like I've been shouting or screaming.

He sighs softly. "No, not the faculty. Just the students."

"Did you watch it?"

"No. It was deleted before any of the staff could see it."

I laugh. "Of course, it was."

"Kellan says that—"

"I know what was on the video, you don't have to rehash it."

"Did you ever talk to anyone after the accident?"

"I didn't have time. When do I need to leave?"

"Leave?"

I roll over and look at Counselor Clarke. "Warren said if there was another clash between me and—" My throat closes up. I can't say her name. It hurts to even *think* it. "Well, he said if there was another clash, he was throwing me out."

They shouldn't throw her out. This wasn't her fault.

"Under the circumstances, Principal Warren has decided that he's going to put you under restrictions until Spring break."

"Under the circumstances?"

"The way you reacted yesterday. You've had problems over the years, but never like that. After speaking with Principal Warren, he agrees that you have a lot of trauma from your past. Trauma that you've never faced or dealt with. Whoever posted that recording knew what it would cause. With the constant clashes between you and Ms. Gray, it set a pattern in your head. So whenever something negative happens to you … Eli, it was *always* going to send you in her direction."

I laugh again, the sound brittle and harsh in the small room. "You have no fucking idea."

"Actually, I do. Kellan told me everything."

My eyes snap open. "He fucking did *what?*"

***

They release me from medical two days later. It's Sunday, I think. Or maybe it's Monday. I'm not entirely sure. I spent a lot of time sleeping and have lost track of the days. A guard walks with me across the school grounds to the dorm. I'm told it's for protection. I'm pretty sure they don't mean mine.

Security rounds have been increased around the campus during the day and in the evening.

Kellan has told Principal Warren *almost* everything but not *absolutely* everything like Counselor Clarke thinks. He shared that Arabella is being bullied by an unknown person and that antagonizing me is something she is being forced to do. He added that I am reacting in the hopes that whoever is behind it will see she is doing what they want and eventually leave her alone.

He didn't tell them that Zoey also received texts demanding she fulfill instructions or that we think her refusal got her murdered.

They think it's coming from someone outside of school. Someone who wants to take my family down, and is trying to use me and Arabella to do it. Their reasoning is because of the video footage of my mom and the funeral. Counselor Clarke thinks everything they've done was to build up to that video and send me into a rage. Their hope being I would hurt Arabella, which they could then use to extort money from my dad.

It's an interesting theory.

I don't think they're right, though.

But it *does* mean they're not throwing me out of school. Instead, they're arranging for further therapy sessions with someone experienced in PTSD trauma once we return after spring break.

I don't need fucking therapy. I just need all this bullshit to stop.

98

Arabella

I take one last glance around the empty dorm room, then drop the key on top of the dresser. My suitcases are packed with everything I own. I'm not planning on coming back after spring break.

Elena and Elliot will be disappointed, and part of me is sad I won't graduate, but my life is worth more than good grades. Being here isn't an option anymore. I can't stay in Eli's volatile orbit, and I don't want to be forced to perform actions I don't want to do. Not if I want to keep my sanity.

There's a knock at my door. With a heavy sigh, I walk over to open it. There's a smartly dressed man with a stoic expression standing on the other side.

"Miss Gray? I'm here to drive you home."

"Do you mind giving me a hand with these down to the car?" I gesture at my suitcases.

He nods. "Sure, I can."

I heave on one of the backpacks, and he takes the other one. Armed with two suitcases each, we wheel them out of the room and along the hallway.

"This is a lot for a week off," he says.

I give a little laugh. "You know what girls are like."

The school will be informed of my decision after I tell my mother and stepdad. I'm done with the school, and the threat to my life. I just want to slip away before anyone, especially my blackmailer, realizes what's happening. Counselor Clarke and Principal Warren are so sure that it's something to do with Eli's dad, but that doesn't explain why they targeted Zoey. She was Eli's friend, not his stepsister. Nothing makes sense anymore.

A sleek black car is waiting outside the building. He takes my cases without comment and puts them in the trunk. I climb into the back of the vehicle, close the door and click on my seatbelt. I'm thankful Elena arranged everything for me. At least it was one thing I didn't have to worry about.

The driver gets in behind the wheel, closes his door, and glances at me through the mirror. "Ready, Miss?"

"Yes, thanks."

My gaze turns to the tinted windows and the students off to have fun over spring break. I know I should feel jealous, but all I have is emptiness.

I dig my earbuds out of my bag, slip them in and press play. I lose myself in the lyrics of 'Traitor' by Daughtry. As the car pulls away, the privacy glass slides up between me and the driver. I rest my head against the window and close my eyes.

Goodbye, Churchill Bradley Academy. Thanks for nothing.

I need to look toward the future. Before I came here, I had a plan. My life mapped out in front of me. Things will change now. I'll be safe. Away from all the danger and bullshit.

***

Sitting up from where I'm slumped against the door, I rub a hand over my face.

What time is it? How long have I been asleep?

I check the time on my cell. It's been four hours since we left the school. We should be in the Hamptons already, but when I look out of the window I frown—nothing of the passing scenery beyond looks familiar.

The privacy glass is up between me and the driver, sealing me into the back of the car alone.

I lean forward and try to peer through the dark glass. I can't see a thing, so I tap on it. "Hello?"

No reply.

I knock again. "Hello?"

Nothing.

Unease swirls through me. Scrolling through my phone, I find Elena's cell number and hit dial. The call doesn't connect. There's a no signal symbol at the top of the screen.

No, no. no. What's going on?

I reach for the handle of the door and try to open it, but it's locked, so I attempt the same with the door on the other side. The windows won't even lower when I jab the button.

I slam my fist against the partition window. "Let me out! Can you hear me?"

No one replies.

"Let me out, you bastard." My spine ramrod straight, and my heart pounds.

"This isn't funny," I shout. "If this is some kind of sick joke, I'm not laughing."

Why isn't he responding to me?

The driver was sent by Elena to take me home. He should respond to my shouts.

The blood freezes in my veins.

But what if this isn't my real driver?

I need to get out of the car.

My body is vibrating with fear. I can't breathe, my thoughts freefalling with every bad thing that could happen.

Do they know I'm not going back to school? Are they finally going to kill me as they did Zoey? I thought I could escape. Be free of it all, but they're not going to let me go.

My throat closes up, and I sob. Tears blur my vision, cresting in my eyes to tumble down my cheeks.

Whatever happens, I'll go down fighting. I'm not going to let them do it while I cower on the ground. I'll make them bleed first. Leave them with scars.

The scenery outside of the car starts to slow its movement.

I suck in a steading breath.

Think!

There are trees surrounding us on either side outside the vehicle.

Somewhere remote to get rid of my body?

The thought almost sends me spiraling into pure terror, but I push through it, clinging to a thread of sanity. When the car stops, I tense further. The door on my left swings open, and a guy dressed all in black and wearing a ski mask leans in.

I kick him in the face—*hard*. The second he staggers back, swearing, I launch myself from the seat, hit him savagely with one flailing fist, and run.

There's a shout behind me. I don't stop, taking off through the trees. Heart in my mouth, I run as fast as my legs will take me.

I can't let him catch me.

Adrenaline keeps me moving, driving me through the sea of never-ending trees. I have no idea where I'm going, but as long as it's away from my kidnapper I don't care. My breath comes out in short sharp bursts, the cold air biting at my lungs.

Something heavy plows into my back. The force is enough to send me flying forward and obliterating my balance. Legs giving out, I fall, hitting the dirt, pain rushing like a shockwave through my body. A weight lands on top of me, pinning me down. Screaming and struggling, I buck my hips.

A hand wraps around my throat, squeezing tightly.

He's going to snap my neck.

"Stop fucking fighting," a voice growls in my ear.

49

Eli

"And you're set on this? You can't think of any other way?" Kellan twirls his car keys around one finger.

"I've spent all week trying to think of another way. This is all I have. It makes sense."

"No, Eli, it doesn't make any fucking sense at all."

"It makes sense to *me*. If you don't want to do it, just say, so and I'll figure it out myself."

"Fuck that. You know I'm going to help you. I just need to make sure you're not doing this from some crazy headspace."

"I'm not crazy." My voice is soft. "I think I'm actually more clear-headed than I've been in weeks."

"Maybe crazy is the wrong word." He unlocks his car and we both climb in. I had my car sent back home after Arabella keyed it, so I'm relying on Kellan to drive. "Desperate might be a better description."

I laugh quietly at that. "Maybe. A little bit."

He reverses out of his parking space and drives off the school grounds. I turn on his stereo and connect it to my phone. A few seconds later, 'Bath Salts' by Highly Suspect blares through the speakers.

"You know you shouldn't play this kind of music when I'm driving. It makes me put my foot on the gas." Kellan lowers the volume so he can talk to me.

I tip my head against the seat and close my eyes. "It also keeps you awake. There's a five-hour journey ahead."

"Oh, I see. *You're* going to nap, while I drive."

"I think I'm going to need all the sleep I can get before we arrive."

He chuckles. "Yep, you're definitely going to be sleeping with one eye open for the next week."

"Do you *really* think it's a bad idea?" I straighten.

"It's a fucking abysmal idea, but you're right. It's the only option you have, so we'll run with it and see what happens."

***

Her knee barely narrowly misses connecting with my dick, and I shift position, straddling her waist.

"Fuck's sake, stop it!" I grab her wrists and pin her hands above her head, while I pull off the ski mask with my free hand. "It's me."

The remaining color drains from her face, and her struggles become wild as she tries to buck me off her body. I expected her to fight, to scream, to try and escape. I am prepared for all of that. After what happened the last time she saw me, it's no surprise.

And it's why I did things this way. She would never have agreed to speak to me if I'd asked.

"Ari, please."

She spits in my face, hurling curses, and somehow manages to get one hand free. There's a sharp sting across my cheek as she rakes her nails down it.

"Get off me. You bastard. Get *away* from me!"

Her hand slams into my chest twice before I can catch hold and resecure it above her head with the other. "*Listen* to me."

But she doesn't. She's too busy screaming at me.

"Ari, it's okay." I release her hands and roll off her, rising to my feet. “I’m not going to hurt you.”

The second she’s free of me, she twists, scrambles to her feet and takes off. I let her go. We’re in the middle of a forest, with nothing other than trees and wildlife for miles around. There’s nowhere she can run. And with the noise she’s making, it’s not going to be hard to find her when she finally runs out of steam.

I follow in her direction at a slightly slower pace, calling her name occasionally, in the hopes that she’ll slow down or stop. But she doesn’t. Because it wouldn’t be Arabella if she didn’t choose flight over fight.

She keeps running for what feels like hours, before eventually slowing to a walk.

When she cries out, I swear beneath my breath and pick up speed to find her sprawled in the dirt. A quick glance around tells me what happened. In her headlong dash to escape me, she tripped over a tree root.

“The Lodge is approximately two miles in that direction,” I jerk my chin to the left. “If you haven’t twisted your ankle, we can get inside before the sun sets and all the noise you’re making brings out the bears.”

“Fuck you. I’d rather be eaten by a fucking bear than be here with you.”

“I know that.” I move closer, and raise both my hands, palm out, when she shrinks away. “I swear, Ari, I’m not going to hurt you. I just want to check your ankle.”

“If you touch me, I’ll scream.”

“If I don’t touch you, you’ll scream. Screaming seems to be the outcome, no matter what right now."

"Where's the driver? What did you do with him?"

"I didn't *do* anything with him, unless you include hiring him to drive you here in the first place."

"No, Elena organized a car."

"Maybe she did, but not the one you climbed into. Is your ankle sore? Can you stand?"

"I'll fucking crawl if I have to, if it means I can get away from you."

I scratch my jaw. "We're twenty-five miles inside Savage River State Forest. I don't think you want to crawl that far. My family has a hunting lodge here, so we can fight in comfort." My gaze drops to her leg. "And make sure you haven't permanently damaged your ankle."

50

Arabella

My stomach drops.

We're in the middle of fucking nowhere. He's kidnapped me and intends to keep me hostage. If I wasn't so frightened, I'd laugh. Why is the universe trying to torture me? No, not the universe, just my evil stepbrother.

Eli stands over me and offers a hand, but I ignore it.

Rolling onto my hands and knees, I steady myself. "I'm not going anywhere with you. I'm going back to the driver."

He drops his arm to his side. "He's gone."

I test my ankle cautiously, grimacing as it throbs in discomfort. "What do you mean he's *gone*?"

"I paid him to drop you off and leave."

I hobble forward to lean against the trunk of a tree for support, trying to think through my anger and panic. "Then I'll go back for my bag and call—"

"Kellan took your bag, along with both our cell phones."

"Kellan?" I echo.

"He dropped me off. We're out here alone for the next week."

All of spring break? Eli intends to keep me captive that long? *Why?* Is he going to finish what he started and choke the life out of me?

"You're fucking insane!" I limp around the tree when he makes a move toward me, the thought of him touching me sending a wave of sickness through me.

He stops and shakes his head. "How many more times do I have to tell you I'm not going to hurt you."

"How about never, because we both know you're a liar?" I limp in the opposite direction.

"Where are you going?"

"Away from you."

"The cabin is that way."

I don't bother to turn and look. "I don't fucking care."

"You don't want to be out here on your own at night. You'll get lost with no food or shelter. Bears are coming out of hibernation, and they're going to be hungry."

I falter at his words. He'd said something about bears earlier. What else lurks in these woods?

Eli or a bear?

Which one would I rather face because both will more than likely kill me?

"It's warm, safe," he continues, his voice low and calm. "There's food and bedrooms."

And locks on the doors?

Think, Arabella. Use your head.

Whatever game he wants to play, I am not going to take part in it. All I can hope is that there's a phone or radio at our destination. Something I can use to call for help and get away from this psycho.

I grit my teeth against the pain in my ankle and shuffle around to face him. "Fine."

"Here." He holds out a stick. "Something for you to lean on."

I snatch it out of his hand, and limp in the direction he points.

My ankle hurts, not that I'm going to admit that to *him*, and I move slowly. I'm not going to ask him for help.

Eli keeps pace beside me. "I know you're angry with me—"

"You tried to strangle me. You wanted to kill me. I think we're beyond angry at this point. I just want you to leave me alone."

"I can't do that."

I turn my head to stare at him as we walk. "What are we, Eli? In your head?"

He rakes a hand through his hair and sighs. "We're complicated."

My stomach clenches at the last word. "Complicated?" My laugh is discordant. "This isn't complicated! This is *toxic*. I'm not doing this with you anymore."

"Ari—"

"No! You're not making things better by doing this. It just makes it worse. I don't want you near me anymore. I can't stand it. Why couldn't you just let me go? Don't you see this is just going to make me hate you more?" My voice breaks on the last few words. I blink rapidly, tears threatening.

I *will not* cry in front of him.

That's exactly what he wants. This is just another way for him to grind me down and hurt me again.

51

Eli

The sun has set by the time we reach the cabin. Arabella hasn't spoken a single word, refused all offers of help when she stumbled, and bored a hole into the side of my head the entire way. I pat the pockets of my hoodie until I find the keys and unlock the door.

"Come inside and sit down."

If everything has gone as I planned, the groundskeeper should have been here to power up the generator and supply firewood, as well as bring the food and clothing I ordered. Moving past her, I throw open the door at the opposite end of the living room and enter the kitchen. A quick check of the cabinets shows that all the food is there, and when I pull open the refrigerator, the interior light flickers on.

I nod to myself. Everything looks good. I take out a large bottle of water and set up the small coffee maker. Then, leaving that to heat up, I go back into the other room. Arabella is perched on the edge of one of the armchairs, poised and ready to flee. I keep my distance and move around her to the door set in the wall on the right from the kitchen. Beyond that, there's a hallway leading to three bedrooms and a bathroom. I go into one and take the pillow off the bed and one of the throws.

"I'm going to push the coffee table closer to you and put this pillow on top, so you can elevate your ankle. Are you cold? I have a blanket."

"I can't get my sneaker off." She won't look at me.

I move closer. "Can I take a look?"

When she doesn't reply, I crouch and carefully slide my fingers around her calf. She hisses.

"Can you lift it?" I guide her leg up and onto the table, then unthread the laces in her sneaker. "Doing okay?"

I glance up at her. She's pale, bottom lip caught between her teeth, but she doesn't answer me.

"I'm going to ease the shoe off your foot and then roll your pants leg up so I can have a closer look."

Her eyes are wet with tears by the time I finally get her shoe off.

"Good girl. Almost done."

I probe around a little, then stand. "I don't think it's broken. It's not swollen. I'll get you some ice. That should draw out any bruising. If you rest for a few hours, I'm sure it'll be fine."

"Like I have any other choice." Her voice is bitter.

"Your mom knows you're here with me. So does my dad. And Kellan, as well as the driver I hired. I can't murder you and hide the body without someone questioning where you've gone. I'd be the prime suspect."

"That's hardly comforting."

"Would you have agreed to talk to me if I'd asked?"

"Of course not. You're a fucking monster."

I wave a hand, not reacting to her words. "There you go then. What other choice did I have?"

"The one any *normal* person would make."

"Oh? And what's that?" I walk into the kitchen and pull out a bag of ice. I take a handful of cubes and wrap them in a dishcloth.

"To *leave me alone!*"

I press the ice to her ankle. "Hold it there." When her hand takes hold of it, I move mine. "Would you like coffee?"

"Stop behaving like this is okay!"

"I know it's not okay, Ari—"

"Don't call me that."

I can't stop a sigh. I knew this was going to be difficult. That she wouldn't be happy with my actions. I just thought that—

I almost laugh out loud.

What did I think? Nothing, that's what. Nothing beyond how if we were alone here at the cabin, she'd have to talk to me.

"Are you cold? I can light the fire, if you want me to."

"Aren't you *listening?* The only thing I want is to get away from *you.*"

"No, I understand that." I walk to the front door and lock it, then pocket the key.

"Did you just lock me in here with you?"

"Only until morning. I don't want you out there in the dark, and I don't want a random hungry bear coming inside. I'll unlock the door in the morning, and you can take a look around if your ankle feels better."

Walking back to the door leading to the kitchen, I prop one shoulder against the frame. "I'm going to make coffee, and then go to my room. There are three bedrooms. Take the second door on the left when you're ready for bed. There's a lock on the inside. The one on the right is mine, the first left is the bathroom. The third door is my dad's bedroom. If you need anything, you can call me. Or help yourself to the food or drink in the kitchen."

I make her a drink while I do my own, even though she hasn't said she wanted one, and place it beside her foot. She doesn't speak or acknowledge me.

Maybe Kellan is right. Maybe this is a fucking stupid idea. But it's the only one I've got, so I have to see it through.

52

Arabella

I keep my attention on the cabin wall and away from Eli. The fact that he's acting so calmly is freaking me out. This quiet version of him is not what I'm used to.

"What happens at the end of the week?" I can't stay silent any longer.

"Kellan comes and picks us up." His voice is quiet.

The silence stretches between us.

Eli sighs. "You know where I am if you need me."

Out of the corner of my eye, I watch him retreat through the building. I don't move or react until I hear a door close somewhere down the hallway.

He wants to talk? *Talk?*

What exactly does he think we have to say to each other? I don't believe for a second that Elena and his dad know that we are here. Eli is lying. He *must* be. There's no way either of our parents would have agreed to this.

My attention lands on the coffee mug by my foot. If he thinks I'm going to drink it, he's crazy. I clench my jaw, remembering the laxatives he'd forced down my throat.

Keeping the bag of ice pressed firmly against my ankle, I carefully swing my leg off the pillow on the table. When I stand, I have to bite my lip to stop myself from crying out when pain shoots up my leg. I need to rest it, but I can't, not yet. I hobble across the room to the kitchen and rummage through the cabinets.

There's more than enough food to last the week. The refrigerator is just as packed. The coffee machine is bubbling quietly, so I find a mug and make a fresh drink. Moving back to the cabinets, I grab a packet of potato chips and a pack of cookies. I leave the snacks on the counter while I forage around, searching for a landline phone or radio. There's nothing in the kitchen. I come up empty in the main room as well.

"Fuck." My shoulders sag and I close my eyes. Eli has stranded us here with no outside contact. If something happens, we have no way to call for help.

My ankle is throbbing more, the longer I stand, so I gather my food and limp along the hallway. When I pass the room Eli said is his, I glare at the door.

Maybe he has a phone or radio in there? He must have *something* in case of an emergency. I'll have to search it when I get a chance.

My thoughts jump to my phone and bag, both in Kellan's possession now. He has Zoey's diary in his hands. Maybe he won't realize what it is? He's seen me with it before and not said anything.

If he works out what it is and tells Eli … he's going to be angry I kept it from him. Will he lose his temper again and lash out? I feel like I'm sitting on a ticking time bomb and waiting for it to explode.

The furniture inside the bedroom Eli said I can use is rustic and comfortable. Everything screams comfort and luxury. I shoot the lock on the door and move around the bed so I can place my snacks and drink on the bedside table. Easing myself onto the bed, I groan and relax into the mattress.

I have to survive a week.

Seven days of forced proximity.

I've been by myself plenty of times before.

If Eli thinks I'm going to rely on him for anything, he's going to be disappointed.

53

Eli

I'm sitting at the breakfast bar eating a bowl of cereal when she appears the next morning.

"Morning, Ari. There's coffee in the pot if you want some. Help yourself to whatever you want for breakfast. I wasn't sure what you'd like so there's cereal, or bread for toast. I also picked up ingredients for pancakes, or there's bacon and eggs if you'd prefer."

She ignores me, and takes a glass out of a cabinet, then fills it with milk from the refrigerator.

"You're not limping. That's good. I guess you didn't sprain it, after all."

Still nothing.

Okay. It's only been twelve hours. I can't expect her to behave like I didn't almost kill her. Not without earning her trust again. My eyes follow her as she takes out a plate, finds the bread and puts two slices into the toaster, then reopens the refrigerator to take out the butter.

"Ari."

Other than a slight stiffening of her shoulders, I might as well not be speaking for all the attention she pays me.

When the toast pops up, she spreads the butter over it, cuts it into neat triangles, then gathers up the plate, her drink and disappears back to the bedroom.

Well, that went better than expected.

I finish my cereal, wash up the bowl and spoon, and leave it on the drainer, then walk down the hallway to her room. Tapping on the door, I call her name.

"Ari, we need to talk."

Silence.

My hand hovers over the doorknob. I could unlock it and walk inside, but that wouldn't give the right impression. I want her to trust me, not continue to believe I'm going to hurt her. To prove that, I need to give her the space she wants, the time to think things through, to get to the same place I've reached over the past week.

I retrace my steps back into the kitchen, gather up the sketchbook I left on the breakfast bar and take it through to the living room. At some point, she's going to have to talk to me. Until then, I'll sketch and plan, and wait.

She reappears at lunchtime, drifting like a ghost into the kitchen. I keep my head down over my sketchpad and watch her out of the corner of my eye while she makes a sandwich. She doesn't go back to her room, but eats it, standing up in the kitchen. When she's done, she discovers the dishwasher, loads it, but doesn't switch it on.

She pauses on her way through the living room, turns, and walks to the front door.

"Don't go far," I tell her.

She stops but doesn't turn. "Am I a prisoner?"

"No, but like I said yesterday, bears are coming out of hibernation. They're going to be hungry and looking for an easy meal."

She pulls open the door and walks out.

I flick my lip ring with my tongue.

I should let her walk her anger off.

But what if she loses her way?

If I follow her, she'll think I'm stalking her.

If I don't follow her, she could disturb a bear.

Fuck. Scrubbing a hand down my face, I set my sketchbook to one side, stand, and search out my sneakers. I pull on a hoodie and set off after her.

She must walk for at least an hour, and I follow a safe distance behind … until she stops and spins.

"I know you're there. Why are you following me?"

I step forward. "Because I know the area, and you don't. I don't want you to get lost."

"Why did you bring me here?"

"I told you why. We need to talk."

"I don't *want* to talk to you. Don't you get it?" Her fingers curl into fists. "I don't even want to *look* at you. You make me sick!"

"I know." My voice is soft. "I'm sorry, Ari."

Her lip curls. "You're *sorry?* The *monster* is sorry? For *what?* What are you sorry for, Eli? For almost killing me or for not finishing the job?"

"I can't change what happened, but if you—"

"Leave me alone." She reaches down, scoops up a handful of rocks and throws them at me.

I don't even try to avoid them, and they hit my chest and arms before bouncing off and falling to the ground.

"I can't leave you alone. Not out here. Come back to the cabin. Let me explain."

"*Explain?*" Her laughter is shrill. "You mean twist the truth until

I don't know what's real and what's pretend?"

"No, I—"

"I said leave me alone!" She spins away and sets off again.

I shove my hands into my pockets and follow her.

59

Arabella

Shoulders hunched, I walk until my legs hurt, aware of Eli shadowing me the whole way. The anger inside me seethes and builds. He's trapped me here, and now he won't leave me be. I'm pretty sure he's just worried I might find someone to help me escape.

"Ari, enough. Stop," Eli calls from some distance behind me. "You've been walking in a circle for hours. There's nothing out here."

"You're lying." I snap, not turning around or slowing my pace. "There must be another cabin out here somewhere."

"There isn't. My dad bought the place because it was so remote."

I huff. "Of course, he did."

"Let's head back."

Fingers close around my arm, and I flinch away. Swiveling, I find Eli right behind me. I shove him away. "You're insane!"

He rubs his face with one hand. "I'm just trying to keep you safe."

"Safe? *Safe*?" I stare into his beautiful face, his slashing cheekbones and black lashes framing his green eyes. "You broke me."

Eli doesn't say a word.

My anger boils over, coursing like molten lava through my veins. "You made my life miserable. I was choking on air while you tormented and bullied me."

His jaw flexes. "I was protecting you."

"Protecting me?" I give a scornful laugh. "Maybe in your screwed-up head, but in reality, *you're* the villain, Eli. The bad guy.

The *bully*. You turned my world into a living hell."

"I know, and I'm sorry."

"Sorry?" My lips curl at the word, and I step closer to him, clenching my hands into fists. "Do you think your apology makes what you did better? That I'm going to magically forget what you did? Pretend the bruises you left on my skin never happened?"

His gaze slides away from my face. "Just give me a chance—"

Something hot and unstable snaps inside me. I punch him. My fist bounces off his chest. Eli doesn't react, which only makes me angrier.

"I hate you." I hit him again. "Hate you. *Hate* you."

I rain blow after blow into his chest, chanting the words. He staggers back a little but doesn't stop me, doesn't retaliate, doesn't even defend himself. He feels solid and unmovable. The fact that he won't crumble and break the way I did, only drives my fury higher. I punch him until my hands hurt, and the strength behind my blows weakens.

"Fuck you," I choke out, tears welling in my eyes.

I drop my head forward and rest my forehead against his chest.

Why won't he break? Why is he still standing?

"Ari." Eli's voice is pained.

"Why should I ever give you a chance? I trusted you once, and you hurt me." Arms encircle me, but I step back, out of his reach. "No, leave me alone."

Tears blur my vision as I walk away from him. I need space. I can't think past the primal rage that's goading me to make him suffer, like he's made me suffer.

Why is he doing this to me? Does he like seeing me like this?

Does he get off on it?

"Ari, wait."

I ignore his call.

"For fuck's sake. *Arabella*." An arm wraps around my waist, lifting me off my feet.

I dig my fingernails into his wrist. "Get off me."

"Keep your voice down. There's a bear."

His voice in my ear is low, rough with warning. My attention snaps to the trees. And there it is. He's not lying. Black fur covering its body, the bear is up on its hind legs, swaying this way and that as it watches us.

My fury evaporates, morphing into fear, and I freeze in Eli's arms. "Oh my god."

"We're going to go back toward the cabin," he whispers, still holding me tight.

"What if it follows?"

"It won't."

"And how the hell do you know that? Are you some kind of bear expert now?"

"It's more frightened of us than we are of it."

"It has teeth and claws." I don't pull away when he releases my waist and grabs my hand. "And it looks hungry."

He tugs me backward, but I keep my eyes locked on the creature. "Ari, move!"

"We're going to get eaten alive, and it's going to be all your fault."

"Yeah, just add it to the list."

55

Eli

I'm pretty confident the bear isn't going to attack us. It's not a grizzly. Black bears are more timid. If I was alone, I'd step forward and shout, but something tells me that if I do, Ari will think I'm trying to get the bear to *kill* her to save me the job. So, instead, I keep a tight grip on her hand and slowly move us backward.

The bear watches, its head high, nose twitching as it sniffs, but it doesn't move, and step by slow step we inch out of its view.

"We should run." Ari's voice is trembling.

"We should definitely *not* run. Just keep moving. You walked in a circle, so we're not far from the cabin."

"But—"

"I know it goes against everything in your nature, baby, but you *have* to trust me right now." I clamp my mouth shut.

Fuck. Did I just call her baby?

I keep watching for the bear, while guiding her back, and when I feel confident that it's not following us, I turn so I can lead her to the cabin.

It takes us a while to get there, and she hangs onto my hand the entire way, starting at any noise. When we finally reach the cabin, she bolts for the door and runs inside. I don't follow her straight away, taking a walk around the outside of the property to check there are no bears nearby and to make sure the smaller building holding the generator is locked up so nothing can get in there. When I'm sure everything is as it should be, I return to the cabin and go inside.

There's no sign of Ari. I guess she's gone to her room. I lock the front door, then walk into the kitchen to start the coffee machine.

I need caffeine.

Lots of it.

First, though, I start a fire. There's a chill in the air, and if Ari *does* decide to venture out of her room, I'd like the place to be warm.

I'm crouching in front of the hearth when I hear a footstep behind me. Glancing over my shoulder, I'm just in time to see Ari disappear into the kitchen. A few minutes later, the smell of bacon frying fills the air.

I smile to myself.

Ari likes to cook, so when I was making my plan to bring her here, I made sure all her favorite foods and ingredients would be available. We're stuck here for a week. If she has something to do that she enjoys, I'm hoping she might concentrate more on that than plotting my death.

My stomach grumbles, reminding me I haven't eaten since the half sandwich I put together at lunchtime.

I should have thought this through a little more thoroughly because the smells coming from the kitchen are torture. I don't know what she's throwing together, but I am willing to bet half of my fortune that there's none for me. Unless, of course, she finds a way to poison it.

I chuckle, thinking about the little mantra we've thrown at each other.

Feed Me. Fuck Me. Fight Me.

Right now, the only one she's doing is fighting me. Although, it's mostly a silent war since she's barely acknowledging my existence.

After the fire is lit, I make my way into the kitchen. Ari is sitting at the breakfast bar, tucking into her food. I take the bowl from the drainer, where I'd left it that morning, grab the cereal box and fill it, then add milk, and find a spoon. I don't hang around or try to talk to her but go back into the living room and drop onto the couch, so I can prop my feet on the coffee table.

When I've finished my cereal, I set the bowl to one side, pull my sketch pad toward me, and pick up the pencil. Flicking to a blank page, I close my eyes and build up the picture of the bear in my head, then start drawing.

"Let me guess. You're sketching a scene where the bear rips me apart while you watch and laugh."

I glance up to find Arabella standing in the doorway. I give her a half smile.

"If I was going to draw you being ravaged, it'd be by me, not a bear. And the only death involved would be *la petite mort*."

56

Arabella

Insidious memories of the last time we'd fucked whisper through my head. The tomb, where I'd clawed and bit him like a wild animal. It hadn't been enough to rid myself of the explosive emotions he kept evoking inside me. Eli and I might be drawn together, but everything between us is tainted.

I stifle the urge to knock the faint smile off his face by curling my fingers into my palms.

Eli's gaze drops to my clenched fists. "Are you getting ready to claw me, Kitten?"

His words send a jolt of … *something* … through me. "I'm not a kitten."

"Yes, you are. A cute ball of fluff, with razor-sharp murder mittens … when she finds her courage to use them."

I roll my eyes. "Shut up."

"Getting you to purr is my favorite thing to do," he continues. "And when you hate-fuck me, it's like riding a living storm."

I snatch up a cushion from a chair and throw it at his head. "I said, *shut up*."

He catches the cushion easily. "I love the way you mark my skin with your teeth and nails. You're the only girl I've been with who's done that."

I clench my hands tighter. "You fucked half of the female population at the school, right?"

Eli quirks an eyebrow. "Jealous?"

"In your dreams, asshole."

I don't want to hear about who else he's been with or remember how it felt when we were together. Or how good the sex made me feel.

Grabbing another cushion from a different seat, I launch myself at him with it and smack him in the face. As I bring it back to hit him again, he uses the one I'd thrown at him to whack me gently in the chest. An irritated growl rips from my throat, and I beat him over the head with mine while he continues his assault on my torso.

This is getting me nowhere.

When I realize he's not hitting me as hard as I am him, I step back, dropping my cushion. My chest is heaving from the effort, and my jaw is aching from being clenched so hard. "I'd rather be mauled by the bear than be ravaged by you."

Eli tilts his head to the side and smiles. "Liar."

"You're impossible."

"And you're scared of letting all those emotions you have bottled up out," he replies, his eyes studying my face. "Do they frighten you, Ari? Are you scared of losing control? Is that why you stopped hitting me?"

I wrap my arms around my waist and back away from him. "No—"

Eli gets up off the couch. "You can be vulnerable in front of me, Kitten. I'm not going to use it against you. You've been keeping yourself together for so long. Let go. Let yourself fall. I promise to catch you."

I shake my head, my heart stopping and starting in my chest. I've already been helpless and exposed in front of him once, when he found me in the chapel with my insides ripped to shreds. Where had that gotten me? Nowhere. He just turned on me again. Became my nightmare.

I flee along the hallway toward my room.

"I'm not going to let you ignore me forever, Ari."

***

I jerk awake, shaking and sweating. It takes me a second to remember I'm not in my dorm but in the cabin where Eli is holding me hostage. The nightmare is still fresh in my thoughts, and I shudder. I'd been tied up, sightless, helpless. Hands touched my body, and every caress had been agony, leaving me screaming over and over.

I check the clock on the wall. It's only been a couple of hours since I fled to the room. I roll onto my side. I'm bored, but the thought of running into another bear prevents me from going outside. There's nothing to do, and I'm already feeling restless. All the times I'd been at home alone, I had things to keep me occupied. The closet and dresser here might be filled with brand-new clothes I like, but Eli has made sure I have nothing to keep me occupied.

Just another form of control. A way to get me to talk to him.

I climb off the bed and move to the door. Twisting the handle, I step out into the hallway. Eli is sprawled on the couch with his eyes closed. I tiptoe along the hallway and make my way toward his bedroom.

There has to be a phone or radio—*something* he's using to stay in contact with Kellan. I just have to find it and call for help. The door creaks for a split second as I open it. I screw my eyes closed and hold my breath, waiting for him to wake up and start shouting. Nothing stirs—no movement or sound. I relax a little and slip into the room, leaving the door ajar.

His room is a lot like mine. The same tasteful, expensive furniture.

There's a hoodie draped over the end of the mattress, and his bed is a rumpled mess. I search every inch of the space but find no sign of a phone. It's not hidden in any of the drawers or under his pillows.

My attention shifts to the pile of sketchbooks. He has his fucking drawings to keep him busy while I have nothing but my thoughts. I send them flying off the table and feel a twinge of guilt the second they hit the floor. Scrambling to pick them up, my hand freezes over the first one that's fallen open. There's a picture of me—and it's not like the violent one I'd seen before.

No, in this one, my head is bent over a book, and my bottom lip is caught between my teeth. I turn the page. In the next sketch, I'm asleep on a bed with my hand tucked under my cheek. I flick through the pages. Each one is a drawing of me. Portraits caught in candid moments of my life.

57

Eli

The familiar creak of my bedroom door infiltrates the dream I'm in, and my eyes snap open. I frown, then relax back against the couch. I guess Arabella is taking a chance and searching my room while I'm out here. I'm not going to stop her. I have nothing to hide. I *want* her to know who I am. If she can figure that out by rummaging through my stuff, she's welcome to do it.

I've spent the past week sorting through what had happened after watching the video that was uploaded. Of talking to Kellan, Principal Warren, and Counselor Clarke, I'd pieced together the sequence of events. Talking about it with the three of them brought me to the realization that the entire time since I returned to Churchill Bradley, whoever was messaging Arabella has been instilling a habit in me. By forcing me to react to everything she did, and punishing her when I didn't, it had been drilled into me that I *had* to hurt her in order to save her.

Kellan thinks that the end game has always been that video. It contained triggers I've ignored for years and, combining those with the driving need to keep Ari alive, they turned me into the monster I've been accused of being.

But until Ari is ready to listen, I can't explain any of that to her. When she finally acknowledged me, spoke to me, and *fought* with me, it gave me hope that we will get there. It'll just take time and patience on my part. Something I'm not really good at, but I'm going to try my best because, otherwise, I might just lose everything that matters to me.

When my door creaks again, I close my eyes, so she doesn't know I'm awake and let her make her escape. She was in there for a while. I have no idea what she saw. Definitely my clothes—nothing exciting to find there. My sketchbooks, maybe?

Maybe she went through my underwear. My lips twitch at the visual of her digging through my dresser.

I know she's going to be looking for a cell phone, or some other way to communicate with the outside world, but she won't find any. I wasn't lying when I said Kellan has taken all our phones. If she'd give me five minutes of her time, I would tell her why.

I drift back off to sleep, still thinking about all the things I need to tell her.

***

The sound of rain hitting the roof wakes me. I push upright off the couch, rubbing the back of my neck to ease the stiffness. The room is in darkness, and as I swing around to put my feet on the floor, it's lit up by lightning through the window. A low rumble of thunder follows shortly after.

Yawning, I make sure everywhere is locked up and then walk down the hallway to my bedroom. I pull off my hoodie, and toss it on top of the dresser, step out of my sweats and climb into bed. I have three sketchbooks on the nightstand, so I take the top one, and flick through it.

It's full of pictures of Arabella. I find an empty page and set pencil to paper, sketching out an image of her from today. Her back to me in the kitchen as she makes her dinner, hair up in a messy ponytail, head turned so her profile is visible. Her nose screwed up as she concentrates.

A smile tugs my lips up as the image takes shape.

Long thick eyelashes curve over eyes narrowed in concentration. The fingers of one hand are drumming on the counter beside the stovetop as she fries the bacon.

Thunder rumbles overhead, and I climb out of bed to throw open the curtains and watch the storm. There's a gap between the lightning and the thunder, so the storm isn't overhead yet, but it's getting closer. With each flash of lightning, I see the trees surrounding the cabin swaying in the wind.

A noise mixes in with the thunder and I frown, turning toward the door. *Was that a scream?* When it doesn't happen again, I decide I must have imagined it. No real surprise with the storm raging outside.

I drag the curtains closed, climb back into bed and switch off the light. Settling back against the pillows, I close my eyes.

58

Arabella

A flash of lightning illuminates the room in white, showing me the shape of Eli on the bed beneath the blanket. Thunder booms overhead a split second later, and blind terror has me diving for the mattress.

"What the—"

Ignoring Eli's surprise, I flip back the blanket and scramble beneath it. I drag it back over us both, and burrow into his side with it over my head.

"Ari?" His voice is cautious.

When I don't reply, a hand lightly touches my shoulder. "Ari, what are you doing?"

Another roar of thunder rounds and I grab at his chest like a frightened child, a whimper leaving my lips.

I'm six years old again, alone in the house with no power, the wind howling eerily outside in the middle of the night. Elena promised to be back from visiting a friend hours ago. One hour slid into three, and she's still not home. I'm shaking so hard my teeth are rattling, and my heart feels as though it might just burst from my chest. I'm too scared to run next door and bang on Mrs. Goldmann's front door for help. What if I get stuck outside? Where did Mommy go? Why did she leave me? I wasn't a bad girl, so why isn't she here keeping me safe?

Strong arms wind around me, pulling me on top of a hard chest. "You're shaking. What's wrong?"

The words penetrate the memories I'm trapped in.

I'm not in the house in Michigan waiting for Elena to return. I'm stuck in the middle of nowhere with my stepbrother.

I cling tightly to him and bury my face into the side of his neck. "Th-thunder."

A hand slips under the hem of my t-shirt and strokes up and down my spine. "Are you scared of the storm, Kitten?"

I nod helplessly, the old trauma of being abandoned clawing at my insides.

"It's not going to hurt you." His chest rumbles beneath me as he talks.

I make a sound of disagreement. "I ca-can't. Pl-please don't ma-make me go. I'll be go-good."

My voice comes out small and weak, childlike. I hate how it sounds. As if I'm about to cry. My throat aches, tears threatening to fall if he sends me away.

Eli's lips gently brush my forehead. "Don't worry, Kitten. You can stay as long as you like. I'll keep you safe from the storm."

A tiny part of me wants to argue and push him away. I should refuse his comfort and the safety of his arms. The stronger, more primal terror that's driving me doesn't care. He feels solid and secure—a haven in the dark. A warm body to thaw the chill that has invaded my limbs. I don't want to be on my own. Not in a strange place.

The patter of the rain outside against the window is a continuous percussion against the glass, the wind shrieking through the trees.

Thunder booms, shaking the windowpanes, and Eli hugs me tighter when I give a little scream. "It's okay, baby. I got you."

"D-don't le-let go," I beg him.

"I won't."

We lay there for what feels like hours, with the tempest raging outside the cabin.

Eli whispers soft words against my hair, but I barely catch any of them, so caught up with the chaos in my head. There's no thought of trying to sleep. No way to relax.

Eventually, the thunder lessens, the noise becoming nothing more than angry rumbles far off in the distance. The tension holding my body tense relaxes its grip, and piece by piece, I relax against Eli's heat.

Neither of us move.

I'm too exhausted and drained, still feeling anxious. His bed is warm. *He* is warm, and he makes a comfortable pillow. Taking in a breath, I inhale his scent. His hands are still running over my back and down my sides under my t-shirt. There's nothing sexual in it, no dark motive, and I don't feel threatened. It's comforting, *soothing*.

"Thanks," I whisper against his throat. "I woke up, and the thunder was so loud, and I didn't know where I was."

"Shhh, it's okay. Why are you scared of storms?"

"I don't really know. I've always been frightened of them."

"What did you do back home when you had one?"

"I'd find somewhere to hide under my bed or make a nest of blankets in my closet. Fear would paralyze me. If I had the door closed, it would muffle some of the sounds. As I got bigger, listening to music on my headphones helped. I know it's a dumb thing to be frightened off."

"Having fears isn't dumb, Ari. Everyone is scared of something. It's part of being human."

A strange sense of unreality sweeps over me. Why does it feel easier to talk to him surrounded by darkness? Maybe because it reminds me of Sin. Confiding in him had been easier when I hadn't been able to see him. When he'd been nothing but a raspy whisper in my ear.

"Why do you have drawings of me?" I blurt out.

Eli's hand snakes up to tangle in my hair, his finger massaging my scalp slowly and rhythmically. "Everyone has an obsession. You're mine."

So far, that hasn't been a good thing. I shiver at the thought, but it soon fades under his caressing touch.

We fall silent.

I've almost drifted off to sleep when he speaks again. "I know everything between us is fucked up, but we need to talk."

Stretching against him, I dissolve back into a languid, sleepy puddle. "Not everything that's broken can be fixed."

"Maybe not, but there are still some things you need to know."

"What do you want from me, Eli?"

He strokes his fingers down my spine, bringing it to a stop just above the swell of my buttocks. "Just listen to me, Kitten. Can you do that, please?"

I'm silent for a beat. I don't want the tension between us to return. I like this warm, dark world we're lying in. But there's a tone in his voice that reaches to something deep inside me. "Okay, fine. Talk."

59

Eli

"Did you know that if you count the seconds between the lightning and thunderclap, it tells you how close the storm is?"

"What?" Her head lifts from where it's buried against my throat.

I know it's not what she expected me to say, but I hadn't expected her to agree to talk, so I need a moment to get my thoughts together.

"Five seconds is one mile. Ten seconds is two miles." I pause when a flash of lightning brightens the room, not as bright as it has been, but enough to see the shape of her burrowed beneath the sheets.

"Count, Ari."

She reaches thirty before there's a faint rumble of thunder.

"Six miles away," I tell her. "It's traveling away from us now."

"How do you know that?"

"Because not long ago the lightning and thunder were almost instantaneous."

"No, I mean about the counting."

I shift my position slightly, so she's lying half on me instead of using me as a bodyboard. "My mom told me when I was little, and I was scared of a storm."

"Oh." Her head drops back onto my shoulder.

My fingers run up and down her spine. I flick my lip ring with my tongue, then suck in a deep breath.

"I'm sorry I scared you. I didn't mean to. I thought wearing the ski mask would make you realize it was me, *Sin*. I didn't think you'd be so fucking scared."

"I thought it was them … coming to kill me like Zoey." I can feel her heart hammering where she's pressed against my chest.

"I realized that almost the second you ran. I swear, Ari, I didn't mean to scare you like that. But I needed to stop you from going home and bring you somewhere no one knows about."

"Why?"

I stroke my other hand through her hair. "Kellan thought about it first. We were talking about the texts and how they always seemed to know where you were in relation to me. He thinks they have a tracker on your cell. We know … well, we're pretty sure … that they cloned your cell, which is how they knew you were talking to Miles. With a tracker, they could confirm you were going to wherever they directed you. That's why Kellan took our phones. If they're not here, they can't be tracked."

"They?"

"If they're tracking yours, there's a chance they are tracking mine as well. Kellan put some kind of signal blocker in the car during the ride here, so they have no idea what direction you went in once you left Churchill Bradley. Without your cell, they have no way to contact you or find you." My fingers stop their path up along her spine. "I'm not willing to play their game anymore, Ari. They got what they wanted, and I almost killed you. I'm not taking that risk again."

"What did they want?"

I laugh, even though it's not funny. "I've spent this past week talking to the school therapist, Principal Warren, and Kellan. All three think that the things they were making you do, trying to get me to react, were all to build up to that last video. They wanted me to hurt you … in front of everyone. To prove I'm the monster they call me. And, fucking idiot that I am, I walked right into it and let it happen."

"But you hurt me even when I didn't do anything to you." The tremor in her voice is like a knife to the gut.

"I'm sorry." I press my lips to her hair. "You have no idea how fucking sorry I am. I convinced myself that if I proved to whoever was watching that you meant nothing, that I *hated* you the same way I did when you first joined the school, then they'd stop targeting you. But they were a step ahead of me all the fucking time. They *knew* I'd decide to do that. And it made everything so much fucking easier for them.

"After the last time … I knew that something had to change, but I needed to get you to talk to me. Bringing you here, where there are no distractions, no one from school to interrupt us, I thought we could finally figure some things out."

"What things?"

I press my palm against her back, securing her in place, and roll onto my side, so we're facing each other, and tip her face up with a finger beneath her chin.

"Well, first, whether we can ever get on the same page on this thing between us."

"There is no *thing* between us."

"Oh, Kitten, you know that's not true."

"Don't." She turns her face away.

"Don't what?"

"Don't call me Kitten. You're not *Sin*. It was all a lie."

"Yes, I am. It's who I became for *you*. Who I *wanted* to be. Something *other* than the monster."

"That's not true. You did all that to humiliate me."

This is it. That defining moment where the truth would either set us on the right track or end us forever. I take a breath.

"At first, I did. You're right. My plan was to do what these strangers are doing. To take videos and photographs and release them to everyone. To prove that you were the daughter of a gold-digger, and just as bad. But the more time I spent with you, as Sin, the more I started to wonder what the real truth was. I read your diaries, and they didn't match with the idea of you I had in my head."

I trace over her lips with one finger. "And then I kissed you, and you were sweet and hesitant and *hungry* … and I was in over my head before I even realized what was happening. So, I cut you off, stopped contacting you because I knew I couldn't go through with my plan. I couldn't do that to you."

"Why did you change your mind?"

"I couldn't fucking stay away from you. I wanted your kisses, your moans. I dreamed about the way you responded to me, and I needed more of it. That night … before we went home for Thanksgiving … I was going to give you what you wanted, what you'd asked for … but you called me *Sin*." I think back to that night, the way the realization that she wanted Sin and not *me* had cut deep and shake my head. "I wanted you to want *me*, Eli, not the fantasy I was building out of your deepest desires."

60

Arabella

"You wanted me to want *you*?" My thoughts race, and I struggle with his words. "But you hated me and bullied me all the time."

His finger caresses my cheek. "Think about it, Ari. I stopped bullying you for a while. Don't you remember?"

The recollection stirs, and I nod in the dark. "You just kept staring at me like a psycho, but that was before I asked you … I mean Sin to have sex with me."

"I'm glad you can finally see us as the same person."

"You used my fantasies to seduce me."

"You grew stronger, more confident." Eli points out. "I was so proud watching you stand up for yourself against everyone … against *me*."

I curl my fingers against the muscles of his bare chest. "Were you ever going to come back to me as Sin? If things hadn't happened over Thanksgiving?"

"I don't know, but I don't think I would have been able to stay away from you. When we had sex, and I realized you were a virgin …. the signs had been there when I played with you when I was Sin … I should have seen them."

"I'd promised Miles I would keep his secret, and I didn't want to break it."

"Not even to your fantasy lover?"

"I almost told you a couple of times," I whisper. "But I couldn't betray my friend's trust."

"I would have been gentler with you if I'd known the truth."

Even though he can't see my expression in the dark, I turn my face away. "If I hadn't drunk the vodka, we wouldn't have had sex."

"Your virginity was always going to be mine to take. It was just a matter of time." The hand Eli has on my cheek slides down to my chin. "You belonged to me the first time you responded to my dare."

I don't resist when he brings my head back to face him. "Eli—"

"Shh, it's okay." Lips brush over mine. "You know it's the truth, Kitten."

Because he is Sin.

Even if things had happened differently, Eli was the one who I wanted. I just hadn't known it. He was the one I'd fallen in love with. My heart aches inside my chest. I bridge the gap between us and snuggle into his warmth, closing my eyes.

Eli wraps his arms around me. "Ari, I—"

"I'm so tired." The safety of his arms is making me sleepy.

He doesn't finish what he's about to say, his words coming out with a little sigh.

A hand strokes my hair. "Go to sleep. We'll talk some more tomorrow."

"Okay."

"Promise me you won't run away?"

"And get eaten by a bear? No thanks."

Eli chuckles. "Guess you're stuck with me then."

I don't reply but smile against his chest. His hands continue to caress me, and my eyes grow heavy with sleep. Cocooned in the dark beneath the blanket with Eli holding me feels like the safest place in the world. My nose scrunches up sleepily. It shouldn't feel this right.

It's the last thought I have before I drift off to sleep.

61

Eli

I untangle myself from Ari's arms and slip out of the bed. She grumbles, a frown pulling her brows together and I freeze beside the bed, but she doesn't wake, rolling over to bury her face into my pillow. I grab my sweats and t-shirt from on top of the dresser and creep out of the room.

I take a quick shower, pull on my clothes and sneakers, and go outside to see if the storm has caused any damage. The ground is wet, but during my walk around, it doesn't look like anything has been destroyed. I check inside the building where the generators are, making sure there are no leaks in the roof, and then do a perimeter check. The trees surrounding the cabin all seem to have survived the storm with nothing more than a few broken branches, and I gather them up and put them in the wood store to dry out.

When I go back into the cabin, sounds reach me from the kitchen. I stick my head around the door to discover Arabella in front of one of the cabinets, studying the contents.

"Morning. I did a quick after-storm check. Nothing is damaged outside. It's still very wet out there, though, so I don't recommend going for a walk today." As much as I want to greet her with a kiss, I don't, reaching past her to take down a bowl and the box of cereal. "I'll get the fire going, if you're cold."

When she shakes her head, I fill the bowl, add milk, grab a spoon, and take a seat at the table.

"I didn't realize you were such a huge fan of Cheerios."

I pause with the spoon halfway to my mouth and turn my head to find her looking at me.

"As far as cereals go, they're probably one of the best."

"It's all I've seen you eat since we got here."

I grin. "Didn't think you were paying me that much attention."

Her gaze drops to my mouth and then returns to my eyes. "What else have you eaten?"

"I had a peanut butter and jelly sandwich yesterday for lunch."

She frowns at me but doesn't say anything else. I eat my cereal while she makes toast, then takes the seat beside me. Neither of us speak. I wouldn't say we eat in a companionable silence because tension is thick in the air. I'm not sure whether it's because she's waiting for me to do or say something, or because she feels awkward about climbing into bed with me during the storm.

When I stand to walk across to the sink, she grabs my arm. I stop and look at her.

"What do you want from me?" It's not the first time she's asked me that question. I have the impression it's one she'll continue to repeat until she hears what she wants to hear, or she believes the answers I give her.

My gaze tracks over her face, and I set down the bowl so I can brush a finger over her lips. "Whatever you're willing to give me."

She opens her mouth, drawing in a breath to speak and I shake my head.

"No, hear me out. If you want to talk, we'll do that. I'll talk about anything you want; answer any questions you have. If you want to fight, we can fight. Hit me. Scream at me. Whatever you need to get it out. If you want silence, I'll stay quiet. If you want to be left alone, I'll stay in my room. Other than needing you to stay here and not walk through the woods alone, *you're* in control here, Ari. Whatever *you want,* that's what I'll do."

"What do *you* want?"

I flick my lip ring with my tongue. "I want you to forgive me. I want you to give me a second chance. I want you to trust me. But I know it's not going to be easy, and I know I need to earn it. I just need to know I have a chance."

62

Arabella

He wants me to forgive him after everything that's happened?

I search his expression, but he doesn't grin or smile.

"I'm really in control, and you'll do *whatever* I want?"

Eli nods. "*Anything*."

A tiny voice in my head reminds me of how he'd held me last night during the storm. How he'd comforted me when I needed it. But now it's daylight and the storm has gone, and the anger and humiliation I've had to endure at his hands for weeks are stronger.

I fold my arms and raise my chin. "Get on your knees and kiss my shoes."

Something I can't define flickers in his eyes, but he doesn't move.

I shake my head and laugh. "So, it was all bullshi—"

Eli descends to the floor to kneel in front of me. Shocked, all I can do is watch as he places his hands on the wood and lowers further until he plants his lips on my shoe. Sitting back on his heels, he stares up at me.

"Anything else?"

"You did it."

"I'm serious, Ari. Whatever it takes to get you to forgive me, I'll do it."

His words have my heart doing a weird little flip-flop in my chest, but I ignore it. I'm not about to forgive him with a snap of a finger. Not after all the pain and misery he put me through.

I chew on my bottom lip for a second. "Okay, I want you to be my devoted servant for the next two days."

He's still on the floor at my feet, watching me, a lock of hair curling on his forehead, his stunning face tipped up to me. Eli looks like a beautiful angel, but I'm aware of the darkness that lurks beneath. I've touched it, tasted it, and been branded by it so many times that it's now a permanent scar beneath my skin. I wait for him to disagree, to protest, but he doesn't.

He smiles. "I can do that."

"You're agreeing to do whatever I command for forty-eight hours?"

"If that's what you want, Kitten. I'm all yours." The slight huskiness of his voice has my body tingling and my heart flip-flopping a second time.

I move away from him. "You can start by running me a bath."

I sink onto the couch, bring my legs up and tuck them beneath me.

Eli gets to his feet. "You're going to enjoy this, aren't you?"

I don't even try to hide my grin. "This was your plan, remember? You're the one who said you'd do anything for me."

"Do you want some scented bubble bath in the water?"

I shake my head. "No, thanks."

Tongue darting out, he flicks his tongue piercing against his teeth before walking off in the direction of the bathroom. I listen as his footsteps recede and bite my lip.

Eli at my command … I can't deny how delicious that sounds. How much can I make him pay for tormenting me for so long?

I sit daydreaming about my revenge, mind turning over everything I could make him do, while I wait for him to return.

"Your bath is ready."

Eli's call from the doorway tugs me from my thoughts. I walk toward him, following as he leads the way back to the bathroom. The air is heavy with warmth, steam curling from the water in the tub. There are two large white fluffy towels on the counter beside the sink.

"Stay," I command when he makes a move to leave. "Stand by the wall."

I don't wait to see if he complies. Kicking off my sneakers, I peel off my socks. With my back to Eli, I shove down my sweats and panties in one go. There's a groan behind me when I bend over at the waist to pull them off my feet. I unzip my hoodie and tug off my t-shirt, then climb into the tub. I moan softly as the hot water laps at my skin and sink into it until every part of me is immersed. I lift my gaze to search out Eli. He's leaning against the wall, watching me through narrowed eyes.

I deliberately asked for no bubbles so he could see every inch of me—my pale skin and the bruises around my wrists and on my hip, the marks of others fading from my flesh. I want him to see them. The ones he'd given me and the others that my night attacker had left.

I keep my attention locked on his face. "Don't you like what you see?"

Eli's gaze moves over my body, jaw tight. "You know you're beautiful, Kitten."

I lift a finger and trail it lazily down between my breasts, over my stomach, and circle my navel. He tracks the movement all the way down to between my legs.

This is the boy who destroyed me.

A boy who spent months shaping my world into a nightmare.

The boy who hated me at first sight.

Getting my forgiveness isn't going to be easy for him.

He wants whatever I'm willing to give him.

And a part of me wants to torture him.

Let's see how long it takes him to regret his words.

63

Eli

She thinks she's punishing me by making me look at her body while she runs her hands over it, but the truth of it is I *like* looking at her. Watching her take her own pleasure makes me hard. But when she forgets the scared little girl she's being, and embraces the tigress hiding beneath her skin, *that* turns me on like nothing else.

A small part of me questions the life choices that have brought me to this point. How did I reach a place where a girl I hated becomes a girl I'm obsessed with to the point where I'll do absolutely anything to make her feel safe and in control?

If she needs to order me around, torment me, make me crawl around the floor after her like a pet fucking dog, to bring out the strong woman I know she is, then I'll do it, and smile while I serve her every whim.

Her soft moan drags my attention back to her. Her eyes are partially closed, her nipples poking out of the water, and her fingers are buried between her legs.

"Eli."

"Yes, Hellcat?"

Her eyes fly open and find me, a blush creeping up over her throat and cheeks. I hide a smile as the realization hits that she isn't calling for me but moaning my name while she makes herself come. She blinks, breasts lifting with her quick breaths as she shudders through her climax.

"Wash my hair." Her voice is shaky.

I push away from the wall and stroll toward her. "You'll have to sit up."

She moves, splashing water over the sides of the tub. "Wait. First, I want you to wash me."

I nod and reach for the washcloth.

"No, use your hands." She hands me the liquid soap.

"You want my hands on your body, Hellcat?"

"I want you to wash me like a good boy."

I laugh quietly at that. There's a brightness in her eyes, a slight tilt to her lips, as she looks at me, *challenges* me to do what she wants.

I nod. "Okay then."

I peel off my hoodie and toss it in the corner, take the soap from her waiting hand and squeeze some into my palm and then smooth it over her shoulder. She leans forward, and I gather up her hair with my free hand so I can soap over her back, and then let the damp heavy weight of it fall. It spreads out in the water behind her.

My fingers stroke over her skin, across her shoulders, over her arms, and slide down her spine. My fingertips skim over the sides of her breasts, across her stomach, dip into her navel.

The water sloshes over the sides again as she shifts so she can lay back, her eyes drifting closed. "Lower."

My fingers slip lower. Over her hips, her thighs, down to her knees.

I'm not washing her anymore. I'm not even pretending. I'm remembering her curves, her shape, all those little secret places that shouldn't be erogenous zones but are. The backs of her knees, her calves, the soles of her feet.

She sighs, not stopping me when I make my way back up her legs, my palms smoothing over her inner thighs. My tongue snakes out to toy with my lip ring as I slip one finger between the soft puffy lips of her pussy. She lets out a small moan when I make contact with her clit, and then she sits bolt upright, knocking my hand away.

"No, I never gave you permission to do that. Go and wait in the other room."

"Whatever you want, Kitten." I dry my hands on a towel, grab my hoodie, and walk out of the bathroom.

My dick is trying to escape from my sweats. It's so fucking hard and sensitive that I'm pretty sure just one touch from her and I'll be done. My lips twitch at the thought. She'd get such a fucking kick out of knowing that. I'm not sure she truly understands how deeply embedded under my skin she is.

I settle onto the couch and pick up the sketchpad I left on the coffee table. I'm sketching an image of her in the tub when she comes out, skin still flushed, wrapped in one of the fluffy towels.

"Go and pick out some clothes for me."

I stand. "Anything in particular?"

"Something comfortable."

I toss the pad down and walk down to her bedroom. It takes me a couple of minutes to pick out clothes, but I finally settle on a pair of shorts and a strappy top. I *think* they're pajamas. She didn't mention underwear, so I skip those. She'll learn quickly that when she gives me orders, she's going to need to be specific, or I *will* take advantage of the loopholes she leaves me.

She's standing where I left her when I return to the living room. My sketchpad is in her hand, and she's looking at the drawing I've half finished.

"Why do you keep drawing me?"

I hand her the shorts and top. "Because you're perfect."

"Nobody's perfect." She drops the towel and I swallow a groan.

"You're perfect *to me*, then."

She drags on the shorts and t-shirt. The pale pink top strains against her breasts, while the shorts cling to her hips and ass the way I want to. I've never been fucking jealous of cotton before.

"Do you want me to light the fire? Are you cold?" My eyes are on her nipples, clearly outlined through her top.

"A little. But I want you to take off your t-shirt first."

My shoulders stiffen. "Ari—"

"You said anything I want. *That's* what I want."

Her blue eyes meet mine, and there's awareness there, the knowledge that she *knows* how I feel about removing my top. I've humiliated her, *hurt* her so many times that she needs to do the same.

I opened the door to this.

I *deserve* it.

Clenching my jaw, I reach back and pull the shirt over my head.

"Turn around."

I suck in a deep breath, and turn around, closing my eyes as I present her with my back.

69

Arabella

I stare at the crisscross pattern over Eli's back. His shoulders are stiff, and the tension in his muscles is clear. He hates being exposed. I remember the way he'd reacted when I'd had to take a photo of his scars.

You're perfect to me.

Does he really believe that, or is he just trying to sweet-talk me?

"Ari." His voice is hoarse.

"Shh." Reaching out, I stroke the marks lightly with my fingertips.

He shudders beneath my touch but doesn't turn around. Slowly, carefully, I trace each one, gliding over the marks with a featherlight touch. I made him take off his t-shirt because I knew he'd be uncomfortable, but the more I stare at the marred flesh, the stronger guilt worms its way through me. Moving closer, I replace my fingers with my lips. Eli sucks in a harsh breath at the first press of my mouth to his skin. I explore the scars all over again, kissing and licking, taking my time to learn them, waiting for him to decide he's not going to comply anymore and stop me. But he doesn't and by the time I'm done, his head has dropped forward, and fine tremors are rolling through his body.

"Keep your t-shirt off," I tell him quietly. "Start a fire."

It takes a second for Eli to move, as though he's still lost in whatever headspace my touch sent him to.

I curl up on the couch while he busies himself in front of the fireplace. My gaze greedily takes in every inch of him, his tattooed flesh and the muscles moving fluidly beneath. The scars he has don't detract from his appeal. If anything, at least for me, they enhance it. Eli isn't flawless, he's perfectly imperfect.

The flames leap to life on the wood in the fireplace, spreading over the rest in little rivers of orange. He brushes his hands down the front of his sweatpants and rises to his feet.

When he moves to join me on the couch, I shake my head. "Kneel on the floor."

"As you wish." He drops to sit by my feet. His jaw is tight, and he won't meet my gaze.

Maybe I should let him cover up again? He's not happy.

I shake off the idea. Pursing my lips, I study him for a moment and then wiggle the toes of one foot toward him. "Massage my feet."

His hand curls around my ankle and he rests my foot on his thigh. He rubs over my skin, starting at the tip of my big toe, then up to my ankle before returning to my toes. The firm pressure he's using softens along the arch and down to my heel. One of his thumbs presses a point at the center of my foot, and my pussy throbs in response. A moan of pleasure leaves my lips before I can stop it. When he does it a second time, my eyes roll up into the back of my head.

He chuckles. "Do you like that, Hellcat?"

"How—" I moan as he does it again.

"You'd be surprised how many erogenous zones we have." His thumbs sweep upward to my toes. "They connect to different parts of our body."

I moan in bliss, and melt back into the cushions, when he turns the same careful attention to my other foot. My attention slips to the bulge I can see in the front of his sweatpants.

Is he enjoying what he's doing? Does he like being under my control? Or is it the fact I'm letting him touch me?

"Take off the rest of your clothes," I order him, my voice shaky.

It's warm enough in the room that he shouldn't be too cold. He doesn't have to stay completely naked for long, just until he's done what I wanted.

He tips his head to the side. "You want me naked?"

I nod. "All of it off."

Eli shifts around to strip out of his sweatpants and boxer briefs in one go. Naked on the floor in front of me, his long thick erection bobs upward. My whole body flushes in response to his excitement. It's a beautiful and dangerous sight.

I remember how it felt to have him inside me.

"Touch yourself."

His eyes stay on mine for a heated moment, then he spreads his thighs. One hand wraps around his cock.

"Make yourself come for me." I lick my lips and moan when he strokes himself.

He's naked, *hard*, and touching himself … all for my amusement.

A drop of pre-cum slides down the tip, coating the head as he works his hand up and down. His breath is coming out in harsh pants, and I'm mesmerized by the taut concentration on his face as he chases a release I've ordered him to take. My pussy pulses needily, but I try to ignore it. Maybe having him do this was a bad idea. I want to touch myself again, but instead, I watch him watching me.

The muscles in his arms flex as he pumps his cock, his movements becoming faster, harder, and harsher.

"Fuck." The word is a raspy curse.

Hips bucking forward, he comes with a tortured groan, spilling his seed all over the wooden floor. He doesn't stop until he's stroked out every last drop. He runs his other hand through his hair, breathing heavily.

65

Eli

My heart is pounding against my ribs, and I'm lightheaded. Whether that's from the intensity of my orgasm, of having Ari's eyes on me while I get myself off, or because I'm naked, with my scars on display, I can't say.

I focus on getting my breathing under control, lowering my head, and bracing my hand against the floor, while I suck in oxygen. When I open my eyes, there's a foot in front of my face. She wiggles her toes.

"Kiss."

"Good thing I don't have a problem with feet, huh?" My voice is wry. I press my lips to her feet, kissing each toe.

Tipping my head slightly, I glance up to find her watching me.

"I don't have a foot fetish," I tell her, then flick my tongue over her toes. "But if this is your kink, and you want me to mouth-fuck your toes, you should tell me."

Her eyes widen, lips parting, and she jerks her foot away, shaking her head. "Clean up the mess you've made."

I push to my feet and walk into the kitchen. The skin between my shoulders is prickling with the awareness that her eyes are on me, on the scars littering my back. I find some paper towels, then go back and clean up the floor. Once that's done, I toss the towels into the trash and kneel beside the couch.

"How many of the girls at school have you slept with?"

I shrug. "I don't keep count. A few?"

"The cheer squad?"

"Most of them. Not always sex, though. Linda sucked my dick, so has Lacy."

"I didn't ask for names." She scowls at me.

I incline my head. "Sorry, Hellcat. I'll keep my responses focused solely on your question."

"Did you like it?"

"Like what?" It's my turn to frown.

"Having sex with them."

There's no right answer to that question. If I say yes, she'll be angry. If I say no, she'll say I'm lying. Which I would be because at the time … I opt for honesty.

"Sure. When it was happening, I enjoyed it."

"Did you meet them at the cemetery?"

"No."

"Did you give them the same dares you gave me?"

"Never."

"I've read that submissives sit with their legs apart and their palms resting on their thighs."

I hike one eyebrow. She waves a hand. I laugh. She's sitting on the couch like a little fucking queen. All she needs is a crown.

"Oh, Kitten." I shake my head. "I promised to be your servant for forty-eight hours. I *never* said I'd be submissive. That's not in my nature."

She pouts, and I really have to fight against the urge to kiss it off her mouth.

"Why do you give me so many nicknames?"

"The situation dictates which one I use."

"And what does *this* one dictate? Why are you calling me Kitten right now?"

"Because that's what I see in your eyes. My little playful kitten who's testing her claws. If I hadn't promised to do what you want—" I snap my mouth closed with an audible click of my teeth.

She leans forward. "No. Please, finish that sentence."

When I don't reply, she uncurls herself from the corner of the couch and comes to stand in front of me. I let my gaze run up her legs, over the shorts covering her pussy, then tip my head back to search out her face.

"Tell me what you were going to say."

I lick my lips, flicking my tongue piercing against my teeth. "If I hadn't promised to do what you want, the way you're behaving would have you on your back while I feed you my dick until you purr for me."

Small white teeth bite down into her bottom lip and she swallows, then spins away.

"I'm hungry. I want pancakes. Make them for me."

Fuck.

"I've never made pancakes. I wouldn't know where to start."

"Because you've always had a cook who made everything for you? What would you do if you had to live alone? You'd starve to death."

"I'd order in or eat out at a restaurant."

"I saw a recipe book in the kitchen. Find one for pancakes and make them for me."

I rise to my feet slowly.

"You can put your pants back on. No underwear or shirt, though. I want you to be commando and shirtless for the next two days."

My jaw clenches, but I reach for my sweats and pull them on, then walk into the kitchen.

How the fuck am I supposed to get around this?

I find the recipe book in a drawer and stare down at it. I don't want to touch it. Definitely don't want to fucking open it. I know what I'm going to find inside and I'm not sure I can handle it.

"Ari—"

"Pancakes, Eli." Her tone is imperious.

She has no fucking clue what's she asking me to do. My heart is in my throat, and my mouth is dry. I lick my lips, flick my lip ring, and turn toward the door.

"Ari—" My voice comes out as a hoarse croak.

"You're going to fall at the first hurdle? Just because you don't know how to make pancakes?" She sounds disappointed. "I should have known better than to think you'd even try once I asked you to do something you don't already know inside and out."

I press my lips together and turn back, eyeing the recipe book like it's a venomous snake. The three steps it takes me to put myself in front of it again feel like miles. I stare down at it, then slowly reach into the drawer to take it out.

My hand is shaking. I make a fist, digging my nails into my palm, then try again. This time I manage to touch it, but then I take a step back.

I can't. I can't fucking do it.

I retreat, grunting when my back collides with the doorframe.

"Could you write a recipe down instead? Use one of the pages from my sketchpad."

Not that it'll make it any easier for me to do what she wants, but it'll cause a different problem. One I can deal with.

"For god's sake, Eli. Just use the recipe book."

"I can't. I'm sorry, Ari. But I can't do it."

"Why not?"

"Please. I'll do anything else you want, but not this. I *can't* do this. There are going to be notes. Photographs."

"Of course, there is. It's a recipe book!"

"No. You don't understand. It's my mom's."

66

Arabella

I stare at his pale face, his eyes full of pain and devastation.

My annoyance at his refusal morphs into understanding. "Sure, I can write it down for you."

He takes a hard, shaky breath. "Okay."

My heart screams out for the boy who'd lost his mother. The part of him who still grieves for the parent he lost and hasn't had a chance to mourn or heal properly. As much as I want to make him obey me, I don't like to see him like this. Vulnerable Eli is not what I'm used to.

I step forward and put myself in front of him. "We need flour, sugar, baking powder, an egg, butter, milk, and vegetable oil."

He nods unsteadily and crosses the kitchen. His hands are trembling as he reaches for the refrigerator door. I catch him glancing at the book over his shoulder, his eyes haunted.

I open the drawer and rummage around inside it. When I find a notepad and a pen, I take them out, and slide the drawer closed, leaving the book inside.

His shoulders relax a little, and he sets the ingredients out on the counter, one at a time. I find all the other items we need to make pancakes, then scribble the instructions down and place the piece of paper in front of him.

Eli glances at it for a moment. "Eggs."

"One egg. Maybe you should measure out the flour first." I hand him an empty cup. "That can get a bit messy. You'll need a cup and a half. Then we'll add three and a half teaspoons of baking powder."

His attention shifts to the cup, but he doesn't take it.

I frown. "Come on, Eli. It's not going to bite you. Just think of the possibilities if you can learn to cook at least one thing for yourself, without any help."

Taking it from me, he places it on the counter but doesn't reach for the bag of flour.

"Eli?"

He blinks, drawing in a sharp breath. "Yeah?"

I touch his shoulder gently. "Are you okay?"

When he hesitates, I worry my lip with my teeth. "Look, you don't have to make me the pancakes. Not if they bring back memories you don't want to face. I … I can't imagine what it's like to lose a parent the way you did."

He closes his eyes, blowing out a breath. "My mom would cook for us whenever we were here." His lips quirk up. "She called me her little helper."

"That must have been nice."

"It was." He laughs, but there's no humor in the sound. "Actually, it annoyed the fuck out of me."

My hand wanders down his back, stroking over his scars. "Maybe one day in the future, you'll be able to open the recipe book and cook something she used to make you. Relive the happy memories you have instead of living in the bad ones."

He swallows. "Yeah. One day."

I drop my hand and rest my hip against the counter. "So, pancakes?"

Eli turns his head, his gaze meeting mine. "I can't."

"It's okay. I understand."

"No, you don't."

I smile faintly. "Your mom—"

"It's not that." He huffs out a breath. "I can't weigh the flour."

I laugh. "You just measure it in the cup. It's easy."

"For you, maybe."

"For anyone."

Eli's lips thin and he looks almost … embarrassed. "Ari, I …" He scrubs a hand down his face. "I can't do it. I have dyscalculia."

67

Eli

"Dys-what?" She blinks at me.

My fingers drum on the countertop next to the list of ingredients.

"You know what dyslexia is, right?"

"Yes, I know that one."

"Dyscalculia is similar, but it's a problem with numbers instead of words."

"But … you always get A's in math."

"*Kellan* gets A's." My voice is dry. "It's going to be easier to show you." I pick up the cup and examine it. "You said a cup and a half, right?"

She nods. I pour flour into the cup until it's full.

"That's one cup." Looking around, I reach for the bowl and dump it in. "Now what?"

"Another half cup."

"Right." I look at the flour and then the cup. "I don't know how much I need to put in for half a cup."

She takes the bag of flour from me and measures out the amount she wants, then adds it to the flour already in the bowl. I pick up the list of ingredients.

"See, the problem is the numbers you've written down …" I run my finger down the list. "They're just meaningless symbols right now."

"Right now?"

"Sometimes they're clear." I give her a half smile. "When stress levels are low. But if I'm tense, or stressed, or even tired … it might as well be a foreign language."

"That must be difficult." She reaches past me for the baking powder. "We need three and a half teaspoons of this."

I pull open the drawer with the silverware and study the contents. "Which one?"

She frowns at me. "This isn't a trick, is it? You knew exactly what piece of silverware to use when we dined out with your dad and Elena."

"That's only because they're placed in a specific order, and I learned it as a kid. I couldn't tell you what any of them are called. That has nothing to do with my disability, and everything to do with me being too fucking lazy to care."

"Teaspoon is the smallest spoon." She points, and I lift one out and hand it to her. "Is it just counting and measuring, then?"

I shake my head and stretch out my arm, turning it so it's palm up. With my left hand, I tap my inner right wrist, and then do the same on my left. There are two small tattoos there. The letters L and R. Her fingers trace over them.

"I have a pretty good internal sense of direction. I can take a walk through the woods and find my way back easily enough, but if I'm asked to specifically go left or right, my mind sometimes blanks. Time is another problem. I have to set alarms. I can tell you I'll be there in ten minutes, or half an hour, but unless that alarm is set, you might see me in two minutes or three hours."

She continues combining ingredients while I explain, then pauses to look at me. "That day in class … when we were called up to answer the math equation. You answered it."

I shake my head. "*You* answered it. If you recall, I made you hold the marker with me. I didn't write the answer, you did."

"Oh!" Stepping around me, she fiddles with the knob on the stovetop until one of the rings lights. "Can you get the pan down for me?"

I reach up for the pan she wants and place it on the stove. She adds a drop of oil, then hands me the bowl full of ingredients and a wooden spoon. "Mix it up."

"Yes, ma'am."

While I mix the batter, she takes out two plates and sets them on the breakfast bar.

"That's enough. Now we need to pour a quarter cup of the batter into the pan."

"A quarter?"

"There are measuring cups we can get. We can write on them what each measurement is … in words."

I move to stand behind her and rest my hand over hers as she scoops some of the pancake batter up. She glances at me but doesn't stop me when I rest my other hand on her hip.

"Now we watch for the edges to dry and bubbles to form. In two or three minutes, we'll flip it."

I dip my head and press a kiss against her ear. "Thank you."

"For what?"

"I don't know. Doing this?" I kiss my way down her throat to her shoulder.

She leans back against me briefly, then pulls away. "Stop that." She swats my hand, which is creeping up over her waist, with the back of a spoon. "You're not forgiven yet."

"It's not been forty-eight hours yet?" I bury my face in her hair.

"No. Flip the pancake."

I lean past her to take hold of the frying pan and toss the pancake, then return my attention to kissing her throat.

"Don't make me punish you, Eli Travers."

"Hmmm. What kind of punishment are we talking about here?"

She huffs a laugh. "I'll eat all the pancakes and you can have cereal again … Wait." She twists to face me. "Is that why you've been eating cereal for the past two days?"

I wave a hand toward the microwave. "It's got an analog dial. I can't figure it out."

"Why didn't you *say* something?"

I smile, brushing hair away from her face. "You weren't talking to me, remember?" I loop my arms around her waist. "Look at it this way. If I don't behave, you can just starve me for the rest of the week."

68

Arabella

We're back to the playful version of Eli I got to know at Christmas. Is it a deflection because of what he's just told me? Admitting to a vulnerability I had no idea he had.

I thought I knew him, and now I'm discovering I don't. He has layers I hadn't known were there before. Not just the scary side, but the weaknesses he's kept hidden. Every day he's surrounded by numbers, struggling with a disability no one knows he has.

"You shouldn't give me ideas like that. I might just starve you." I smile, winding my arms around his neck. "Kiss me."

Eli doesn't hesitate to dip his head and press his lips to mine at my command. It's soft and sweet, not what I'm used to when we're together. The second I make a small noise of protest in my throat, the nature of the kiss shifts to something darker. It becomes sharper, desperate, and thinly controlled. My tongue plays with his, tasting the heat in his mouth, our teeth clashing. He kisses me like he knows how much I crave it. A drug I've been hooked on since the first time his lips found mine months ago. He moves forward an inch, welding the line of our bodies together so I can feel the hardness of his cock swelling in the front of his sweatpants.

We break apart, breathing hard, neither of us saying a word.

I drown in his eyes as he stares down at me, and I don't know what to say. This isn't how I planned the day to go. I'm still angry with him, but at the same time, things are shifting.

Tongue darting out, he flicks his lip piercing. "Pancake."

"Pancake?" I echo dazedly.

The corners of his mouth curve up in a smile. "Ari, the—"

My eyes widen. "Oh! The pancake!"

I twist in his arms to rescue the pan and tip the pancake onto one of the plates. I'm relieved to see it's not burnt.

"Can you find something to go on top of them? Maple syrup, butter, or fruit?"

Eli moves up behind me, his hands finding my hips again. "Is there anything you want in particular? I can see if we have it."

"No, whatever you find will do." As I pour some more of the batter into the pan, I can feel his breath on the side of my neck. His teeth bite down hard into my skin. My groin clenches and a throbbing ignites in my pussy. Eyes closing at the sharp pain, I moan, leaning back into him. He soothes the sting with a kiss before stepping away.

I try to concentrate on making more pancakes, but all my focus is on the boy rummaging around on the shelves of the refrigerator. Even when I'm supposed to be angry with him, my body still wants him.

He moves to the sink and runs the water. I glance over from transferring another pancake onto a plate to see what he has. There's a bowl of strawberries in his hand, and he's washing a handful of the berries.

When I meet his gaze, he's smirking. "You like strawberries, don't you, Kitten?"

My cheeks grow hot, remembering the time in the tomb when I'd begged him as Sin to fuck me. He fed me strawberries that night.

I tear my attention away and refocus on the pan in front of me.

"You know I do."

I cook until all the batter is gone and there's a stack of pancakes on each plate. Eli places a few strawberries on top of them. Grabbing some silverware from one of the drawers, we carry everything to the kitchen table and make ourselves comfortable. Eli cuts into one of the fluffy golden circles and takes a bite. A smile blooms over my face when he moans around the piece in his mouth.

"These are so good. I had no idea you could cook like this."

I shrug. "It was a skill I had to learn from an early age. I enjoy it. Cooking is one of my favorite things to do. I've always found it relaxing. A stress reliever when I need it the most."

Eli pauses with the fork halfway to his mouth. "And you haven't been able to do that a lot since you moved in with us."

I slice the knife into one of my pancakes. "I got to bake at Christmas, but that was the first time since we came to live in the Hamptons. It's not like I can do it at school, either. Everything is prepared for us."

"You could always open a restaurant."

"I'm not *that* talented with food, and I don't want to do it as a job. I have my twenty-year plan." I pop the pancake into my mouth and chew.

Eli nods. "To become a fashion designer."

Swallowing, I narrow my eyes. "You only know that because you read my diary."

"And I gave it back to you."

"You know that doesn't make it better. It was private."

When I glance away from him, he touches his fingers to my

cheek and catches my chin in his grip. Slowly he coaxes my face back around to his. He's holding a strawberry in his other hand.

He brings it to my lips. "Bite."

I arch an eyebrow. "You're not the one in charge here."

"It's just a strawberry, Ari."

"We both know it's more than that."

He rubs the piece of fruit against the fullness of my bottom lip. "I'm just asking you to try it."

I resist for a beat before taking a bite, the sweetness exploding in my mouth. A trickle of juice escapes, and my tongue snakes out to lick it up. His eyes are dark as they track the movement, the intensity in them stalling my breath in my throat.

"More." The demand leaves him on a rough growl.

"Eli—"

He pushes the strawberry into my mouth, and I'm forced to take another little bite. This time when the sticky sweet juice coats my lips, he captures it with a kiss.

69

Eli

The heady combination of strawberries and Ari's lips makes my dick hard. I groan against her mouth.

"Tell me to stop kissing you."

She leans closer, chasing my lips with hers. I shift forward on my seat, lift her off her chair and onto my lap. Her arms loop around my neck, her tongue darts into my mouth, and I stop trying to resist the temptation she poses.

My hand lifts, cups her jaw and tilts her head back, then slides down to wrap around her throat. She immediately stiffens and pushes at my chest.

"Let me go." She doesn't wait for me to release her but shoves away and scrambles off my lap.

Picking up her plate, she moves over to the trash can and dumps the remaining pancakes into it.

"Ari?"

She shakes her head and walks out of the kitchen. I stand and follow her.

"What did I do? Because I obviously did something wrong. If you don't tell me, I can't fix it."

She spins to face me. "I just need you to leave me alone for a little while. I need to process everything you've told me."

I think back over the last few minutes. She asked me to kiss her. I complied.

"Ari—"

"You tried to strangle me, Eli. And when you touched my throat, it brought it all back."

The words are delivered tonelessly. A heavy weight rests in the pit of my stomach.

"Okay." I give her a slow nod. "I'll give you some space."

I grab my sketchpad on the way past and walk down the hallway to my room. Once I'm inside, I drop onto my bed and close my eyes. There's a pressure building inside my head. One caused by my own fucked-up decisions.

I'm not sure we can ever get past what I did. Kellan warned me I was taking things too far. But I didn't listen. I was too caught up in what happened to Zoey, what *could* happen to Arabella, to realize I was becoming the thing I feared the most—the thing that was most dangerous to her.

The Monster of Churchill Bradley Academy.

70

Arabella

As soon as I hear Eli's door close, I touch my throat and swallow hard. The fury on his face when he attacked me is imprinted in my mind. I try to rub away the feel of his fingers against my skin.

His hands are crushing the breath from my body. I can't move. I'm clawing at his wrists in desperation with my nails, but he just won't let me go. He's going to kill me.

A tremor runs through my body as the memory shifts.

People are screaming. Eli is on the floor straddling Garrett, whose face is a red mess. I'm begging him to stop, unable to get more than a whisper out past my lips. There's so much blood.

Pressing a hand to my mouth, I collapse down onto the couch. My heart is pounding against my ribs, and I can't stop shaking. I hug my knees to my chest. I'd been fine until Eli gripped my throat. The second he squeezed, I was catapulted back to that day. I bury my face against my knees and try to breathe through the panic fluttering on the edge of my mind. I struggle with it, clinging on, not wanting to go over the edge into a full-blown panic attack.

How do I trust him when I know what he's capable of? The violence when he snaps.

He said whoever was blackmailing me had trained him to react whenever I did something to him. They *wanted* him to attack me after the video they posted. It's sick and twisted. Who would have the knowledge to manipulate and execute such a plan?

I focus my thoughts on the question instead of my fear.

My gaze moves to the fireplace, and I stare into the flames. The longer I watch them dance and crackle, the more the tension eases from my shoulders.

This game that's being played with us was set in motion months ago, meticulously constructed to unfold bit by bit, with us as pawns on the chessboard. They wanted everyone to see Eli as a true monster, and they'd achieved their aim.

Who?

Who hates Eli that much, and why? It has to be someone who knows him well. His moods and triggers. The fact he has dyscalculia but has been hiding it from everyone. They've been pulling his strings just as they pulled mine.

But no one had gotten to know me. Not properly.

Chewing on my lip, I turn the question over in my head. My blackmailer knew what buttons to press to make me obey them.

Had I really been that easy to read?

They'd made me a victim and preyed on my weaknesses.

What happens when the week is up? Is Eli going back to school? Maybe I should tell him that I don't intend to go back.

But I'm not sure I can deal with him right now. The moment we shared has been shattered, and it's left me cold and shaken. I want the confidence that was stolen from me back. I want to be the same Arabella Gray who'd been baking cookies when Eli Travers first walked into my life.

The future looms, murky and uncertain before me.

71

Eli

I step into the hallway and move through the cabin. I can hear Ari pottering around in the kitchen, but I don't go there. Instead, I pull open the front door.

"I'm just going to get some firewood," I call and walk outside before she answers me.

It isn't really a lie. I *will* collect some firewood on my way back, but first, I need to clear my head.

I take a slow walk around the outside of the cabin, then veer off into the woods. I spent every year of my life here with my mom and dad, before she died, and could wander the woods for hours without getting lost. I have no intention of going too far, though, just in case Arabella needs me or gets it into her head to come looking for me.

I walk far enough into the woods that I can't see the cabin, then stop and lean against a tree, tipping my head back to look up at the sky through the leaves.

Who the fuck was behind those texts? And why did they use Arabella to goad me?

The answer to the second question is easy. She's the perfect target. She doesn't have any close ties to anyone at school, no one to confide in, which makes her easy to alienate. When it looked like she had found someone in Miles, they put a stop to it.

But that should mean she is the target and not me, surely?

Is Kellan wrong? Maybe *she* is the target. Like Zoey was. Maybe it's not about me at all.

Then why have both girls been targeted? I'm the only connection that links them. No, it makes sense for it to be me. Which takes me back to the question of *why?* What do they want from me? What do they stand to gain from goading me to react in an aggressive way toward Arabella?

I shake my head.

Nothing about this makes sense. Not without knowing who it is. And I haven't figured out *that* puzzle piece yet.

Pushing away from the tree trunk, I walk aimlessly for a little while longer, hands shoved deep into my pockets, until my steps take me back to the cabin.

I don't know how long I've been out, but the sun is setting when I finally open the door and step inside. The smell hits my nose the second I enter, and my stomach lets out a loud grumble.

"Ari?"

She comes out of the kitchen, wiping her hands. "You've been out for hours."

"Have I? I didn't realize." Without my cell to set an alarm on, I have no way of keeping track of the time while I'm out.

"I was worried you might have been eaten by a bear."

"Worried or hoped?" I smile when she glances at me. "I'm joking. Pretty sure death by bear wouldn't be painful or long enough."

"I made dinner."

"Oh?" I follow her through to the kitchen and prop myself against the doorframe to watch as she bends and opens the oven door.

When she straightens, she has a dish balanced between the

oven mitts.

"What's that?"

"Mac and cheese." She sets it down. "Can you set the table, please?"

"Yes, ma'am." I take out plates and silverware, and she fills them with the food.

"Sit down and eat." She pulls out a chair and takes a seat.

I study her for a second, then turn and open a door to take out a bottle of wine.

"I think white would go with mac and cheese," I say and pop the cork.

Finding two glasses, I fill them both and place one beside her plate. "Would you prefer it if I ate in my room?"

She shakes her head. "No."

I take the seat opposite her, and we eat in silence until Ari lets her fork drop to the plate with a clatter.

"Do you have *any* idea who could be behind the texts?"

I take a sip of wine. "None."

"It has to be someone who knows you well. How else would they have known you have dyscalculia?"

"Maybe they don't and just know I hate math."

"You hate most of the classes we take, except art. Why target math?"

She has a point. "Maybe because it's the only class where the teacher doesn't ask me to take part. It's no great leap to think making me stand up and take part is going to irritate me."

"Surely that means it's someone from our class, then?"

"Maybe. Most of the faculty know I have dyscalculia. It's why they don't really complain if I'm late or skip a class."

She lifts her glass and rolls it over her lips before taking a sip. I lick my lips, watching as she swallows the pale liquid.

"Apart from Zoey, has this ever happened before?"

"I don't think so."

"You don't … you don't think Kellan would do it, do you?"

"*Kellan*?"

"It makes sense, if you think about it." She's talking so fast that the words are tripping over each other. "He knows everything about you. Maybe he doesn't like you spending time with anyone else. The texts didn't start until after we … well … you know."

"It's not Kellan."

"Are you sure?"

"It's *not* Kellan, Arabella." I drop my fork and stand. "Thanks for the food. I'm going to bed."

72

Arabella

"No, wait!" I push my chair back and rush after him before he can leave. "I'm just trying to work out who could be behind all this."

Eli doesn't turn to look at me, his shoulders tight. "Kellan is my best friend. It's not him."

"Who else can it be?" Frustration swells inside me. "You started at the school years before me. I don't know anything about your past there. Maybe Principal Warren is right, and it's linked to your dad."

"My parents met at the Academy."

"They did?"

Eli glances at me over his shoulder. "Dad knew she was the one for him after she yelled at him for getting her wet."

Heat rises in my cheeks, and I have to press my fingers to my mouth to stop myself from laughing, but it escapes anyway. "Oh my god. Too much information!"

The frown on his expression turns into amusement. "Not *that* kind of wet. There was a rainstorm, and she was walking along the path beside the road. He drove through a puddle and soaked her."

I toy with the hem of my tank top. "See, I didn't know they attended Churchill Bradley Academy until you just told me."

Eli swivels around to face me, flicking his tongue piercing and watching me with stormy eyes. "I don't think it's anything to do with my dad."

I move back to the table and pick up our plates. "Then, who's your enemy, Eli? Who hates you the most?"

He laughs. "You know what it's like at the school, Ari. You've seen it with your own eyes. *Everybody* hates me. Even the ones who want to fuck me."

I scrape our leftover mac and cheese into the trash can. "But what was it like before the accident? What was your life like?"

Eli watches as I place the plates and silverware in the sink. "You know we have a dishwasher right there next to you."

"Washing up helps me think. There's also a sense of achievement when you finish." I turn on the faucet to fill the bowl with water and add dish soap.

Eli refills our glasses. "Life was perfect. Mom and Dad were very social. Hosting pool parties and barbecues for our neighbors and their friends. There was always something going on."

"So, you had interaction with other kids?" I run a sponge across one of the plates. "I noticed, at Christmas, there were a bunch of students from the school at the Country Club."

"My mom used to set up playdates." He takes a sip of wine.

Rinsing off the plate, I stack it in the dish rack. "With who?"

"Tina and Bret when we were small. For a while it was me and Jace. Then later, when I was older, Brad, Garrett, and Evan would always tag along with Jace. We were friends … until we weren't. But our parents kept putting us all together, and hoped we'd bond. There were a bunch of others, but they didn't go to Churchill Bradley, and I rarely see them now. When we started at Churchill Bradley Academy, they all joined the football or swim teams. I was just the shy kid who liked to draw."

Shy Eli.

I try to imagine what he'd been like, but the image is poisoned with the monster I'd come to fear.

Eli sighs and scrubs a hand over his face. "I'm going to bed."

"Okay." I don't try to stop him this time, focusing on the dirty silverware instead.

He drains the rest of the wine in his glass and disappears through the door.

I take my time with the finishing up the dishes, dry everything and then put it all away. My wine glass is still on the table, half-full, the bottle beside it.

We're no closer to working out who our nemesis is than we were yesterday. Maybe it's more than one person? Why else refer to themselves as 'us' when they text me?

Everything is knotted together like a messy ball of twine. Trying to find the relevant threads to the truth is proving to be difficult.

When I finish my drink, I refill my glass. I need something to numb me enough that I'll just pass out. If I don't, then I'll just wake sobbing from the nightmares that have been steadily getting worse every time I close my eyes. The fact that the person who tied me up in the middle of the night is still out there leaves me unnerved and anxious.

I take my glass and the bottle to the couch. The fire is nothing more than embers now, but warmth still lingers in the air. I'm not sure how long I sit there, gazing into the glowing fireplace and sipping wine, before I hear the patter of rain against the windows.

Please don't let there be another thunderstorm.

I drown my anxiety with alcohol. By the time I've finished most of the bottle, I'm feeling lighter, but the worry of there being another potential thunderstorm remains, even though, so far, there hasn't been a single rumble.

I don't want to be alone, and the wine hasn't helped me forget anything. Not in the way I want it to.

I stagger up off the couch, and scurry along the hallway. When I reach Eli's door, I open it quietly and sneak inside. The room is in inky blackness, but I know the direction of the bed. As soon as my knees hit the mattress, I crawl onto it and worm my way beneath the blanket.

"Ari?" Eli's voice is soft.

Wiggling toward him in the dark, I wrap my arms around his chest. "I want to sleep here tonight."

A hand strokes my hip. "There's no storm."

"I know." I skim one hand over the contours of his body, along his shoulder to his neck. Sliding my fingers into the hair at the back of his head, I tilt my face upward, my lips clumsily find his and I kiss him, tasting the heat of his mouth when he opens for me. He kisses me back, cupping my jaw. My free hand roams over his chest, side, and hips—neediness flaring to life inside me. My pussy pulses with an eagerness to be filled.

Eli groans against my mouth. "What are you doing, Hellcat?"

"I want to be with you." I roll my hips against his thigh and rub myself into the side of his body with a little giggle. "Touch me. Please touch me. Make me forget everything, Eli. Put your cock inside me. I want your hands all over me and your mouth between my legs. Fuck me. Please, fuck me, so I don't have nightmares tonight."

73

Eli

Her mouth presses hot, wet kisses to my jaw, my shoulder, over my chest. Her tongue flicks over my nipple, and I hiss.

"Eli, please. I need you." She clutches my wrist and pushes my hand between her legs over the thin cotton of her shorts. "Right here."

The material is wet, soaked with her desire, and my fingers move of their own accord, pressing against her pussy. She moans, nips at my nipple, and rubs against my hand.

"So good. Yesss," she hisses. "I need more. Please, touch me, Eli. I need you so much."

I roll, pinning her beneath me, and push one leg between hers, trapping my hand against her pussy. She rocks against me and lifts her arms to wind them around my neck to pull my head down to hers. I let her. Our lips meet, meld, and devour each other with a heat, an intensity that takes over.

Her hands run down my back, over my spine, and back up again. For once, I don't care that she's touching my scars, that I have no shirt on. She's shown me that they don't matter to her, that it doesn't change how much she wants me. Her touch sends a shudder through my entire body. It's such an unusual sensation to have someone stroking a part of me that I've never allowed to be touched. But I like it. I like that her hands are on me.

My mouth leaves hers to kiss a path along her jaw to her ear and nip the lobe. A throaty moan leaves her lips, hardening my dick.

"Do you want me?" My voice is a raspy whisper.

Her nails dig into my ass, and her legs part to lift and wrap around my hips so she can rub against my dick. "So much." She peppers kisses over my shoulder. "Feed me. Fuck me. Fight me. The three F's." She giggles. "I fought you. I fed you. Now I want to fuck you." The words end in a little hiccup, and I pull back to frown down at her.

"Are you drunk?"

"No!"

I reach behind me and pull her hands off my ass to pin them above her head. Holding them there with one hand, I reach for the lamp on the nightstand with the other and flick it on. She blinks up at me. Her eyes are bright, slightly unfocused. I drop my head against her shoulder, and sigh.

"Fuck's sake. How much of the wine did you drink after I left you?"

Her lips curve into a pout. "Just a little bit."

"How much is a little bit?"

"Maybe the rest of the bottle."

I groan. "You're killing me, Kitten."

"I'd rather be fucking you."

"Only when you're drunk." I roll off her and sit up, twisting to place my feet on the floor.

"Where are you going?"

"To make coffee."

"But I don't want coffee." There's a sulky tone to her voice that would be funny at any other time.

"And I don't want to be screamed at tomorrow morning when you're sober and decide I took advantage of you again."

"You're not taking advantage of me. I'm an adult. I can make decisions for myself." Her protest is ruined by another little hiccup.

I turn and rest one knee on the bed so I can lean over her. Gripping her chin, I turn her head to me and press a hard kiss to her lips. "You're also a fucking lightweight when it comes to alcohol. When you're sober, if you still want me to fuck you, we can revisit this."

"I'm not drunk," she protests. "I'm just a little …" The pout turns into a brilliant smile. "*Tipsy!*" She reaches up to run her finger along the stubble coating my jaw, reminding me I haven't shaved in a couple of days. "It's so rough. I like how it feels against my skin. I want to feel it between my legs."

I turn my face into her palm and kiss it. "Come and drink some coffee with me."

"I'd rather sit on your face."

A begrudging laugh escapes me. "Baby, you're going to be the fucking death of me." I break away from her again and straighten. "How about this? We'll have coffee, and then if you still want to, I'll bury my face into your pussy and make you come on my tongue all night long."

"Promise?" She hiccups again.

"I swear on my life. I'll do whatever you want, for as long as you want, as long as you're sober when you ask me." I hold out a hand. "Deal?"

She eyes my fingers, then wraps hers around them. "Deal!"

I tug her off the bed and lead her back along the hallway to the kitchen. She perches at the breakfast bar while I set up the coffee machine.

"How can you do that if you have problems with measurements?"

I glance over at her. She has her chin propped up on her hand and is watching me.

I take out a filter sheet and show it to her. "There's a fill line, so I know how much to put in."

"When did you realize you had a problem with numbers?"

I scoop coffee into the machine, close the lid and hit the power button. "I think my mom figured it out first. I remember her adapting how she'd explain distance. Instead of numbers, she'd use landmarks as a reference point. Mom arranged for me to see someone, but she did it in such a way that I didn't know I was being tested for something. I just thought it was the same for everyone. It wasn't really until I went to Churchill Bradley and became friends with Kellan, that I realized it wasn't."

"Who else knows?"

"Kellan, the faculty." I shrug. "I don't know if my dad knows or ever noticed. He was at work a lot when I was growing up, and it was usually just me and Mom at home. By the time Mom died, I'd become adept at working around it." I fill two mugs, add cream and sugar to Ari's and take them both across to her. "I'm not ashamed of it, Ari. I don't *hide* it. It's just not something that comes up in conversation. Because I've always lived with it, I'm used to adapting things as I go, so I don't really pay attention to it, unless I'm in a situation where I have no choice. It's entirely possible other people know and haven't commented on it."

79

Arabella

I take the mug from Eli and curl my fingers around it. "Someone must have figured it out."

He places his own on the bar and taps the rim of my mug. "Drink."

Scrunching up my nose, I sigh. "If I drink it all, we can go back to bed, right? You aren't going to change your mind?"

"I've already promised you we will, if that's still what you want."

I take a gulp of the liquid and then hiss. "It's hot."

He shakes his head and chuckles. "Of course, it's hot. As much as you want to play, Kitten, you need to slow down."

I pout. "But I want to fuck."

"Sober up first." He takes a sip of his drink.

"You no fair," I grumble, blowing on the coffee to try and cool it faster.

"I told you; I'm not fucking you until I know you're sober."

"But my body aches," I whine. "It feels so empty. You've addicted me to sex."

"Drink." The word comes out in a guttural growl.

Between blowing on it to cool it down and taking small sips, I manage to finish every last drop. Eli watches me, leaning against the breakfast bar, drinking his own and studying my face.

Once I'm done, I show him my empty mug, grinning. "All gone!"

"How are you feeling?"

"Still horny." I slip off my seat, and wrap my arms around the back of his neck. "Now, will you fuck me?"

He brushes his nose gently against mine. "I'll make you come, but my dick isn't going inside you tonight."

"Why not?"

"Because you don't sober up that quickly, Ari. You might be thinking a little clearer, but I'm making a promise to both of us right now that I will *never* fuck you when you're drunk."

A tiny whine leaves my throat. "But I want you to."

"No." His voice is firm.

"Eli—"

"You want my mouth on your pussy or not?"

"You know I do."

"Then don't fight me on this."

I roll my eyes and huff. "Fine, but I'm still sleeping in your bed tonight."

He smiles. "Kitten, I wouldn't want you anywhere else."

He pulls me into his body and kisses me hard, his tongue dueling with mine and making my head spin. Hands moving to my ass, he lifts me, forcing my legs to wrap around his hips. I nip and kiss his neck as he carries me back through the cabin. Cool sheets meet my back when he lays me on his bed.

I strip quickly and reach for him. "Touch me, Eli."

Groaning, he descends into my arms, and I wrap my legs around him. I like his weight. It feels right, his hard edges to my soft ones. I palm his face, and I kiss him boldly, wantonly, taking what I need.

He moves against me, his hardness rubbing against me through his sweatpants, and I arch into him, seeking to satisfy the throbbing in my core. His lips move down my jaw, kissing and biting.

I grab his hand, push it beneath my shorts, and press his fingers to my pussy. "I need you, Eli."

His fingertips stroke along my sensitive flesh. "I thought you wanted my mouth on you."

I shudder at the contact. "After. You promised me all night."

"I got you, baby." He pushes a finger inside me.

Clutching at his shoulders, I groan, tilting my hips to welcome it deeper.

Eli pumps it in and out of me. "Fuck, you're so wet."

His thumb circles my clit, and the building pressure climbs within me.

Another finger joins the first, and I grind against them. "More. I need more."

"Ride my hand." He captures my mouth in a fierce kiss.

I writhe as a third finger slips inside me. My moans are smothered by his mouth, as it ravages mine. Our tongues dance together, fighting for dominance.

My nails rake down one side of his back as an orgasm slams into me. Eli doesn't stop rubbing my clit, drawing every last response from my body. When I relax back into the mattress, he pulls his hand from between my legs and licks his fingers.

"How many orgasms are you planning on making me give you?"

I giggle. "A million."

"You're definitely trying to kill me."

"Did you think I was going to stab you? Or smother you with a pillow."

Eli laughs. "The idea crossed my mind when we first arrived."

I hum, and then smile. "Death by giving orgasms."

Nudging his shoulder, I get him to roll onto his back, and then I straddle his waist.

He stares up at me, eyes narrow. "What are you doing?"

"Don't you like having me on top of you?" I move my hips in a slow, smooth circle and feel his cock twitch beneath his sweatpants.

"You know I do, but if you want my mouth, you need to sit on my face."

Ignoring him, I continue gyrating against the hard ridged length, enjoying the friction.

I want to tease him. Torment him. Make him as lost to the need to have me as I feel when I'm around him.

My rhythm grows faster, desperate, until I'm mindlessly grinding over him. "Please, please. I want you inside me."

"Ari—"

"I need it so bad."

His hands jerk up to grip my hips. "Baby, you need to stop."

I throw my head back, but I don't stop my movements. "No. Give me what I want. I'll drive you mad until I get it. Fill me up with your cum. Do it, Eli. I know you want it to."

75

Eli

The girl writhing around on top of me is torturing me. Killing me slowly with the heat of her body, her soft moans, her pleas to have my dick inside her.

Reaching up, I tangle a hand into her hair and pull her head back down to mine, rolling to pin her beneath me as our mouths collide. Her hand snakes between our bodies to shove beneath the waistband of my sweats. I pull it out, shaking my head.

"But I want—"

I cover her mouth with my hand. "Multiple orgasms from my fingers and mouth. That was the agreement."

"But, Eli—"

"Eli's not here right now," I whisper, bracing myself on one hand to stare down at her. "Only Sin." I run my tongue over her lips. "And he doesn't fuck you."

I slide down her body, pull her shorts off, toss them to one side, and settle between her thighs. The first sweep of my tongue over her clit arches her back off the mattress. Her hands fall into my hair, fingers curling against my scalp. A contented sound rumbles up my throat at her cries, at the taste of her on my tongue.

She tugs at my hair, begging and pleading, sobbing, and moaning, while I feast on her. My fingers join my tongue, sliding through her wetness until I can push two inside her and thrust them in and out while my tongue flicks, licks, and strokes over her clit.

Words are spilling from her lips, unintelligible moans interspersed with my name. *Not* Sin, but *me*.

Eli.

Her hips buck, fingernails scraping over my scalp as she falls over the edge. I lift my head and press a kiss to her trembling thigh.

"Count for me, Kitten."

"Two." The number is a breathy whisper.

"Good girl."

***

Dawn is rising when she finally pleads with me to stop. Her body is shaking and slick with sweat. I've kept my word and managed to stay inside my sweats. But her lips are swollen from my kisses, and she lost count of her orgasms around six or seven. Her skin is flushed, and her eyes are heavy when she rolls onto her side to look at me.

"I'm not drunk now."

I prop my head up on one hand and reach out to brush her hair away from her face. "Drunk on orgasms. Still not fucking you."

Her hand cups my dick through my pants. "But you're hard."

"Fucking stone," I agree.

"I could help with that." She gives a gentle squeeze.

"You could, but not until you're sober."

She slides closer and hooks her leg around my hip so she can rub against my dick. "Sleep naked with me."

"No. You're a bad girl who wants to do naughty things to me while I'm asleep." I cup her ass and pull her closer so I can grind my erection against her pussy.

Her eyes roll up, eyelashes fluttering closed, as she moans at the sensation.

"I was warned about girls like you," I whisper, thrusting against her. "Greedy for my dick. Corrupting my innocence."

She snorts a laugh at my claim, her fingers tracing up my back, and opens her eyes to search out mine. "What if I wake you up sucking your cock?"

"What time is it?"

She blinks at my question but looks at the wall where the pale light of dawn shines onto the clock hanging there.

"Four in the morning."

"If you sleep until eight, I won't complain if I wake up with my dick in your mouth."

"Four hours." She sighs and buries her face against my throat. "That's too long."

"But long enough to convince me you're sober enough to be responsible for your decisions."

"When did you become the responsible one?" She pulls back to look at me.

"When I thought we shared something special only to discover when I woke up that I took your virginity while you were drunk, and you accused me of raping you."

She has the grace to blush, eyelashes lowering to shield her eyes. "I'm sorry."

I tilt her head up and kiss the tip of her nose. "I'm not blaming you, Kitten. I just need you to be sober before I put my dick in you again. I gave you my word that I wouldn't fuck you while you're drunk. If I break that promise, what chance do I stand of you believing anything else I say?"

Wrapping my arm around her waist, I settle onto my back and draw her into my side. "Try and get some sleep now. Maybe we can take a walk tomorrow, get some fresh air, work up an appetite." I kiss the top of her head. "Maybe you can bake some cookies?"

She nestles against me, lips brushing over my throat as she speaks. "Are you asking me to cook something for you?"

"If I say yes, will you refuse?" Sleep is making my eyes heavy, but I fight to stay awake until I get my answer.

"I won't refuse."

I'm smiling when sleep finally pulls me under.

76

Arabella

I peel down Eli's sweatpants as slowly as I can, trying not to wake him. It's eight-thirty in the morning, and he's still dead to the world. I woke up from a dreamless sleep, snuggled against his chest, sober, and every inch of me relaxed. I don't feel a single bit of regret for last night in the cold light of day.

I get his sweats down to his knees before giving up and crawling between his legs. His rock-hard erection is thick and long. Licking my lips, I wrap my hand around it and swipe my tongue over the tip of his cock.

I keep my eyes on Eli's face.

He doesn't move.

I smile.

Engulfing the top with my mouth, I pump his length with my hand. A groan rumbles up from his throat, his hips shifting restlessly. I swirl my tongue and bob my head, taking him deeper inside my mouth.

"Fuck." Fingers tangle in my hair, and our gazes clash.

His eyes are no more than slits, but I can see the gleam of his irises from beneath his thick lashes.

"Suck," he commands.

I do, sliding up and down his length, taking as much of him as I can.

His teeth sink into his bottom lip. "Yeah, just like that. Dirty girl."

He fists his hand in my hair but doesn't try to adjust my pace. Working his cock like my favorite lollipop, I maintain eye contact.

I want to see him fall apart. Know that I'm the one that makes him lose control.

His hips thrust up, joining the rhythm I've set until he's fucking my throat at a rough pace.

"There's nothing more beautiful than seeing my dick disappearing into your mouth." His lips part on a groan, neck arching on the pillow. "Don't stop, Hellcat."

His fingers tighten in my hair, but I ignore the sting. His cock jerks in my mouth, his movements becoming less smooth and more desperate. A beat later, a tortured groan rips from him, and his cum fills my mouth.

His grip is firm on my hair, holding me in place. "Swallow it all."

I suck him dry until his cock is softening in my mouth.

His fingers slide from my hair, and he flings his arms over his face to cover his eyes. "That's one hell of a wake-up call."

I kiss his hip. "I guess you deserved an orgasm after all the ones you gave me last night."

Eli peers at me from beneath his arm. "No regrets?"

"No." I shake my head. "I wanted you to touch me. It wasn't the same as Christmas. I might have been tipsy, but I was in control."

He's silent for a moment, studying my expression. "I'm still not going to fuck you."

His attention jumps to my bare breasts as I sit up between his spread legs. "But you said—"

"I know what I said." Eli raises his upper half off the bed, resting back on his elbows. "We have the rest of the week to talk and get to know each other. Do you want to spend all of it in bed?"

A sense of vulnerability washes over me at his words. I grab the blanket and tug it around my body. "Don't you want me that way anymore?"

Eli runs a hand through his hair. "Of course, I do. I'm fucking hard as a rock around you every second of every fucking day. You invade my dreams, my fantasies. You're so deep under my skin that it's like you've become a part of me."

I stare at him open-mouthed. "So, you *do* still want to have sex with me?"

He flops down onto his back, laughing quietly. "I've created a monster."

I snatch up one of the pillows and hit him in the chest with it. "I am not."

He pulls it out of my hands before I can hit him again. "Maybe you're just addicted to me."

I am, but I haven't admitted it out loud to him. Do I really want him to know what kind of power he has over me?

I climb off the bed and wrap the blanket around me like a toga.

Eli doesn't move from the mattress. "Where are you going?"

I stop at the door and glance back at him. "I'm going to take a shower and get dressed."

"Ari?" His call halts me.

Footsteps sound behind me, but I don't turn. "You drive me crazy."

He presses against my back, winding an arm around my waist. "I know. But I don't know how to be any other way."

I sigh. "If you want to talk, then we can do it over breakfast."

"Thank you." His lips touch the side of my neck, and I shiver.

My stomach flutters in response. "For what?"

Eli places a kiss on my shoulder this time. "Not letting me starve."

Clutching the blanket to my breasts, I glance at him. "Don't get too comfortable. The week isn't over yet."

77

Eli

Fingers slide through my hair, and I look up from the sketch in front of me. I smile at Ari as she moves past where I'm sitting at the kitchen table to reach the stove.

We've settled into an odd routine over the past three days. Days are spent talking and learning about each other. Our interests, our childhood, our dreams for the future. Nights are spent learning other things. How to touch, *where* to touch, to give the most pleasure.

We still haven't had sex, much to her annoyance. I don't know why I'm putting it off. I want her, *all* of her, but something is stopping me from taking that last step. That doesn't stop her from trying to change my mind, though.

"Hungry?"

"If you're cooking, then I'm starving."

She laughs. "Saying all the right things." She opens the oven door and takes out the dish. "Baked ziti for dinner. And I made cookies earlier to snack on later." She looks over her shoulder at me. "Could you set the table, please?"

I flip closed my sketchbook and clear the table of my pencils, wipe it over with a cloth, then set out two plates, silverware, and open a bottle of wine. Moving up behind her, I wrap an arm around her waist and bury my face into the curve of her throat.

"Ari, I—"

"Unless you're about to throw me over your shoulder, toss me onto the nearest surface and ravish me, wash your hands and sit down."

I laugh, press a kiss to her shoulder, and step back. "Sorry, babe. I need food, otherwise, I'll be too weak to make you scream my name later."

I follow her to the table and wait while she portions out the food, then hold out her chair for her.

"Would madame like wine?" I toss a tea towel across my arm and hold up the wine bottle.

She laughs up at me, and nods. I fill both our glasses, then settle on the chair beside her.

"Fun fact," I tell her as she scoops up a forkful of food. "We've known each other for six months."

"It seems longer." She chews and swallows. "Wait. How do you know? I thought you couldn't do math."

"It's March. I know, up here …" I tap the side of my head. "... that September to March is six months. It doesn't really mean anything to me, but I know what it is. When I first went to Churchill Bradley, my mom taught me how long it was between the semesters, so I knew when I would go home. So, September to December is three months. January to March is three months, and then March to June is three months."

I lift my glass and tilt it toward her. "The point I'm making is it's been six months since you burst into my life and turned it upside down."

"I think if anyone's life was turned upside down, it was mine." She softens the words with a smile.

I put my glass down and drag my chair closer to her. Taking the fork out of her hand I place it on her plate and curl my fingers around hers.

"I'm sorry, Ari. I was stupid, cruel, and wrong. I behaved badly and made what should have been an exciting thing for you awful and frightening." I lift her fingers to my lips and kiss each one. "How can I make it up to you?" I waggle my eyebrows.

She laughs, pulls her fingers free and palms my cheek, her thumb sweeping over my bottom lip. "I like this version of you."

***

I wake up early Sunday morning. Ari is wrapped around me, face buried against my throat and one leg thrown across mine. She's fast asleep, her breathing soft and steady. We didn't get to sleep until late, after spending yet another day talking and then crawling into bed together.

Easing onto my side, I press a path of kisses along her shoulder, up her throat, over her jaw until I reach her lips.

"Time to wake up, baby."

Her brows pleat and she grumbles softly.

"Kellan is getting here early. Do you want to be in bed when he arrives? Especially if he's with Miles."

Her arms tighten around me. "Can't we just stay here and never go back?"

I kiss the corner of her mouth. "I wish we could. But we'll run out of food. And without a cell phone or a car, we can't get more."

"I didn't plan on going back. I packed everything."

"I know. We saw the cases. Don't worry, Kellan will bring it all with him. And you have a load of new clothes as well."

Her eyelashes flutter, and then her blue eyes lock on mine. "You bought all the clothes here for me, didn't you?"

I nod. "I wasn't sure what you'd want, so I just stuck with sweats and t-shirts."

Her fingers stroke down my back, over my hip and round to curl around my dick. "Did I ever thank you for the clothes?"

I let her push me onto my back.

"Even if you did, I'd be more than happy for you to thank me again."

78

Arabella

Strong arms wrap around me from behind. I turn in Eli's embrace, and bury my face in his chest, its warmth familiar and comforting to me now.

He hugs me tightly. "It's going to be okay."

"How do you know that?" I reply quietly. "You don't know what's going to happen."

He runs one hand up and down my back. "Ari, trust me."

A tempest of emotion threatens to turn me inside out. I'm only going back to Churchill Bradley Academy because he convinced me to stay and graduate.

Fingers touch my chin, and he tilts my face up to his. "The school knows about what happened." His lips brush over mine, sending a delicious shiver down my spine. "The faculty will be watching over us." A kiss to the tip of my nose. "Whoever your blackmailers are, they won't be able to get to you." His mouth skims along my jaw. "You'll be safe."

I shake my head. "They got to me before. There's no guarantee it won't happen again. Nothing stopped them from hurting Zoey."

Pain washes over his expression. "We don't know, for sure, what happened to her."

"I do."

"How?"

I bite my lip. It's time to tell him the truth. "I had her diary."

Eli's eyes widen. "*Zoey's* diary?

I nod.

He releases me from the hug and steps back, putting distance between us. "What do you mean by *had*?"

I feel cold at the loss of his touch and cross my arms. "It was in my bag. The one that Kellan took when we arrived here."

"Where did you find it?"

"In the chapel. It was hidden under one of the pews."

Emotions shift and change over his expression too fluidly for me to catch. "How long have you had it? Why didn't you tell me?"

My gaze drops to the floor at the bite in his tone. "I-I didn't know if I could trust you."

"Jesus Christ, it could have the answers we need."

"I read some of it … You were right. She was being forced to do dares. They were making her do things—"

"I told you that Zoey told us about the dares."

"But I don't think she told you everything."

"What the fuck are you talking about?" Frustration is clear in his tone.

"She was scared. They were hurting and threatening people she cared about. She was too frightened to tell you and Kellan because she knew she was being watched."

His eyes are bright, sharp with anger. "I can't believe you kept this from me."

I swallow hard. "I was going to tell you."

"*When*? Before or after you left the school."

"Eli—"

He shakes his head when I try to touch him. "I need to finish packing."

"I'm sorry!" I call.

He stops in the doorway and turns, jaw tight. "You should have told me."

I don't try and stop him from leaving this time. Maybe he's right, and I should have shown them the diary, but he'd been making my life hell. Zoey's words had been one thing that had kept me going in my darkest moments.

I haul the suitcase off the bed, and grab my coat, then take everything with me into the main room. I leave everything by the couch and do one last check on the kitchen to make sure everything has been cleaned and put away. Walking back into the main room, I chew my lip and glance toward the hallway.

Maybe I should talk to Eli. Apologize again. I don't want him to be angry with me. Not when I'm being sent back into hell.

"Hey, Bella. I'm glad to see you didn't kill Eli and bury his body in the woods. We let ourselves in."

I spin at the sound of Kellan's voice and find him standing right behind me.

"It came close to that a few times." My attention shifts to the boy beside him. "What are you doing here?"

Miles huffs dramatically. "No *'how are you? Thank you for coming to my rescue.'*"

Smiling, I give them both a quick hug. "It's good to see you."

"Kellan thought it would be a good idea if I drove you back to the school. So no one sees you all arriving at the same time."

Kellan waves his hand. "It's just a precaution."

A wave of unease flows over me. "I guess that makes sense."

His attention shifts to the doorway behind me. "So, did you two lovebirds fuck and make up?"

"Did you find Zoey's diary in Arabella's bag?" Eli crosses the room, eyes on Kellan.

"I did," Kellan confirms. "You don't look happy about it."

"I only found out about it a few minutes ago." His words are clipped.

Miles' gaze bounces between the two of us. "Let's get your suitcases in the trunk of my car."

I'm torn between wanting to talk to Eli and needing to run and hide from his temper. I've seen what happens when he loses control. Although the rational part of my brain is telling me he won't hurt me, the echoes of the attack from before linger in my mind.

Miles grabs the hand of one suitcase, while I take the other.

"Are you okay?" he asks when we're outside.

"Yeah." My smile is weak.

"You look pale."

"Eli didn't know I had Zoey's diary. He's angry at me for not telling him sooner."

We round his car, and he pops the trunk. He lifts the suitcases and slots them in next to his own.

"I got snacks for the five-hour journey back." He locks the trunk and smiles at me.

I try to muster up some excitement, but anxiety is a heavy weight in the pit of my stomach. "Great."

I turn at the sound of footsteps. Kellan and Eli are walking toward us. Eli halts directly in front of me and stares down into my face.

"You and Miles go first. We'll leave in an hour."

Shoving my hands into the pockets of my coat, I curl them into fists. "Okay."

"No going to the chapel or the cemetery. You stay where people can see you."

"I promise, no wandering off."

He lifts his hand and cradles the left side of my face. "I'll see you soon."

I nuzzle against the warmth of his palm. "Okay."

His hand drops away, and he steps back to join his friend. I suck in a breath, refusing to let the emotions inside overwhelm me. It's going to be fine. Everything will be different. I'm going to be safe.

Once I'm in the car, I click my seatbelt on. Miles chatters as he starts the engine, but all my focus is on the dark-haired boy with green eyes, watching me moodily from in front of the cabin. I wave, but Eli just nods in response. I keep my gaze locked on him, turning in my seat until he vanishes from view.

79

Eli

Once the car is out of view, I turn and find Kellan studying me, eyes narrow.

"What?"

"I was expecting to see more damage, to be honest. You look pretty good for someone who just spent a week with a girl who wouldn't have pissed on you if you'd been on fire."

"Golden showers are *not* my kink."

"Interesting that you don't deny the fire part, though."

I shrug. "She burns me alive every time she touches me."

Kellan's laughter echoes around the clearing.

"What's funny?"

"I told you months ago you were in love with her. You kept denying it."

I roll my eyes and walk back inside the cabin. Kellan follows me.

"Seriously, though. Did you figure things out?"

"I think we still have a few sharp edges to sand down, but yeah … I think we're in a good place. Took a while, and I wasn't sure it would happen at first." I stop in the center of the kitchen and turn to face him. "Do you have the diary with you?"

"In the car."

"Anything in there that could help us?"

"Maybe, maybe not. We need to get with Arabella and see how much of what she was made to do matches what they wanted to do. There might be things we don't know about. One thing it does confirm is that *you're* the main target. Zoey seemed to think that whoever it was wanted to break up our friendship. They asked her to come between us. Flirt with us both, set us against each other for her attention and affection. Make you jealous and angry as often as possible."

"It makes no sense."

"To *us*, it makes no sense. But we don't have all the answers. There's something we're missing that will tell us why this is happening."

"Did you find anything on our cell phones?"

I reach into a cabinet to take down two mugs and busy myself making coffee for us both.

"There was a tracer app on Arabella's. That girl has no fucking idea of cyber security. No passwords, nothing hidden. I don't know how the tracer got on there. Someone could have installed it while she was away from her cell. It could have been sent to her via text. But it was installed just before Thanksgiving. Oddly, around the time the first video was leaked."

"So, when the cell I gave her went missing?"

"That would be about right. One bit of good news though. There was nothing on your cell."

"Did you pick up the new phones?"

"I did. They're also in the car. I also arranged for new numbers and transferred all the cell numbers you need into yours."

I hand him a mug. "It's got to be another student."

He pauses with the drink partway to his mouth. "How'd you figure that?"

"It doesn't make sense for it to be any of the staff."

"What about the people behind the real dares?"

I snort. "You know it's Principal Warren behind those."

"Not for certain."

"Of course, it is. Him and the rest of the teachers who've been there for at least ten years. They do it as a bit of harmless fun. By telling us to *not* do them, it guarantees that we will. Why do you think they're all such ridiculous dares? *And* why security never looks too closely at students sneaking around after hours."

"Still doesn't mean it's him."

I roll my eyes. "Where do you think I stole the paper from? It's kept in the bottom drawer of his desk, along with the fountain pen he uses to write them." I pause for a drink. "Anyway, the dares have been going on since my dad was there. He told me it was the faculty who do it. It's handed down to the most senior member of staff whenever the one who was in charge of it retires. Warren was a math teacher when Dad was there. When Principal Garner retired, Warren got the position and took over the dares.

"Why do you think there are so many rumors about them? The faculty makes up shit that has happened to students. Do a search for some of the names they use in the stories of kids who didn't do the dares and had shit happen to them. None of them fucking exist."

"And how long have you been sitting on *that* little gem of information?"

"I thought you knew."

"*Now* I do. Okay, so we scrub any teachers you've clashed with off the list. Are you sure?"

"Positive. It doesn't feel like something a teacher would do. They'd be more likely to cause shit for me through education. Alienating me from other people wouldn't make any difference to them. And, anyway, I don't clash with teachers all that often. Does Zoey mention any teachers in her diary?"

Kellan shakes his head. "She got along well with all of them."

"Another reason I don't think it's any of the faculty."

"Okay, okay. You've made your point. So that leaves all the students."

I shake my head. "It leaves *our* year and maybe the two below us at most. None of the others were there when my mom died, and I was dubbed the monster. I'm leaning toward it being someone in our year, maybe two or three working together."

"So, we're looking at Miles' old buddies. What about Jace? He had a thing for Arabella."

"Not for Zoey though. She was friendly with the entire group of them."

"Especially Tina." Kellan's voice is dry. "Don't suppose this is a case of spite? Tina wanting payback for taking Zoey away from her?"

"I didn't take Zoey away from anyone."

"*I* know that. Jilted lover situation? Jealousy?"

"How does that link to Arabella?"

"Easy target?"

I flick my lip ring, thinking it over. None of those reasons feel right. I shake my head. "No. I don't think that's it."

He blows out a breath. "Then we're back to square one. With no fucking clue and no way of working it out."

"Oh, we'll work it out." My voice is soft. "The game has changed. Now we're playing by *my* rules."

***

"Fuck. Fucking fuck!"

Kellan's curse snaps me out of the doze I was in. Popping an earbud out, I look at him. "What's wrong?"

"I think I have a flat tire." He pulls off the road and parks. "Fucking thing." He throws open the door, unclips his seatbelt and climbs out.

I meet him at the back of the car. "You *do* have a spare, right?" The look he throws at me makes me chuckle. "Fine. Flashlight?"

"In the trunk with the jack." He pops the lid, and we haul out the suitcases, flip back the carpet and take out the spare wheel. "Not how I wanted to spend Sunday evening," he mutters as he takes it around to the side of the car.

It takes both of us to get the wheel off and replace it, and we're both covered in dirt and oil by the time we're done.

"How far from school are we?" I ask once we're back inside.

"Another three hours, give or take. We better hope security on the gates are in good moods; otherwise, we might have to drive into town and stay in a hotel for the night."

"They'll let us in." I rest my head against the back of the seat. "Wake me when we get there."

80

Arabella

The gates of Churchill Bradley Academy come into sight, and the emotions inside me solidify into a cold, hard lump in my chest. I wrap my arms around myself and bow my head. There's a song playing quietly on the radio, but I can barely hear the words.

The longer we drove, the more the stolen moments I had with Eli grew cold and faded. All my worries and fears have come roaring back. I don't know what to expect. For the past week, I've been cocooned, protected from the harsh reality, and I've enjoyed being with Eli. I was *happy*. More like the Arabella Gray I'd been before arriving at Churchill Bradley. We'd shared things—fragile, precious moments.

But then, two miles into the journey, I learned that Kellan didn't give Miles my phone, only my bag with my wallet inside. With no way to contact Eli at all, it left my mind open to all the negative thoughts again.

"You okay?"

Miles' soft voice breaks through my thoughts. "I just—I wasn't planning on coming back."

He glances at me, then returns his attention to the road as security waves us through. "You didn't have to come back, Arabella. You know that, right?"

"I do, but Eli pointed out that I might not get accepted for an internship or college if I don't graduate."

"I can see his point. Churchill Bradley is ranked up there with

Harvard and Yale. It looks good on your resume and will open doors for you."

"If I survive until graduation."

"Hey, none of that. You've got me, Kellan, and Eli looking out for you."

"I've heard that before."

"I am!" he insists. "I'm keeping an eye on everyone surrounding Lacy and Brad."

I turn and stare at him. "You're *spying* on them?"

A faint smile appears on his lips. "It was Kellan's idea."

"What if they figure out you're watching them?"

Miles snorts. "None of them have figured out I'm gay in all the years we've been hanging out. I wouldn't worry about it."

Even with his assurance, worries niggle at me. "I don't want you to get hurt."

"I'll be fine. I'm in contact with Kellan all the time, and just like you, I've been ordered not to wander around on my own without plenty of people around. In fact, I promised I'd text him as soon as we got here."

"Kellan?"

Miles laughs as he pulls smoothly into a parking spot in the car lot. "He's cute when he pretends not to be concerned about me."

"You make a good couple."

"Yeah, we do."

It's hard not to smile at his happiness. I unclip my seatbelt and climb out of the passenger side, while Miles gets out of his side and opens the trunk. It takes us three trips to get everything to the dorm building. My door is unlocked, and my room key is on the dresser, right where I left it.

After insisting to Miles that I'll be okay, he agrees to go and unpack his own stuff and leave me alone. I open my cases. I don't want to stand still. It only leads to thinking, and I'm already jittery. Once I'm done, I go through my things again, organizing them into types of clothes and colors. It feels strange not having Eli with me, not being able to stop whatever I'm doing to search him out for a kiss, or just to lean against him and soak up his warmth. I've grown used to his presence, the touch of his hands, his kisses on my neck. It's as though I've left a piece of myself behind at the cabin. It's going to be strange sleeping in a bed alone tonight. I'm so used to having his body wrapped around mine all night long.

He'll be here soon.

That one thought sends warmth spreading through my body. I know he's angry at me for not telling him about the diary, but it will pass. He'll forgive me.

Are you sure about that?

"He will." I say the words out loud.

And what version of Eli will he be when he gets here?

The stray thought worries me. I've discovered so many versions of Eli that I don't know what to expect.

He's the monster of the school and has an image to uphold.

Will the affectionate, teasing version of Eli I got used to at the cabin be gone?

***

The questions and fears are still tumbling through my head when I go down for dinner that evening. It's busy with a lot of the students already back, but some familiar faces are still missing. There's no sign of the two faces I'm looking for—Eli and Kellan aren't at their usual table.

Where are they?

I see Miles with Lacy, Tina, Brad, Maggie, Bret, Garrett, and Evan. Garrett glances my way, his face still a bruised mess, and waves. Bret elbows him in the ribs, but he ignores him.

I wave back, guilt for the beating he'd taken from Eli washing over me, but I'm relieved to see a friendly face.

Lacy sends me an unfriendly glare before she whispers something in Tina's ear. The other cheerleader looks my way, and laughs. My stomach twists.

Why did I imagine this time around it would ever be different? I've been kidding myself into thinking all the bad stuff would magically go away.

Ducking my head, I join the line for food, my attention darting to the doorway every time someone enters. There's *still* no sign of Eli or Kellan. I hate that I can't text them. Surely Miles would tell me if something was wrong, though?

Uncertainty circles like a vulture in my head. What if he's been told *not* to tell me?

I linger over my food, barely aware of what I'm putting in my mouth. Students come and go while I sit at a table alone, waiting.

Eli never shows.

My heart is heavy in my chest when I finally give up and head back to my dorm room.

81

Eli

After changing the tire, Kellan announces we need to stop for gas. *That* turns into grabbing something to eat. Of course, Kellan isn't satisfied with something from the gas station. He wants to find a restaurant, which means we have to drive into the next town we reach. And when we finally leave the restaurant, and get back on the road, we hit a traffic jam caused by a crash further up the road.

By the time we pull up to the gates of Churchill Bradley, it's after midnight, and I'm grinding my teeth in frustration. It takes another fuck knows how long to get our cases to our room. I'm halfway out of the door when Kellan calls my name.

"Where are you going?"

"To let Ari know we're back."

"Eli, it's almost one-thirty in the morning. Let the girl sleep. You'll see her tomorrow."

"But—"

He raps his knuckles against my forehead. "Start thinking with this head instead of the little one."

I scowl at him. "It's not little, thank you very much."

"And I'm sure Bella thoroughly enjoys what you do with it, but it doesn't change the fact that she'll be asleep, and you can't just go waltzing up there to announce yourself." He leans forward and inhales. "Plus, you stink of dirt and car fumes. Take a shower, then go to bed."

"But—"

"You said that already." He steps past me and closes the door. "Don't make me lock it and swallow the key, Eli. I'll do it, and then you'll have to listen to me bitch about it until I shit it out." He leans against the door, folds his arms, and cocks an eyebrow. "Well?"

I glare at him for a moment longer, then blow out a breath. "Fine!"

"That's a good boy." He pushes away from the door and pats my cheek. "We *will* housebreak you, even if it kills us."

I roll my eyes and throw open a suitcase to pull out clean clothes, then head into the bathroom to take a shower. I leave the door open, so I can talk to Kellan while I wash.

"Did you give Miles the cell for Ari?"

"No. I thought you'd want to give it to her." He snickers. "Like I'm sure you've been giving everything else to her this week."

"You're such a fucking child sometimes."

"It stops you from turning into a broody, miserable fucker. Without me, you'd be less of a person and more of an antisocial monster."

"Thanks."

Kellan using the term '*monster*' doesn't bother me the way it does when anyone else says it. And he's not wrong. Without him around, I probably would have truly become the monster they call me a long time ago.

I come out of the shower, a towel wrapped around my waist and rub at my hair with a second one. Kellan is sprawled on his bed, messing with his cell. His gaze lifts and scans over me, and a smile tips up his lips.

"Nice war wounds."

"Hmm?"

"Those little teeth marks covering your ribs. She's a biter, I see."

"Oh." I laugh. "Yeah, she bites. But that's okay, because so do I."

***

"Fuck." A thud joins the curse, and I lift my head off my pillow to search out the source of the sound.

Kellan is hopping around the room, dragging on jeans.

"Where's the fire?" I roll onto my back, yawning.

"It's almost ten. We've missed first class."

"What? Fuck!" I shoot upright and join him in scrambling for clothes.

We fight for the bathroom to wash and brush our teeth.

"You have art," Kellan tells me around his toothbrush. "Two-hour class, working on your sculpture. I'll come and grab you at lunchtime. I've set an alarm on your cell."

"If you see Ari—"

"She also has art, so it's unlikely I will. But if I do cross her path, I'll tell her to meet you for lunch."

We separate on the path outside the dorm. Kellan sets off at a jog toward the computer building, and I skirt around the outside of the gym to hit the side entrance that will take me to the room I'm using for my sculpture.

Pulling the dust sheet off, I step back and examine it. It's almost finished. I need to finish the monster's feet, where they're gripping the rock beneath him. His hands curving around the girl in his arms also need some final detail, as well as the wings spread out around them.

I run my finger over it, searching for sharp edges, then reach for my earbuds, tap play on my music and get to work.

The alarm on my cell goes off at the same time as the door swings open to allow Kellan inside.

"Lunch time already?"

"Time flies when you're having fun." He props his shoulder against the doorframe, hands pushed deep into the pockets of his jeans. His face is missing its usual smile.

"Everything okay?"

"What?" He straightens. "Oh, yeah. Just hungry. Ready to go?"

"Just let me clean up." I gather up the tools I've been using and drape the dust sheet back over the sculpture, then sweep up the floor.

Turning, I nod. "Okay, I'm done." I lock up behind us and walk with Kellan down the hallway and outside. "Did you see Ari?"

82

Arabella

There's still no sign of Eli or Kellan when I come down to breakfast on Monday morning.

Are they avoiding me?

Gnawing apprehension is twisting me into knots.

Why doesn't Eli want to see me? Is it because I didn't tell him about Zoey's diary? What if his plan is for it to be like before?

I don't want him to bully me again because he thinks it will protect me. That is not the reason I came back.

My head is a mess by the time the first bell sounds. I've hardly touched my breakfast because I feel nauseous. Pushing it aside, I head for first class.

I'm almost at my locker when a shoulder slams into mine from behind. Shoved into the row of lockers to my right, I hit them hard.

"Watch it, freak." Lacy snaps, walking past me. "I don't even know why the school has more security patrolling the dorm at night. No one wants a dirty skank like you."

Brad laughs beside her. "Maybe it's just to keep her in her room and protect the rest of us."

I move away from where I'm leaning against a locker, but Bret rests a hand beside my head, preventing my escape. "Ready to get down on your knees and worship my cock, yet?"

Garrett appears out of nowhere and shoves his friend away from me. "Dude, leave her alone."

My actions dictate how they see me. They've always judged me on how I behave.

Damaged. Broken. Victim.

I don't want to wear those labels anymore. I'm *not* ruined, I'm a survivor.

Gritting my teeth, I raise my chin. "Lacy told me there wasn't much down there to suck on. Sorry but I'm not interested, Bret."

Garrett shoots me a surprised look and then laughs while Bret turns cherry red. I note the fact he doesn't deny being with Lacy.

"What the fuck, babe?" Brad snaps.

"I don't know what the fuck she's talking about." Lacy's voice comes out shrill and high. "The only dick I've sucked is yours."

"Funny, that's not what Eli says," I call over my shoulder as I walk away.

Not waiting to see what happens, I slip into the classroom and take my seat.

Eli and Kellan don't turn up.

Dread settles and grows inside me.

Mrs. Winters arrives, and the class starts. Focusing on the class proves difficult, and I spend most of the time staring into space, my thoughts filled with where Eli could be. I'm so wrapped up in my head that I don't realize when the class ends until someone knocks into my desk.

Art is next, and after talking to the teacher, I head for the room I share with two other girls. My ballgown is waiting. I haven't worked on it for weeks. It's something I can lose myself in for the next few hours as I bring something beautiful to life. Something that the dares, the blackmail and the hatred directed at me from the other students can't ruin.

Eli

I don't see Ari when we first walk into the cafeteria, so I follow Kellan into the line for food. He frowns at me. I usually go straight to our table.

"I want to look at what cakes they have." My voice comes out defensive, and he snorts.

"Don't bullshit me. There's a better view of the room from here. Look in the far corner. That's her usual seat."

My eyes shift in the direction he nods toward, and sure enough, there she is. There's a tray of food in front of her, which she's pushing around the plate with a fork and a distinct lack of enthusiasm. I take a step forward.

"What about your cake selection?" Kellan's voice drips with humor.

"Fuck off."

His laughter follows me as I stalk across the floor. Students fall silent as I pass them, and I briefly wonder what they're seeing, how I must look. My gaze is focused on the blonde head in front of me. When I reach her table and my shadow falls over her, she raises her head.

Her eyes widen when she sees me.

"Stand up." I deliver the instruction in a clipped tone.

"Where—"

"Stand. Up."

Students are whispering around us. I know they're waiting for me to hurt her, to lash out, to humiliate her. When I smile, she turns pale and scrambles to her feet. Fear flashes across her face, replaced quickly by determination and defiance. She's ready to fight me, to do battle, and my tongue sweeps over my lips.

"What are you doing, Arabella?" I tilt my head and lift an eyebrow.

"I don't know what you mean. I'm just having lunch." Her eyes dart past me, and I'm certain she's looking for an escape.

I shake my head and tut. Before she can react, my shoulder hits her stomach and I toss her up into a fireman's lift. She shrieks, hands hitting my back. I give her ass a light swat with my palm.

Everyone is silent around us, staring as I stride across to my usual table, where Kellan is sitting and watching, shoulders shaking with his laughter.

Dropping Ari onto the table, I push her thighs apart and step between them, press two fingers beneath her chin to tip her head up and kiss her.

The room collectively gasps.

Her lips part beneath mine, and her hands lift to loop around my neck. I step closer, fingers threading into her hair so I can angle her head better. My tongue strokes over her lips, and I draw back slightly.

"That's better." I smile down at her.

"I thought you were avoiding me."

My smile fades into a frown

"Avoiding you? No. Why would I do that?"

She shrugs, looking uncomfortable. "I don't know. I just …"

"You let the fuckers get into your head," I finish softly. "The car got a flat. We didn't get back here until after midnight. Then Kellan wouldn't let me come and find you. We slept through the alarms this morning, so I went straight into art." I press another kiss to her lips. "I'm definitely not avoiding you." I kiss a path along her jaw. "In fact, after classes end today, I want you to pick out some clothes and stay with me instead of upstairs in your room."

"Really?"

I kiss the tip of her nose. "Really. I got used to having you in my bed." My smile broadens. "Quite liked waking up with my dick in your mouth, as well."

She turns pink. I laugh.

"As much as I am getting endless entertainment out of the gaping fish faces all around us right now, do you think you could hurry it along? Just tell the girl you love her, so I can eat my lunch." Kellan's words are loud in the silence of the cafeteria.

It's Ari's turn to laugh. A laugh that fades when I don't join in. I'm staring down at her, my tongue flicking at my lip ring. Her tongue snakes out to wet her lips.

"Eli?"

"I have something for you." Reaching into my pocket, I pull out a little black box and hold it out to her. "Two somethings, actually, but open this one first."

She frowns and takes it from me but doesn't open it.

"It won't bite."

When she lifts the lid, her lips part. The charm bracelet she lost all those months ago is nestled on the black velvet inside.

"Before you say anything, I didn't take it. I found it in front of Zoey's plaque just before spring break. I was going to give it to you during the week, but everything was so messed up, and I wasn't sure you'd believe me when I explained, so I didn't—" Her lips cover mine, cutting me off.

When she finally pulls away, she lifts a hand to stroke over my jaw. "Thank you."

I press my lips to her palm, then reach into my pocket again. "Second thing." I hold out a box similar to the first.

When she opens this one, her gasp is audible. A fine silver chain lays on the velvet, with a small padlock connecting the two halves. I reach up to touch the larger one around my neck.

"Just before my mom died, she gave me this. She explained that the padlock stood for security and safety. I never want you to feel anything but safe, Ari." I run a finger over her lips. "This is my promise. No matter what, you can trust me to keep you safe."

Her eyes are shining, wet with tears when she lifts her face to search out my eyes. "Why?"

My smile is faint. "Haven't you figured that out yet?"

She shakes her head.

"Because I love you. First as Sin, and then as Eli. And I'm done pretending I don't."

89

Arabella

Eli loves me.

I can't stop smiling. "I love you too."

He crushes me against him and kisses me fiercely. When we break apart, we're both breathing heavily. Nothing else exists but the boy in front of me. I'm still not sure if this is real or if I'm dreaming. I might splinter apart from the sheer emotion I'm feeling. After giving me such a scare moments ago, I'm stunned by his declaration.

I look down at the necklace. "Will you help me put it on?"

He takes it carefully out from its bed of velvet and fastens it around my neck. "There."

I stroke over the padlock with my fingertips. "It's perfect. I'm never taking it off."

Eli smiles. "I can't wait to see you naked with it on."

"If you're lucky, you might just get your wish tonight."

He kisses the end of my nose. "No more keeping things to yourself."

I clutch the boxes to my chest. "I promise."

"Good girl."

"Get a room," Kellan says. "Some of us are trying to eat."

It's enough to have reality filtering back. Shocked faces are staring at us from all around the cafeteria. Lacy's jaw is practically on the ground. Everyone looks stunned at what's unfolded between us.

I try not to laugh. Eli helps me off the table, then pulls me down onto his lap when he sits in his chair. "This, right here, is your place now."

I loop my arms around his neck, and he hugs me to his chest. "Are you sure this is a good idea?"

"I'm done playing their game, and so are you. We're together. I'm not going to lose you, Ari. If you're where I can see you all the time, they won't be able to force you to do anything."

"You're serious about me moving into your dorm room?"

"One hundred percent."

Kellan rolls his eyes. "Don't mind me. I'm just his roommate."

"If you don't want me—"

"Don't be ridiculous. Eli is right. Keeping you close is safer."

Eli's mouth finds the side of my neck, and kisses along it. "You can relax, Kitten. No more fear. No more being alone. You're exactly where you're supposed to be now."

I want to stay frozen in this moment forever. Eli has made a claim in front of the entire school.

I'm his.

He's mine.

I'm in the arms of the Monster of Churchill Bradley Academy, and there's nowhere else I'd rather be.

85

Eli

"What do you want to do?" We're walking across the grass to the dorm building after the final class of the day. "Go and grab your stuff now or wait until after dinner?"

"Let's do it now. Work up an appetite."

I stop on the path and pull her around to face me. "I can think of more entertaining ways to work up an appetite."

She aims a light punch at my shoulder. "Is sex all you think about?"

I widen my eyes. "I was talking about going for a run. You're the one with sex on the brain. You're going to wear me out. I've created a fucking monster."

"You absolutely were not!"

"Correct me if I'm wrong, but I'm pretty sure *you* were the one trying to get into my pants all week. I was the one having to fight to keep my purity intact."

Her jaw drops but she recovers fast. "Purity? *You*?"

I nod. "Absolutely. It was a constant battle to keep my pants on while a certain someone dry-humped me as often as possible."

She shakes her head. "For that, I should make you sleep alone."

I smirk. "You can try."

"Is that a challenge?" Her blue eyes are dancing as she looks up at me.

"You think you can hold out longer than I can? Baby, I've just denied you for an entire week. My self-control is unbreakable."

She tosses her head and sniffs. "I wasn't even *trying*."

"Sure." I grab her hand and start walking again. "Okay, you're on. Let's see how strong your willpower is."

"We need stakes to make it interesting."

A laugh bursts out of me, and I send her a sidelong glance. "Is that a competitive streak I'm sensing, Hellcat?

There's a smile teasing her lips, and the fingers of her free hand are toying with the padlock around her throat. It makes my entire body heat up. "What are we playing for?"

"You get my dick if you win."

"What do you get if you win?"

"Your pussy." I squeeze her fingers. "There are no losers in this game, Kitten."

"You can't have a contest without the loser needing to do something," she protests.

I push open the door and step back to allow her inside before me, then follow her into the hallway of the dorm building.

"Okay. If I win, you have to let me fuck you on the desk before a class tomorrow."

"And if I win?"

"I have to fuck you on a desk before class tomorrow."

"Eli!" She punches my shoulder again.

I stop, turn and back her against the wall, hands either side of her head. Schooling my expression into a blank mask, I lower my head until our lips are millimeters apart.

"If I win." I drop my voice to a whisper; one she recognizes as the lover she'd taken in the dark. Her eyes darken, lips parting. "I'll edge you all morning but won't let you come. Then I'm going to fuck you on your desk with no condom, and you'll have to sit in class full of my cum until it's over." I press a kiss to the corner of her mouth. "After class is over, you'll walk to the nearest restroom to clean up, and take off your panties. At lunchtime, you'll join me at my table and sit on my lap so I can play with your pussy while I eat lunch."

"What if I win?" Her voice is breathless.

"You won't, but if you do, I'll do whatever you want for a week." I smile and nip her bottom lip. "Rules of the game. Touching, kissing, teasing is all on the table. When you beg me to fuck you, I win."

"You'll be the one doing the begging." Her fingers slip under my shirt and stroke up my back.

"It's cute that you think you stand a chance." I step into her body, letting her feel how hard my dick is, and lick my lips. "Red or green, Hellcat?"

Her soft gasp at my question sends a shot of lust through my veins. "Green."

***

It takes four trips from her floor to mine to bring down everything she wants. We could have left it in her room, but she's worried someone might go into it again and destroy things. I can't argue with her logic. They've been in there before, and now we're openly antagonizing them.

I sprawl on my bed and watch as she puts her clothes away in my closet and dresser. I'm already regretting the challenge, especially when every time she stretches up, I catch a glimpse of bare creamy skin.

"You should do that naked," I suggest, and she glances at me.

My dick goes ramrod stiff when she peels off her t-shirt, leaving her in a sheer bra that leaves nothing to the imagination. I recognize it. It's one of the sets I bought for her while we were at the cabin.

"Are you wearing the matching panties?"

She pushes down the legs of her sweats and steps out of them, then turns to face me. My gaze moves over her, pausing on the nipples pushing against the material of her bra, and then down over her stomach to her pussy. There's a slight damp patch on the panties.

"You like being on display, don't you, Kitten?"

"You read my diary. You tell me." She goes back to unpacking.

I swing my legs off the bed and stand, then move up behind her. Placing my hands on her hips, I hold her still and press my dick against her ass, while I kiss a path over her shoulder.

"I think you still have too many clothes on." I drag down the strap of her bra. "Take the rest off." I open my mouth over the pulse beating in her throat and suck hard on her skin.

She moans softly, tilting her head and leaning back against me.

"I'm going to mark you, so everyone knows you belong to me," I whisper, moving to another spot on her throat.

My palm slides over her stomach and up to her breast. I brush my thumb over the hard little tip, then pinch it. Her arm lifts, loops around my neck and pulls me more firmly against her throat.

"Do you like that?" I bite my way up to her ear. "Are you wet? Do you want my dick?" I nip her earlobe.

"I can feel how hard you are." She turns and presses one hand against my dick. "Are you begging to fuck me, Eli?"

I grind my erection against her palm, and smile. "Not even close, Kitten."

Arabella

I stroke his cock through his sweatpants, the anticipation of feeling it inside me growing, and smile up at him. "Hmm, you're so hard."

Eli teases my mouth with his lips. "Does it make you ache? Do you want me buried inside you? All you have to do is ask me to fuck you."

I thrust my tongue into his mouth, and kiss him savagely, still caressing his hardness through the material. The second he deepens the kiss, I drop my hand and step away. "If you want my pussy, then you're going to have to beg for it."

Eli grins and shakes his head. "Not going to happen."

I move to the bed and bend over, giving him a view of my ass, and glance at him. "Are you sure about that?"

His eyes roam over me as I wiggle my ass at him. "It's tempting."

"You've never fucked me from behind before." I remind him. "You could fist my hair and make me scream your name,"

"Show me how much you want my dick."

The low, rough words send a shiver down my spine and my body heats up.

I drop down onto his bed and stretch out with my arms above my head. Arching, I push my breasts upwards in the lace bra. Eli licks his lips, grabs the chair beside his desk, and moves it so he can sit facing the mattress.

Does he want a show? I'll give him one.

I sit up and crawl toward him, positioning myself on the edge of the bed so I can spread my legs. I cup my breasts through my bra.

"You're not going to break me, Hellcat." Eli palms himself through his sweatpants

My hand trails down between my breasts, over my belly, and between my legs. I stroke along the damp scrap of lace. "We'll see about that."

Eli sits back and pulls his cock out from beneath the waistband of his sweatpants. "Is this what you want?" He strokes himself from tip to base and back again.

Rising off the bed, I hook my fingers in my panties and peel them down my legs. Once they pool at my ankles, I kick them aside and retake my seat, spreading my thighs again.

I meet his hungry gaze. "Is this what *you* want, Eli?"

"Play with yourself." His voice is husky.

I run my fingers through my soaked center, then push a single finger inside. Lust slides over every inch of me as Eli pumps his cock into his palm.

I pinch my nipple, dragging the material of the bra down until my breasts are free, and find my clit so I can rub it. "It feels so good."

He groans, hand picking up speed.

I lick my lips. "My pussy would be so much better than your hand. Just imagine sinking inside me."

I slip another finger inside me and slide them in and out. A nerve ticks in Eli's jaw.

A sense of power washes over me. I want him to lose control. To pin me to the bed and fuck my brains out after denying me all last week.

"Don't come," I moan, rocking my hips up to meet my thrusting fingers.

His eyes meet mine, his hand slowing down. "If you get to orgasm, then so do I, Hellcat."

I rub my clit harder, my breath stuttering in my throat. "You have to save it all for me."

Eli grips his cock, his attention locked between my legs. "Fuck."

My hips undulate against the mattress, I bite my lip. "Every inch of you is mine. I want all of it."

Having him watch me getting off is the hottest thing in the world. It's intense, and I've never felt as wanton as I do right now. My orgasm builds and builds, faster, sharper, until I'm right on the edge of tumbling over. My pussy clenches, and I come hard.

"Eli. Oh god! Eli!" I throw my head back, the sheer force of my release blinding me for a split second. Pleasure overwhelms me, leaving me a twitching mess.

87

Eli

Fucking Christ. I'm tempted to let her win just so I can put us both out of our misery. Gathering up the tattered edges of my willpower, I force myself to tuck my dick back into my pants, then crook a finger.

"Come here."

She slides off the bed and moves toward me, hips swaying.

"Give me your fingers." I tap my lips.

She lifts her hand and presses one finger against my mouth. I suck it in, licking the evidence of her orgasm off. "Another." She slides that finger free and replaces it with the second. I roll my tongue around it, flicking and licking, then slowly release it.

"When I've fucked you in class tomorrow and my cum is dripping from your pussy, I want you to wait until everyone is in the room and then dip your fingers into it, get them good and soaked, then lick them clean."

I wind an arm around her waist and pull her to stand between my legs. "I'm going to paint your body with it, rub it into your nipples, and over your lips so that every time you take a breath or lick your lips, you remember who's marked you." I lean forward and lick over one taut nipple.

"Eli." My name is a moan.

"Right here, Kitten. All you have to do is reach out and take me." I take her hand and press it to the front of my sweats where my dick is straining against them. "Climb on, take me out and fuck me. You know you want to."

Her hand flexes, *squeezes*, and then she steps away, her eyes narrowing. "*You* take it out and fuck me."

I lean back in my chair, and smile at her. "I can do this all night."

"So can I." She lifts her hands to cup her breasts, lifting them until her nipple brushes my lips. "We both know you're imagining how good it'll feel to be inside me. You want that, don't you? You want to pin me down, spread my legs wide and fuck me hard."

She turns away, walking back to the bed, and climbs on, giving me a flash of her pussy as she lowers her head to the pillows, keeping her ass in the air.

"Open your legs. Show me how wet you are. That orgasm you gave yourself wasn't enough, was it, baby? It didn't even take the edge off." Her legs widen, and I can see the arousal on her thighs.

Fuck. I'm not sure how long I can keep this going. Maybe she is going to win. My dick is aching with the need to be inside her. I shove a hand down into my sweats and wrap my fist around it.

"Are you wishing your hand was my mouth, Eli? Do you want to fuck my throat until you come?" She licks two fingers and reaches between her legs to stroke her clit. "Don't you want to fill me up, Eli? I'm right here, naked and wet and ready. My mouth, my pussy, my ass. What would you like? You can fill whichever hole you want. All you have to do is ask to fuck me."

Her legs spread wider, and she pushes her fingers into her pussy. Her hips rock against them. My jaw clenches.

Fuck.

"Use three fingers." My demand is rough.

She does, and moans at the sensation.

"Still not full enough, are you, Kitten? You need my dick to go deep inside you. To hit that spot only I can reach."

"My fingers … are doing … just fine." She pants the words.

"But you need more." My hand is stroking my dick in time with her fingers. "You want my tongue on your clit, my dick driving into your pussy, my finger in your ass. You want me to suck on your nipples. You want me to bite them while you claw at me. You want your legs wrapped around my waist while I drive you into the mattress."

"Eli … oh god … Eli."

"Say it."

Her hips are jerking, breath coming in small bursts. If she doesn't fucking beg soon, I'm not going to be able to hold out.

I stand, pushing my sweats down my legs and kick out of them. It takes me three steps to reach the bed. My palm strokes over her ass.

"Fuck your fingers harder. Add a fourth. Stretch yourself open for me." I bend to lick over her thigh, bite into her ass, and she whimpers. "Tell me to fuck you."

I reach between her legs and stroke a finger over her clit. Her hips buck.

"Oh god."

"There's no god here, Kitten. Just a monster. But if you ask me, I can answer all your prayers." I pinch her clit. She's soaking wet, her arousal dripping over my fingers. I coat them in her juices, then lean forward to press my finger against her lips. "Taste how much you want me, Ari."

Her tongue flicks out, licks over my fingertip. “Eli.”

“Tell me.”

I pull her fingers free from her pussy and flatten them to the mattress. “No more touching until you say please.”

“Nooo,” she moans. “I was so close. I need to come.”

“I can make you come. But you have to ask for it.”

I kiss a path down her spine, dip my tongue between her ass cheeks and down to her pussy. “You’re so wet, Kitten. So ready. Just think how much you want me. I’d slide right in and fill you up, just the way you need me to. Do you want me to pin you down? Pull your hair? Tell me you want to come on my dick. Does your pretty little pussy ache, Kitten? Does it need to be filled, owned, *worshiped*? I can give you that.” I palm her pussy, slide two fingers either side of her clit and spread her open. “Your clit is desperate to be touched, isn’t it, baby? Just one touch … that’s all it would take. Tell me you want me.”

88

Arabella

Clawing at the blankets, I can't stop shaking with desperate need. "I want … I want."

"Say it."

His touch is driving me mad. "No." The word leaves me on a whine.

"Fucking say it."

His hand vanishes from my pussy, and I whimper. A second later, something hard drives between the wet lips of my pussy. Eli's long, thick cock has my insides melting with the need to feel it claiming me, but he doesn't enter me as I crave.

"Give in." He grinds himself against me. "You know you want to."

I shake my head. "You say it."

"You're so goddamn stubborn." He glides through my wetness over and over.

My pussy is aching, desperate to be filled, and the emptiness tears a frantic moan from my throat. "I won't let you win."

"All we're doing is driving each other insane."

Eyes rolling back in my head, I rock back as Eli dry humps me. "Fuck me."

"Are you giving in?"

"No."

A hand comes down on my ass cheek, making me yelp. "You don't get my dick until you beg."

"You're such an asshole."

"You're the one who agreed to this challenge."

"You enjoy torturing me."

He thrusts slowly. "You're the one who started all this. I can do this all night long, keeping you on edge."

"So … so can I." I force the words out through a moan.

"Last week, I wasn't even trying to make you lose your mind."

"Liar."

"Kitten, you were the one desperate to have sex."

"So were you."

"I'll have you a babbling, horny, soaked mess beneath me in a few hours."

Hours.

Eli is playing for keeps this time. I'm going to explode if we don't have sex. That's all it takes for me to lose it.

"Fuck me. Please fuck me. Please, please, please."

"Finally, halle-fucking-luja." Eli snarls behind me, finds my entrance and slams into me hard.

I cry out and drop my head to the pillows.

"So fucking good."

"More." My demand is met with another wild shove of his cock inside me.

His hands grip my hips as he rams into me in short, sharp thrusts. It's feral and brutal, and I love every second of it. The way he fucks me is the mirror of how I've been feeling all week while he was holding back from doing no more than touching and kissing me. It's as if he's letting me know that he needs this just as much as I do.

He wraps an arm around my waist, pulling me back until I'm in a kneeling position on his lap. The position sends his cock sliding into me deeper, and my pussy flutters around his length.

He bites down on the side of my neck. "Who does this pussy belong to?"

"You." I pant.

"That's right, Kitten. Don't you ever forget that." He sets a merciless pace pounding into me over and over. He possesses me—*claims* me.

Reaching back over his shoulders, I tangle my finger in his hair. He captures my mouth with his, our tongues mimicking the thrust of his body into mine. We kiss and kiss, feral twists of our lips. Our movements shift, becoming more frantic and unsteady.

He fists my hair and pushes me forward until I'm on my hands and knees on the mattress again. I'm shoved forward along the bed as he pistons forward into me.

"I … Eli …" Gripping onto the blankets, I scream out his name as an orgasm rocks through me in intense waves.

Eli slams his hips forward, riding out my release, and then fucks me as fast and as hard as he can.

89

Eli

"I think we missed dinner." My fingers trace a lazy pattern up and down Ari's spine.

She's curled into my side, alternating between stroking over the tattoos on my chest and kissing whatever bare skin she can reach. "I'd offer to cook, but I don't think they would let me."

"I'll order something. What do you want?" I slide out from beneath her and sit up, looking for my pants.

"Did Kellan give you your cell back? I meant to ask you about that."

"Oh … fuck. I forgot." I spot my sweats on the floor, stand, and pull them on. "I had him pick us up a new phone each and set new numbers."

I scan the room until I spot the box with Arabella's cell in it. Walking over, I pick it up and toss it to her.

"Kellan confirmed there *was* a tracker on your other phone. They were using it to keep up with your location, who you were talking to, and what you were doing with your cell."

Her eyes are wide as they stare at me. "Really?"

"Open the box." I lean against the wall and fold my arms, my gaze on her face as she opens the box.

She laughs when she discovers the case her new phone is nestled inside.

"I had it designed for you. The drawing is mine." I push away from the wall and move back to the bed to sit on the edge.

"You designed it?" She echoes my words.

"I thought it was appropriate."

The case is black. On the back is a kitten with horns sticking up behind its ears. A tarnished halo hangs off one of them. Beneath it, the words "Fight Me" are written.

"Oh my god. I love it!" She throws herself at me, peppering my face with kisses.

Laughing, I lift her onto my lap and wind an arm around her waist. "So … food?"

"Are you sure security will allow it?"

"As long as I give them enough money, sure." I reach for my cell on the nightstand and flick through the various options. "What do you want? Pizza, burgers, Chinese, something else?"

"Burger, milkshake, and fries."

"You got it. Let me check where Kellan is and see if he wants anything." I tap into messages and send one to him. His reply comes through almost immediately.

`Kellan: Yes. Miles, too. Just order two of my usual. We'll be up in ten minutes. I assume it's safe and you're not going to blind my poor innocent eyes with naked shenanigans?`

`Me: Fuck. Off.`

`Kellan: Love you too.`

I stand, carrying Ari with me, and set her on her feet, then lightly pat her ass. "Better put some clothes on unless you want to stay naked and give Kellan ideas."

"Definitely not. That was a one-time deal."

"You didn't enjoy it?" I pull open my dresser and take out a clean t-shirt.

"You know I enjoyed it. I just don't want to do it again."

"A threesome was in your diary. You wrote about that a lot."

There's a long silence, and when I finally turn, she's staring at me.

"All the things you did as Sin … it was all stuff I wrote about … fantasized about. But you hated me, so why?"

I shrug. "I told you. I planned to use it to send you running from here, but the more tastes I got of you, the more I realized I couldn't do it. And then it became a point of just wanting to let you experience all those things."

I reach out and stroke a finger over her lips, down her throat, circle one nipple, and down further until I can slide it between her legs. "Like tomorrow, when I flip up the skirt you're going to wear and fuck you before math." I push my finger inside her. "You're going to ride my dick and have to muffle your screams. I'm going to make you come just before the bell sounds and the door opens to let Mr. Drake and the rest of the class in." I add a second finger. "Your body is still going to be clenching and pulsing and throbbing while they're taking their seats." I pull my fingers free, run them over her lips, then kiss her. "Just like you wrote about."

90

Arabella

Biting my lip, I squirm on my seat, my body still twitching from the orgasms Eli gave me. He did exactly what he promised. After waking me early and edging me with his mouth and hands, we'd left for class thirty minutes before it started. Then he'd fucked me on my desk, his hand over my mouth, smothering my moans and cries. I loved every second of it, especially when he'd bitten my neck.

I press my legs together, staring down at my textbook. I can't concentrate, every move I make reminding me that I'm full of his cum. I'm sure people are looking my way, checking out the marks and bites all over my throat. They're all over my body, not just where people can see them.

Eli is going out of his way to mark his territory. The hickeys on my neck are visible for all to see.

Does anyone know what we've done? Have they guessed he fucked me like an animal in the classroom before the bell had rung?

"Miss Gray, are you feeling well? You look a little flushed?"

Head snapping up, I meet the teacher's concerned stare. "It's just a little warm in here."

"Do you need to step outside for a moment?"

"No, Mr. Drake."

He frowns. "Speak up if you change your mind."

"Yes, sir."

The second his attention returns to the whiteboard, I glance in

Eli's direction. The look of approval shining in his eyes sends heat through me. He mouths the words 'good girl.'

After class is over, you'll walk to the nearest restroom to clean up, and take off your panties. At lunchtime, you'll join me at my table and sit on my lap so I can play with your pussy while I eat lunch.

Remembering his command, I tear my gaze away from his face and back to my book. We're back to playing games, and I like it. The anticipation and the thrill are a drug I've missed. This time, though, knowing that Eli loves me makes it all the sweeter. I reach for the little padlock dangling on its chain around my neck and stroke the pad of my thumb over it.

Maybe we're safe, and the nightmare has finally ended.

When I peek over at Eli a second time, Lacy is watching me through narrowed eyes. The look of pure hate on her expression sends my gaze back to my desk. It's enough to leave me shaken and dissolve some of the warmth coursing through my veins.

I keep my focus on the teacher and my book for the rest of the class. When the bell rings, I sit and wait for most of the students to filter out before me. I'm aware of Eli and Kellan still lounging at their desks. They're both playing with their phones, and neither of them look my way.

I pack away my things and hurry from the classroom, aiming straight for the girls' restroom. Locked inside one of the stalls, I peel off my panties. With Eli telling me what he planned to do, I'd had time to plan—packing wet wipes and a plastic bag to store my cum soaked underwear in. I clean up and flush the toilet, then straighten my skirt. I'm thankful Eli let me pick the knee-length and not the thigh-high one he'd teased me about. I'm less likely to flash anyone my bare pussy as long as I don't bend over too much.

When I unlock the door and step out, the smile on my lips drops away.

Lacy looks me up and down. "I don't know what your game is, but Eli Travers is mine."

I walk past her to the sink and wash my hands. "Last time I looked, your boyfriend was Brad."

"I thought you'd learned your lesson by now. You're nothing, Arabella. We rule the school, and you do as we tell you." Her lip curls.

A chill crawls down my spine at her words, so familiar and yet not quite the same. "Who's we?"

Is she the one behind the blackmail?

She snorts and flips back her hair. "Duh, the cheerleaders and the jocks. The *popular* kids. I don't know how you got your hooks into Eli, but it ends here."

I dry my hands and turn to her. "Why are you so interested in Eli?"

"I told you he's mine."

"Why?"

"He's always been mine. Brad ... He's a puppy. Eli is a tiger. I know which one I'd rather have in my bed."

I caress the hickeys on the side of my neck. "Eli is a beast in bed."

Her eyes narrow into slits. "You're going to dump him at lunch in front of the whole cafeteria. Make it painful and unpleasant."

"Are you serious?" My gaze slices toward the door of the restroom and back.

Lacy laughs. "Totally. It's not like he's going to be heartbroken.

Eli might have said the L word, but he could never love someone like you. He needs a queen like me."

Anger snaps through me, sharp and hot, obliterating the small voice of common sense telling me to be careful.

Who the fuck does she think she is?

I walk forward until I get right up in her face. "Eli is *mine*. He loves *me*."

The confidence in her expression falters, and she takes a step back.

"He can't keep his hands, mouth, or dick off *me*. I'm not dumping him for you or anyone else. And if you don't like that, it's your problem, not mine. You might think you're something special, Lacy, but you're not." I shove past her, open the restroom door and step out into the hallway.

Kellan and Eli are waiting for me a little further down. Eli's gaze meets mine, and I give him a shaky smile. The warmth in his green eyes makes my insides melt.

Lacy is wrong. Eli does love me.

His attention shifts to something behind me, and he frowns. It's the only warning I get. A hand slams into my back, shoving me forward into a passing crowd of students. I go flying, but one of the boys catches me before I hit the ground.

"You little bitch." Lacy's shriek echoes down the hallway.

As I turn, she comes at me with her nails. It takes a split second for me to realize she's going for the necklace Eli gave me. I lift one hand to protect it, and swing my other.

The crack of my palm across her cheek is loud in the sudden silence. "If you ever threaten me or try to touch me again, you'll regret it."

91

Eli

Kellan stops me, one hand on my arm, as I move toward Arabella and Lacy.

"She needs to do this alone." His voice is low in my ear. "If you rush in and rescue her every time she's targeted, it'll just make them more determined. Let her fight this battle, Eli. She's not weak. She just needs to figure it out for herself."

It takes every ounce of self-control I have not to shake him off when Lacy launches herself at Arabella. But my concern is unnecessary. Ari's hand flashes up and connects with Lacy's cheek in a loud slap, which echoes along the hallway.

"If you ever threaten me or try to touch me again, you'll regret it." The threat is delivered in a cool tone, and then she turns, eyes searching me out.

Kellan's hand drops and we both move forward to meet her. For a brief second, I look past her to where Lacy is standing, hand pressed to her cheek, eyes burning as she stares at us, then I shift my gaze down to Ari. I stroke a finger down her cheek, over her lips, then dip my head to kiss her, just a quick press of lips; otherwise, I'll end up dragging her somewhere private for more.

"I like it when my little Hellcat comes out to play," I murmur against her mouth, then straighten, so I can wrap my arm around her shoulders and tuck her into my side. "What was Lacy's drama?"

Her hand slides around my waist and squeezes my hip.

"Apparently, you belong to her."

"I do? I don't recall getting that memo."

"It's okay. I cleared up her misunderstanding."

I stop in the middle of the hallway and turn to face her. "Yes. You did. And I'm so fucking proud of you for it." I drop my arm from her shoulder and take her hand. "We've done the 'fuck me' part, you did the 'fight me' part, so I guess it's time for the 'feed me' part of the day." I lift her hand to my mouth and kiss her fingers, one by one. "Ready for me to play with my food?"

She turns scarlet. "You said at lunchtime. It's only ten."

"Lunch, mid-morning snack. What's the difference?" I shrug. "I'm hungry now." I tug her toward the doors which lead outside.

"You're hungry?" Kellan catches up with us.

I grin. Ari's cheeks darken further. Kellan rolls his eyes, then slaps my shoulder. "Fine. You go and do nasty things to your girl in public. I've got somewhere to be."

I swing my head to look at him. "Oh? Where are you going?"

He smiles. "Just a couple of things I need to do. I'll see you in English." He picks up speed and moves ahead of us.

I stare after him, flicking my tongue piercing against my teeth.

"Is he okay?" Ari's voice draws my attention back down to her.

"Hmmm? Oh … yeah." But I'm not convinced. He's up to something, I just don't know what it is. "Come on. Snack time."

***

Kellan doesn't show up for English *or* lunch. Ari checks our room when she goes back to put on a pair of panties for the rest of the day, and reports that he's not in there, either. When I text him to ask where he is, I get a winking emoji in reply.

Is he fucking around on Miles? I know he's not *with* the swim team captain, because he's sitting opposite me. Kellan has always been a bit of a free spirit where sex is concerned. I can't recall him ever being in a committed monogamous relationship. But I know from the way Miles reacted when he walked in on the three of us, that the swim captain isn't like that. He wants commitment, and if Kellan is getting his kicks elsewhere, then it won't be long before Miles walks away from him.

"Do you think whoever it is still texts my other cell?" Ari's voice is quiet.

Me and Miles both look at her.

"They don't know I have a new cell. What if they were texting throughout spring break? I feel like we're just waiting for something to happen. What if they think I'm just ignoring them?"

"I'll ask Kellan. He'll know if your cell has received any texts." Maybe that's what has him preoccupied. I know he's been trying to find a way to trace where the texts were coming from.

I pull out my cell again.

`ME: Where are you?`

`Kellan: Standing in the doorway, admiring how hot the three of you look.`

I look up and, sure enough, Kellan is leaning against the doorframe, thumbs hooked into the belt loops of his jeans and smirking at me. When our eyes meet, he pushes away and walks across the floor to drop down in a chair beside Miles.

"Hello, darling." He leans across to plant a kiss on Miles' cheek.

The swim captain doesn't even react, which is a huge step for him.

"Are you out in the open now?" Ari asks, her gaze darting between them.

"I haven't made a big announcement or anything," Miles replies. "But I've stopped pretending. If my parents find out …" He shrugs. "It's going to happen at some point."

"And I'm so rich, he can just be my trophy boyfriend if they cut him off," Kellan adds. "I'll pay all his bills, as long as he keeps doing that thing with his tongue that I like so much."

Miles' cheeks turn pink. Ari laughs softly and reaches across to place her hand on top of his. "They're as bad as each other, aren't they? It's no wonder they're friends."

"No, we're friends because Eli walked in on me trying to hang myself about a week after I got here and drove me insane until I agreed not to kill myself." Kellan's tone is light, playful, and I can see from the expression on both Miles' and Ari's faces that it takes a moment or two for his words to sink in.

"He was doing it wrong," I say into the silence, my voice similar to Kellan's. "The knot he used would have come undone the second he stepped off the chair. All he would have gained from it was a sprained ankle."

"Eli spent an hour lecturing me on how I should research the correct way to make a noose. Told me I lacked commitment to my plan. Then described what would happen if I was successful. Finding out you piss and shit yourself turned me off the idea. I don't want anyone's last memory of me to be that I shit my pants." He grins at me. "Could you imagine? Those jeans cost four hundred dollars."

"I offered him an old pair of sweats to do it in, but he declined. Decided he'd rather annoy me for the rest of the school year instead."

"Anyway, it's a good thing I changed my mind; otherwise, Eli would have joined me a few years later."

We share a look, then Kellan grins. "Look how shocked they both are." He bumps Miles' shoulder with his own. "It was years ago. Neither of us are suicidal these days." He winks at me. "Eli leans more toward homicidal."

92

Arabella

"Was that story true? The one you told us yesterday about Kellan?" I haven't been able to stop thinking about how they joked about it.

Eli's lips pause on their path along my neck. "Yes."

We're making out in one of the empty storage rooms, skipping the last class of the day.

I curl my fingers in the hair at the nape of his neck and pull him closer. "You're a good friend."

Eli hums against my skin, the vibration going right down to my pussy. "He puts up with me."

"He loves you like a brother."

"I know, and I love him too." He licks my neck, hands busy teasing my breasts.

"Don't let Miles hear you say that. He might get the wrong impression." I wrap my legs tighter around his waist, drawing him against me where I'm sitting on the bench. "Did you ask him about the messages?"

"Messages?" He sounds distracted.

I smile. "From my old phone."

"Didn't get the chance."

"Not last night?"

"I was kind of busy fucking you into the mattress last night." He growls and bites down on my shoulder.

The sharp pain makes me gasp and my eyes roll back. "You need to ask him."

"Don't worry about it."

I dig my nails into his back under his hoodie and claw them down his spine. He moans.

"After everything that's happened, I can't help but worry about it."

His breath ghosts against my lips, but he stops short of kissing me. "They would have found a way to contact you by now. There have been no notes in your locker. No unknown messages to your new number."

"It's only been three days since we got back from spring break."

Eli silences me with a kiss, tongue plunging into my mouth. He cups my cheeks, savaging my lips until my toes curl.

He rips his mouth away from mine. "Fuck, Ari. What are you doing to me?"

A rustling noise and foil tearing is followed by him flipping up my skirt in the dark. A hand touches the heat between my legs and pushes my panties aside. I clutch his shoulders, and moan as the tip of his cock invades my pussy. He doesn't stop until he's seated as deeply as he'll go. My inner walls clench around him, and I savor the way his cock feels inside me.

He drops his head to my shoulder. "Let's stay like this forever."

"I know you're just trying to distract me." I moan as he thrusts slowly in and out of me.

"This is not a distraction."

"We were only going to make out. You don't want me to think about the texts."

Eli's hands move to my hips. "Kellan is handling it."

I kiss and nip my way up to his jaw. "I want to know what's going on."

"It's not your concern."

I exhale. "Eli—"

His pace doesn't change, thrusting in and out in languid, torturous movements as he fucks me. "All you need to think about is graduating and coming all over my dick."

I dig my fingernails into his ass, pulling him deeper inside me. "You can't use sex as an excuse not to tell me anything."

"It's not an excuse."

"I'm not going to let you keep me out of the loop."

Eli's grip tightens roughly around my hips. "If I don't tell you, you don't really have any choice."

"That's not fair."

"Kitten, after everything you went through, I don't want to see you getting hurt all over again."

I swear I can hear a smile in his voice, but it only fuels my irritation. "I'm stronger than I was before."

His movements pick up speed, making the bench creak beneath me. "I know you are, but that doesn't stop me from wanting to protect you."

I close my eyes, losing myself in the pleasure building inside me. "You can't protect me from everything."

"Maybe not, but I can from this."

"Maybe I'll just ask Kellan myself."

He pauses, mid-thrust. "Ari—"

"No." I cut him off before he can try to order me around again.

"You're not hiding things from me. You made me promise to be open and honest. That goes two ways."

Eli swears under his breath and starts to fuck me again, this time pumping into me fiercely. Wrapping my arms around his neck, I bury my fingers in his hair. He's angry, and I can feel every inch of his frustration in the way he takes me. He doesn't like my decision, but I'm not going to let him talk me out of it. I need to know everything. He needs to learn that he can't keep me wrapped up in cotton wool, like something fragile and delicate.

My inner walls clench around his length, my orgasm claiming me. His mouth finds mine, swallowing my cry as I come undone in his arms.

He growls against my lips, pushing his cock inside me as far as my body will allow, as he finds his own release. Our ragged breathing is heavy in the dark of the closet.

I hug him tightly. "I'm glad we could have this talk."

He gives a soft laugh as he pulls out of my body and steps back. A second later, light explodes into life above me. Blinking fast, I try to dispel the black spots dancing before my eyes. When my vision finally clears, Eli is rolling the used condom off his cock.

"We'll talk to Kellan together." He ties a knot in it, and tucks himself away in the front of his sweatpants. "Okay?"

I ease myself off the bench and lower my skirt. "Deal."

"Don't think you're always going to get your own way, Kitten."

Running my fingers up his chest, I glance up at him through my eyelashes.

"Don't be grumpy with me. You know I'm right about keeping

me in the loop. You're already with me every second of the day."

Eli rakes a hand through his hair. "And yet you're still worrying about it."

My playful mood dims. "Of course, I am. They punished me before for not doing what I was ordered. They hurt Miles. Went through my things, stalked me, taunted me. Even with you and Kellan at my side all the time, the thought of them still watching me leaves me sick. I lived with this for months, Eli. My fear of it won't just magically disappear."

His gaze drops from mine. "Ari—"

The last bell rings out from the hallway outside.

"We should go and get dinner. I'm hungry." Not waiting for him to finish what he was about to say, I open the storage closet door and step outside into the empty hallway.

93

Eli

"Ari's asking questions."

Kellan looks up from the laptop he's taking apart. "About what?"

"Whether we've made any progress on who's behind the texts."

He scratches his jaw. "What did you tell her?"

"That we'd talk to you."

He makes a show of peering behind me. "I don't see her."

"Kell." His name is a growl.

"You can't keep her protected forever, but okay. I'll tell you what I know, and you can decide what you want to share with her. Where is she?"

"Out on a run with Miles. I was banned from going along." My lips twitch. "She seems to think I might drag her into the woods and have my wicked way with her."

"Is she wrong?"

"Maybe not. Still don't like it, though."

"She'll be fine with Miles." He pushes the laptop to one side. "Okay, the texts are coming from somewhere inside the school. So that rules out anyone that isn't at Churchill Bradley."

"How do you know? There's no way of tracking the location of a cell number."

"No, but the timing of the texts and the instructions in them make it clear that whoever was sending them could *see* both you and Arabella."

"They had a tracker on her phone."

"Yes, but they didn't on yours, and they knew if you were in the same room or not." He stands and crosses to the mini refrigerator in the corner of the room, stoops, and takes out two bottles of water. Handing one to me, he sits back down. "*But*, and this is the weird part, the texts aren't always from the same person."

"But they come from the same number."

He nods. "I ran the phrases through a piece of software that flags up similarities in sentence structure. It uses algorithms to—" He looks at me and laughs. "Your eyes are glazing over. Okay, let's just leave it as it's clever, and given enough data, it can tell if two pieces of text are written by different people. I didn't have enough data for it to tell me for sure … until spring break."

"What happened then?"

"She stopped responding to their texts." He pauses for a mouthful of water. "See, *that* brought out the primary person behind this whole thing. During spring break, they wanted her to carry on goading you. Stupid things like break into your bedroom at home, destroy your sketchbooks, slash your clothes. Damage stuff in the house and blame it on you. When she didn't respond, they started threatening her."

"But she didn't see the messages."

Kellan nods. "And neither of you were where they expected you to be."

"In the Hamptons."

"That's right. And then it took another turn. Threats to climb through her bedroom window, reminders of what they did to her in the dorm when they tied her up. The wording changed, became more aggressive when they discovered neither of you were there. One of the texts demanded to know where she was, where *you* were. And *that* narrows it down further. Because it means they were local to the house and know where you live."

"And now?"

One side of his mouth lifts. "I replied to one of the texts on Monday, pretending to be Arabella. I told them I left the cell here and didn't get any of their messages, but that it was over and that she wasn't going to do what they wanted anymore."

"So why haven't they retaliated yet?"

"Because she … *I* … am still talking to them. I have them convinced that she's with you just so she can break your monstrous little heart and destroy you as payback for the shit you've done to her. It's eased them off a little. They're waiting and watching to see what happens."

"And while that's going on …"

"They're leaving more and more clues about who they might be. They're here in school. They share classes with you both, which makes them seniors. And …" He licks his lips. "I'm pretty sure it's the same person who killed Zoey."

I stiffen. "Why?"

"Zoey's diary. The things they wanted her to do are so similar to the texts Arabella has been getting. All targeted at alienating you. Her last entry talks about going to the cemetery because her anonymous texter wanted to meet and talk and explain why they needed her to do these things."

"But no name?"

He shakes his head. "Zoey was sure it was someone male, though.

She made a note in her diary about the way they phrased things and said it was definitely a masculine way of speaking."

"So, what's the next step?"

"To get them to the point where they want to meet and explain themselves."

Arabella

"Come on, Bella."

Jogging along behind Miles, as we hit the tree line, I try to keep up. "Slow down."

The shadows stretch with the setting sun, casting everything in sepia tones as nighttime draws closer.

Throwing a look over his shoulder at me, he changes his speed to match my own. "Sorry."

"Are you sure you want to do a lap of the cemetery?"

"We're safe together."

I keep my breath steady as my feet pound over the dirt path. "Has Kellan said anything to you about my old phone?"

"No. Why?"

"I want to know what's happening."

"I'm sure Eli will tell you."

My attention shifts to the gates of the cemetery, which loom up ahead as the bench comes into sight. "I'm not so sure."

"Kellan has been very distracted lately."

"I thought he was spending more time with you."

Miles shakes his head. "Not as much as I would like."

A movement at the corner of my eye snaps my attention toward the trees on my left. Pace faltering, I catch sight of a face peeking out from behind a tree.

"There's someone—" Before I can finish, Bret emerges from his hiding place.

Miles stops beside me as Kevin, Evan, and Jace also appear. "Hey. What's up, guys?"

"Did you think we wouldn't find out, Cavanaugh?" Jace sneers. "That someone wouldn't see you with your little boyfriend."

Miles stiffens beside me. "Guys, please."

The note of fear in his voice makes me grab his hand, and I tug him backward away from them. "Who he's seeing doesn't have anything to do with you."

Bret takes a step toward me. "Shut your mouth, Gray."

"No. Leave him alone."

Evan shakes his head and grins. "Not until we're done with him."

They don't want to talk; they want to cause pain. Is it because Miles is gay? It's the only thing that makes sense. The fact that he's been hiding it and was caught sneaking around with Kellan must be fueling their hate.

I squeeze his hand tight. "Run."

Miles doesn't have to be told twice. He takes off beside me, legs pumping to keep pace with my mad dash. Shouts erupt behind us. Pounding feet chase us along the path back toward the school. Heart in my mouth, adrenaline coursing through my veins, I don't look back.

"Fuck. Fuck. Fuck." Miles chants as the end of the trees comes into view.

"Don't stop." I pant. "We're almost there."

Bursting out of the trees and onto the grass, we head toward the dorm building at a run. The few students milling around glance in our direction. Garrett is beside the main door to the dorm when we reach it. He takes one look at my face and then gestures at the door.

"Go. Get inside."

"Did you know about this?" I glance back as the group of jocks emerges from the trees.

"They didn't tell me about the ambush. I heard Tina mention it to Linda. I was coming to warn you."

Miles grabs my arm. "Bella, come on!"

We hurry into the building and make our way to Eli's room. I throw open the door without knocking, shove Miles inside, then close and lock it behind us. Eli's head lifts from where he's sitting, a sketchbook on his lap, and frowns at us.

"Is that Bella?" Kellan calls, poking his head out of the bathroom door.

"Some of the jocks just tried to ambush us." My heart is still beating wildly in my chest.

Discarding the sketchbook, Eli uncoils from the bed. "Are you okay?"

I nod. "They were after Miles."

Kellan steps out of the bathroom, a towel wrapped around his hips. "Did they hurt you?"

Miles doesn't resist when Kellan pulls him into his arms.

"No, Bella got me the hell out of there. I should have known something like this was going to happen."

"It's not your fault that they're all fucking homophobic."

"I've lied to them for years."

"Out of fear," Kellan reminds him.

Eli takes my hand and leads me toward his bed. Sitting down on the edge of the mattress, he pulls me onto his lap and hugs me tightly. "I knew I should have gone for a run with you."

I loop my arms around his neck, and press my face into the side of his neck. "I told you they weren't after me."

"I spoke to Kellan about the texts."

I stiffen. "Without me?"

Eli's lips brush my cheek. "Don't be angry with me, Kitten."

Miles and Kellan are talking quietly, but all my focus is on Eli.

I shift on his lap and palm his cheek to pull his head around to meet his gaze. "What did he say?"

"He checked the phone. They were contacting you over spring break and weren't happy when you didn't respond. It's someone in our year. At least, that's his guess. They live in the Hamptons too."

"How do you know that?"

Eli's smile is faint. "Because they checked to see if we were at the house."

The thought of them peering in through my bedroom window makes my skin crawl. "Oh my god."

"Don't worry." His arms tighten around me. "Kellan messaged them pretending to be you and explained you'd left the phone at the school over the break. They keep leaving clues he's been following."

"You mean he's close to finding out who's behind it all?"

Eli nods. "Yes, Kitten. I think he is."

95

Eli

Miles stays with Kellan in our dorm room that night. Once the lights are out, I can hear them talking quietly across the room.

"Do you want me to go down to your room and grab some stuff?" I roll over to face Kellan's bed. "You don't have to go back there."

"Thanks, Eli. I'll see how it goes during class tomorrow."

"Well, if you need me to … I'm more than happy to remind them why they've been scared of me for the last four years."

Warm lips press against my back, and hands slide around my waist, dipping down. I catch Ari's wrist before her fingers find my dick.

"We have company, Hellcat. I don't think Miles wants to see us fucking tonight."

"I don't mind watching," Kellan's voice sounds through the darkness, then he grunts.

"Miles just hit you, didn't he?"

Ari buries her face against the back of my neck, and I can feel her body shaking as she laughs.

"Get some sleep. We'll figure it out tomorrow."

They go back to talking quietly to each other, and I shift around so I'm facing Arabella. She scoots closer, burrowing into the warmth of my body.

"How are we supposed to act normal tomorrow? They chased us through the woods. Who knows what might have happened if they'd caught up."

I stroke my hand down her back. "I doubt they would have done anything. They just wanted to scare him. I'll take a walk down to his room in the morning and see if Bret wants to face me."

I wind an arm around her waist and roll onto my back, pulling her onto me. "Get some sleep, Kitten."

***

There's no answer when I bang on the room Miles shares with Bret before classes start the next morning. I don't know if that's because Bret is hiding inside or because he's left for breakfast early. I shout that I'll see him in class, just in case he *is* hiding, and then catch up to Kellan, Ari, and Miles, who are on their way down for breakfast.

None of the boys who chased Miles are at their table when we walk into the cafeteria, but the cheerleaders are there. Lacy's eyes are on Ari as we walk past her and her friends. Ari's head turns, and her lips tilt up into a smirk. A moment later, she stops, steps in front of me and pulls my head down to kiss me.

I don't resist, cupping the back of her head with one hand and tangling my tongue with hers. When we break apart, Ari's eyes drift to Lacy again, and that smirk returns. I laugh softly, link my fingers with hers, and we continue to our table. Kellan and Miles join us a few minutes later, two trays stacked high with enough food for the four of us.

"Nice territorial display," Kellan says to Ari as he takes a seat.

She shrugs. "I'm tired of being scared of what they might do."

A shadow falls across the table, and all four of us look up to find Garrett hovering.

"Mind if I join you?" He doesn't wait for an answer but slips onto the seat on the opposite side of Ari. "Are you okay?"

"What the fuck do—" My growl is cut off by Arabella's hand on my arm.

"Garrett got us into the dorm building last night. If he hadn't been there, they might have caught up to us."

I lean past Ari to glare at him. "Seems like a huge coincidence that you just happened to be there."

He shakes his head. "I heard what they planned and was on my way to warn you. Then I spotted Bella and Miles running out of the woods."

"Eli." Ari's voice is soft. "Garrett was the only one who tried to help me the last few weeks before spring break."

I know what she's saying. He supported her while I was busy trying to break her. My tongue slips out to toy with my lip ring. His face still holds remnants of bruising from the beating I gave him, but he holds my gaze steadily.

"I'm sorry for—" I wave a hand toward his face. "I wasn't thinking straight."

"I figured that out. At the time, it was fucking scary. I thought you were going to kill me."

"If Kellan hadn't turned up, I might have. I think that was the point." I look at Kellan and hike an eyebrow. He shrugs. I turn to Ari. "Do you trust him?"

She doesn't even hesitate. "Yes."

"What about you, Miles?"

He looks from Garrett to me, and then at Kellan. "I don't know," he says slowly. "He was just as shitty to Bella as everyone else for a long time."

"Yeah, I was," Garrett replies.

"So why did you stop?" Miles nails him with a glare.

Garrett's eyes shift to me. "I already told Bella this. When you hit her …" He shakes his head. "It was too much. It crossed a line. Before that, everything the guys were doing … it was harmless teasing. But you—"

"*Fucking harmless teasing?*" I snarl.

"No, I know. Looking back, it was anything but that. But at the time, I thought everyone was just fooling around. You know, pranking the new girl." He sighs. "But it got too dark. It stopped being funny. And then you were getting worse, more dangerous, and she looked ill. When you hit her," he repeats the words softly. "It was like blinders fell off my eyes, and I could see how awful people were being to her."

"You didn't stop being friends with them, though." Miles sounds angry.

"They're idiots, but yeah, they're still my friends."

"What about now?"

"What do you mean?" Garrett frowns at the swim captain.

"They're fucking homophobic. They were going to attack me yesterday."

Garrett's frown turns into shock. "That's not—Miles, no. That's not why they were coming for you."

"What other fucking reason is there?"

Garrett looks around the table, then returns his attention to Miles. "Miles, we've known you're gay for years. No one cares. We just didn't say anything because *you* didn't say anything. They were chasing you yesterday because they think you've chosen Eli and Kellan over them."

96

Arabella

Miles is pale. "You *know*?"

Garrett shrugs. "I mean, a couple of us started to think you might be bi after you hooked up with Bella."

"He did that to keep Jace off my back," I tell him. "He was coming on strong, and I didn't like it. So, they were after Miles because he's friends with us?"

"Who the fuck cares what they think," Eli growls from beside me. "We aren't their entertainment."

"Just watch your back." Garrett's words are directed at Miles. "I've never seen them this pissed off before. I wouldn't stay in your room with Bret—"

"Is he the one fueling this?" Kellan cuts in, his attention on the jock's face.

Garrett nods. "He's angry at his roommate's defection to the other side."

My chest tightens, anger sparking. "We aren't on sides. This isn't a war."

"That's not how Lacy and Brad see it."

"This is insane." I dart a glance at Lacy and her friends. "I wish I'd never been her roommate."

"You might have ended up with someone else if she hadn't requested to take you."

Eli freezes beside me and eyes the jock. "Lacy *asked* to be

Arabella's roommate?"

"According to Linda."

Garrett's words send my thoughts into a spin. "But why? No one knew who I was when I first arrived."

"Lacy did." His voice is low and serious. "I overheard her telling Maggie that she knew you were being sent to the school by Eli's dad. His marriage to your mom was all over the Country Club before you even arrived."

"So, it wasn't a coincidence," Eli says. "Her ending up in Zoey's old room was planned from the start."

Garrett frowns. "What does Zoey have to do with anything?"

Kellan smiles tightly. "Nothing."

I kick him under the table and nod at Garrett. *Tell him.*

Narrowing his eyes, he shakes his head. *No.*

Eli takes my hand and squeezes it gently in a warning. *Trust Kellan.*

They don't want Garrett to know about the texts or how everything is linked to Zoey's death. Do they suspect him even after I've told them I trust him?

"Shit."

Miles' mutter sends my attention to the cafeteria door. Bret, Kevin, Brad, Jace, and Evan are standing there. The stares they give us are chilling. Brad's lips twist with a look of disapproval.

Eli moves his hand around the back of my chair as he leans back. "They aren't going to do anything. Not with us all sitting here."

Miles swallows hard. "Are you sure?"

Eli's hand plays with the end of my ponytail. "Positive. Are you staying or going, Garrett?"

The other jock hesitates for a split second. “Staying.”

“You sure? You’ve seen how they’ve treated Miles because of our friendship with him.”

Brow furrowing, he searches my expression, his mouth tight. “You’re right, Arabella. We aren’t on different sides. I want to be your friend, and if I want to sit with you, then real friends wouldn’t turn on me for that decision.”

The group of jocks move to join the cheerleaders at their table. As soon as they sit down, Lacy starts whispering to her boyfriend. A thick tension fills the cafeteria, the students around us glancing up uneasily as if they sense it too.

Kellan wraps an arm around Miles’ shoulders and places a kiss on his cheek. “I think we should go and move your stuff into our dorm room.”

“Agreed.” Eli’s tongue flicks out to play with his lip ring.

“I can help. We’ll get his things moved quicker with the five of us helping before Bret comes back,” Garrett offers.

I remain silent as we all rise from the table. I take Eli’s hand as we walk toward the door. The sensation of being watched burns into a spot right between my shoulder blades, but I don’t glance back.

Even with Eli’s reassurances that we’re safe because he can remind them why they all fear him, I can’t shake the horrible sense of foreboding that’s weighing down on me.

97

Eli

We have everything out of Miles' room and in ours before the bell rings to signify the first class of the day. When we reach the room for math, Mr. Drake is already in there, but tension is thick in the air as we take our seats. I purposely slow down when I reach Bret's desk and hold his eyes as I move past him, a small smile tipping up one side of my mouth. His throat moves as he swallows, and his eyes dart away from mine.

The group of jocks are the first out of the room when the class ends, but Lacy and the cheerleaders linger. I grab my bag and Ari's, take her hand and walk across the room, only to stop when Lacy steps in front of us.

"Whatever she's doing to keep your attention, I can do it better." Her gaze moves over the bites I've left on Arabella's throat. "You like to mark your prey, but why stop at just using your teeth? I know you like knives, Eli. I'd let you use one on me."

"Because I drink the blood of my victims, right?" My voice is dry.

"I'll do anything you want." She runs her fingers up the front of my shirt.

I brush her hand off me, and glance down at Ari. "What do you think? Do you want to play with her, Kitten?"

"I'm not gay," Lacy says before Ari can speak.

"You said, you'd do anything I want. What if I want to give you to Ari as a pet?" I glance around, looking for Miles. "Do you still have that collar and leash I gave you?"

"Probably. Somewhere."

"Lacy here wants to be our new pet."

"No, wait. I never said that."

"You said, *anything* I want. I want to give my girl here the chance to pay you back for all the shit you've done to her."

Lacy's cheeks turn red. She takes a step back, smile dropping away. "Fuck you."

I look her up and down, then smile. "Not in this lifetime." I guide Arabella past her and out into the hallway.

"Do you want to grab your art stuff and bring it to the room I'm working in?"

Arabella shakes her head. "The two girls I'm sharing a room with aren't cheerleaders. I've never had any problems with them before. I think I'll be okay."

"I don't like you being alone."

"The room I use is off the main art studio. Mr. McIntyre is in there the entire time. I won't be alone. I won't leave until one of you come and meet me."

"I'm in the main studio, so I'll be nearby," Miles adds, coming up beside me. "Garrett is in computer studies with Kellan. The only one who'll be alone is you."

I laugh. "I'll be fine."

"What if more than one of them corners you."

"I'd like to see them try."

"Don't be too overconfident, Eli," he persists. "I think you should stay in the room until we come for you."

I look from him to Ari, who's nodding. "You agree with him?"

"He's right. You are the only one who will be alone."

I reach out and cup her cheek. "Okay. I'll stay there until you come for me. I'll keep the door locked and text you once I get there." I kiss her lips, savoring the contact, then draw away. "Deal?"

She curls her fingers into the front of my shirt and drags me back to her. "Promise me you'll stay there until we come for you." Her voice is fierce.

I run my nose along hers. "I promise."

We part ways outside the main building, and I turn toward the building where my sculpture is while the others go in the opposite direction to the art studio and computer science department. As I skirt the side of the gymnasium, someone calls my name. I turn just as Jace runs around the corner. He skids to a stop a few feet away.

"I need to talk to you."

"Fuck off."

"Seriously, Eli. I *need* to—"

"If you don't turn around and disappear, the beating I gave you back home will look like fucking foreplay." I take a step toward him.

"Eli—"

"One." Another step puts me within arm's reach.

He tenses, fingers curling into fists.

"Do you want me to break your arm in such a way you'll never play football again?"

"Fuck. Fine. Don't say I didn't fucking try!" He spins and runs back the way he came.

98

Arabella

We spend the evening locked away in the room. I'm snuggled into Eli's side, and only half listening to the movie that's playing on the TV. Miles and Kellan are on the other bed making out. Four pizza boxes are strewn on the desk next to empty drink cans.

They're taking the threat on Miles seriously, and it makes me wonder if something has been said in the texts on my old phone. When I asked Kellan to show me, he'd just smiled and shook his head.

Is there something happening I don't know about?

A moan sounds over the noise of the TV, and I peek across at the two boys. Kellan has his hand down the front of Mile's sweatpants, their tongues tangling together.

"Enjoying the show, Kitten?" Eli murmurs.

Cheeks heating at being caught, I tear my attention away from them. "What? I …"

His hand smooths up over my stomach and cups my breast, thumb stroking over one hard nipple.

"So, you're a voyeur as well as an exhibitionist."

"No."

He chuckles at my denial. "It's okay to admit you are. There's nothing wrong with it." He pinches my nipple.

"Fine." I bite his shoulder gently. "I find it hot watching two guys making out."

"You mean seeing *me* make out," Kellan calls across the room. "Don't worry, Bella. I know the truth."

Miles groans. "I'm not having sex with you while they watch."

"Counter-offer." Kellan sits up. "What about them having sex while *we* watch?"

"I don't want to watch Arabella having sex, thank you very much."

Kellan laughs. "Killjoy."

Eli drops a kiss on the top of my head. "Looks like no one is getting fucked this evening, then."

"We didn't think this through, did we?" Kellan flops onto his back.

"Two couples in one room. With one person who isn't into being watched … No, we didn't." Eli agrees, sounding more amused than irritated.

"I'm sorry. I just … it doesn't …" Miles stammers.

Eli waves a hand. "It's fine. Not everyone is comfortable being naked around each other the way me and Kellan are. And seeing Ari naked isn't going to do anything for you, since she doesn't have a dick."

"We could put a sock on the door when the room is being used," Miles suggests, face bright red as he rolls onto his side to face us. "Some of the jocks do that when they have a girl over."

"Or how about you and I go find somewhere tomorrow night to spend alone?" Kellan spoons his boyfriend from behind and kisses his neck. "Tomorrow is Friday. Once the last class is over, we can drive into town and book a room at the hotel."

Miles' expression lights up as he turns in his arms. "Really?"

"We can come back Saturday after breakfast."

"I'd love that."

Eli yelps when I pinch his side. "Why didn't you think of that?"

Capturing my wrist, he pretends to scowl down at me. "You want to go and have sex in a hotel again?"

"I remember the last time was pretty fun."

"You mean when I stripped you, then fucked you on the balcony in full view of the parking lot?"

I hook my free arm around his neck and pull him down for a kiss. His lips capture mine as he presses me down onto the mattress, the weight of his body pinning me in place.

"Oh my god, please wait until tomorrow." Miles grouses a second later, before a pillow hits us.

Laughing against Eli's mouth, I break the kiss. "Okay, fine. I'm sure we can all wait that long to get what we want."

"Speak for yourself." Eli's fingers dip beneath the sheets to find my pussy.

***

"Come on. I'm hungry." I tug on Eli's hand and pull him along the hallway until we're out of the dorm building. Miles and Kellan are beside us, holding hands.

"Slow down." Eli laughs. "I'll make sure you get breakfast. I promised to feed you."

I stop so I can turn around and curl my arms around his neck. "And fight me and fuck me."

"Tonight." He drops a kiss onto my parted lips, his tongue darting between them quickly. "All night long, my little Hellcat."

"It's always the quiet ones," Kellan murmurs to Miles. "They look innocent, but under all the shy exterior, they're horny sex fiends."

I roll my eyes. "Like you and your boyfriend aren't excited to be getting some alone time too."

Lifting their joined hands, Miles kisses Kellan's knuckles. "It's the best thing in the world right now. I honestly can't wait for tonight."

I swear, for a second, Kellan blushes.

The jocks are already in the cafeteria when we arrive. Lacy, Tina, Maggie, and Linda are in the line for food. I half expect them to cause trouble, but apart from a few daggered glares, they stay on their side of the room. Garrett joins us when he arrives for breakfast. He doesn't seem bothered when his friends glower at him. Jace is doing his best to bore a hole into the side of Eli's head. It's creepy as fuck, but Eli just ignores him.

Lacy directs a few snide comments at me once we're in class, but all I do is smile. I'm not alone anymore. Not isolated. No matter what she says, she can't shake my feelings for Eli. She's just a jealous bitch.

The rest of the day passes in a blur.

Eli makes me go to dinner in the cafeteria, even after Miles and Kellan leave early to drive to town. He lingers over coffee, and I'm sure he's doing it on purpose. By the time we go up to his room, I'm buzzing with anticipation.

Eli kicks the door closed behind us. "Alone at last."

Leading him to the bed, I push him down onto the mattress. "I've been waiting for this all day. Get naked."

He licks his lips. "Miss Gray, are you trying to take advantage of me?"

I straddle his lap and slip my hands into the front of his sweatpants so I can curl my fingers around his cock. “Oh, I’m going to do very bad things to you, Mr. Travers.”

He drops his head back against the pillow and closes his eyes. “Promises. Promises.”

I plan to make tonight one that Eli will remember forever.

99

Eli

My cell chimes just as I reach the chapel. Stopping outside, I pull it out.

Kitten: Where did you go?

Me: Kellan asked me to meet him in the chapel. He said he found something and wanted to show me. I didn't want to wake you.

Kitten: I'm coming to meet you. I want to be there, too.

I blow out a breath, but don't try and talk her out of it.

Me: Find Garrett first. Don't walk through the woods alone.

I pocket my cell and push open the doors to the chapel.

"Kell?" I step inside. "What was so mysterious that we had to meet here?" When he doesn't reply, I call his name again. "Kellan?" My voice echoes around the interior.

I pull out my cell and check the message he'd sent me, just in case I misread it. But no, it clearly tells me to meet him here.

"Kellan, stop fucking around." Moving deeper inside, I head up the aisle between the rows of pews, and then I spot him. I roll my eyes. "Really?"

He's sprawled out on top of the altar, head turned toward me. He watches me, a slight smile on his face, as I move closer, but he doesn't speak.

"What did you find? Something else of Zoey's?" I sigh when he still doesn't reply. "Enough with the dramatics, just fucking—" A sound to my left cuts me off, and I tilt my head searching it out. It sounds like a muffled shout.

"Is someone else here?"

There it is again. There's *definitely* someone else in here. Ignoring Kellan, I walk along one of the pews, listening for the sound again.

"Kellan, who else is here?" He ignores me, and his lack of response makes the hairs on the back of my neck stand up. "Kell?"

I start to turn back to my friend, when what sounds like a muffled shout echoes around the chapel. I stop and spin.

There.

I turn and walk toward the pulpit on the far left of where the altar is. A shape comes into view, and it takes me a second for my brain to catch up with what my eyes are seeing.

"*Miles*?" I pick up speed and drop to my knees in front of the swim captain. There's a gag wrapped around his mouth, and his hands and feet are tied together. "What the fuck?"

He mumbles something, eyes widening, and he jerks his head forward. Something cold touches my throat, and I freeze in the middle of reaching for the gag.

"What the fuck is it about you that makes people want to be your friend? No matter what I fucking do, you won't fucking leave."

The voice is recognizable, yet there's something off about it.

"Everyone believes you're the fucking monster I called you. They believe you do all the bad things that happen around here. But they *still* fucking talk to you. They all want to be your fucking friend."

The blade he's holding taps lightly against my throat. "Stand up."

Miles is shaking his head, trying to say *something*, but I can't figure it out.

"It'll be okay. Just hold tight," I tell him, then stand.

"Fucking slowly." The tip of the knife digs into my throat, just above my jugular.

Holding my hands out to my sides, I ease upwards.

"You know, I've asked everyone what it is about you. Why they fucking like you so much. They all deny it, but I can see it in their eyes. They can't hide it from me. All the girls want you; all the boys want to *be* you. I've done fucking everything you have. I'm *better* than you are, but all I hear is Eli, Eli, *fucking Eli*."

"Can I turn around?" I know who it is, but I'm finding it hard to believe. I need to see to be sure.

"No, you fucking can't."

"Okay." I keep my voice calm. "So, what do you want to do?"

"I want to fucking get rid of you, that's what I want to do. You had everything. A happy family, friends, parties. Everything I should have had. I thought after your mom died, they'd finally see how you didn't deserve it. But they all wanted to help you, be your friend. Poor *fucking* Eli. He lost his mom. *Wah wah. Boo hoo.* Not even looking like a fucking monster stopped people from wanting to be your friend. I had to be on the go fucking constantly, making sure everyone saw you as a monster. But Kellan wouldn't listen, and then Zoey decided that she liked you more than she liked me."

The blade digs deeper. "She refused to admit she was fucking you. And then she stopped playing the game, so I had to punish her."

The words send a chill down my spine.

"Did you kill Zoey?"

"No, *you* did! I asked her to meet me, but she refused to listen. All she wanted to talk about was how you weren't the person everyone thought you were. That you were sweet, and nice, and kind. I couldn't let her tell people that, could I?"

"So, you killed her."

"No! You fucking killed her because you have to be the one in control, the one that owns everything. It's all your fucking fault. And then you had to make it worse, didn't you? You weren't supposed to fucking *like* the little bitch. You were supposed to hurt her. And then everyone would see what I see."

"Ari—Arabella?"

"I did everything, fucking *everything,* to set up that scene. You attacked her, attacked Garrett, and you still didn't get sent away. You're still the fucking golden boy of Churchill Bradley." His voice changes, turns flat. "So, I did what I had to do."

My tongue snakes out to lick dry lips. My heart is fucking hammering against my ribs. My eyes are glued to Miles, who is shaking his head, tears spilling down his cheeks.

"What did you do?" I force the question out. I already know the answer. Deep down, I'd known it the minute I stepped inside, I just didn't want to acknowledge it.

"You didn't protect your knight, Eli. You should have protected your knight."

"What did you *do*?" I need him to say it. I don't want him to fucking say it.

Miles' shoulders are shaking with the force of his sobs. I absently note the blood dripping from his wrists as he twists them against the rope, trying to get free.

"I took your knight out of the game."

Something hits me from behind and sends me crashing into Miles. By the time I regain my balance and spin, he's gone. My gaze darts to the altar where Kellan is lying. He hasn't moved, hasn't changed position.

I don't want to go any closer. Don't want to see the proof of what I already know, and my feet drag against the stone floor, inch by inch, until I'm in front of him. There's a lump in my throat. My vision is blurry. I can't focus.

With a shaking hand, I reach out and press two fingers to the pulse in his throat.

"Kell?"

Nothing.

"*Kell*!" I shake him. His head rolls back and forth. "Kellan, fucking wake up." My hand slides down his chest, and against his ribs. "Kellan, talk to me. Kell? Don't do this. Please don't do this." I dip my head and rest my forehead against his. "Please, Kellan. Please talk to me. Don't do this. Please don't do this. Wake up."

100

Arabella

"Are you sure he said the chapel?" Garrett scans the trees.

I check the message on my phone. "That's what he said."

As the stone building comes into view, I see no sign of anyone. I'm not sure why Kellan asked Eli to meet him out here, but it must be important. I'm angry that Eli left me sleeping instead of waking me. If he'd told me, we could have come together.

A voice shouting breaks the silence from inside.

"Stay here," Garrett orders.

I ignore him and run toward the door, not listening when he calls after me. Rushing up the steps, I burst into the chapel and stop dead in my tracks. Eli is standing at the altar, shouting and shaking the boy sprawled on top of the stone.

Kellan's eyes are open, but he's not moving. The light spilling in from the stain-glass windows paints them both in a rainbow of colors that's both beautiful and macabre.

Why isn't he moving?

Eli shouts Kellan's name, his voice breaking, pressing his forehead to his friend's. Every single movement is frantic and driven with desperation. My attention moves to the red covering his hands.

Blood.

Eli has blood all over his hands. Why is there blood on his hands? The longer I stare, the more into focus the scene comes. Kellan's top is covered in red … in blood.

This can't be real.

"Eli?" My voice is barely a whisper, my lips feel numb.

"Oh my god." Garrett's shocked voice beside me snaps me from my daze.

Together, we move as one toward them, rounding the altar to get to Kellan. Eli's gaze is locked on the unmoving boy, and he doesn't acknowledge either of us when we stop beside him.

Garrett touches Kellan's neck, searching for a pulse. When his eyes meet mine, they're full of anguish, and he shakes his head.

Lips trembling, fighting against tears, I wind my arms around Eli's waist. "Eli." My voice shakes. "Eli, he's gone."

"No! No!" He snarls the words and shoves me away from him. "Shut your fucking mouth. He's not gone."

I reach for him again and hug him from behind. "Baby, we need to call someone. We need to tell them he's here."

Twisting, he thrusts me backward, his eyes wild. "Shut up. Shut up! You're lying. Kellan is not gone. He's *not* gone."

I don't try to touch him again. "I'm so, so sorry."

Garrett releases a shaky breath, his phone in his other hand. "I'm calling security."

I nod. A noise distracts me, and I search through the murky dimness until I find the source. A pair of tear-stained eyes are staring at me bleakly, and it takes me a second to register that I'm seeing Miles.

I hurry over, crouch down in front of him, and rip the gag out of his mouth. "Who did this? Who did this?"

Bowing his head forward into my chest, he sobs hysterically. I wrap my arms around him, my tears finally spilling free to drip down my face. I run my hands over every inch of Miles, searching for wounds but find none.

Behind me, I can hear Garrett arguing with Eli, who's shouting at him to leave Kellan alone.

That he'll wake up.

That he's just resting.

That he's not dead.

How did this happen? How did we get here?

Yesterday we'd been happy, and now we'd woken up and walked straight into a nightmare.

I kneel on the dusty stone floor and hold Miles as he weeps. He tries to talk, but nothing he says makes sense. Leaning back, I carefully untie the rope around his wrists, grimacing when I see the bleeding welts it's left on his skin.

"Is he okay?" Garrett's voice is low and anxious. "We should have help arriving soon."

I sniff, wipe my eyes and suck in a deep breath, trying to get my emotions under control. "I think so. You ... are you sure Kellan is—" I can't say it, my throat locking up.

He nods. "I can't get through to Eli."

"Let me try again." Rising unsteadily, I scrub the wetness from my cheeks, leaving Garrett to comfort my other friend.

Eli hasn't moved, cradling Kellan's face, shoulders hunched and shaking. "Kell … get up. Come on. Please, just get up."

"Please, baby. You have to let him go." My voice wobbles, as I touch his shoulder.

"No! Never! You hear me? Never. He was pretending to be you. He was trying to find out who your blackmailer was. He shouldn't be here. He shouldn't fucking be here."

He doesn't even look at me, throwing out one hand to drive me away. The force is enough to send me backward into the nearest pew. His words are like spikes in my chest. Collapsing down onto the seat, my heart breaks as I watch my boyfriend desperately trying to bring his best friend back to life.

Kellan is gone. It should have been me, not him.

Eli blurs before my eyes as fresh tears spill free. My throat is tight, I can't breathe, can barely *see* through my tears.

Shouts come from outside, followed closely by a dozen security men charging into the chapel. Garrett intercepts them and informs them of what we've found while I return to Miles' side. Slumping down beside him against the stone wall, I wrap my arm around his shoulders. He leans into me and rests his head on my shoulder, still crying quietly.

Two of the security men move to talk to Eli, but he just shakes his head when they tell him to come away from the body. They share a look and reach for his arms. He turns on them like a wild animal, swinging his fists, snarling, and snapping his teeth. It takes four of them to physically drag him, kicking and screaming, away from Kellan's body.

Garrett stands by, watching. Whatever strength that has been keeping him from breaking is finally reaching its limit. Tears fill his eyes, and he crumbles to his knees, succumbing to shock and grief.

I can't stop shaking, chilled right through to my bones with my own emotions. Silently, I beg the universe to press rewind to last night.

I want to go back.

To stop before this moment can happen and shatter all our lives.

"Evan," Miles whispers hoarsely in my ear. "It was Evan who did this."

101

Eli

"Kell!" My eyes snap open.

"Shh. Just relax." A female voice, one that is vaguely familiar, sounds next to my ear. "Lay back. Stop struggling."

"Where's Kellan?" The words come out as a rough bark.

There's a beat of silence. "Your father is on his way."

"*Where. Is. Kellan?*" My gaze zeroes in on the nurse leaning over me.

She looks away. "The police are at the scene now. They'll arrange for him to be taken—"

"He's been *left* there?" I try to sit up again but can't go further than sitting up. Glancing down, I discover I've been handcuffed to the bed. "What the fuck?"

"You were out of control." A new voice. I swing my head around and spot Garrett standing by the door. "They're shutting the school for a few weeks and sending everyone home."

"Where's Evan?"

Garrett shakes his head. "No one can find him."

I yank on the cuff holding me in place. "I need to go back to the chapel."

"The police have it cordoned off. There's a detective waiting outside to speak to you. Do you feel up to it?"

I rattle the handcuff. "Don't have much fucking choice, do I?"

"I'll let them know."

He disappears out of the door and is replaced by an older man who flashes his badge at me.

"Detective Parker." He moves closer to the bed. "How about I remove those?" He flicks a finger against one of the cuffs around my wrist.

"Please."

"Your name is Eli Travers, right? I've been informed that Kellan Fraser was your closest friend. Would that be correct?" He removes the handcuffs and clips them to his belt.

My heart falters in my chest, and a heavy wave of nausea rolls through me. "Yeah."

"Can you talk me through what happened?"

"He texted me to meet him. I … When I got there … he … I …" I squeeze my eyes closed. "I'm sorry, I can't," I whisper.

"That's alright. It's okay, Son. If you're not ready, we can talk another day."

"I'm taking him home. You are more than welcome to come and see him in a couple of days."

"Dad?" I hate the way my voice breaks at the sound of his voice. "Dad, I tried to save him. But I was too late. I couldn't bring him back. I couldn't—"

"It's okay." Arms envelop me, and I breathe in the familiar scent of my dad's cologne. "Let's get you out of here. The car is outside. Elena and Arabella are waiting."

Something churns in my stomach. "Ari … Is she okay?"

"Shook up. Upset. Let's just get you guys home, okay?"

"I need to go back to my room. There's something I have to get."

"They've locked down the school."

"I'm going to my room." I twist around and place my feet on the ground, then stand.

Another wave of nausea threatens. The image of Kellan lying on the altar flashes through my mind, and I sway, pressing a hand to my mouth.

"Eli?"

My dad calling my name is the last thing I hear before I lurch for the bathroom and throw up.

102

Arabella

"Are you okay?"

Looking toward the front of the car, I meet my mother's gaze. I rest my cheek against the cold glass of the door window.

"I'm fine."

"It's okay not to be."

I want to scream and shout. I want to tear the school apart, find Evan and demand to know why he's done all these things.

Why did he kill Kellan? Why did he take one of my friends away?

My bottom lip quivers. "How am I supposed to feel? One of my friends is dead."

"Angry, confused, sad."

I screw my eyes shut and sigh. "Guilty?"

She shifts on the front passenger seat, making the leather creak. "This was not your fault."

An image of Kellan on the altar and the raw pain on Eli's face flashes in my head.

"You don't know that. Kellan is dead because of me," I say the words softly, knowing if I say them any louder, all the emotions I'm holding in might just rip me apart.

"Bella, open your eyes."

I shake my head.

"Sweetheart, look at me." This time her demand is firmer.

I meet her gaze. She searches my face, her expression serious.

"You're not responsible for what happened."

Yes, I am. Kellan had that phone because of me. He was talking to the blackmailer because of me. He shouldn't have been at the chapel. He shouldn't be the one who's dead.

My head aches with all the thoughts I can't switch off. "Is Miles okay?"

"The police took him to the hospital under armed guard. He'll be protected."

"I still can't believe Evan was responsible for all of this."

"Was he one of your friends?" There's a note of curiosity in Elena's tone.

I frown. "No, I mean, I guess he was in my circle when I was hanging out with the cheerleaders. He was always so quiet. He followed one of the other boys around all the time."

"You don't know why he snapped?"

I shake my head. "I think Miles knows, but the police took him before he could tell me."

She offers me a sad smile. "You're safe now, Bella."

I don't return it, unable to shake the coldness that's been hanging over me since the chapel. "Am I?"

"He's eighteen, alone, and on the run. The authorities will catch him in no time."

I wish I had her confidence. There's no way Evan did all this on his own. He must have had help.

Who? The other jocks? The cheerleaders? Teachers?

My head spins with the possibilities.

"Everything is going to be okay," my mother continues. "Once we have both of you home, you'll see."

A hysterical little laugh rises in my throat. "Do you think that's going to fix all this? That we'll be back to normal in a couple of weeks? Eli held his *dead* best friend in his arms. There was so much b-blood." My voice wobbles and my eyes burn. "Ev-everything's bro-broken."

A sob bursts from my chest, and I bury my face in my hands. Shaking, my heart breaks all over again. I cry, all my sorrow and anguish pouring out with my pain.

Images hit me one by one.

Kellan kissing Miles. Kellan laughing. Kellan smiling. Kellan holding me when I had a panic attack. Kellan sitting beside me when I'd been all alone. Kellan teasing me. Kellan dancing with me.

Kellan ... Kellan ... Kellan.

He's gone, and he's not coming back.

Arms envelop me, and I blindly go into them. Wrapping my arms around her waist, I sob against my mother's shoulder.

"I've got you, Bella. I've got you," she croons into my hair. "Let it all out, honey. We'll get you both through this."

Her gentle words just make me cry harder.

They can't fix this.

Nothing will.

Eli has lost his best friend, and there's nothing I can do.

And, after today, I might have just lost Eli too.

103

Eli

I move quietly around my dorm room, avoiding Kellan's side as much as I can. I'm not ready to deal with that, with seeing the things he's left scattered around. My dad is a quiet presence behind me, standing in the doorway while I pack up my sketch pads, pencils, and my favorite clothes. I don't see anything belonging to Arabella. She must have already been back to pack her things.

Once I'm done, I turn to finally look at Kellan's side of the room. There's something I need to get. I know where he hid it, I'm just not sure I can do it. But I need to, in case anyone comes in while we're away to clear out his things. I don't *think* they will. My dad said that he's requested the room is locked up until he or someone he sends can come to clear it out, and the school agreed.

My gaze moves over his bed, the discarded laptop in pieces on the table and then to his closet. Sucking in a breath, I cross the room and throw it open.

"Eli?"

"There's something I need to get." I crouch and pull out a box, flip open the lid and check the contents, then seal it closed again, and straighten. Tucking it under my arm, I grab the suitcase I've packed and move to the door. "Okay."

There's a lump in my throat stopping me from saying anything else, and the soft click as my dad closes the door behind me makes me flinch. We don't talk on our way down the stairs and along the hallway to the main doors. There are other students milling around, and I have brief glimpses of red eyes, crying, and whispered words as I pass them. I don't stop or acknowledge anyone, keeping my attention focused solely on putting one foot in front of the other until we are outside.

My dad's black sedan is parked in front of the doors, with the trunk open. I toss in my suitcase, place Kellan's box beside it, then move around to the side of the car. The door is open, waiting for me to climb inside, like the gaping black abyss inside my chest is waiting to swallow me whole.

Digging a hand into a pocket, I pull out my earbuds and push them in, then flick through the music on my cell. A moment later, 'I'm ok' by Call Me Karizma fills my ears. I take in another steadying break, then slide onto the seat.

My eyes connect with Arabella's, and something lurches inside me. I turn away. I can't do it. I can't speak to her right now. I am barely keeping it together in front of my dad. If I hear the pain in *her* voice …

I swallow, forcing down the lump that's rising further up my throat, and stare out of the window. The sound of a car door slamming, followed by the engine roaring to life, sounds over my music, and then we're pulling away from the school.

Away from the events of the past twenty-four hours.

Away from Kellan.

Arabella

"Here we are," Elena announces as she opens the front door of the house.

She's trying too hard. Her fake attempt at happiness only turns my stomach. I've had four hours of Eli ignoring me, pretending like I don't exist. While he's lost himself in his music, I've been going crazy in my head, reliving the moment I found him and Kellan over and over.

I wheel two of my suitcases into the main hallway and leave them by the wall. The maids rush past us to help Elliot and Eli with the rest of our bags.

Elliot walks in with a couple more bags. "How about some lunch? You both must be starving."

Eli doesn't reply. His earbuds are still in, and his attention is on anything but me. He clearly doesn't want to be around me. He's dealing with things in his own way.

Alone and shutting me out.

Does he blame me? Does he hate me?

I give his dad a weak smile. "I'm not hungry."

Elena gently touches my arm. "Did you eat breakfast?"

"No. I can't face food right now."

"Sweetheart, you have to eat something."

I move to the stairs. "I'm going to my room."

"Arabella."

I ignore my mother's call and take the steps two at a time. I don't bother with my bags. Everything in them is a reminder of Kellan. I'm still reeling from everything that's happened, and I'm not sure when I'm going to stop.

Quiet voices talk below me, but I don't pay attention to what they are saying. All I'm focused on is escaping. I reach my room and open the door, slip inside it, and rest against the wood.

Now that I'm finally alone, the silence closes in on me. Sorrow drowns my brain, and a painful breath catches in my throat.

Don't think.

I wipe a hand over my eyes, blinking hard to keep back the tears, and step away from the door. Digging out my cell, I open the conversation I have with Miles and send him a text.

`Me: How are you doing? I'm here if you want to talk.`

I wait for a beat, but there's no reply.

Maybe he's resting? Or he just doesn't want to talk after what happened.

I drop the cell onto the bed and glance around my room. The restless urge to keep moving drives me to my closet, where I stare at the half-unpacked boxes. I grab the first one and pull it out. Kneeling beside it, I lift the lid and pluck the books out to stack them on the floor. I sort through them, putting them in order before transferring them to the empty bookshelf by the wall. When the box is empty, I move on to the next one. I've just finished with the third box when there's a tap at my door.

"Come in." My voice sounds flat, empty of emotion.

Elliot's head appears around the door, and he steps inside. "I brought you a sandwich. Cheese and tomato. And a cup of tea."

The thought of food makes me feel nauseous.

I spare him a glance before returning to the contents of the box in front of me. "Thanks."

He places the tray he's carrying on my desk by the wall. "I see you're finally unpacking. Better late than never, right?"

I cradle my music box against my chest and carry it over to the bookcase.

Elliot watches me, his expression troubled. "If there's anything you need, Arabella, all you have to do is ask. Your mother and I are here for you both."

I swallow past the lump in my throat. "Eli needs you more than I do."

"My son has locked himself in his room and won't talk to anyone."

"He's hurting. Kellan … it's still raw."

He sighs. "I know that. We've … had a hard time communicating since his mother died. After my heart attack, things started to change for the better. Now … I'm frightened I might have lost him for good this time."

Just like I've lost him.

How do we find our way back from here?

I draw an unsteady breath into my lungs, and return to my boxes. "I'm sorry. I … I need to get this done."

Elliot studies me for a long silent moment, then nods. "Keeping busy? I did the same thing when my first wife died."

Our eyes meet and hold, and I'm sure I see a flash of understanding in his gaze. As if he knows that if I stop, I'm going to fall apart all over again, and I just can't handle that right now.

He clears his throat. "I'll leave you to it. We're hoping you and Eli will join us for dinner this evening."

Kneeling, I unwrap a snow globe from my box. "Maybe."

His footsteps move across the room and then halt. "We might not have been the best parents in the world to either of you, but you and Eli are not alone, I promise."

The door clicks shut. I hunch my shoulders, grief hitting me in a wave.

Don't think. Don't feel. I can't stop moving.

I refocus on the box in front of me.

Eli

It's been two days since I left Churchill Bradley, and four days since I left my best friend, cold and lifeless, on the altar in the chapel.

Four days.

Ninety-six hours.

Five thousand, seven hundred and sixty minutes.

Like you worked out that math for yourself. Kellan's voice is a dry whisper inside my head.

"Of course, I didn't. I asked Google." The sound of my own voice surprises me and I open my eyes.

I'm lying on my back on the floor in my bedroom, surrounded by empty beer bottles and half-smoked joints. Pages torn out of my sketch pad litter the carpet. Sketches of Kellan, of the chapel, of Miles, and Evan.

I've spent the last two days drunk and high, sketching the scene from Saturday feverishly over and over, trying to get all the details right. I have to guess how Evan looked since I wasn't facing him, but I could hear him. His voice should have *told* me, warned me what he'd done.

Why hadn't I fucking realized sooner?

"Eli?" My name is followed by a tap on the door. "Detective Parker is here. Do you think you could come down and talk to him?"

I grope around the floor, lifting bottle after bottle until I find one with some beer left in it and lift it to my lips. Once it's empty, I drop it and push to my feet. The room spins, and it takes me a couple of attempts to reach the door. Squinting, I take a guess at which of the three doorknobs is the correct one and make a grab for it. I'm wrong, but my knuckles hit the right one, so I adjust my aim and clutch at it, then pull open the door.

My dad is standing in the hallway. He sighs when he sees me.

"What?" I reach deep inside and pull out a smirk.

"Nothing. The detective is in my study. Do you want to take a shower and change first?"

"Nope." I pop the P.

Stepping out of the room, I stagger past my dad and walk down the hallway. I manage to mostly stay in a straight line. The stairs present a minor inconvenience, and I stumble down at least five of them before regaining my balance.

"Eli." My dad's hand curves around my arm, stopping me from diving headfirst down the final few steps. "If you're not ready to do this …"

"I'm fine." Maybe if I say it often enough, I will be.

"You don't have to pretend."

"I'm not." My voice is clipped. "You said your study?"

He sighs again but doesn't try to change my mind. He reaches past me to open the door to his study and walks in, leaving me to follow.

"Detective Parker, can we make this quick? I don't think my son is really in the right—"

"Have you found him?" I push past my dad and nail the detective seated beside the desk with a glare.

"Not yet. I need you to talk me through what happened when you went to the chapel. Do you think you could do that for me?"

"Sit down, Eli." My dad waves to a second chair and skirts around the desk to sit.

I flop heavily onto the seat he indicated and stretch my legs out in front of me. "I got a text from Kellan asking me to meet him …"

***

I step out of the study, pulling the door closed behind me. A quick glance up and down the hallway tells me no one is around. My shoulders sag, and I lean against the wall and close my eyes.

I managed to keep it together through the whole interview with the detective, describing what I walked into, everything Evan said to me, and then discovering Kellan's body. My eyes are burning, my throat is raw, and I want nothing more than to retreat to my room and crawl under the sheets to hide away.

But I can't. Talking to the detective has reminded me that there are things I need to do. I suck in a deep breath, push away from the wall and open my eyes … just in time to see Arabella walk around the corner.

Fuck.

I haven't seen her since the car ride back home.

She stops when she spots me, and we stare at each other. Her eyes are red rimmed, her face pale. I think she might have lost weight. She's discarded the rebellious goth look she's been using and reverted to her yoga pants and hoodie outfit. Her hair is up in a ponytail and her face is bare of makeup. Not that she ever needed makeup to look pretty.

"Eli."

The anguish in her voice twists my stomach into knots. I can't comfort her, not right now. Not when I can't even comfort myself. I can't smile and tell her everything will be okay. I can't assure her that Evan will be found.

I can't fucking do anything.

All I can do is lower my head and stride past her without speaking because, on top of everything else, I can't bear to see the pity in her eyes when she looks at me.

Arabella

Rawness stretches his features taut, and the pain I'm carrying inside me screams out in response. He looks pale. His eyes are hollow and empty. His hair is messy, and he's lost weight in his face. The t-shirt and sweatpants he's wearing are crumpled, and it doesn't look as though he's showered this morning.

I tried knocking on his door yesterday, but he didn't answer.

"Eli." I can barely get his name to leave my lips.

His head drops, and he walks past me without a word. It's as though there's an invisible shield around him, keeping everyone at bay.

I want to comfort him. Seek my own relief in his arms, but I don't know how to reach him. We're islands apart, and the gap between us is only growing.

My heart aches at the rejection. Touching the padlock hanging around my neck, I have to force my legs to keep moving forward. I knock on the study door and enter at the sound of Elliot's voice.

"Ah, Arabella." Elliot smiles. "This is Detective Parker. He has a few questions for you."

"Okay." I close the door behind me and take a seat. "Have you found Evan yet?"

The detective shakes his head. "No, ma'am."

"It's been days! Surely you must have some idea where he is?"

"His family hasn't had any contact with him. He hasn't gotten in touch with any of his friends—"

"Then you need to put more manpower into this," Elliot cuts in. "Eli and Arabella might be eighteen, legal adults, but they're still just *kids*. They need to feel safe."

"We're doing everything we can." Detective Parker assures him, his tone level and calm. "Ma'am, I'd like you to tell me what happened when you reached the chapel."

I've been trying not to think about it, and now he's asking me to relive the nightmare all over again. I lower my gaze to the floor.

"If you need a moment, I can wait."

How much did Eli tell them? Does his dad know that we were together? That we've been dating for a few days? That I've been having sex with my stepbrother?

"No, it's fine." My voice comes out in a croak. "I … I texted Eli to see where he was, and he told me Kellan had asked to meet him at the chapel."

***

Forty minutes later, I slip out of the study, emotionally drained and sick to my stomach. The detective had made me go through the events over and over. He wanted to know where Eli had been standing. How Kellan was positioned. If I'd seen Evan. Every word, every single detail, was pulled from my memory until I'd been stuck in the moment. The threat of a panic attack ended the interrogation when Elliot stepped in. Making my way unsteadily along the hallway, I walk up the stairs.

They haven't found Evan. Where could the bastard be?

The thought plagues me as I head back to my room. Music is blaring out from behind Eli's door, a heavy rock song where the singer is screaming out the lyrics.

I slam my bedroom door shut and pull my cell out of my pocket to text Miles.

`Me: They haven't located Evan.`

He hasn't answered any of my messages, but I've kept on sending them anyway. I continue to type as I drop down onto the bed.

`Me: The detective I talked to said he hasn't been in contact with his dad or any of his friends. How much do you want to bet one of them is lying?`

`Me: He was the closest to Jace. I wonder if he knows where he is.`

I chew on my lip, staring up at the ceiling. Maybe Elliot could tell me where his house is?

`Me: I might visit him and ask him.`

A text pops up on my screen.

`Miles: Bella, please don't do anything stupid.`

It takes me a second to get my emotions under control at seeing a reply from him, finally.

`Me: Evan needs to be caught.`

`Miles: Let the authorities deal with it. Please just drop it. You don't know what it was like, Bella. Evan is insane. Let it go.`

`Me: I can't.`

`Miles: Promise me you're not going to do anything?`

My fingers hover over the screen, knowing in my heart that I can't promise him that.

`Miles: For fuck's sake, this isn't a game! He`

murdered Zoey and Kellan.

I sigh.

Me: Fine. Okay.

Miles: I'll text you again soon. I'm not supposed to be talking to anyone from school.

No matter what I've promised, I'm not sure I can just sit here. I don't want to feel helpless anymore. Kellan's killer is out there somewhere, and someone has to know where he is.

107

Eli

'Outrun Myself' by Jack Kays is playing through my speakers. I'm standing beneath the shower, the water falling over me in a heated spray. I have one hand braced against the wall, and my tears mingle with the water, washing away down the drain.

I don't recall feeling this empty, this *dead* inside, when my mom died. Maybe it's because I was younger. I don't know.

Throwing my head back, I scrub a hand over my face and into my hair. I need to get control of myself.

Wash. Shave. Get dressed. Go downstairs.

I list the steps I need to take.

I rub my hand over the eight days' worth of growth on my chin.

Fuck it. I'm not shaving.

Sucking in a breath, I follow the first step and wash, then step out of the shower and wrap a towel around my waist.

What's next?

Get dressed, idiot. Kellan rolls his eyes inside my head. *Can't have a funeral without you there, can I?*

"I don't want you to have a funeral at all. I want this all to be a big fucking joke." I grab a second towel and dry my hair, then walk into the bedroom.

There's a suit laid out on my bed. Black pants, black shirt, black tie, and a black jacket.

"I'm going to look like a fucking undertaker."

But you'll wear it because it's what I want.

It was a shock to discover that Kellan had left instructions with his lawyer for what would happen if he died. Turns out he set everything up just after his eighteenth birthday, even the unconventional funeral he wants. I don't know why I was surprised to discover that. Kellan has always been someone who has plans in place for everything. That's why it's him who's dead and not me.

A stab of pain knifes through my heart. It should have been me lying on the altar, not him.

Stop it. Get dressed, stop fucking moping, and go downstairs.

I toss the towels to one side and pull on the clothes. Buttoning the shirt, I walk over to the full-length mirror on the closet door, so I can knot the tie. Once I'm dressed, I slip my feet into boots and pull open the door … just as Arabella comes out of her room a few doors down.

She's dressed in a black knee-length dress and flat shoes. Her hair is in some kind of intricate braid down her back. She meets my gaze.

"Eli."

That one word. My name. Her voice. It unravels something inside me, and I reduce the distance between us and palm her cheeks.

"I'm sorry," I whisper.

Her hands lift, glide over my shoulders and down my chest. She shakes her head. "You have nothing to be sorry for." Her fingers find my tie and smooth over it. "Can I walk down with you?"

I drop my hands from her face and link my fingers with hers. We walk along the hallway and down the stairs in silence. When we reach my dad's study, my steps falter and my tongue flicks out to toy with my lip ring.

Ari's fingers squeeze mine.

"It's okay."

I glance at her and swallow. "It's not. It'll never be okay again." I raise her fingers to my lips. "But it'll get easier."

I reach for the door and push it open. My dad, Elena, and a stranger are inside.

"Eli. Arabella. Come in and sit down." My dad's voice is somber. "This is Jackson Merrit, Kellan's lawyer and executor of his will."

The older man smiles sadly. "This won't take long. I know you have a difficult day ahead." He takes out an envelope from his pocket. "Kellan, as you know, was orphaned when he was a child. His parents' entire estate was left in trust for him, which he gained access to on his eighteenth birthday. While he does have family, none of them were close to him. When he turned eighteen, being the diligent young man he is … was … he arranged his own will for, in his words, the very likely event of him dying young."

My eyes close, the lump in my throat solidifying.

"Kellan made his wishes very clear. Twenty million was to be divided between his two aunts and uncle. The rest of the money, as well as all his material assets, is yours, Eli."

There's a rushing sound in my ears, and then warm fingers touch my cheek. "Eli?"

My eyes snap open and lock on blue ones, cloudy with concern.

"I'm okay." I *have* to be okay; otherwise, I won't make it through the rest of the day.

"Kellan added a clause to his will that if any of his relations try to contest it, everything reverts to you, and they get nothing." The lawyer reaches into another pocket. "He also left you this and said you should read it after his funeral." He holds it out to me.

I eye it but make no move to take it from him. Ari leans forward. "I'll take it and give it to him later."

"I know this is something you don't want to think about right now, so I'll arrange an appointment for you to sign all the relevant documentation."

I nod. Everyone around me stands.

"I'm sorry for your loss." The lawyer shakes my dad's hand, then Elena's and leaves the room.

"We'll leave you alone for a minute." My dad's hand pats my shoulder and then he's gone, taking Elena with him.

Arabella moves to stand in front of me. "The car will be here soon."

I tip my head back, eyes tracking over her face. "The day you met me must be carved out as the worst day of your life in your mind."

Her head tilts and she reaches out to adjust my tie, then pats my chest. "It wasn't your best first impression," she tells me softly. "But you grew on me." She holds out her hand. "Ready to go?"

"No?"

She catches my hands in hers and tugs me until I stand, then reaches up to press a gentle kiss against my lips. "It's time to say goodbye, Eli."

108

Arabella

My mom and Elliot are waiting for us when we exit the room. The letter Kellan's lawyer gave me is safely tucked away in my pocket for Eli to read later.

Elena's gaze lingers on mine and Eli's clasped hands, but she doesn't say a word.

Emotions try to overwhelm me, but I count silently to ten and push them back down. I want to be strong for Eli. He's finally spoken to me, and even though I'm still hurting, I don't want to destroy this fragile bond between us. This isn't about what I'm feeling right now. Today Eli has to say goodbye to his best friend.

"The car is here," Elliot says.

Eli tenses beside me, but I squeeze his hand in reassurance and lead him forward. "Come on."

He resists for a second before he gives in and allows me to guide him toward the main door. I'm not sure where the strength is coming from inside me, but I cling to it, focusing on a need to see this through. The driver waiting for us outside is wearing a stoic expression. He opens the rear door of the car as we approach and waits for us to slip inside, with Elliot and Elena joining us, before closing it with a bang.

No one speaks.

We all sit in silence, the grief that shrouds us a heavy weight over my shoulders. Eli doesn't let go of my hand. If I'm his anchor to get through the next few hours, I'm not going to leave his side. My heart is bleeding a river in my chest, but I will myself not to shed a tear.

I need to be strong for Eli.

"If you need anything, son, I'm here," Elliot murmurs. "Elena too."

Eli swallows hard, and he nods. "Thanks."

His exhausted eyes meet mine, and I offer him a small smile. "We're all here for you."

His lips lift as if he's trying to smile but fall before it can take shape. "I know."

I want to hug him tight, but I remain still beside him. As much as I want to take away his pain, I can't.

The drive to the crematorium seems to take forever. A countless number of mourners dressed in black are waiting around outside when we arrive. People stop and glance our way as we get out of the vehicle, all their eyes on Eli.

Ignoring them, I lean into him, offering my support. "We need to go inside, okay?"

He nods.

I take charge again and guide him toward the steps and up to the doors. As much as I'm guessing he doesn't want to face this, he needs it in order to move on and heal. The somber interior of the crematorium has been decorated with white flowers. When I take a deep breath, the perfume is sickly sweet to my nose. Light pours in through the stained-glass windows leaving puddles of color over the cold marble floor. It's beautiful, but it also stirs unpleasant memories.

Kellan on the altar, bathed in a rainbow, his eyes staring glassily ahead.

Don't think.

Eli is screaming his name over and over.

Don't cry.

Eli's hands covered in blood, and Kellan's chest soaked in red.

Keep moving.

We're directed forward up to the seats of pews to the front. Elliot slips in first, then Elena, until I'm sandwiched between her and Eli. Familiar faces surround us—students and teachers from the school. Others I don't recognize that, I guess, are Kellan's family. So many people here paying their respects to a boy whose life was cut short too soon.

I can't bring myself to look up at the sleek black closed coffin or the photograph of Kellan that's just above it. Instead, I focus on the boy beside me, keeping the icy hand that's still clinging to mine in my lap. I stroke my thumb over his skin and try my best to warm it up. The rhythmic motion soothes a little of my nerves.

Eli sits staring ahead, his eyes locked on the coffin.

Sadness resonates between us—a thread connecting us at this one single point in time.

Goodbye, Kellan. I'm so sorry. It should have never ended this way.

I let the grief flow through me, breaking down the walls I've built so high until I taste the kiss of my tears on my lips as they roll down my cheeks and drip off my chin.

109

Eli

The ceremony goes on and on. People stand up and say words. They might as well be speaking a foreign language for all the attention I pay them. My focus doesn't shift from the coffin until everyone stands.

I don't want to come back as a zombie. So, make sure they burn my body to ashes.

What if I die first?

Don't be ridiculous. I'm going to die long before you. Monsters live forever, Eli. The pretty ones die young.

Are you saying I'm not pretty?

Of course not. Just not as pretty as I am. Anyway, you need to make sure they do it properly. I want everyone to watch while I burn. You'll do that for me, won't you?

You're so fucking morbid, Kell.

Memories of the conversation we had over the pros and cons of burial or cremation run through my head while the coffin moves slowly into the furnace behind the curtains.

As the coffin disappears, my throat tightens. My heart is beating out a rapid rhythm against my ribs. I can't breathe. I can't watch while my friend burns. I need to get out.

Pulling my hand free from Arabella's, I push past her.

"Eli?" She whispers my name, and I shake my head but don't stop moving.

My vision is swimming, weaving in and out, and I collide with more than one person on my way to the doors. The crisp spring air hits me as I step outside, and I suck in breath after breath, filling my lungs until they ache from the pressure. My eyes are burning. My hands are shaking. I don't know whether I want to cry or drink, but something has got to give. Something needs to be done.

"Eli?" The voice snaps my spine taut. It's not Ari, or my dad.

I turn around slowly and my gaze locks onto brown hair. A small part of me registers that he looks as tired as I feel, but I push that aside. I don't give a fuck how he looks, how he feels.

"What are you doing here?" My voice comes out flat and clipped.

"We might not have been close, but I never wanted to see him dead."

There's something about his voice, his stance. My eyes narrow.

"You knew." It isn't a question.

"No, I—"

"Don't lie." I step forward and curl my fingers into the front of his shirt to haul him closer to me. "You *fucking* knew." My voice is as empty as my soul.

He pales.

"Eli, I tried to—"

"You knew Evan was behind everything. You knew he was the one driving Ari to target me. You. Fucking. Knew."

He grips my wrist and tries to pull free. I shake my head.

"Oh no, Black. You're not getting off so easily this time." I emphasize that warning by spinning and pinning him to the wall.

"I tried to talk to you!"

"You didn't fucking try hard enough." I'm not even angry. I feel *nothing*. So, when my fist buries itself into his chest, I do it with full clarity of my actions. "You knew it was Evan, and you stood there and let him ruin lives. I hope it was fucking worth it." I hit him again … and again … and again.

He doesn't fight back. Doesn't try to stop me. Just stares at me out of eyes full of guilt and misery.

Blood explodes outward when I split his lip, but he *still* doesn't try and defend himself. I release his shirt, and he slides down the wall until he's sitting on the ground. It doesn't stop me. I crouch and send another punch into his face.

And then I'm being hauled backward. I don't resist, don't fight to get free. I just hold Jace's gaze with mine.

"You knew," I say softly, shake off the people hanging onto me, and stalk away.

Arabella catches up to me just as I step through the gates of the cemetery. She doesn't speak, slipping her hand around my arm, and keeping pace as I stalk along the sidewalk. I walk aimlessly, taking random turns, until eventually, she pulls me to a stop.

"There's a small gathering being held at the Country Club. Do you want to go?"

I shake my head. "Kellan hated that place."

"Do you want to go home? I can call an Uber."

I nod and lean against the wall.

She pulls out her cell and taps around. "It'll be here in a couple of minutes."

A touch to the back of my hand has me looking down. She's holding my left hand, fingers stroking over my knuckles.

"For someone who needs their hands to produce art, you don't take very good care of them."

I look at the bloodied mess I've made of them, and shrug.

"Let's get you home and cleaned up."

***

She leads me upstairs to my room, makes no comment on the beer bottles and joints littering the floor and walks into my bathroom. I let her wash the blood from my hands.

I bite back a bitter laugh. All I ever see is blood on my hands. Kellan's blood. It's stained my skin, my *soul*. I'll never *not* see his blood.

When she's done, she takes my hand and we walk back into my bedroom. "Do you need anything?"

"Kellan's letter."

She catches her bottom lip between her teeth. "Are you sure you want that now?"

I hold out my hand. She stares at me for a moment longer, then reaches into her pocket and takes out the envelope.

I take it from her, turn, and sit on my bed. As she moves toward the door, I lift my head.

"Stay?"

She sinks onto the bed beside me.

Tearing open the envelope, I pull out the sheet of paper. The sight of Kellan's bold handwriting sends a sharp stab of pain through the ever-present numbness. I shove it away and focus on the words.

Eli

If you're reading this, then I'm dead.

cue dramatic pause here

I've always wanted to write a letter with that opening. I'm not sitting here cracking up over it!

But seriously, if you're reading this note written by my eighteen-year-old self, then I died young like I predicted, and it was before I fell in love, got married, etc., blah blah. That means you get everything. Everything important anyway. I know you don't care about the money. At least, not at this point in time. But I want you to have it, anyway, even if this isn't the final letter and I live longer because I don't do something stupid which ends my life. Which, let's be honest, isn't going to happen because if you're not around to talk me out of it, I do stupid shit all the time. Even then, this part of my will won't change. You're the closest thing to family I have. Forget the fuckers who stick around because they want what I have. You stick around because of who I am.

Where was I? Oh, yeah. My eighteen-year-old self wants you to know that I love you. Not in the want to get in your pants and fuck your delicious, crazy brains out kind of love. Don't be ridiculous. You're not my type. Too broody. I try to stop you from getting stuck inside your own head, but I'm no longer here to do that, so I need you to hear this.

Find someone who gets you. Eli. Someone who sees beyond the monster you think you have to be. Someone who isn't scared of your snapping and snarling.

Someone just like me. in fact.

But with girl parts.

Love you. my beautiful monster.

Kellan

The sheet drops from my hand to the floor, and I close my eyes. Warm fingers touch my cheek.

"Are you okay?"

I shake my head.

"Do you want to talk?"

Another headshake.

"What can I do?"

I force my eyes to open and look at her.

"I think I'm broken, Ari," I whisper. "I don't feel anything. I should be sad, right? Or angry. I should have felt *something* when I hit Jace. But there was nothing there. Just a fucking great big *nothing.*"

The fingers on my cheek move to stroke along my jaw. "It's going to take time, that's all." Her palm cups my cheek and forces my head around to face her. "Let me help you."

She stands and moves around until she can climb onto my lap. Her legs slip either side of mine, and she returns her palms to my face to tip my head up. Her head dips, her lips brushing over mine.

"Do you feel that?" Her voice is a whisper. Her tongue flicks out to lick over my lips. "You're so cold. Let me warm you up."

My eyes close as her lips move over mine and slowly … so *fucking* slowly … the warmth of her body chases away the cold of mine.

"Ari." When my lips part to say her name, her tongue dips inside, finds mine and strokes against it.

My hands close over her hips, and just like that, flames erupt, licking over my skin, until it becomes an inferno.

I twist until she's on her back and I'm above her. Our mouths clash, my teeth sinking into her bottom lip until the coppery taste of her blood fills my mouth. She groans, hands sliding down my back to drag the hem of my shirt out of my pants. Her fingers reverse their path, nails raking up my spine.

"Do it again." The demand bursts from my throat like a growl. It's the first thing I've fucking felt in *days*.

She complies, and the sting as she breaks through my skin triggers something inside me. I drag down the front of her dress and capture one nipple between my teeth, nipping sharply until she cries out and arches up. My hand finds the bottom of her skirt, and I drag it up until I can wrap my fingers around her thigh and hook her leg over my hip. My dick is straining against my pants, demanding to be freed, and I grind against her.

"Eli." Her throaty moan feeds my rising hunger, and I hook my fingers into her panties and drag them down her legs.

Sliding down the bed, I give her no warning before I bury my face between her thighs and push my tongue into her pussy. My fingers are biting into her thighs, holding her still as she writhes against my mouth.

There is nothing gentle about my mouth's attack on her. I feast on her like I'm starving, and her pussy is the only thing that will sate my hunger. Her fingers claw at my hair, pulling and scratching while my tongue fucks her relentlessly into an orgasm.

When she falls over the edge, I rear up and unbuckle the belt at my hips, drag it off, and unzip my pants.

"Condom?" My question is a low growl.

She shakes her head. "Just fuck me."

I don't need to hear anything more and I thrust inside her.

110

Arabella

Eli thrusts into me over and over, his movements harsh, almost cruel. I take what he gives me, knowing this is what he needs, and I'm ready to give him everything. Wrapping my legs around his hips, I rake my nails down his back, making him hiss.

He pumps into me harder in response, ramming me mercilessly into the mattress. His teeth bite along my jaw and my neck, sinking into my shoulder until it hurts.

I moan his name, fingers tangling in his hair, but I don't try and stop him.

"Hurt me," I pant when his lips brush the skin he's marked. "Hurt me as much as you need. Fuck me like you hate me."

Rearing up, his hand closes around my throat and squeezes. Fear seeps up, but I keep my gaze locked on Eli's.

He pulls out, then slams back into me in one deep thrust.

"You want me to use you, Hellcat?"

"Yes." Leaning my head back, I moan, my mind blurring with pleasure and pain.

He lifts my legs over his shoulders, and grinds into me deeper.

"Do you want to take away my pain?"

My fingers claw at the sheets beneath me. "I want you to feel. Don't stop. Please don't stop. Feel me."

The look on his face should be terrifying, but I'm not frightened of him. Eli fucks me like a madman. It's savage, vicious. As though he's trying to reignite the emotions frozen inside him or suck out all of mine.

My legs are still over his shoulders as he drops down to brace himself over me on the bed with his hands. His pupils are dilated in unadulterated hunger. He pounds into me over and over in a steady rhythm, making the bed shake. I grab his ass in both hands and dig my nails into him. His lips pull back, baring his teeth, and he rolls his hips and rams into me harder.

An orgasm slams into me out of nowhere, arching my back and tearing a scream from my lips. Eli doesn't break his pace, his jaw tight, expression tense.

I let him use my body, until he finally stiffens and finds his release. Head thrown back and eyes closed, his whole body bows in what looks like pleasure and torture.

Dizzy, panting, I feel his cock pulse inside me, and I groan softly in response. It takes me a second to register that he is shaking.

I frown. "Eli?"

A sound comes from him, and when he lowers his head, his tear-filled eyes find mine. I watch as the beautiful, scarred boy in front of me, who's still buried deep in my body, breaks into pieces. His weight sinks on top of me, and he buries his face against my breasts and weeps.

I gather him into my arms and kiss the top of his head. "I'm here. I have you. You can let go now."

Eli doesn't try to talk, he just cries. My heart aches, and I have to fight back the tears at seeing him so destroyed. I stroke his hair, his shoulder, back, whispering words of comfort. He clings to me as if I'm the only thing in the world stopping him from being completely swept away.

I'm not sure how much time passes before his sobs fade. The muscled body on top of me grows heavy, and finally, his breathing evens out. Glancing down at his pale face, I find his long black eyelashes resting against his cheeks, his face relaxed in sleep. I manage to grab the end of the spare blanket that we've dislodged and is now hanging off the bed. I pull it up, and drape it over us both, covering our bodies from the waist down.

He's exhausted, and I'm not about to wake him. If I have to lay here the rest of the day holding him, I will.

I brush a lock of stray hair off his forehead and smile sadly down at him.

"I love you, Eli Travers. We may not have had a fairytale beginning, but you're my monster, and I wouldn't have it any other way."

He doesn't stir or move. I watch him while he sleeps, glad I can bring him a slither of solace in his grief. If rough sex is what it takes to help him through this, then I'll stay in his bed every night while he mourns.

Panic zips through me when there's a tap at the door. I can't move. Eli's head barely covers my breasts, and the last thing I expected was we'd have company.

As It opens slowly, framing Elliot and Elena in the doorway.

Surprise ripples over Elliot's expression when he sees me on the bed with his son asleep on top of me.

"Arabella, what are you doing?"

My cheeks burn with embarrassment, and I hug the boy in my arms tightly. "Giving him what he needs."

My mother doesn't seem surprised at all. "You're together, aren't you? It's okay, sweetheart. You can tell us."

I sweep my tongue over my lips. "Yes. We're together."

Elliot clears his throat, his shock passing quickly. "Your mother suspected something at Christmas and told me. After the way you two argued, I wasn't sure myself."

Feeling awkward with guilt, I squirm on the bed. "I'm sorry we didn't tell you."

He smiles. "You have nothing to be sorry about."

"You're not angry?"

"No, of course not. I'm just a little confused about how we got here from the bullying and hatred."

Elena pats his arm gently. "I'm sure they'll explain when things are a little better."

Elliot nods. "Eli needs someone right now. He needs *you,* Arabella."

My heart beats a little faster in my chest. "I'll be whatever he needs me to be."

"Let us know if there's anything you need," my mother whispers. "Or Eli."

"Thank you." I mouth, watching them slip back out of the room.

This is not how I imagined our parents finding out that we're together.

Still holding the boy sleeping over me, I lay my head back down on the mattress and close my eyes. I don't want to think about the funeral or the fact Eli beat up Jace. Right at this second, all I want to do is be the support my boyfriend needs.

111

Eli

Consciousness returns slowly. There's something warm under my cheek. A soft repetitive thudding in my ear. I move my head, rubbing my cheek against the warm softness.

"Eli?" The whisper is joined by fingers stroking through my hair.

I frown, forcing my mind to clear itself of the jumbled exhausted mess it's been in.

"Ari?" My voice comes out as a rough croak. Finally, the neurons in my brain fire to life and my lids rise, allowing me to see.

Moonlight shines through the window, bathing everything in a silver glow. I lift my head carefully, *cautiously*. It feels like a heavy weight, but I manage to raise it enough for me to see what I'm lying on.

One pale breast, topped with a perfect pink nipple, fills my gaze. I frown and stretch out a hand, bracing it against the mattress so I can push myself off the body beneath me and roll onto my back.

Fingers stroke over my jaw, my lips, along my throat, and then Ari's face comes into focus as she leans over me.

"Hey." The word is soft, accompanied by a small smile.

I blink up at her, my eyes tracking over her face. Her bottom lip is slightly swollen, and I'm certain there's a small speck of blood in the corner of her mouth. A dark bruise catches my attention, and I redirect my focus to her throat. I follow the line of bites down her neck, over her collarbone, and down to her breasts, where they spill out over the neckline of a black top.

My frown deepens.

"Did I hurt you?"

She shakes her head. I lift a hand and trace it over her lips, then gently push her bottom lip down. Teeth marks indent the pink flesh inside.

"That was me." It wasn't a question. My tongue snakes out to toy with my lip ring. "I made you bleed."

Her tongue licks at my fingertip. "I made you feel. It's a fair trade." I pull my finger away from her lips and fist my hand into her hair, so I can pull her head down to mine. The kiss I place against her lips is gentle. "Thank you."

She draws away slightly, her eyes intense as she stares at me. Tightening my hold on her hair, I tumble her to the mattress and roll to pin her beneath me. She braces her palms against my shoulders, stopping me from lowering my head to capture her mouth.

"I haven't cleaned up since last time."

My brow furrows as I try to decipher her meaning. Then it becomes clear. "Oh. Why not?"

"You collapsed, and I … I didn't want to disturb you."

"How long was I out?"

"Three … maybe four hours?"

"And you stayed with me?"

One side of her mouth tilts up. "In the wet patch, yeah."

The laugh that escapes my lips surprises us both. Her lips part, and then curl up into a full smile. Laughing feels good, seeing her smile feels better. Still chuckling, I dip my head and kiss her.

"I love you, Kitten."

***

I come out of the shower feeling almost human. Ari is sitting cross-legged on my bed, scribbling into a book. I pause in the doorway and look around.

"You tidied up?"

"It stank like a rundown bar in here."

"How do *you* know what a rundown bar smells like?"

She rolls her eyes. "Fine, how I *think* a rundown bar would smell." She unfolds herself from the bed and stands.

I appreciate the view of long bare legs clothed in short pajama shorts and a cropped top that displays her navel and the hint of her breasts. When I reach her face, she's got one eyebrow arched.

"Enjoying the view?"

The smile feels weird on my face, but I don't stop it from forming. "Very much."

The mildly offended look melts away from her face and is replaced with a grin. She crosses the room and rises on her toes to wrap her arms around my neck. Burying her face into the curve of my throat, she breathes in.

"You smell good," she murmurs.

I tweak the end of her hair. "You're just trying to get into my pants again."

Her soft laugh sparks my nerve endings to life. "And that's my cue to tell you that your dad and my mom know about us."

"They … *how*?"

"They walked in while you were asleep."

"Fuck."

She shakes her head and leans back to look up at me. "They're okay about it. It was a bit weird, but they didn't seem annoyed. If you're feeling okay, we could go down and talk to them?"

The hesitancy in her voice is clear. She doesn't know how I'm going to react to the idea. I wind an arm around her waist and pull her closer to me.

"We should do that." My stomach chooses that moment to make some strange, ungodly sound. "What time is it?"

"Almost midnight." She frowns at me. "When did you last eat?"

My silence as I try to remember is answer enough. She pulls out of my embrace. "Put some clothes on. The kitchen staff won't be here, so I can invade their space without them yelling at me." She flaps her hands at me when I don't move fast enough for her. "Clothes, Eli. So, I can feed you."

I toss her a half smile. "Do you promise to fuck me afterward?"

112

Arabella

Seeing Eli smile makes my heart flip-flop in my chest. "As many times as you want me to."

He captures my hand, brings it to his lips and presses a kiss to my knuckles. "Is that a promise?"

I roll my eyes at him and giggle. "Forever and always. Now get dressed. I need to feed you."

He finds some clothes and tugs them on. The second he's presentable, I grab his hand and tug him out of the door along the dark hallway, toward the stairs. A light is on in the reception hall downstairs.

I stop on the bottom step to give Eli a quick kiss, and then head for the kitchen.

It's a surprise to find we're not alone. Elliot and Elena are sitting huddled at the kitchen table with two glasses of milk and a plate of chocolate cookies in front of them.

The second he sees his son, Elliot smiles. "You caught us."

Eli frowns. "Have you been waiting for me to wake up?"

"Maybe a little, but we've grown into the habit of having a warm drink and cookies before bed most nights."

"When his insomnia kicks in." My mom leans into him, laying her head on his shoulder. "One of our little rituals."

I let go of Eli's hand and move toward the kitchen counter. "He's hungry, so I was going to make him something to eat."

Elena gestures at the boy beside me. "Come and join us."

Tongue snaking out, he flicks his lip ring before taking a seat across from them. "Ari told me you guys know about us."

"Elena worked it out before I did," Elliot replies. "I honestly didn't think you were getting along."

I concentrate on gathering eggs, butter, milk, and all the ingredients I need for an omelet, while I half listen to the conversation.

"We weren't," Eli is saying to his dad. "But things changed."

I place everything on the counter, and cross the kitchen to where Eli is sitting, cup his jaw and drop a kiss on his lips. "For the better."

When I turn to leave, he grabs my wrist and hauls me back into his lap, capturing my mouth with an intensity that leaves me breathless.

"Enough." I gasp when he finally frees me. "Let me cook."

"It's nice to see you two together." Elena is holding Elliot's hand on the tabletop. "We never expected this to happen."

"And that's our cue to go back up to bed." Elliot chuckles. "It's late, and we can talk more in the morning. Come on, darling, let's give them some space."

"See you in the morning."

Humming softly to myself, I crack eggs, whisk ingredients together and add everything to the frying pan. Hands find my waist pulling me back into a hard-muscled body.

"I missed this."

"What?"

"You cooking for me."

I smile, waving the spatula at the stove in front of me. "I'll cook for you anytime you want."

Eli kisses my neck, nipping at my skin. "Sounds good to me."

"Go sit down, or you'll never get fed."

"Is that an order?"

"Don't make me spank you." I threaten with a mock growl.

His hand moves to my ass and squeezes it gently. "You shouldn't give me ideas, Kitten."

"Last time you did that, it hurt." In the classroom, in front of everyone. The memory dims my mood a little.

"I can make it pleasurable for you. Done right, you'd be thanking me and begging for more."

When his hands slide around my thighs, I sigh. "Eli."

"Okay, okay." He kisses me a second time and smiles against the curve of my neck. "I'm going."

I plate up the omelets, and carry them to the table, where he's laid out silverware. We eat quietly together, and when I try to wash up, he insists I leave it for the kitchen staff in the morning. Giving in to the heated look in his eyes, we sneak back up to his bedroom hand in hand.

"I need to use the bathroom, then you can ravage me," he announces once we are inside.

He vanishes into the bathroom and closes the door. I take the opportunity to check my cell for messages.

Unknown number: Hey, Arabella, this is Jace. There's something I wanted to tell Eli, but he won't listen to me. I'm hoping I can explain to you, and then you can pass it on.

I stare down at the text with uncertainty.

Me: How did you get my number?

Unknown number: Garrett.

Scrolling through my contacts, I find the jock's number and shoot him a message.

Me: Did you give Jace my number?

Two minutes later, my cell vibrates with a response.

Garrett: Yeah, he wanted to contact you. Apologize for what happened. I hope that's ok? Why are you up so late?

Me: I couldn't sleep. It's fine. Thanks.

Returning to Jace's message, I reread it slowly.

Me: What do you want to tell me?

Unknown number: I was wondering if we could meet up.

I glance at the closed bathroom door, then back down at the screen.

Me: You could just call.

Unknown number: Look, I know I was an asshole to you, but this needs to be said face to face. The least I can do is buy you breakfast.

The thought of Eli getting into another fight with him leaves me cold. He's in a better place than he was yesterday. I don't want to shatter that with whatever Jace wants.

Me: Where?

Unknown number: The Country Club, tomorrow at nine.

Me: Ok, I'll see you then.

I switch off my phone, leave it on the nightstand and climb under the sheets. Once I know what Jace wants, I'll tell Eli. There's no point making him worry. He's been through enough, and if I can protect him from more harm, then I will. It's the least I can do as someone who loves him. Tonight, I'll let him lose himself in my body over and over until he's tired enough to sleep again.

113

Eli

I'm only half awake when the mattress bounces and the warmth of Ari's body moves away from mine. I roll over onto my stomach and let sleep take me back under. She's probably going to the bathroom.

That's the last thing I remember thinking when I next open my eyes to discover her side of the bed still empty and very cold.

"Ari?" She doesn't answer my call.

I lift my head and look around. The bathroom door is open.

"*Ari?*"

Still no reply. Reaching out, I grab my phone. "Time."

The time is ten fifty-six am.

Huh, I've slept in. She must have woken earlier and decided to get up. Rolling out of bed, I drag a hand through my hair, pull on a pair of sweats and the nearest t-shirt, and walk out of the bedroom.

The house is quiet as I walk through it. I wonder if my dad has gone back to work, but then the door to his study swings opens, and Elena steps out.

"Eli!" She smiles. "Arabella said you were still sleeping." Her hand touches my arm. "How do you feel?"

"I'm okay, I think. Is Dad in there?" I jerk my chin toward the room behind her.

She nods and steps to one side. "I'm sure he'd love to see you. I was just going to see if I can talk the cook into making lunch early. Would you like something?"

"No, thanks." I move past her and enter the study, then pause and glance back. "You should probably be here for this conversation."

She follows me inside. My dad looks up as I approach his desk. He stands and strides around to meet me halfway across the room. His hands land on my shoulders and we stare at each other, then he folds me into his arms.

"I'm sorry, son. I know the last few days have been difficult for you."

This close to him, I come to the sudden realization that I'm taller. When did that happen?

"I miss him."

His hand rubs between my shoulders. "I know."

"I'm sorry I was such a dick when Mom died. It must have been worse for you."

"It's okay, Eli. I should never have left you to be responsible for everything, no matter what I was going through." He pulls away and pulls my head close to his. "I love you, son. I need you to know that."

I nod. "I love you, too, Dad." Sucking in a deep breath, I straighten and take a step back. "Ari said you walked in on us."

He chuckles and skirts back around his desk to sit down. "Elena has been saying since Christmas that she was sure you two were sneaking around together, but with the way you were fighting, I wasn't convinced."

"It's been … *gnarly*." I tell him about the way I treated her when she first joined Churchill Bradley, careful to keep any mention of our late-night assignations out of the story. Then I tell them how we started having feelings for each other over Christmas, which leads to the things Ari did when I returned to school.

"So, Evan was behind all those videos being released, the cell being planted in your locker, *and* then blackmailed Arabella to push you to … what?"

I rub a hand down my face. "That's just it. When I got the text to meet Kell …" I pause to lick my lips. "He … Evan, I mean … I'm not sure I got the sense of everything he said, but it seems like he has been trying to take everything that he thought was mine since we were young kids. He kept talking about how I had everything, and he *should* have it all."

"You didn't tell that to the detective."

"I wasn't really thinking about it. But I'm pretty sure he killed Zoey, Dad. He said something about how he tried to talk to her in the cemetery, but he had to punish her. That it was my fault she's dead."

"It's not your fault."

"I know. I *know* it's not. Have they found him?"

Elena shakes her head. "No. He hasn't been home or been in contact with his family."

119

Arabella

Sitting in the back of the Uber, I unlock my phone and find Miles' messages. My heart is hammering behind my ribs, and my hands are shaking with apprehension.

`Me: I'm on my way to meet Jace at the Country Club. You know where I am if things go wrong.`

I hold on to my cell and shift nervously in my seat. It was hard for me to tear myself away from the warmth of Eli's body this morning. I'd left him sleeping soundly, looking peaceful and relaxed.

Maybe I should have told him where I was going.

But he would have tried to stop me, and I need to know what Jace has to say. Whatever he wants to tell Eli, it must be important for him to risk my boyfriend's wrath.

My phone pings.

`Miles: Wait, what? Do you mean Eli doesn't know about this?`

`Me: I didn't want to worry him.`

`Miles: OMG, Arabella, don't do this. Abort. Abort. Have you never watched a serial killer documentary? You are walking into a trap.`

My determination wavers. Maybe this wasn't such a good idea? I should have thought things through properly.

But it's too late, because my destination is drawing closer.

`Me: No, I haven't, and I'm at the Country Club.`

Miles: Turn around and go home.

Me: I'll text you once I'm with Jace.

Miles: I AM TELLING ELI.

Me: Please don't. We are in a public place. There are plenty of people. I'm not a complete idiot.

Miles: You've got five minutes, and then I want another message.

The car rolls to a stop, and I pay the driver, then climb out. A few people are entering the building, and I fall in behind them. The place is busy, with tables full of families out having breakfast together. Once inside, I search for Jace.

He sees me first. He's sporting a black eye and split lip from Eli's beating at the church.

He waves at me from a table tucked in a far corner. I assure myself there's no one else I know around, before weaving through the tables to join him.

He frowns when I stop beside him and snap a photo of us together.

"What are you doing?"

I send it to Miles. "Proof of life."

Me: Not a trap so far :)

Miles: Message me again in five minutes.

Me: Yes, mother.

Miles: I'm serious, Arabella.

Me: ok, ok.

"Is that Eli?"

I take the seat opposite Jace and pin him with a stare. "You wanted to talk. So, talk."

"Are you hungry? I can order you something?" He glances toward a roving server.

I shake my head. "I don't want anything from you but words."

He releases a long slow breath. "I didn't know Evan was going to kill Kellan."

"Is that it?"

"Evan wants to make Eli suffer."

Unease crawls down my spine. "Why?"

Jace's brown eyes lock with mine. "He hates him."

"I kind of figured that out on my own. What I don't understand is why, and how we got to this point."

"You don't understand what it's like."

I glance around warily. "Then tell me."

"Evan gets inside your head. I didn't see it at first. He's been my friend since I was ten."

"What do you mean get inside your head?"

Jace sighs and hunches over his cup. "Whispering. Comments. He always knows what you want to hear. He has a way of making you feel important. Coaxing you to do things and getting you to see stuff his way but letting you believe the idea was your own."

I frown. "We're talking about the same Evan here? The guy who followed you around all the time like your personal puppy?"

"That's the image he wanted everyone to see. The person he became when we started attending the school. He's different when no one is watching. When it's just the two of us."

"You're saying he pretends to be something he's not?"

Jace nods jerkily. "He would joke about the classes we were

taking. How easy they were. Childs play. Nothing slowed him down, not even math. He had keys to the dorms. Knew the routines of all the teachers and security. Some of them were even being blackmailed by him because he knew their dirty little secrets."

My phone pings.

`Miles: Are you still alive?`

`Me: Yes.`

`Miles: How do I know this is Arabella?`

`Me: We're still Daredevil and Elektra.`

`Me: Ok, you've got another five minutes.`

I stare at the boy across the table. "Are you trying to tell me Evan is some kind of evil genius?"

"It was fun at first." Jace's voice lowers to a whisper. "The things we did before you arrived. He would talk Lacy and the cheerleaders into doing stuff. He knew exactly what buttons to push to get someone to carry out his instructions. Then he became obsessed with Zoey when she became friends with Eli and Kellan. I know he stalked her. I found photos of her in one of his drawers."

"Have you told the police all of this?"

"Yes, they know everything." He swallows hard and rakes a hand through his hair. "I swear to you, I don't know where he is. If he's still talking to any of us, I don't know. When he started saying Miles and Garrett were traitors, something clicked inside my head. He wanted us to hurt them."

A nervous tick jumps below his right eye.

"How?"

His gaze drops from mine. "He … he wanted to break Miles' legs in such a way he wouldn't be able to swim again. As for Garrett …"

My mouth is so dry, I really want a drink, but I'm not prepared to stay here long enough to drink it. I lick my lips. I'm not sure I want to hear the rest, but I ask anyway.

"Tell me."

"He said if he lost a hand, he wouldn't be playing sports again. Evan was acting weird for weeks right up until he killed Kellan."

"Weird?"

"Erratic and angry, he kept ranting about Eli. How you weren't doing what he wanted, just like Zoey."

My phone pings, and I glance down at it.

Miles: Are you still alive?

Me: Still kicking.

Miles: I don't know what he's telling you, but I think you should leave now. If you don't, I'm calling the cops.

He's right, it's time to go. I've been here long enough.

Pushing back my chair, I rise. "I need to get back."

Jace stands. "Can I give you a lift back to the house?"

"No, thanks. I'll call an Uber."

"Still don't trust me?" His smile is sad.

I back away from him. "After what happened, you're lucky I turned up at all."

"Bella," Jace calls as I turn to leave. "Warn Eli. I don't think this is over. Evan is fixated on him."

The knowledge sends a sick feeling spiraling through me. I call for an Uber the second I'm outside, and text Miles while I'm waiting for it to arrive.

Me: I'm leaving now.

Miles: Thank fuck for that. What did you learn?

Me: That Evan is a manipulative psychopath.

Miles: I could have told you that.

Me: I'm texting Eli to tell him where I've been.

Miles: Good.

I know I'm about to get into a whole world of trouble, but I don't shy from it. I shoot Eli a text and hope he won't be too mad with me once I get home.

Me: I've been at the Country Club talking to Jace. Please don't be angry with me. We'll talk when I get back.

115

Eli

My cell chimes in my pocket. Pulling it out, I tap on the screen.

`Kitten: I've been at the Country Club talking to Jace. Please don't be angry with me. We'll talk when I get back.`

"*What the fuck?*" I lurch to my feet and stab the call icon. "Are you fucking stupid?" I snarl down the line when she picks up.

"It's fine." Her voice is calm. "I'm on my way back now."

"Jace is—"

"*No*, he's not. I'll explain everything when I'm home."

"Ari—"

"No, Eli. I'm not arguing with you over the phone. I'm already being stared at because everyone can hear you yelling. I'll be home soon, then we'll talk."

She cuts the call and leaves me standing, staring at it. "Fuck's sake."

"What's going on?" My dad's voice draws my eyes up to him.

"Fucking Ari. Did she tell you she was going out?"

"She didn't say anything to me." Dad glances at Elena, who shakes her head.

"She came down earlier and said you were still sleeping. I thought she went back up to your room. Where did she go?"

"To fucking meet Jace."

My dad frowns. "She shouldn't be going out alone, not while that boy is still on the loose. Who knows where he might be hiding."

"Or who's helping him. Jace is his best friend." I walk toward the door. "I'm going to go and get her."

"Slow down. Do you know where she is?"

"She said she was just leaving the Country Club."

"Then the chances are you're going to miss her. There's no point in you driving over there when she's probably already nearly home."

He's not wrong, but I don't like it. I shove my cell back into my pocket and continue out of the study.

"Where are you going?"

"I'm going to wait outside for her."

***

Me: Where are you?

Me: Ari? Fucking answer me.

Me: Where the fuck are you?

I'm pacing up and down the drive when my dad comes out.

"She's not back yet? It's been over an hour."

"She's not answering her messages, either."

"Have you tried calling her?"

"Twice."

I look down at the cell in my hand.

ME: If you don't fucking answer me, I'm going to switch on the tracker Kellan installed on your cell and hunt you down. When I find you, I'm going to punish you.

That gets a response.

Kitten: Sounds kinky.

I frown.

`Me: Where the fuck are you?`

`Kitten: You tell me. You're the one with a tracker.`

I don't have a fucking tracker on her cell. At least, I don't think there is.

`Me: Ari, what are you doing? You said you were coming straight home to talk.`

She doesn't reply immediately, but when her text finally comes through, it turns me cold.

`Kitten: I'm sorry, your little kitten can't come to the phone right now. She's a little tied up.`

A photograph is attached—of Arabella. Her eyes are closed. There's duct tape across her mouth and a bruise forming on her cheek.

`Kitten: Red or green, Eli? Are you ready to play?`

116

Arabella

Consciousness weaves in and out. Darkness meets my eyes when I open them before they close again. Memories stir. A car coming to pick me up. A man wearing a ball cap pulled low over his face.

Evan.

I'd tried to get out of the vehicle, but the doors had been locked. When I wouldn't stop trying to break the window, he pulled over and climbed in the back with me. We fought, and he injected me with something. After that, everything is blank.

I try to lick my lips, but the duct tape over my mouth prevents it. My cheek is throbbing where he hit me. When I try to move, I discover my hands are bound behind my back, and my ankles are tied. My limbs are numb.

I open my eyes, my head still dazed from whatever drug he'd given me. Then everything slides into nothingness again.

A cool breeze caresses my cheek, rousing me to awareness a second time, and I shiver. I snap my eyes shut at the bright light, then squint through narrowed slits.

Evan is smiling down at me. "Don't worry, Zoey. You're safe now."

His finger strokes my cheek, and I flinch away from his touch.

Why is he calling me Zoey?

He lifts me out of the trunk of the car, and a painful prickling sensation spreads through me. I can't even struggle to escape with the way he has me tied up, and he carries me away from the car.

Where are we?

"I'm taking you home." Evan breaks the silence. "We'll never be parted again."

My head lolls against his shoulder, and I search for any sign of something familiar as he walks. He stops abruptly, and lowers me to the ground, then rolls me onto my side. When he turns away, I try to loosen the ropes around my wrists, but none of my efforts to get free are successful. Eyes wide, I watch as he pushes aside a thick overgrown bush and pulls up a metal trap door.

Evan chuckles when he glances my way.

"Eli doesn't know about this way in. The Academy is riddled with tunnels that run every inch of the campus. Old Churchill made sure he had plenty of escape routes out of his precious mansion. We're about a mile from the school."

We're back at Churchill Bradley Academy. How is anyone going to find me here?

Panic tries to swallow me whole, and I close my eyes, breathing through my terror.

"The place is still on lockdown." Evan continues, scooping me back up into his arms. "It's just the two of us."

I'm trapped with a psychopath. What is he going to do with me? Kill me as he did with Kellan and Zoey.

He carries me toward the hole in the ground, and it's only then that I realize there are stone steps leading down into a tunnel. Ignoring my struggles, he descends into the dark.

My breathing is coming out in shallow pants. I need to focus on not hyperventilating, because losing myself to fear won't help me get out of this.

Evan swings me up over his shoulder in a fireman's lift, and closes the trap door above us with a heavy clunk. Thrown into darkness, I shudder as cold air licks my skin. Light bursts into life a second later, the beam of the large flashlight Evan is now holding cuts through the blackness.

I blink, trying to stem the tears threatening to fall as helplessness overtakes me. The only sounds are his footsteps echoing along the tunnel and my harsh breathing.

Oh god, what can I do? He's going to kill me.

Evan doesn't speak, just walks. Time crawls slowly by. Inside my head, I scream out for Eli.

I should never have gone to see Jace. Was he part of this plan? Did he get me there so Evan could snatch me? Miles told me not to trust him. I'm such an idiot.

Eli. Oh god. Eli! He's lost two people he loves already. I can't be the third.

No! I'm not going to die. Whatever it takes to get out of this, I'll do it. I'll claw, bite, and fight until I get myself free.

Evan stops, and metal groans. Light floods in from above. I get a glimpse of more stone steps leading up. He takes them slowly, carrying me back outside. We're back in the woods, only this time, I can see the chapel to my left.

Is that where he is taking me? To put me on the altar like a sacrifice as he did with Kellan?

An image of Kellan flashes through my head.

His eyes are open and glassy. His body is awash with the hues of color streaming in through the stained-glass windows.

Evan kicks the trap door closed, then sets off in the opposite direction to the stone building.

"Don't worry, no one will see us." He pats my ass, and I can't stop a whimper. "The groundskeeper is far on the other side of campus, and the security guards they left stick close to the school. We're all alone out here."

Feeling has returned to my arms and legs. Everything aches. My stomach heaves as I bounce on his shoulder. He weaves through the trees, taking me in a familiar direction. When the cemetery comes into view, dread tries to choke me.

I need to stay calm. Think straight. Don't panic.

He hums softly to himself as he carries me through the gates and past the weathered gravestones. When we reach the door of the tomb, he pushes it open, and makes his way across the stone floor.

I'm dropped carefully onto something soft, and twist my head to look, I find it's a sleeping bag. There are empty cans of beer to my right and discarded food tins. The rest of the space has been decorated with flowers. Lilies—their ghostly white petals bright against the gray of the stone walls.

Has he been using the tunnels to get around the school? How many more are there?

He closes the tomb doors, then turns back to me.

"Home sweet home. I got the lilies just for you. I remembered they were your favorite."

Not mine. Zoey's.

That's who he thinks I am right now.

I watch him, wide-eyed and wary, as he joins me on the sleeping bag. When I try to wiggle away, he stops me with an arm over my waist.

He fists my hair with his free hand. "Don't scream. If you do, I'll have to hurt you. Do you understand?"

I nod jerkily.

Maybe if I pretend to be her, he'll keep me alive long enough for someone to find me.

He peels the duct tape from my mouth. I give him a shaky smile. "I'll be good, I promise."

He cups my chin and rubs his thumb along the side of my jaw. "Do you see now you belong with me and not Eli? He's nothing but trouble."

"Why do you hate him so much?" The question tumbles from me before I can stop it.

"He tried to take Jace from me."

"Jace?"

"We were ten. We were sent around Eli's house to play. He impressed everyone with all the stuff his parents had bought him, and he chose Jace to play a game with him. I saw the fun they had. His mom came in with cookies, and everything was so fucking perfect. It was all a plot to take my friends for Eli."

He's insane.

My lips part as his thumb brushes over them. "Why would he do that?"

Evan's expression darkens. "My mom died when I was four. My dad pretended everything was perfect without her, but it wasn't. I needed to smash the illusion. Show them what it was."

His words leave a cold hard lump inside my chest. "Evan, what did you do?"

"I tampered with their car. Eli was supposed to die that day, with his mom."

"You caused the accident, but … but you were fourteen years old." I can't keep the horror from my voice.

Tilting his head, he studies my face, stroking my cheek and neck with a gentle touch.

"It didn't take much to find the information I needed online. You'd be surprised what you can find if you search hard enough. My dad got suspicious after that. Started asking questions. He'd had glimpses of how clever I was, and I realized then that I would have to play a part. I couldn't let him see all the things I'd done."

I'm shaking, his body pressed into mine, and all I want to do is run as fast and far away from him as I can. I twist my wrists together, still tied behind me, but the ropes bite into my skin.

Keep him talking.

"Eli came back to school after the crash."

Evan grunts. "I thought I'd gotten rid of him, but he just wouldn't fucking die. So, I had to rethink. It was easy enough to spread the name. He became the Monster of Churchill Academy, but it didn't work out as I had planned. He accepted the role I'd given him even when everyone turned their backs on him."

"But Kellan remained his friend."

"Fucking Kellan." His lips curl up. "No matter what I did, that bastard would not walk away. He thought he could trick me. In the end, I proved to him which one of us was smarter."

Another memory hits me.

Kellan is unmoving on the altar while Eli screams his best friend's name begging him to wake up.

Evan groans quietly. "Don't cry, Zoey. I told you you're safe now."

It's only when he wipes away the wetness on my cheek that I register my silent tears. "O-okay."

"Shh." He presses his warm lips to mine.

Everything inside me recoils, but I force myself to remain passive.

117

Eli

My dad is onto the police, speaking to the detective who is dealing with the case. When he ends the call, I swing around to face him.

"Well?"

"They're on their way here. They want to see the texts and the photographs."

"And what are we supposed to do in the meantime? He's going to fucking kill her."

"Eli, you need to stay calm. If you—"

"*Calm*? Did you see the photograph?" I shove my cell in his face. "She's unconscious. What the fuck did he already do to her? How do we know she's not already dead?"

"Eli—"

"Do *not* tell me to calm the fuck down." I'd have said more, only my cell bursts into life. I hit connect without even looking to see who's calling me. "What?"

"It's Miles. Is Bella with you?"

"No, she fucking isn't."

"She went to meet Jace. I made her stay in contact with me the whole time. But then she texted to say she was leaving, and that was the last time I heard from her."

Jace.

Fucking Jace.

"I need to go. I'll call you when I know more."

"Eli, wait. What are you going to do?"

"Find the bastard and end this once and for all."

"What do you mean find … Oh … fuck … Evan's got her?"

I stab at the icons on my phone and forward the text and photograph to him.

"Jace must have organized everything, so the fucker could grab her."

"I don't think so. Look, don't do anything rash. I'm going to call Garrett. He lives near you. I'll send him over to help."

"What the fuck can he do to help?"

"He's a technical wizard. Maybe he can track Ari's cell."

Ari's cell. I twist to look up at my bedroom window. I have the phone up there that Kellan cloned to copy everything that went to her phone. Maybe there's something on there.

"As soon as I figure out where he is, I'm going."

"Wait for Garrett."

"Then tell him to hurry the fuck up." I end the call and race into the house, taking the stairs two at a time to my bedroom.

The box is at the back of my closet. I grab it and sit on the bed. Prising off the lid, I take out the cell.

My tongue strokes over my lips, toys with my lip ring, and then I flick my tongue piercing against my teeth.

Do I want to do this? Do I want to see the final conversation between Kellan and Evan?

Do I have any fucking choice?

I push the power button. It takes a second or two to boot up, but once it's done, I navigate into the messaging app, and scroll up to the day before I walked into the chapel to find my best friend dead.

Unknown number: I know you're not Arabella. Do you think you can fool me?

Cell Number: I'm not trying to fool you.

Unknown number: Then why pretend?

Cell Number: Because you wanted to play a game. Isn't that what I'm giving you?

Unknown number: It's not the game I want to play. Who are you?

Cell Number: Shouldn't I be asking that question?

Unknown number: It doesn't matter. I'll find out. And when I do, you will regret trying to ruin everything.

The final message burns into my mind. Evan had clearly found out it was Kellan and taken steps to remove him.

But how?

I toss the cell down. There's nothing else on there that can help find Arabella. I take out my cell and text Ari's number.

Me: Where are you? Is she alive?

Kitten: Zoey doesn't want you anymore. She's with me. No one wants you.

Zoey?

Me: It's not Zoey you want. It's me. Isn't that what all this has been about? Tell me where you are, and I'll come to you.

Kitten: You're supposed to be clever. You figure out where I am. I'll be waiting.

Me: How am I supposed to do that?

Kitten: What's wrong, monster? Do you need a clue?

Me: Yes.

The reply is a link to YouTube. I click it.

'Under The Graveyard' by Ozzy Osbourne starts to play.

Fuck. I know where he is.

Snatching up my car keys, I run out of my room. There's a redheaded boy walking up the stairs when I hit the top step.

"Eli, what can I do to help?"

"Get out of my way." I keep moving, and he dances to one side when I show no signs of stopping. He follows me out of the house and around to where my car is parked.

"Where are you going?"

"Churchill Bradley."

"Why?

"Because that's where Evan is."

118

Arabella

I bite down on my lip until I taste blood, and will myself not to flinch away from the groping hands. I've kept him rambling on for as long as I can. But then he received a text and his mood changed. His lips are on my neck, kissing and biting at my skin over where Eli has left his marks. His weight is heavy on me, his hand underneath my top as he fondles my breast.

"I'm going to make you forget Eli," he murmurs against my jaw. "Oh, Zoey. You're so beautiful."

"Please stop." My voice comes out in a whine. "I … I have my period."

Evan freezes on top of me. "You do?"

"Yeah, it just started," I lie. "I don't like having sex when I'm bleeding. It's too messy."

He braces his arm on the floor and pushes up to loom over me. "If I can't have your pussy then I'll use your mouth."

He rolls off me, and I heave out a breath. I want to claw at every inch of my skin where he's touched me, scrub it away, so it doesn't exist.

How much longer can I stop him from doing what he's planning? I'm sure we've already been here for hours. I need to get out of here before he stops accepting my excuses.

"Evan?" I tilt my head to look at him. "I need to pee. Can you untie me? I'll … I'll suck your dick afterward, I promise."

He laughs, his expression softening. "I'm sorry. I should have thought of that before. No trying to run away, or I *will* punish you."

"I won't run."

He takes a step toward me, but a beeping from the pocket of his jeans distracts him. Taking out his cell, he checks it.

Dread lurches through me when his face contorts into a grimace.

"What's the matter?"

"Eli is here."

"Eli?" I repeat, hope beating in time with my heart.

His scowl turns into a grin. "He finally wants to play, but I'm not letting him have you again."

"Evan, please."

"Shut the fuck up." He hauls me up.

I scream as loud as I can, thrashing from side to side in his arms, but he doesn't take me far.

I'm dumped down, and my stomach sinks when I stare up at the smooth gray sides. I'm flat, staring up at the roof of the tomb. Whatever is beneath me is lumpy and hard.

No, don't think about it. Don't. Think. About. It.

But I can't stop myself.

He's put me in Churchill's coffin.

I was so focused on him that I hadn't noticed anything different about the rest of the tomb. It must have been open all this time.

"No, please." I shake my head, tears blurring my vision.

He places the flashlight next to me, "Close your eyes, Zoey. I'll come back for you."

"Evan, don't do this." I sob.

He pats my hair, brushing the loose stands out of my face.

"Shhh. Hold your breath as long as you can. Lord Bradley will keep you safe until I come back for you."

He steps back, and a second later, the jarring sound of stone grating against stone fills my ears. The top of the coffin inches across, bit by bit.

"No, no, no." My words morph into a scream.

He seals me in completely, and I scream and scream.

Something white catches the corner of my eye in the glow of the flashlight he's left me. I turn my head, and my gaze latches on to the skull close to my face. The sight of it rips another shriek from my aching throat.

He's left me to suffocate.

How long can I last in here without air?

119

Eli

"The school is locked up. How do you know he's in there?"

We're parked outside the gates, the lights on my car brightening the entire area.

"I just do." We've had this same conversation over and over during the entire drive here.

"We need to wait for the police."

I slant a glare at him and throw open the door. "Fuck that. You shouldn't have fucking called them."

He follows me slowly toward the gates. "Miles was right. Eli, slow down. You're not thinking."

"If I slow down, he's going to kill her."

"You don't know that."

I swing to face him, anger burning through my veins. "Don't I? Why the fuck are you so convinced? Are you working with him, Garrett?"

"What? No! I'm just saying we need to think this through before we go rushing in there."

"I think you either need to shut the fuck up or get back in the car and stay there." I eye the gates, then jump up to grab the top bar and pull myself over the top.

Garrett mutters something behind me, but I don't listen, too focused on climbing over the gates and landing on the other side. There's a soft thump as Garrett lands beside me.

"The police are going to be here soon. They said they'd send someone from the local station."

"Don't care." I set off toward the school.

"Eli." He grabs my arm. "Fucking slow down. He *killed* your friend. He's not going to think twice about trying to kill you or Arabella. Slow down and *think*. Stop rushing. That's going to get one of you killed for sure."

"What do you suggest?" I shake off his hand.

"Security is going to be on the grounds somewhere. We go and find them. They're armed. At the very least, it gives us protection."

I want to dismiss his suggestion, but I know he's right. If we're going to succeed in getting Ari back, we need to take all the help we can get. I just don't want to hang around waiting for the police to show up. Not now we're here.

"Fine. You go and find them. Meet me at the cemetery."

"That wasn't … You should come with me."

"No." I stride away, not waiting to see if he follows me.

"Okay," he calls after me. "But don't do anything until we get there."

I lift a hand, but don't turn around, my eyes focused on the tree line ahead of me.

"Clever, Eli. I knew you'd figure it out." The voice floats to me in the darkness.

"Hiding, Evan?" I stop near the cemetery gates.

"From *you*? You're nothing to be afraid of. A pathetic scared little boy hiding behind the mask of a monster."

I shrug. "You christened me with the name."

"And you wasted it." A shadow detaches from the trees and coalesces into the shape of Evan. He cants his head as he stares at me. “What do they see in you, Eli? I don’t get it.”

“I’m not a puzzle you need to solve.”

“No, you’re the bane of my existence. A cancer that needs to be removed.”

“So come and do it. Or are you a coward?”

He throws back his head and laughs. “Oh, you’d like that, wouldn’t you? Kellan tried that trick. He thought he could fool me into thinking he wanted to talk, and then he tried to kill me.”

“I doubt that. You killed him.” My voice shows no sign of the pain saying those words sends through me.

“*You* killed him. You’re to blame for everything. They would all be alive if you had just fucking died with your mother.”

Cold fingers trace up my spine. “What did you say?”

But he’s not listening.

“All you had to do was fucking die, then everything would have been perfect. Jace would be mine, Kellan would be mine. Zoey would love me, and that little bitch in heat who you’ve been panting over for the last few months would be kneeling at my feet.” His lips tilt up. “She offered to suck my dick, you know. You’re not that special, after all.”

I take a step closer. “Who did?”

“Your little bitch. Your *kitten*.” His voice rises. “*I’ll suck your dick, Evan.*”

“Why would she offer to do that?”

“Because she wants to please me.” He rolls his eyes. “Get with the program, Eli.”

His mood swings, from angry to humorous, are giving me whiplash.

"Why did you kill her, Evan?" I slide another step closer.

He throws out a hand. "Stay over there, Eli. I know what you're doing."

"I'm not doing anything. I'm just trying to understand." … And trying to stall until Garrett shows up.

But what if he isn't going to show up? What if he's working with Evan? What if no one else is here to help?

"Where's Arabella?"

He laughs. "You'll never find her. She's gone for good. All your friends are gone, Eli. You have no one left." He smirks. "How does it feel?"

I squash down the panic at his words. She's not gone. He's got her hidden somewhere. I have to believe that.

"I'm not alone. I have my dad, my stepmom. I have Miles and Garrett. I have Arabella. I'm surrounded by people who love me for who I am. What do you have, Evan?" One more step and I should be within arm's reach of him.

"Lies! No one likes you. I've made sure of that."

"No. You failed." I choose my next words carefully, watching him intently for signs of a reaction. "For all the shit you've done, you failed, Evan. I have everything. *You* have nothing."

He launches himself at me, hands clamping around my throat and squeezing. "You're wrong! I've won. You won't take her away from me."

"I already did. I took them all. They're all with me, Evan. Not you."

His nails dig into my skin, and he screams, spit flying from his mouth. "No! No! No!"

Lights are dancing in front of my eyes, but I don't try to fight him off. I let him rant and scream, listening as he pours out all the hate. Admits to all the terror he caused. Just as my vision begins to dim, my lungs burning with the need for oxygen, he releases me.

I stagger backward, sucking in breath after breath, then lift my head up.

Evan is pinned between two security guards. Garrett stands beside them, pale and wide-eyed. And just beyond them, three police officers are moving toward us.

120

Arabella

"Help." My voice is hoarse, and my breathing is shallow. "Please, someone help me."

I can't get out. The walls are closing in. Sweating and shaking, my throat tightens, and I'm choking. I open my mouth to scream, but the only sound that comes out is a whimper.

I'm going to die.

This was what Evan planned, to leave me trapped with no way out.

Eli is never going to find me in here. Why would anyone look in the coffin? If Evan has gone, why would anyone search it at all?

A hysterical laugh leaves my throat.

I'll just be one more ghost to haunt the cemetery. No one is going to find my body. I'll rot inside here on top of Churchill Bradley himself.

I laugh and laugh until it trails off into hopeless tears.

Maybe I'll just go to sleep, and I won't feel a thing?

"Eli." His name leaves my lips in an agonized whisper. I love him so much, and I should have stayed with him. I wish we'd had more time.

Exhaustion settles over me.

Tears spill down my cheeks, and I close my eyes. "I'm sorry. I'm so sorry."

121

Eli

"Where is she?" I surge toward Evan, who throws his head back and grins at me.

"Somewhere you'll never find her."

"Where the fuck is she?" It's my turn to wrap a hand around his throat.

Hands pull at my wrist, dragging me away from him. I shake them off and surge forward again, only to find myself stopped, held in the grip of two police officers.

Evan laughs.

"Checkmate, Eli. I took your knight, and now I've taken your queen."

"We'll find her."

I snap my head sideways to search out the cop who spoke. "Will you? Like you found him? If it wasn't for me, he'd still be fucking out there." I pull free. "I need to find her."

"She's talking to the angels now, Eli." Evan cackles, lips pulled tight into a distorted grin.

Angels? My gaze jerks in the direction of the chapel, and I take off at a run.

"Eli! Wait!" Garrett's shout doesn't slow me down, and I make it to the chapel in record time. But when I reach the doors, I stop.

What if she's in there?

What if she's on the altar the same way Kellan was?

My heart stutters in my chest.

I can't go through that again.

I can't lose her as well as Kellan.

I push the doors open and step inside. My eyes immediately go to the altar, and a relieved breath escapes me. It's empty.

"Ari?" I call her name softly and walk down the center until I reach the front of the chapel. I avoid the red stain on the altar and keep my attention on places where she could be hidden.

I don't know how long I search, covering the same ground over and over before I admit to myself that she's not here.

Where else?

I walk outside and find Garrett waiting for me. "The police have taken Evan away. Security is searching inside the school for Arabella."

I shake my head. "She's not in there."

"How do you know?"

"I just do." I retrace my steps to the cemetery gates.

"We'd hear her if—"

My eyes cut to him. "Don't fucking say it." I step through the gates and into the cemetery, my gaze sweeping over the stones and plaques. A flash of white catches my eye, and I frown.

"What's that?" We walk over the dirt and come to a stop in front of Zoey's plaque. A bouquet of white flowers is in front of it. Reaching down, I pluck out the card.

It was never meant to end this way. I'm going to fix it. We will be together.

Evan x

"Did he ever talk about Zoey to you?" My fingers rub at the card as I look around.

"Not after she died. But he asked her out before then, and she said no."

"How did he seem?"

"He didn't really react at all."

My gaze moves over Churchill Bradley's tomb, then swings back. "The door is open."

"What?"

"On the tomb." I stride across to it and move down the steps.

"Ari?" My voice echoes around the interior.

I step through and stop abruptly. The place is covered in the same flowers as the bouquet outside. A sleeping bag is laid out beside the coffin, and beer bottles, cans, and food remnants are scattered around.

"I guess this is where he was hiding out." I turn in a slow circle. "*Ari?*"

Garrett moves around, nudging trash aside with his foot. "She's not in here, Eli. There's nowhere to hide."

But something is nagging at me. My tongue creeps out to touch my lip ring. Something isn't right. Closing my eyes, I visualize the interior of the tomb, building it up in my mind.

Wait.

My eyes snap open and I step across to the coffin. One hand brushes over the top.

"There are stone fragments."

"So?"

I slant a look at him. "I've spent a lot of time in here. These are new." I return my attention to the coffin.

Garrett moves up to stand beside me. "You don't think—" His voice is low, stressed.

I don't answer. Instead, I brace my hands against the stone slab and push. A loud grating noise fills the air as stone moves against stone. I shove again.

"Oh my god!" Garrett's shout echoes around the crypt. "Oh my fucking god. She's in there. Bella? *Bella?*"

One more shove and the slab topples off. I'm inside the coffin, my fingers searching for Arabella's pulse before it crashes to the ground.

"Ari? Ari, baby? Open your eyes."

She doesn't move. I can't feel a fucking pulse.

"Ari?"

My mind flashes back to that moment when I discovered Kellan, when I saw the blood, his lifeless eyes.

"Fucking wake up. *Ari!*"

122

Arabella

"Ari, come back to me."

Sucking in a breath at the tortured voice, my eyes snap open.

Eli is kneeling over me inside the tomb, his expression twisted in agony.

Am I dreaming? How can this be real?

My lips part. "Eli?"

"You're alive." The words leave him in a relieved rush, and he pulls me up against his hard, muscled chest.

My bound arms throb in pain, and I cry out.

"You're hurting her," a second familiar voice warns. Garrett.

"Did Evan harm you?" Eli's voice is anxious as he lowers me back down. "Did he touch you? Are you hurt?"

I try to speak, but nothing comes out.

"Garrett, call an ambulance. She's in shock." He turns me on my side carefully and unties my hands and then my ankles.

I can hear Garrett talking on the phone quietly, but all my focus is on the boy above me.

My Nasty Little Monster who holds my heart in his hands.

The Monster of Churchill Bradley Academy saved me.

I should be happy, relieved, but I feel numb.

Why can't I feel anything?

In the middle of rubbing my wrists, he grimaces, fingers tracing over the darkening bruises and the blood seeping from my broken skin.

"It's okay. Everything is okay. The police have Evan. It's over, Ari. It's over."

My head spins, relief finally flooding through my veins.

"Ari?" Eli's voice sounds far away. "Ari? Baby, please stay awake."

I want to obey, but it's like fighting against the tide.

Darkness rushes in, and I hear no more.

***

Consciousness returns, and with it, the feel of a finger stroking my cheek. Sighing, I nuzzle against it sleepily.

"Kitten? Let me see those beautiful blue eyes."

Eyelids lifting, I focus on Eli. He's leaning forward on a plastic chair, dark circles under his eyes and his hair looks like he's been dragging his hands through it. I'm in a narrow bed with a white sheet covering me, in a room I don't recognize.

He lifts my hand and presses his mouth to the bruises ringing my wrist in a kiss. "Hey."

He looks pale and exhausted.

"Hey, yourself." My voice is croaky, and it hurts to swallow. "Where?"

"The hospital." One corner of his mouth tilts up. "You passed out after Garrett and I found you."

"I'm sorry."

"You are never doing anything without telling me ever again. Do you hear me?"

I nod. "Yes."

He threads his fingers through mine. "He could have killed you."

A wave of tiredness washes over me. "I know."

"I could have lost you too." His voice breaks.

I fight against the drowsiness, but my eyes close. "Eli."

"It's okay, Ari." Gentle lips brush over mine. "The doctor said you'd be out of it for a while. My dad and your mom are on their way."

I struggle to hold onto what he's saying. "Don't leave me."

"I'm right here. I'm not going anywhere. You're mine, and I'm never letting you go."

His promise stays with me as I drift into a dreamless sleep.

123

Eli

The next few days pass in a blur of activity. Detective Parker comes to the hospital a couple of times, checking on Ari as well as asking me questions. He tells me that they've taken Lacy, Brad, Jace, Kevin, and Bret in for further questioning because Evan mentioned having them take part in his twisted plans and texts to Arabella. He adds that Evan is looking at murder charges, as well as intent to kill both me and Arabella.

Other than that, he won't share what will happen to them, only that they are looking at charges for aiding a felon, and potentially blackmail as well.

Churchill Bradley Academy's Principal comes by to visit two days into her hospital stay. He tells us that all senior-year students have graduated, and there is no need to return to school. He explains that they're closing for the foreseeable future, while they examine what could have been done to prevent what we experienced.

I could give them a list, but I hold my tongue.

On day four, the doctor tells Arabella that she can go home. My dad insists on bringing a car, so I don't have to drive, and she leans on me the entire way through the hospital and outside. It takes us a while to get there, but she refuses to use a wheelchair. She's still a little cautious and slow. I say nothing. I even manage not to offer to carry her because I know it will be met with snark and glares. She's eager to get out of here, but she wants to do it under her own steam, can't blame her for that.

When we finally reach the car, she settles onto the back seat with a relieved sigh. I drape my arm across her shoulders and draw her closer. I can't stand having even the smallest distance between us right now. Her head drops against my chest, and she curls sideways into me.

I meet my dad's eyes through the mirror as he starts the car. He nods and smiles, then pulls out of the parking lot.

We both doze on the journey back to the house, drifting in and out, having partial conversations which break off, only to resume when we wake again.

When the car engine cuts out, my eyes snap open.

"It's okay." My dad's voice is soft. "We're home."

Elena is standing in the doorway when we climb out of the car. Silently she holds out her arms and wraps Arabella into them. She's been a frequent visitor to the hospital, but I asked her to stay home today and move a few things around for me. After I explained why, she agreed. When Elena finally releases Ari, I take her hand and draw her inside toward the staircase.

"The doctors say you need to keep taking it easier for a few more days," I say as we ascend the stairs. "I've had your stuff moved into my room, so I can keep an eye on you."

As predicted, she rolls her eyes. "I'm fine, Eli."

I stop when we reach the hallway and turn to face her. "You might be, but *I'm* not. I want to be beside you when you fall asleep and find you there when I wake up. I nearly lost you, Ari." I cup her cheeks. "I can't go through that again."

Her arms lift to loop around my neck. "You won't have to."

She's not wrong. I've already arranged to have extra security cameras fitted around the house and grounds. We have trackers installed on both our cells, so we know where each other is at all times, and I have no intention of letting her out of my sight any time soon.

Find out what happens next in ***Dare To Live***

Eulogy For Kellan

By Kim Hafer

In Memory of the One We Lost

To the one who kept the monster entertained until the
princess arrived.
To the one who loved completely despite the ones who went
before him.
To the one whose laugh helped us through each day.
To the one who saw through the smoke and mirrors to the
pattern that would set us free.
To the voice of reason that found us in our darkest moments.
To Kellan, the dark raven watching over us still.

Thank you for reading Dare To Fall. If you'd like to keep up to date with L. Ann & Claire Marta, you can find both of them on Facebook.

L. Ann - https://facebook.com/lannauthor
Claire Marta - https://facebook.com/clairemartabooks

You can also join their active reader groups:-

L. Ann's Literati - https://facebook.com/groups/lannsliterati
Claire's Liquor & Lust - https://facebook.com/groups/clairesliquorandlust

You can find more books by L. Ann and Claire Marta on Amazon in paperback, ebook and audio.

Made in United States
Troutdale, OR
12/28/2023